BITS &
PIECES

ROT & RUIN
BOOK FIVE

BITS &

PIECES

Jonathan Maberry

SIMON & SCHUSTER BFYR

NEW YORK LONDON TORONTO SYDNEY NEW DELHI

SIMON & SCHUSTER BFYR

An imprint of Simon & Schuster Children's Publishing Division
1230 Avenue of the Americas, New York, New York 10020

For information about special discounts for bulk purchases, please contact Simon & Schuster
Special Sales at 1-866-506-1949 or business@simonandschuster.com.
The Simon & Schuster Speakers Bureau can bring authors to your live event.
For more information or to book an event, contact the Simon & Schuster Speakers Bureau
at 1-866-248-3049 or visit our website at www.simonspeakers.com.
Also available in a SIMON & SCHUSTER BFYR hardcover edition
Book design by Laurent Linn.
Zombie Card art by Rob Sacchetto
The text for this book is set in Augustal.
Manufactured in the United States of America
4 6 8 10 9 7 5 3
Library of Congress Cataloging-in-Publication Data
Maberry, Jonathan.
[Short stories. Selections]
Bits & pieces / Jonathan Maberry.
pages cm. — (Rot & ruin ; book five)
Summary: Twenty-two short stories, eleven of which were previously published,
based on the Rot & Ruin series in which fifteen-year-old Benny Imura and his friends
fight a zombie plague in a post-apocalyptic America. Includes a related comic book script.
ISBN 978-1-4814-4418-7 (hardcover) — ISBN 978-1-4814-4419-4 (pbk.)
ISBN 978-1-4814-4420-0 (eBook)
[1. Survival—Fiction. 2. Zombies—Fiction. 3. Bounty hunters—Fiction. 4. Brothers—Fiction.] I. Title.
II. Title: Bits and pieces.
PZ7.M11164Bit 2015
[Fic]—dc23
2014047164

FIRST EDITION

This is for all of the kids and teens
who find the courage to do what is right, to accept
a code of ethics, and to always be warrior smart.

And, as always, for Sara Jo.

ACKNOWLEDGMENTS

Special thanks to Lisa Mandina; librarian Erin Daly and the girls at the Chicopee Library Teen Book Club—Samantha Desrochers, Michelle Rondeau, Amanda Noonan, Laura Hebert, Tiffany Moczydlowski, and Heather Moczydlowski; to Rachael Lavin; to Rachel Tafoya and the students of my Experimental Writing for Teens programs; Michelle Lane; Walker Shefchek; Steven Ard of Kamiakin High School; and Keaton Russell.

CONTENTS

BITS & PIECES

PART ONE

FIRST NIGHT

This Is How the World Ends.

FROM NIX'S JOURNAL

ON FIRST NIGHT
(PRIOR TO *ROT & RUIN*)

My name is Phoenix Riley. My friends call me Nix.

I was born right around the time the world died. A plague turned everyone into zombies. Actual living dead.

No one knows where it started. Or how. Or why.

It spread fast, though. By the time people realized that there was a problem, the problem was biting them. Then everything went crazy. There was a day the survivors call First Night. That was the point at which no one could ignore the problem. No one could say that it wasn't really happening, or even if it was, it wasn't happening here. It was happening everywhere.

The year I was born, the United States
Census Bureau estimated that there
were 6,922,000,000 people alive on planet
Earth. My mom says that probably a
billion people died on First Night. And
over the next few days and weeks,
nearly everybody died. They used to have
something called the "Internet." Before
that went down, the estimates of the
global death toll were at three billion
and climbing. After that there were no
more news reports. There was no one left
to report it. And after the power grids
failed, there was no way to report it.

The world went dark and it went silent.

Except for the sound the dead make.
Moans. Like they're hungry.

And they are hungry. All the time.

They want to eat people.

Animals, too. They'll eat anything alive.
That's why the world's so empty. The
dead rose and they ate everyone.

Well, not everyone, I suppose. My teachers
say that the dead killed enough people

for everything to fall apart. My history teacher said the outbreak destroyed what he called "the infrastructure." Which is police and government and hospitals and like that. My health class teacher says it was disease, malnutrition, and bad water that killed most of the others.

Problem is, no matter how someone dies, they come back to life as a zombie.

Everyone.

Which meant that the survivors kept having to run to find a safe place to hide. And to find food and stuff. To find medicine.

Mom ran. She took me with her.

I used to have a dad, and brothers. I never knew them. I was too little, and when Mom ran . . . she was running _from_ them. Or from what they had become.

Mom doesn't talk about that. I don't think she can.

I grew up in Mountainside. It isn't a real town, or at least it didn't use to be.

Before First Night it was a reservoir built against a mountain wall in Mariposa County in the Sierra Nevada Mountains of central California. Not too far from Yosemite National Park. A bunch of people who were on the run found it. The reservoir had a fence, and that kept the people alive. Then more and more people found it, and when the big panic started to settle down, the people sent out teams to raid local houses and towns and stores for building materials, food, beds, clothes, and all sorts of stuff. They found a construction supply company a few miles from here, and they brought back miles of chain-link fence. Pretty soon they had a kind of town.

That was fourteen years ago.

Since then people have built eight other towns along the Sierra Nevadas. At the New Year's census, the total population of the nine towns here in central California is 28,261. Mom's friend Tom Imura says that there are maybe five hundred to a thousand people living outside the towns. Out in the Rot and Ruin. Out where the zoms are. Loners, scavengers who raid towns for supplies, bounty hunters, and a bunch of crazy monks who live in old gas stations and who think the zoms are the meek who were supposed to inherit the earth. Add them to the people in the towns, and there are still fewer than thirty thousand people left.

Thirty thousand of us and nearly seven billion zoms.

I've never been outside the fence line. Neither have most of the people in town. People here hardly even talk about what's out there. They talk about the other towns as if they're in different countries. We get news from them, and once in a rare while a traveler goes from one town to another. But everything else is the Rot and Ruin.

My mom wants me to live here. To "be content" because I'm safe and alive.

Behind the fences.

In a cage.

Sometimes I think the fence isn't just for keeping the zoms out. I think it's to keep us in. We built it and we locked ourselves in.

I hate it.

I can't live in a cage.

I won't.

But . . . I don't know how to escape the cage when everything outside is the Ruin. Out there, everything wants to kill you. Everyone says that.

Still . . . if I have to live my whole life in a cage, then I know I'll go crazy.

There has to be a way out.

There has to be.

Sunset Hollow

Tom Imura's Story

(This story takes place on First Night,
fourteen years before *Rot & Ruin*)

1

The kid kept crying.

Crying.

Crying.

Blood all over him. Their blood. Not his.

Not Benny's.

Theirs.

He stood on the lawn and stared at the house.

Watching as the fallen lamp inside the room threw goblin shadows on the curtains. Listening to the screams as they filled the night. Filled the room. Spilled out onto the lawn. Punched him in the face and belly and over the heart. Screams that sounded less and less like her. Like Mom.

Less like her.

More like Dad.

Like whatever he was. Whatever *this* was.

Tom Imura stood there, holding the kid. Benny was eighteen months. He could say a few words. "Mom." "Dog." "Foot."

Now all he could do was wail. One long, inarticulate wail that tore into Tom's head. It hit him as hard as Mom's screams.

As hard. But differently.

The front door was open, standing ajar. The back door was unlocked. He'd left through the window, though. The downstairs bedroom on the side of the house. Mom had pushed him out. She'd shoved Benny into his hands and pushed him out.

Into the night.

Into the sound of sirens, of screams, of weeping and praying people, of gunfire and helicopters.

Out here on the lawn.

While she stayed inside.

He'd tried to fight her on it.

He was bigger. Stronger. All those years of jujutsu and karate. She was a middle-aged housewife. He could have forced her out. Could have gone to face the horror that was beating on the bedroom door. The thing that wore Dad's face but had such a hungry, bloody mouth.

Tom could have pulled Mom out of there.

But Mom had one kind of strength, one bit of power that neither black belts nor biceps could hope to fight. It was there on her arm, hidden in that last moment by her white sleeve.

No.

That was a lie he wanted to tell himself.

Not white.

The sleeve was red, and getting redder with every beat of her heart.

That sleeve was her power, and he could not defeat it.

That sleeve and what it hid.

The mark. The wound.

The bite.

It amazed Tom that Dad's teeth could fit that shape. That it was so perfect a match in an otherwise imperfect tumble of events. That it was possible at all.

Benny struggled in his arms. Wailing for Mom.

Tom clutched his little brother to his chest and bathed his face with tears. They stood like that until the last of the screams from inside had faded, faded, and . . .

Even now Tom could not finish that sentence. There was no dictionary in his head that contained the words that would make sense of this.

The screams faded.

Not into silence.

Into moans.

Such hungry, hungry moans.

He had lingered there because it seemed a true sin to leave Mom to this without even a witness. Without mourners.

Mom and Dad.

Inside the house now.

Moaning. Both of them.

Tom Imura staggered to the front door and nearly committed the sin of entry. But Benny was a squirming reminder of all the ways this would kill them both. Body and soul.

Truly. Body and soul.

So Tom reached out and pulled the door closed.

He fumbled in his pocket for the key. He didn't know why. The TV and the Internet said that they couldn't think, that something as simple and ordinary as a doorknob could stop them. Locks weren't necessary.

He locked the door anyway.

And put the key safely in his pocket. It jangled against his own.

He backed away onto the lawn to watch the window again. The curtains moved. Shapes stirred on the other side, but the movements made the wrong kind of sense.

The shapes, though.

God, the shapes.

Dad and Mom.

Tom's knees gave all at once, and he fell to the grass so hard that it shot pain into his groin and up his spine. He almost lost his grip on his brother. Almost. But didn't.

He bent his head, unable to watch those shapes. He closed his eyes and bared his teeth and uttered his own moan. A long, protracted, half-choked sound of loss. Of a hurt that no articulation could possibly express, because the descriptive terms belonged to no human dictionary. Only the lost understand it, and they don't require further explanation. They get it because there is only one language spoken in the blighted place where they live.

Tom actually understood in that moment why the poets called the feeling heart*break*. There was a fracturing, a splintering in his chest. He could feel it.

Benny kicked him with little feet and banged on Tom's face with tiny fists. It hurt, but Tom endured it. As long as it hurt, there was some proof they were both alive.

Still alive.

Still alive.

2

It was Benny Imura who saved his brother Tom.

Little, eighteen-month-old, screaming Benny.

First he nearly got them both killed, but then he saved

them. The universe is perverse and strange like that.

His brother, on his knees, lost in the deep well of the moment, did not hear the sounds behind him. Or if he did, his grief orchestrated them into the same discordant symphony.

So no, he did not separate out the moans behind him from those inside the house. Or the echoes of them inside his head.

That was the soundtrack of the world now.

But Benny could tell the difference.

He was a toddler. Everything was immediate; everything was new. He heard those moans, turned to look past his brother's trembling shoulder, and he saw them.

The shapes.

Detaching themselves from the night shadows.

He knew some of the faces. Recognized them as people who came and smiled at him. People who threw him up in the air or poked his tummy or tweaked his cheeks. People who made faces that made him laugh.

Now, though.

None of them were laughing.

The reaching hands did not seem to want to play or poke or tweak.

Some of the hands were broken. There was blood where fingers should be. There were holes in each of these things. In chests and stomachs and faces.

Their mouths weren't smiling. They were full of teeth, and their teeth were red.

Benny could not even form these basic thoughts, could not actually categorize the rightness and wrongness of what was happening. All he could do was *feel* it. Feel the wrongness. He heard the sounds of hunger. The moans. They were not happy sounds. He had been hungry so many times, he knew. It was why he cried sometimes. For a bottle. For something to eat.

Benny knew only a dozen words.

Most of them were names for food and toys.

He stopped crying and tried to say one of those names.

"Tuh . . . Tuh . . . Tuh . . ."

That was all he could get. "Tom" was too difficult. Not always, just sometimes. It wouldn't fit into his mouth now.

"Tuh . . . Tuh . . . Tuh . . ."

3

It was a strange moment when Tom Imura realized that his baby brother was actually trying to say his name.

Because saying it was also a warning.

A warning was a thought that Tom wouldn't have credited to a kid that young.

Could toddlers even think like that?

A part of Tom's mind stepped out of the moment and looked at the phenomenon as if it were hanging on a wall in a museum. He studied it. Considered it. Posed in thoughtful art-house stances in front of it. All in a fragment of a second so small it could have been hammered in between two of the *Tuh* sounds.

Tom.

That's what Benny was saying.

No. That's what Benny was *screaming*.

Tom jerked upright.

He turned.

He saw what Benny had seen.

Them.

So many of them.

Them.

Coming out of the shadows. Reaching.

Moaning.

Hungry. So hungry.

There was Mrs. Addison from across the street. She was nice but could be mean sometimes. Liked to tell the other ladies on the block how to grow roses, even though hers were only so-so.

Mrs. Addison had no lower lip.

Someone had torn it away. Or . . .

Bitten it?

Right behind her was John Chalker. Industrial chemist. He made solvents for a company that sold drain cleaner. He always brought the smell of his job home on his clothes.

Now he had no clothes. He was naked. Except for his hat.

Why did he still have his hat on and no clothes?

There were bites everywhere. Most of his right forearm was gone. The meat of his hand hung on the bones like a loose glove.

And the little Han girl. Lucy? Lacey? Something like that.

Ten, maybe eleven.

She had no eyes.

They were coming toward Tom and his brother. Reaching with hands. Some of those hands were slashed and bitten. Or gone completely. None of the wounds bled.

Why didn't the wounds bleed?

Why didn't the damn wounds bleed?

"No," said Tom.

Even to his own ears his voice sounded wrong. Way too calm. Way too normal.

Calm and normal were dead concepts. There was no normal.

Or maybe *this* was normal.

Now.

But calm? No, that was gone. That was trashed. That was . . .

Consumed.

The word came into his head, unwanted and unwelcome. Shining with truth. Ugly in its accuracy.

"*Tuh . . . Tuh . . . Tuh . . .*"

Benny's voice was not calm.

It broke Tom.

It broke the spell of stillness.

It broke something in his chest.

Tom's next word was not calm. Might not actually have been a word. It started out as "No," but it changed, warped, splintered, and tore his throat ragged on the way out. A long wail, as unending as the moans of his neighbors. Higher, though, not a monotone. Not a simple statement of need. This was pure denial, and he screamed it at them as they came toward him, pawing the air. For him. For Benny. For anything warm, anything alive.

For meat.

Tom felt himself turn but didn't know how he managed

it. His mind was frozen. His scream kept rising and rising. But his body turned.

And ran.

And ran.

God, he ran.

They, however, were everywhere.

The darkness pulsed with the red and blue of police lights; the banshee wail of sirens tore apart the shadows of the California night, but no police came for him. No help came for them.

The little boy in his arms screamed and screamed and screamed.

Pale shapes lurched toward him from the shadows. Some of them were victims—their wounds still bleeding—still *able* to bleed; their eyes wide with shock and incomprehension. Others were more of *them*.

The things.

The monsters.

Whatever they were.

Tom's car was parked under a streetlamp, washed by the orange glow of the sodium vapor light. He'd come home from the academy, and all his gear was in the trunk. His pistol— which cadets weren't even allowed to carry until after tomorrow's graduation—and his stuff from the dojo. His sword, some fighting sticks.

He slowed, casting around to see if that was the best way to go.

Should he risk it? *Could* he risk it?

The car was at the end of the block. He had the keys, but the streets were clogged with empty emergency vehicles. Even if he got his gear, could he find a way to drive out?

Yes.

No.

Maybe.

Houses were on fire one block over. Fire trucks and crashed cars were like a wall.

But the weapons.

His weapons.

They were right there in the trunk.

Benny screamed. The monsters shambled after him.

"Go!" Mom had said. "Take Benny . . . keep him safe. Go!"

Just . . . go.

He ran to the parked car. Benny was struggling in his arms, hitting him, fighting to try to get free.

Tom held him with one arm—an arm that already ached from carrying his brother—and fished in his pocket for the keys. Found them. Found the lock. Opened the door, popped the trunk.

Gun in the glove compartment. Ammunition in the trunk. Sword, too.

Shapes moved toward him. He could hear their moans. So close. So close.

Tom turned a wild eye toward one as it reached for the child he carried.

He lashed out with a savage kick, driving the thing back. It fell, but it was not hurt. Not in any real sense of being hurt. As soon as it crashed down, it began to crawl toward him.

And in his mind Tom realized that he had thought of it as an *it*. Not a *him*. Not a *person*.

He was already that far gone into this. That's what this had come to.

He and Benny and *them*.

Each of them was an *it* now.

The world was that broken.

It was unreal. Tom understood that this thing was dead. He knew him, too. It was Mr. Harrison from three doors down, and it was also a dead thing.

A monster.

An actual monster.

This was the real world, and there were monsters in it.

Benny kept screaming.

Tom lifted the trunk hood and shoved Benny inside. Then he grabbed his sword. There was no time to remove the trigger lock on the gun. They were coming.

They were here.

Tom slammed the hood, trapping the screaming Benny inside the trunk even as he ripped the sword from its sheath.

All those hands reached for him.

And for the second time, a part of Tom's mind stepped out of the moment and struck a contemplative pose, studying himself, walking around him, observing and forming opinions.

Tom had studied jujutsu and karate since he was little. Kendo, too. He could fight with his hands and feet. He could grapple and wrestle.

He could use a sword.

Twice in his life he'd been in fights. Once in the seventh grade with a kid who was just being a punk. Once in twelfth grade when one of the kids on the hockey team mouthed off to a girl Tom liked. Both fights had been brief. Some shoves, a couple of punches. The other guy went down both times. Not down and out, just down. Nothing big. No real damage.

Never once in his twenty years had Tom Imura fought for his life. Never once had he done serious harm to another person. The drills in the police academy, even the live-fire exercises, were no different from the dojo. It was all a dance. All practice and simulation. No real blood, no genuine intent.

All those years, all those black belts, they in no way prepared him for this moment.

To use a sword on a person. To cut flesh. To draw blood.

To kill.

There is no greater taboo. Only a psychopath disregards it without flinching. Tom was not a psychopath. He was a twenty-year-old Japanese-American police academy cadet. A son. A stepson. A half brother. He was barely a man. He couldn't even legally buy a beer.

He stood in the middle of his own street with a sword in his hands as everyone he knew in his neighborhood came at him. To kill him.

Video games don't prepare you for this.

Watching movies doesn't prepare you.

No training prepares you.

Nothing does.

Nothing.

He said, "Please . . ."

The people with the dead eyes and the slack faces moaned in reply. And they fell on him like a cloud of locusts.

The sword seemed to move of its own accord.

Distantly, Tom could feel his arms lift and swing. He could feel his hands tighten and loosen as the handle shifted within his grip for different cuts. The rising cut. The scarf cut. The lateral cut.

He saw the silver of the blade move like flowing mercury, tracing fire against the night.

He felt the shudder and shock as the weapon hit and sliced and cleaved through bone.

He felt his feet shift and step and pivot; he felt his waist turn, his thighs flex, his heels lift to tilt his mass into the cuts or to allow his knees to wheel him around.

He felt all of this.

He did not understand how any of it could happen when his mind was going blank. None of it came from his will. None of it was directed.

It just happened.

The moaning things came at him.

And his sword devoured them.

4

Three terrible minutes later, Tom unlocked the trunk and opened it.

Benny was cowering in the back of the trunk, huddled against Tom's gym bag. Tears and snot were pasted on his face. Benny opened his mouth to scream again, but he stopped. When he saw Tom, he stopped.

Tom stood there, the sword held loosely in one hand, the keys in the other. He was covered with blood. The sword was covered with blood.

The bodies around the car—more than a dozen of them— were covered with blood.

Benny screamed.

Not because he understood—he was far too young for that—but because the smell of blood reminded him of Dad. Of home. Benny wanted his mom.

He screamed and Tom stood there, trembling from head to toe. Tears broke from his eyes and fell in burning silver lines down his face.

"I'm sorry, Benny," he said in a voice that was as broken as the world.

Tom tore off his blood-splattered shirt. The T-shirt he wore underneath was stained, but not as badly. Tom shivered as he lifted Benny and held him close. Benny beat at him with tiny fists.

"I'm sorry," Tom said again.

All around him was a silent slaughterhouse.

And then it wasn't.

From the sides streets, from open doors, *more* of them came.

More.

More.

Mr. Gaynor from down the block. Old Lady Milhonne from across the street, wearing the same ratty bathrobe she always wore. The Kang kids. Delia and Marie Swanson. Others he didn't know. Even two cops in torn uniforms.

"No more," Tom said as he buried his head in the cleft

between Benny's neck and shoulder. As if there was any comfort there.

No more.

But there was more, and on some level Tom knew there would always be more. This was how it was now. They'd hinted about it on the news. The street where he lived proved it to be true.

5

He kicked his way through them.

He kicked old Mr. Gaynor in the groin and watched the force of the kick bend him in half. It should have put him down. It should have left him in a purple-faced fetal ball.

It didn't.

Gaynor staggered and went down to one knee. His face did not change expression at all. Nothing. Not even a curl of the lip.

Then Gaynor got heavily, awkwardly to his feet and came forward again. Reaching for Benny.

Tom kicked him again. Same spot, even harder.

This time Gaynor didn't even go down to one knee. He tottered backward, caught his balance, and moved forward again.

Tom cursed at him. Shrieked every foul thing he could muster at him.

Benny squealed each time Tom kicked, and he hoped he wasn't crushing his brother as he exerted himself to lash out at the things around him.

He kicked once more, changing it from a front thrust to a

side thrust. Lower. To the knee instead of the groin. The femur broke with the sound of a batter hitting a hard one down the third-base line.

Sharp.

Gaynor went down that time. Not in pain, not yelling. But down. Bone speared through the cotton of his trousers, jagged and white. Tom stared at him, watching the man try to get back up again. Saw gravity pull him down, saw how the ruined scaffolding of shattered bone denied him the chance to stand.

Not pain.

Just broken bone.

Tom backed away, spun. Ran. Holding Benny, who kept screaming.

He dodged between parked cars, jumped over a fallen bike, blundered through a narrow gap in a row of privet hedges, staggered onto the pavement. Two teenagers, strangers, were there on their knees, faces buried in something that glistened and steamed.

A stomach.

Tom couldn't tell who it had been. But he saw the dead hands twitch. The teenagers recoiled from their meal, staring briefly with vacuous stupidity as the half-consumed body began shivering. The corpse tried to sit up, but there were no abdominal muscles left to power that effort. Instead it rolled onto its side, sloshing out intestines like dead snakes. The teenagers got to their feet, turned, looked, and sniffed the night.

Then they turned toward Tom.

And Benny.

Benny screamed and screamed and screamed.

It was then, only then, that the shape of this fit into Tom's mind. Not the cause, not the sense, not the solution.

The shape.

He backed away, turned, and ran again.

The lawns behind him were filled with slow bodies. Some sprawled on the grass like broken starfish, lacking enough of their muscles or tendons to move in any useful way. Others staggered along, relentless and slow.

Tom ran fast, clenching Benny to him, feeling the flutter of his brother's heart against his own chest.

The street ahead was filled with the people who had lived here in Sunset Hollow.

So many of them now.

All of them now.

6

Then another figure stepped out from behind a hedge.

Short, female, pretty. Wearing a torn dress. Wild eyes in a slack face.

She said, "Tom—?"

"Sherrie," he said. Sherrie Tomlinson had gone all through school with him. Second grade through high school. He'd wanted to date her, but she was always a little standoffish. Not cold, just not interested.

Now she came toward him, ignoring his sword, ignoring the blood. She touched his face, his chest, his arms, his mouth.

"Tom? What is it?"

"Sherrie? Are you okay?"

"What is it?" she asked.

"I don't *know*."

He didn't. There were news stories that made no sense. An outbreak in Pennsylvania. Then people getting sick in other places. Anywhere a plane from Philly landed. Anywhere near I-95 and I-76. Spreading out from bus terminals and train stations. The reporters put up numbers. Infected first, then casualties. In single digits. In triple. When Tom was racing back from the police academy, trying to get home, they were talking about blackout zones. Quarantine zones. There were helicopters in the air. Swarms of them. When he got home, the TV was on. Anderson Cooper was yelling—actually yelling—about fuel air bombs being deployed in Philadelphia, Pittsburgh, Baltimore. Other places.

London was about to go dark.

L.A. was on fire.

On *fire*.

That's when he stopped watching TV. That's when they all stopped. It was when Dad came in from the backyard with those bites on his neck.

And it all fell apart.

All sense. All meaning.

All answers.

"What is it?" asked Sherrie.

All Tom could do was shake his head.

"What is it?"

He looked at her. Looked for wounds. For bites.

"What is it?" she repeated. And repeated it again. *"What is it?"*

And Tom realized that the question was all Sherrie had left. She didn't want an answer. Couldn't really use one. She was like a machine left on after its usefulness was done. An organic recording device replaying a loop.

"What is it? What is it?" Varied only by the infrequent use of his name. "What is it, Tom?"

The only other changes were in the hysterical notes that ebbed and flowed.

The inflection, the stresses put on different words as something in her head misfired.

"What is *it*?"

"What *is* it?"

"*What* is it?"

Like that. Repeated over and over again. A litany for an apocalyptic service without a church.

It reminded Tom of that old song.

"What's the Frequency, Kenneth?"

REM. From an album called *Monster*.

Now there was irony.

"What's the Frequency, Kenneth?"

The title was a reference from an attack by two unknown assailants on a newsman. Dan Rather. Someone Tom's father used to watch. Someone his older brother, Sam, used to know. They kept whaling on Rather and demanding, "Kenneth, what's the frequency?"

Only Sherrie's message was simpler.

"What is it?"

Tom didn't have a word for it.

"Infection" was too shallow, and this ran a lot deeper.

"Pandemic" was a TV word. It seemed clinical despite its

implications. A word like that was too big and didn't seem to belong to this world. Not the world of the police academy; not here in sleepy little Sunset Hollow.

"What is it, Tom?"

The guy on Fox News called it the end of days. Like he was a biblical prophet. Called it that and then walked off to leave dead air.

End of days.

Tom couldn't tell Sherrie that this was the end of days. It was the end of today. And maybe it was the end of a lot of things.

But the end? The actual end?

Even now Tom didn't want to go all the way there.

He moved on, walking faster in hopes that she'd stop following him. She didn't. Sherrie walked with legs that chopped along like scissors. "What is it, Tom?"

She seemed to be settling into that now. Using his name. Latching onto him. Maybe because she thought that he knew where he was going.

He said, "I don't know."

But it was clear Sherrie didn't hear him. Or maybe *couldn't*.

Benny kept squirming, and Tom felt heat against his hip. Wet heat. Leaky diaper.

Damn.

Only pee, but still.

How do you change a diaper during the end of the world? What's the procedure there?

"What is it, Tom?"

He wheeled around, wanting to scream at her. To tell her to shut up. To hit her, to knock those stupid words out of her mouth. To break that lipstick structure so it couldn't hold the words anymore.

She recoiled from him, eyes suddenly huge. In a small and plaintive voice she asked, "What is it, Tom?"

Then the bushes trembled and parted.

There were more of them.

Them.

"Sherrie," Tom said quickly, "go to my car. It's right over there. It's unlocked."

"What is it?"

"Get in the damn car."

He pushed her away, fumbled with the door handle, pushed Benny inside. No time for car seats. Let them give him a ticket. A ticket would be nice.

"Sherrie, come on!"

She looked at him as if he was speaking a language composed of nonsense words. Vertical frown lines appeared between her brows.

"What is it?" she asked.

The people were coming now.

Many more of them.

Most of them strangers now. People from other parts of the town. Coming through yards and across lawns.

Coming.

Coming.

"Jesus, Sherrie, get in the damn car!"

She stepped back from him, shaking her head, almost smiling the way people do when they think you just don't get it.

"Sherrie—no!"

She backed one step too far.

Tom made a grab for her.

Ten hands grabbed her too. Her arms, her clothes, her hair.

"What is it, Tom?" she asked once more. Then she was gone.

Gone.

Sickened, horrified, Tom spun away and staggered toward the car. He thrust his sword into the passenger foot well and slid behind the wheel. Pulled the door shut as hands reached for him. Clawed at the door, at the glass.

It took forever to find the ignition slot, even though it was where it always was.

Behind him, Benny kept screaming.

The moans of the people outside were impossibly loud.

He turned the key.

He put the car in drive.

He broke his headlights and smashed his grille and crushed both fenders getting down the street. The bodies flew away from him. They rolled over his hood, cracked the windows with slack elbows and cheeks and chins. They lay like broken dolls in the lurid glow of his taillights.

7

Tom and Benny headed for L.A.

They were still eighty miles out when the guy on the emergency broadcast network said that the city was gone.

Gone.

Far in the west, way over the mountains, even at that distance, Tom could see the glow. The big, ugly, orange cloud bank that rose high into the air and spread itself out to ignite the roots of heaven.

He was too far away to hear it.

The nuclear shock wave would have hit the mountains anyway. Hit and bounced high and troubled the sky above them.

But the car went dead.

So did his cell phone and the radio.

All around him the lights went out.

Tom knew the letters. He'd read them somewhere. EMP. But he forgot what they stood for.

That didn't matter. He understood what they meant.

The city was gone.

An accident?

An attempt to stop the spread?

He sat in his dead car and watched the blackness beyond the cracked windshield and wondered if he would ever know. On the backseat, Benny was silent. Tom turned and looked at him. His brother was asleep. Exhausted and out.

Or . . .

A cold hand stabbed into Tom's chest and clamped around his heart.

Was Benny sleeping?

Was he?

Was he?

Tom turned and knelt on the seat. Reaching over into the shadows back there was so much harder than anything else he'd had to do. Harder than leaving Mom and Dad.

Harder than using his sword on the neighbors.

This was Benny.

This was his baby brother.

This was everything that he had left. This was the only thing that was going to hold him to the world.

No.

God, no.

His mouth shaped the words, but he made no sound at all.

He did not dare.

If Benny was sleeping, he didn't want to wake him.

If Benny was not sleeping, then he didn't want to wake that, either.

He reached across a million miles of darkness.

Please, he begged.

Of God, if God was even listening. If God was even God.

Please.

Of the world, of the night.

Please.

How many other voices had said that, screamed that, begged that? How many people had clung to that word as the darkness and the deadness and the hunger came for them?

How many?

The math was simple.

Everyone he knew.

Except him. Except Benny.

Please.

He touched Benny's face. His brother's cheeks were cool.

Cool or cold?

He couldn't tell.

Then he placed his palm flat on Benny's chest. Trying to feel something. Anything. A breath. A beat.

He waited.

And around him the night seemed to scream.

He waited.

This time he said it aloud.

"Please."

In the backseat, Benny Imura heard his brother's voice and woke up.

Began to cry.

Not moan.

Cry.

Tom laid his forehead on the seat back, held his hand against his brother's trembling chest, and wept.

FROM NIX'S JOURNAL

ON TOM IMURA
(BEFORE *ROT & RUIN*)

Tom hated it when anyone said that he was a hero.

He _was_ a hero, but he always said he wasn't.

My mom thinks he is. I think Mom is in love with him. So is Mrs. Murphy, who runs the Wash-N-Soak over on Cranberry Street. So is Jenn, the librarian at school. And Lupita and her sister. They make knives and tools, and Tom is in their store all the time. They stand at the window and stare at him when he leaves. I mean total googly-eyed stare.

Even the mayor's wife, Mrs. Kirsch, stares at him a lot. I've seen it when I go over to the Imura place to hang out with Benny. Mrs. Kirsch seems to find a lot of

reasons to come out in the yard whenever
Tom's out there working in his garden or
just coming back from a run. And don't
get me started on what happens when
Tom's out back with his swords.

Tom uses swords. It's a thing with him.
He calls it <u>kenjutsu</u>, which is a Japanese
word (I looked it up) that means "the art
of the sword." It's what the samurai,
the warriors of ancient Japan, used to
practice. Tom started studying it, and
some unarmed stuff called jujutsu and
karate, way back before First Night. He
started when he was a little kid. His dad
was born in Japan, and so was his older
brother, Sam. They're both dead now. Sam
went missing during First Night, and
Tom and Benny's dad died during the
outbreak. Benny's mom, too. She wasn't
Tom's mom, though. Both of Tom's parents
were Japanese, but his real mom died
of cancer. His dad married an Irish-
American lady, so that makes Benny
his stepbrother. Or half brother. Not sure
which is right. (NOTE: Look that up.)

Anyway, when Tom's outside training with
his sword, he sometimes does it with no
shirt on. It's funny, but when he wears

a shirt he looks kind of skinny, but when he takes it off, he's got all these muscles. They aren't huge—not like Mr. Williams, who has muscles on his muscles on his muscles. Tom's muscles are more like Mr. Olivetti, our gym teacher at school.

When Tom's in his yard working with his sword, Mrs. Kirsch seems to find a lot of reasons to water her flowers, even if it just rained. Or to put seed in the bird feeder, even after they've migrated south. Sometimes she has her friends over. They sit on the porch and seem to drink a lot of wine no matter what time of day it is.

I don't get it. I mean, sure, Tom's cute, but he's <u>old</u>. If he was twenty on First Night, then he's at least thirty-four. That's almost as old as my mom. Kind of gross.

Now Benny . . .

Yeah, that's different.

He's older too, but only by a year. He just turned fifteen.

Benny's so cute. God.

He doesn't mess around with swords, though. And he can't stand Tom. He thinks Tom's a jerk. He thinks Tom ran away and didn't try to help their folks when the outbreak happened.

Benny said he ran away and left them there to die.

Benny hates Tom.

I asked Mom about that, and she said that Benny's wrong. She says Tom is a hero because he saved Benny. That he saved a lot of people.

I don't know what to believe. Benny seems so sure.

It makes me wonder, though . . . what exactly _is_ a hero?

I'll have to look that up too.

Jack and Jill

Stebbins County, Pennsylvania

During the Outbreak
(On First Night, fourteen years before *Rot & Ruin*)

1

Jack Porter was twelve going on never grow up.

He was one of the walking dead.

He knew it. Everyone knew it.

Remission was not a reprieve; it just put you in a longer line at the airport. Jack had seen what happened to his cousin, Toby. Three remissions in three years. Hope pushed Toby into a corner and beat the crap out of him each time. Toby was a ghost in third grade, a skeleton in fourth grade, a withered thing in a bed by the end of fifth grade, and bones in a box before sixth grade even started. All that hope had accomplished was to make everyone more afraid.

Now it was Jack's turn.

Chemo, radiation. Bone marrow transplants. Even surgery.

Like they say in the movies, life sucks, and then you die.

So, yeah, life sucked.

What there was of it.

What there was left.

Jack sat cross-legged on the edge of his bed, watching the weatherman on TV talk about the big storm that was about to hit. He kept going on and on about the dangers of floods, and there was a continuous scroll across the bottom of the screen that listed the evacuation shelters.

Jack ate dry Honey Nut Cheerios out of a bowl and thought

about floods. The east bend of the river was three hundred feet from the house. Uncle Roger liked to say that they were a football field away, back door to muddy banks. Twice the river had flooded enough for there to be some small wavelets licking at the bottom step of the porch. But there hadn't ever been a storm as bad as what they were predicting, at least not in Jack's lifetime. The last storm big enough to flood the whole farm had been in 1931. Jack knew that because they showed flood maps on TV. The weather guy was really into it. He seemed jazzed by the idea that a lot of Stebbins County could be flooded out.

Jack was kind of jazzed about it too.

It beat the crap out of rotting away. Remission or not, Jack was certain that he could feel himself die, cell by cell. He dreamed about that, thought about it. Wrote in his journal about it. Did everything but talk about it.

Not even to Jill. Jack and Jill had sworn an oath years ago to tell each other everything, no secrets. Not one. But that was before Jack got sick. That was back when they were two peas in a pod. Alike in everything, except that Jack was a boy and Jill was a girl. Back then, back when they'd made that pact, they were just kids. You could barely tell one from the other except in the bath.

Years ago. A lifetime ago, as Jack saw it.

The sickness changed everything. There were some secrets the dying were allowed to keep to themselves.

Jack watched the Doppler radar of the coming storm and smiled. He had an earbud nestled into one ear and was also listening to Magic Marti on the radio. She was hyped about the storm too, sounding as excited as Jack felt.

"*Despite heavy winds, the storm front is slowing down and looks like it's going to park right on the Maryland/Pennsylvania border, with Stebbins County taking the brunt of it. They're calling for torrential rains and strong winds, along with severe flooding. And here's a twist . . . even though this is a November storm, warm air masses from the south are bringing significant lightning, and so far there have been several serious strikes. Air traffic is being diverted around the storm.*"

Jack nodded along with her words as if it was music playing in his ear.

Big storm. Big flood?

He hoped so.

The levees along the river were half-assed, or at least that's how Dad always described them.

"Wouldn't take much more than a good piss to flood 'em out," Dad was fond of saying, and he said it every time they got a bad storm. The levees never flooded out, and Jack wondered if this was the sort of thing people said to prevent something bad from happening. Like telling an actor to break a leg.

On the TV they showed the levees, and a guy described as a civil engineer puffed out his chest and said that Pennsylvania levees were much better than the kind that had failed in Louisiana. Stronger, better maintained.

Jack wondered what Dad would say about that. Dad wasn't much for the kind of experts news shows trotted out. "Bunch of pansy-ass know-nothings."

The news people seemed to agree, because after the

segment with the engineer, the anchor with the plastic hair pretty much tore down everything the man had to say.

"Although the levees in Stebbins County are considered above average for the region, the latest computer models say that this storm is only going to get stronger."

Jack wasn't sure if that was a logical statement, but he liked its potential. The storm was getting bigger, and that was exciting.

But again he wondered what it would be like to have all that water—that great, heaving mass of coldness—come crashing in through all the windows and doors. Jack's bedroom was on the ground floor, a concession to how easily he got tired climbing steps. The house was 115 years old. It creaked in a light wind. No way it could stand up to a million gallons of water, Jack was positive of that.

If it happened, he wondered what he would do.

Stay here in his room and let the house fall down around him.

No, that sounded like it would hurt. Jack could deal with pain—he had to—but he didn't like it.

Maybe he could go into the living room and wait for it. On the couch, or on the floor in front of the TV. If the TV and the power were still on. Just sit there and wait for the black tide to come calling.

How quick would it be?

Would it hurt to drown?

Would he be scared?

Sure, but rotting was worse.

He munched a palmful of Cheerios and prayed that the river would come for him.

2

"Mom said I can't stay home today," grumped Jill as she came into Jack's room. She dropped her book bag on the floor and kicked it.

"Why not?"

"She said the weatherman's never right. She said the storm'll pass us."

"Magic Marti says it's going to kick our butts," said Jack.

As if to counterpoint his comment, there was a low rumble of thunder way off to the west.

Jill sighed and sat next to him on the edge of the bed. She no longer looked like his twin. She had a round face and was starting to grow boobs. Her hair was as black as crow's wings, and even though Mom didn't let her wear makeup—not until she was in junior high, and even then it was going to be an argument—Jill had pink cheeks, pink lips, and every boy in sixth grade was in love with her. Jill didn't seem to care much about that. She didn't try to dress like the middle school girls, or like Maddy Simpson, who was the same age but who had pretty big boobs and dressed like she was in an MTV rap video. Uncle Roger had a ten-dollar bet going that Maddy was going to be pregnant before she ever got within shooting distance of a diploma. Jack and Jill both agreed. Everyone did.

Jill dressed like a farm girl. Jeans and a sweatshirt, often the same kind of sweatshirt Jack wore. Today she had on an olive drab US Army shirt. Jack wore his with pajama bottoms. Aunt Linda had been in the army, but she'd died in Afghanistan three years ago.

They sat together, staring blankly at the TV screen for a while. Jack cut her a sly sideways look and saw that her face was slack, eyes empty. He understood why, and it made him sad.

Jill wasn't dealing well with the cancer. He was afraid of what would happen to her after he died. And Jack had no illusions about whether the current remission was going to be the one that took. When he looked into his own future, either in dreams, prayers, or when lost in thought, there was an end to the road. It went on a bit further, and there was a big wall of black nothingness.

It sucked, sure, but he'd lived with it so long that he had found a kind of peace with it. Why go kicking and screaming into the dark if none of that would change anything?

Jill, on the other hand, that was different. She had to live, she had to keep going. Jack watched TV a lot, he saw the episodes of Dr. Phil and other shows where they talked about death and dying. He knew that some people believed that the dying had an obligation to their loved ones who would survive them.

Jack didn't want Jill to suffer after he died, but he didn't know what he could do about it. He told her once about his dreams of the big black nothing.

"It's like a wave that comes and just sweeps me away," he'd told her.

"That sounds awful," she replied, tears springing into her eyes, but Jack assured her that it wasn't.

"No," he said, "'cause once the nothing takes you, there's no more pain."

"But there's no more *you*!"

He grinned. "How do you know? No one knows what's

on the other side of that wall." He shrugged. "Maybe it'll be something cool. Something nice."

"How could it be nice?" Jill had demanded.

This was right after the cancer had come back the last time, before the current remission. Jack was so frail that he barely made a dent in his own hospital bed. He touched the wires and tubes that ran from his pencil-thin arm to the machines behind him. "It's got to be nicer than this."

Nicer than this.

That was the last time they'd had a real conversation about the sickness, or about death. That was nine months ago. Jack stopped talking to her about those things and instead did what he could to ease her down so that when the nothing took him, she'd still be able to stand.

He nudged her and held out the bowl of cereal. Without even looking at it, she took a handful and began eating them, one at a time, smashing them angrily between her teeth.

Eventually she said, "It's not fair."

"I know." Just as he knew that they were having two separate conversations at the same time. It was often that way with them.

They crunched and glared at the TV.

"If it gets bad," Jack said, "they'll let everyone go."

But she shook her head. "I want to stay home. I want to hang out here and watch it on TV."

"You'll be *in* it," he said.

"Not the same thing. It's better on TV."

Jack ate some Cheerios and nodded. Everything was more fun on TV. Real life didn't have commentary, and it didn't have playback. Watching a storm beat standing in one while you waited for the school bus to splash water on you. It beat the smells of sixty soaking-wet kids on a crowded bus, and bumper-to-bumper traffic waiting for your driveway.

As if in response to that thought, there was a muffled honk from outside.

"Bus," said Jack.

"Crap," said Jill. She stood up. "Text me. Let me know what's happening."

"Sure."

Jill began flouncing out of the room, but then she stopped in the doorway and looked back at him. She looked from him to the TV screen and back again. She wore a funny half smile.

"What—?" he asked.

Jill studied him without answering long enough for the bus driver to get pissed and really lay on the horn.

"I mean it," she said. "Text me."

"I already said I would."

Jill chewed her lip, then turned and headed out of the house and up the winding drive to the road where the big yellow bus waited.

Jack wondered what that was all about.

3

Mom came into his room in the middle of the morning, carrying a tray with two hot corn muffins smeared with butter and honey and a big glass of water.

"You hungry?" she asked, setting the tray down on the bed between them.

"Sure," said Jack, though he wasn't. His appetite was better than it had been all summer, and even though he was done with chemo for a while, he only liked to nibble. The Cheerios were perfect, and it was their crunch more than anything that he liked.

But he took a plate with one of the muffins, sniffed, pasted a smile on his mouth, and took a small bite. Jack knew from experience that Mom needed to see him eat. It was more important to her to make sure that he was eating than it was to see him eat much. He thought he understood that. Appetite was a sign of health, or remission. Cancer patients in the full burn of the disease didn't have much of an appetite. Jack knew that very well.

As he chewed, Mom tore open a couple of packs of vitamin C powder and poured them into his water glass.

"Tropical mix," she announced, but Jack had already smelled it. It wasn't as good as the tangerine, but it was okay. He accepted the glass, waited for the fizz to settle down, and then took a sip to wash down the corn muffin.

Thunder rumbled again and rattled the windows.

"It's getting closer," said Jack. When his mother didn't comment, he asked, "Will Jilly be okay?"

Before Mom could reply, the first fat raindrops splatted on the glass. She picked up the remote to raise the volume. The regular weatherman was no longer giving the updates. Instead it was the anchorman, the guy from Pittsburgh with all the teeth and the plastic-looking hair.

"Mom—?" Jack asked again.

"Shh, let me listen."

The newsman said, "Officials are urging residents to

prepare for a powerful storm that slammed eastern Ohio yesterday, tore along the northern edge of West Virginia, and is currently grinding its way along the Maryland-Pennsylvania border."

There was a quick cutaway to a scientist-looking guy that Jack had seen a dozen times this morning. Dr. Gustus, a professor from some university. "The storm is unusually intense for this time of year, spinning up into what is clearly a high-precipitation supercell, which is an especially dangerous type of storm. Since the storm's mesocyclone is wrapped with heavy rains, it can hide a tornado from view until the funnel touches down. These supercells are also known for their tendency to produce more frequent cloud-to-ground and intracloud lightning than the other types of storms. The system weakened briefly overnight, following computer models of similar storms in this region. However, what we are seeing now is an unfortunate combination of elements that could result in a major upgrade of this weather pattern."

The professor gave a bunch more technical information that Jack was pretty sure no one really understood, and then the image cut back to the reporter with the plastic hair, who contrived to look grave and concerned. "This storm will produce flooding rains, high winds, downed trees—on houses, cars, power lines—and widespread power outages. Make sure you have plenty of candles and flashlights with fresh batteries because, folks, you're going to need 'em." He actually smiled when he said that.

Jack suddenly shivered.

Mom noticed it and wrapped her arm around his bony

shoulders. "Hey, now . . . don't worry. We'll be safe here."

He made an agreeing noise but did not bother to correct her. He wasn't frightened of the storm's power. He was hoping it would become one of those Category 5 things like they showed on Syfy. Or a bigger one. Big enough to tear the house to sticks and let the waters of the river sweep him away from pain and sickness. Being killed in a super storm was so delightful that it made him shiver and raised goose bumps all along his arms. Lasting through the rain and wind so that he was back to where—and what—he was . . . that was far more frightening. Being suddenly dead was better than dying.

On the other hand . . .

"What about Jill?"

"She'll be fine," said Mom, though her tone was less than convincing.

"Mom . . . ?"

Mom was a thin, pretty woman whose black hair had started going gray around the time of the first diagnosis. Now it was more gray than black, and there were dark circles under her eyes. Jill looked a little like Mom and would probably grow up to look a lot like her. Jack looked like her too, right down to the dark circles under the eyes that looked out at him every morning from the bathroom mirror.

"Mom," Jack said tentatively, "Jill *is* going to be all right, isn't she?"

"She's in school. If it gets bad, they'll bus the kids home."

"Shouldn't someone go get her?"

Mom looked at the open bedroom door. "Your dad and Uncle Roger are in town, buying the pipes for the new irrigation system. They'll see how bad it is, and if they have to, they'll get her." She smiled, and Jack thought that it was every bit as false as the smile he'd given her a minute ago. "Jill will be fine. Don't stress yourself out about it. You know it's not good for you."

"Okay," he said, resisting the urge to shake his head. He loved his mom, but she really didn't understand him at all.

"You should get some rest," she said. "After you finish your muffin, why not take a little nap?"

Jeez-us, he thought. She was always saying stuff like that. Take a nap, get some rest. *I'm going to be dead for a long time. Let me be awake as much as I can for now.*

"Sure," he said. "Maybe in a bit."

Mom smiled brightly, as if they had sealed a deal. She kissed him on the head and went out of his room, closing the door three-quarters of the way. She never closed it all the way, so Jack got up and did that for himself.

Jack nibbled another micro-bite of the muffin, sighed, and set it down. He broke it up on the plate so it looked like he'd really savaged it. Then he drank the vitamin water, set the glass down, and stretched out on his stomach to watch the news.

Rain drummed on the roof like nervous fingertips, and the wind was whistling through the trees. The storm was coming for sure. No way it was going to veer.

Jack lay there in the blue glow of the TV and the brown shadows of his thoughts. He'd been dying for so long that he could barely remember what living felt like. Only Jill's smile sometimes brought those memories back. Running together down the long lanes of cultivated crops. Waging war with broken ears of corn, and trying to juggle fist-size pumpkins. Jill was never any good at juggling, and she laughed so hard when Jack managed to get three pumpkins going that he started laughing too and dropped the gourds right on his head.

He sighed, and it almost hitched into a sob.

He wanted to laugh again. Not careful laughs, like now, but real gut-busters like he used to. He wanted to run. God, how he wanted to run. That was something he hadn't been able to do for over a year now. Not since the last surgery. And never again. Best he could manage was a hobbling half run like Gran used to when the Millers' dog got into her herb garden.

Jack closed his eyes and thought about the storm. About a flood.

He really wanted Jill to come home. He loved his sister, and maybe today he'd open up and tell her what really went on in his head. Would she like that? Would she want to know?

Those were tricky questions, and he didn't have answers to them.

Nor did he have an answer to why he wanted Jill home *and* wanted the flood at the same time. That was stupid. That was selfish.

"I'm dying," he whispered to the shadows.

Dying people were supposed to get what they wanted, weren't they? Trips to Disney, a letter from a celebrity. All that Make-A-Wish stuff. He wanted to see his sister and then let the storm take him away. Without hurting her, of course. Or Mom, or Dad, or Uncle Roger.

He sighed again.

Wishes were stupid. They never came true.

4

Jack was drowsing when he heard his mother cry out.

A single, strident "No!"

Jack scrambled out of bed and opened his door a careful inch to try to catch the conversation Mom was having on the phone. She was in the big room down the hall, the one she and Dad used as the farm office.

"Is she okay? God, Steve, tell me she's okay!"

Those words froze Jack to the spot.

He mouthed the name.

"Jill . . ."

"Oh my God," cried Mom, "does she need to go to the hospital? What? How can the hospital be closed? Steve . . . how can the damn hospital be—"

Mom stopped to listen, but Jack could see her body change, stiffening with fear and tension. She had the phone to her ear and her other hand at her throat.

"Oh God, Steve. What *happened*? Who did this? Oh, come on, Steve, that's ridiculous. . . . Steve . . ."

Jack could hear Dad's voice but not his words. He was yelling. Almost screaming.

"Did you call the police?" Mom demanded. She listened for an answer, and whatever it was, it was clear to Jack that it shocked her. She staggered backward and sat down hard on a wooden chair. "*Shooting?* Who was shooting?"

More yelling, none of it clear.

Shooting? Jack stared at Mom as if he was peering into a different world from anything he knew. He tried to put the things he'd heard into some shape that made sense, but no picture formed.

"Jesus Christ!" shrieked Mom. "Steve . . . forget about, forget about everything. Just get my baby home. Get yourself home. I have a first aid kit here and . . . oh yes, God, Steve . . . I love you, too. Hurry!"

She lowered the phone and stared at it as if the device had done her some unspeakable harm. Her eyes were wide, but she didn't seem to be looking at anything.

"Mom . . . ?" Jack said softly, stepping out into the hall. "What's happening? What's wrong?"

As soon as she looked up, Mom's eyes filled with tears. She cried out his name, and he rushed to her as she flew to him. Mom was always so careful with him, holding him as if he had bird bones that would snap with the slightest pressure, but right then she clutched him to her chest with all her strength. He could feel her trembling, could feel the heat of her panic through the cotton of her dress.

"It's Jilly," said Mom, and her voice broke into sobs. "There was a fight at the school. Someone *bit* her."

"Bit—?" asked Jack, not sure he'd really heard that.

Lightning flashed outside and thunder exploded overhead.

5

Mom ran around for a couple of minutes, grabbing first aid stuff. There was always a lot of it on a farm, and Jack knew how to dress a wound and treat for shock. Then she fetched candles and matches, flashlights and a Coleman lantern. Big storms always knocked out the power in town, and Mom was always ready.

The storm kept getting bigger, rattling the old bones of the house, making the window glass chatter like teeth.

"What's taking them so damn *long*?" Mom said, and she said it every couple of minutes.

Jack turned on the big TV in the living room.

"Mom!" he called. "They have it on the news."

She came running into the room with an armful of clean towels and stopped in the middle of the floor to watch. What they saw did not make much sense. The picture showed the Stebbins Little School, which was both the elementary school and the town's evacuation shelter. It was on high ground, and it had been built during an era when Americans worried about nuclear bombs and Russian air raids. Stuff Jack barely even knew about.

In front of the school was the guest parking lot, which was also where the buses picked up and dropped off the kids. Usually there were lines of yellow buses standing in neat rows, or moving like a slow train as they pulled to the front, loaded or unloaded, then moved forward to catch up with the previous bus. There was nothing neat and orderly about the big yellow vehicles now.

The heavy downpour made everything vague and fuzzy, but Jack could nevertheless see that the buses stood in haphazard lines in the parking lot and in the street. Cars were slotted in everywhere to create a total gridlock. One of the buses lay on its side.

Two were burning.

All around, inside and out, were people. Running, staggering, lying sprawled, fighting.

Not even the thunder and the rain could drown out the sounds of screams.

And gunfire.

"Mom . . . ?" asked Jack. "What's happening?"

But Mom had nothing to stay. The bundle of towels fell softly to the floor by her feet.

She ran to the table by the couch, snatched up the phone, and called 911. Jack stood so close that he could hear the rings.

Seven. Eight. On the ninth ring there was a clicking sound and then a thump, as if someone had picked up the phone and dropped it.

Mom said, "Hello—?" Jack pressed close to hear.

The sounds from the other end were confused, and Jack tried to make sense of them. The scuff of a shoe? A soft, heavy bump as if someone had banged into a desk with their thighs. And a sound like someone makes when they're asleep. Low and without any meaning.

"Flower," called Mom. Flower was the secretary and dispatcher at the police station. She'd gone to high school with Mom. "Flower—are you there? Can you hear me?"

If there was a response, Jack couldn't hear it.

"Flower—come on, girl, I need some help. There was some kind of problem at the school, and Steve's bringing Jilly back with a bad bite. He tried to take her to the hospital, but it was closed and there were barricades set up. We need an ambulance. . . ."

Flower finally replied.

It wasn't words, just a long, deep, aching moan that came crawling down the phone lines. Mom jerked the handset away from her ear, staring at it with horror and fear. Jack heard that sound, and it chilled him to the bones.

Not because it was so alien and unnatural . . . but because he recognized it. He knew that sound. He absolutely knew it.

He'd heard Toby make it a couple of times during those last days, when the cancer was so bad that they had to keep Toby down in a dark pool of drugs. Painkillers didn't really work at that level. The pain was everywhere. It was the whole universe, because every single particle of your body knows that it's being consumed. The cancer is winning, it's devouring you, and you get to a point where it's so big and you're so small that you can't even yell at it anymore. You can't curse at it or shout at it or tell it that you won't let it win. It already has won, and you know it. In those moments, those last crumbling moments, all you can do—all you can *say*—is throw noise at it. It's not meaningless, even though it sounds like that. When Jack first heard those sounds coming out of Toby, he thought that it was just noise, just a grunt or a moan. But those sounds *do* have meaning. So much meaning. Too much meaning. They're filled with all the need in the world.

The need to live, even though the dark is everywhere, inside and out.

The need to survive, even though you know you can't.

The need to have just another hour, just another minute, but your clock is broken and all the time has leaked out.

The need to not be devoured.

Even though you already are.

The need.

Need.

That moan, the one Jack heard at Toby's bedside and the

one he heard now over the phone line from Flower, was just that. Need.

It was the sound Jack sometimes made in his dreams. Practicing for when it would be the only sound he could make.

Mom said, "Flower . . . ?"

But this time her voice was small. Little-kid small.

There were no more sounds from the other end, and Mom replaced the handset as carefully as if it was something that could wake up and bite her.

She suddenly seemed to notice Jack standing there, and she hoisted up as fake a smile as Jack had ever seen.

"It'll be okay," she said. "It's the storm causing trouble with the phone lines."

The lie was silly and weak, but they both accepted it because there was nothing else they could do.

Then Jack saw the headlights, turning off River Road onto their driveway.

"They're here!" he cried, and rushed for the door, but Mom pushed past him, jerked the door open, and ran out onto the porch.

"Stay back," she yelled as he began to follow.

Jack stopped in the doorway. Rain slashed at Mom as she stood on the top step, silhouetted by the headlights as Dad's big Dodge Durango splashed through the water that completely covered the road. His brights were on, and Jack had to shield his eyes behind his hands. The pickup raced all the way up the half-mile drive and slewed sideways to a stop that sent muddy rainwater onto the porch, slapping wet across Mom's legs. She didn't care; she was already running down the steps toward the car.

The doors flew open, and Dad jumped out from behind the wheel and ran around the front of the truck. Uncle Roger had something in his arms. Something that was limp and wrapped in a blanket that looked like it was soaked with oil. Only it wasn't oil, and Jack knew it. Lightning flashed continually, and in its stark glow the oily black became gleaming red.

Dad took the bundle from him and rushed through ankle-deep mud toward the porch. Mom reached him and tugged back the cloth. Jack could see the tattered sleeve of an olive-drab sweatshirt and one ice-pale hand streaked with crooked lines of red.

Mom screamed.

Jack did too, even though he could not see what she saw. Mom had said that she'd been bitten . . . but this couldn't be a bite. Not with this much blood. Not with Jill not moving.

"JILL!"

He ran out onto the porch and down the steps and into the teeth of the storm.

"Get back," screeched Mom as she and Dad bulled their way past him onto the porch and into the house. Nobody wiped their feet.

Roger caught up with him. He was bare-chested despite the cold and had his undershirt wrapped around his left arm. In the glare of the lightning, his skin looked milk white.

"What is it? What's happening? What's wrong with Jill?" demanded Jack, but Uncle Roger grabbed him by the shoulder and shoved him toward the house.

"Get inside," he growled. *"Now."*

Jack staggered toward the steps and lost his balance. He dropped to his knees in the mud, but Uncle Roger caught him under the armpit and hauled him roughly to his feet and pushed him up the steps. All the while, Uncle Roger kept looking over his shoulder. Jack twisted around to see what he was looking at. The bursts of lightning made everything look weird, and for a moment he thought that there were people at the far end of the road, but when the next bolt forked through the sky, he saw that it was only cornstalks battered by the wind.

Only that.

"Get inside," urged Roger. "It's not safe out here."

Jack looked at him. Roger was soaked to the skin. His face was swollen, as if he'd been punched, and the shirt wrapped around his left arm was soaked through with blood.

It's not safe out here.

Jack knew for certain that his uncle was not referring to the weather.

The lightning flashed again, and the shadows in the corn seemed wrong.

All wrong.

6

Jack stood silent and unnoticed in the corner of the living room, like a ghost haunting his own family. No one spoke to him, no one looked in his direction. Not even Jill.

As soon as they'd come in, Dad had laid Jill down on the couch. No time even to put a sheet under her. Rainwater pooled under the couch in pink puddles. Uncle Roger stood behind the couch, looking down at Mom and Dad as they used rags soaked with fresh water and alcohol to sponge away mud and blood. Mom snipped away the sleeves of the torn and ragged army sweatshirt.

"It was like something off the news. It was like one of those riots you see on TV," said Roger. His eyes were glassy, and his voice had a distant quality, as if his body and his thoughts were in separate rooms. "People just going crazy for no reason. Good people. People we know. I saw Dix Howard take a tire iron out of his car and lay into Joe Fielding, the baseball coach from the high school. Just laid into him, swinging on him like he was a total stranger. Beat the crap out of him too. Joe's glasses went flying off his face, and his nose was just bursting with blood. Crazy stuff."

"Give me the peroxide," said Mom, working furiously. "There's another little bite on her wrist."

"The big one's not that bad," Dad said, speaking over her rather than to her. "Looks like it missed the artery. But Jilly's always been a bleeder."

"It was like that when we drove up," said Uncle Roger, continuing his account even though he had no audience. Jack didn't think that his uncle was speaking to him. Or . . . to anyone. He was speaking because he needed to get it out of his head, as if that was going to help make sense of it. "With the rain and all, it was hard to tell what was going on. Not at first. Just buses and cars parked every which way and lots of people running and shouting. We thought there'd been an accident. You know people panic when there's an accident and kids are involved. They run around like chickens with their heads cut off, screaming and making a fuss instead of doing what needs to be done. So Steve and I got out of the truck and started pushing our way into the crowd. To find Jill and to, you know, see if we could do something. To help."

Jack took a small step forward, trying to catch a peek at Jill. She was still unconscious, her face small and gray. Mom and Dad seemed to have eight hands each as they cleaned and swabbed and dabbed. The worst wound was the one on her forearm. It was ugly, and it wasn't just one of those bites when someone squeezes their teeth on you; no, there was actual skin missing. Someone had taken a bite *out* of Jill, and that was a whole other thing. Jack could see that the edges of the ragged flesh were stained with something dark and gooey.

"What's all that black stuff?" asked Mom as she probed the bite. "Is that oil?"

"No," barked Dad, "it's coming out of her like pus. Christ, I don't know what it is. Some kind of infection. Don't get it on you. Give me the alcohol."

Jack kept staring at the black goo, and he thought he could see something move inside it. Like tiny threadlike worms.

Uncle Roger kept talking, his voice level and detached. "We saw her teacher, Mrs. Grayson, lying on the ground, and two kids were kneeling over her. I—I thought they were praying. Or . . . something. They had their heads bowed, but when I pulled one back to try to see if the teacher was okay . . ."

Roger stopped talking. He raised his injured left hand and stared at it as if it didn't belong to him, as if the memory of that injury couldn't belong to his experience. The bandage was red with blood, but Jack could see some of the black stuff on him, too. On the bandages and on his skin.

"Somebody bit you?" asked Jack, and Roger twitched and turned toward him. He stared down with huge eyes. "Is that what happened?"

Roger slowly nodded. "It was that girl who wears all that makeup. Maddy Simpson. She bared her teeth at me like she was some kind of animal, and she just . . . she just . . ."

He shook his head.

"Maddy?" murmured Jack. "What did you do?"

Roger's eyes slid away. "I . . . um . . . I made her let go. You know? She was acting all crazy and I had to make her let go. I had to . . ."

Jack did not ask what exactly Uncle Roger had done to free himself of Maddy Simpson's white teeth. His clothes and face were splashed with blood, and the truth of it was in his eyes. It made Jack want to run and hide.

But he couldn't leave.

He had to know.

And he had to be there when Jill woke up.

Roger stumbled his way back into his story. "It wasn't just her. It was everybody. Everybody was going crazy. People kept rushing at us. Nobody was making any sense, and the rain would not stop battering us. You couldn't see, couldn't even think. We—we—we had to find Jill, you know?"

"But what *is* it?" asked Jack. "Is it rabies?"

Dad, Mom, and Roger all looked at him, then at one another.

"Rabies don't come on that fast," said Dad. "This was happening right away. I saw some people go down really hurt. Throat wounds and such. Thought they were dead, but then they got back up again and started attacking people. That's how fast this works." He shook his head. "Not any damn rabies."

"Maybe it's one of them terrorist things," said Roger.

Mom and Dad stiffened and stared at him, and Jack could see new doubt and fear blossom in their eyes.

"What kind of thing?" asked Dad.

Roger licked his lips. "Some kind of nerve gas, maybe? One of those—whaddya call 'em?—*weaponized* things. Like in the movies. Anthrax or Ebola or something. Something that drives people nuts."

"It's not Ebola," snapped Mom.

"Maybe it's a toxic spill or something," Roger ventured. It was clear to Jack that Roger really needed to have this be something ordinary enough to have a name.

So did Jack. If it had a name, then maybe Jill would be okay.

Roger said, "Or maybe it's—"

Mom cut him off. "Put on the TV. Maybe there's something."

"I got it," said Jack, happy to have something to do. He snatched the remote off the coffee table and pressed the button. The TV had been on local news when they'd turned it off, but when the picture came on, all it showed was a stationary text page that read:

WE ARE EXPERIENCING
A TEMPORARY INTERRUPTION IN SERVICE
PLEASE STAND BY

"Go to CNN," suggested Roger, but Jack was already surfing through the stations. They had Comcast cable. Eight hundred stations, including high-def.

The same text was on every single one.

"What the hell?" said Roger indignantly. "We have friggin' *digital*. How can all the stations' feeds be out?"

"Maybe it's the cable channel," said Jack. "Everything goes through them, right?"

"It's the storm," said Dad.

"No," said Mom, but she didn't explain. She bent over Jill and peered closer at the black goo around her wounds. "Oh my God, Steve, there's something in there. Some kind of—"

Jill suddenly opened her eyes.

Everyone froze.

Jill looked up at Mom and Dad, then Uncle Roger, and then finally at Jack.

"Jack . . . ," she said in a faint whisper, lifting her uninjured hand toward him, "I had the strangest dream."

"Jilly?" Jack murmured in a voice that had suddenly gone as dry as bones. He reached a tentative hand toward her. But as Jack's fingers lightly brushed his sister's, Dad suddenly smacked his hand away.

"Don't!" he warned.

Jill's eyes were all wrong. The green of her irises had darkened to a rust and the whites had flushed to crimson. A black tear broke from the corner of her eye and wriggled its way down her cheek. Tiny white things twisted and squirmed in the goo.

Mom choked back a scream and actually recoiled from Jill.

Roger whispered, "God almighty . . . what *is* that stuff? What's wrong with her?"

"Jack—?" called Jill. "You look all funny. Why are you wearing red makeup?"

Her voice had a dreamy, distant quality. Almost musical in its lilt, like the way people sometimes spoke in dreams. Jack absently touched his face, as if it was his skin and not her vision that was painted with blood.

"Steve," said Mom in an urgent whisper, "we have to get her to a doctor. Right now."

"We can't, honey, the storm—"

"We *have* to. Damn it, Steve, I can't lose both my babies."

She suddenly gasped at her own words and cut a look at Jack, reaching for him with hands that were covered in Jill's blood. "Oh God . . . Jack . . . sweetie, I didn't mean—."

"No," said Jack, "it's okay. We *have* to save Jill. We have to."

Mom and Dad both looked at him for a few terrible seconds, and there was such pain in their eyes that Jack wanted to turn away. But he didn't. What Mom had said did not hurt him as much as it hurt her. She didn't know it, but Jack had heard her say those kinds of things before. Late at night when she and Dad sat together on the couch and cried and talked about what they were going to do after he was dead. He knew that they'd long ago given up real hope. Hope was fragile and cancer was a monster.

Fresh tears brimmed in Mom's eyes, and Jack could almost feel something pass between them. Some understanding, some acceptance. There was an odd little flicker of relief as if she grasped what Jack knew about his own future. And Jack wondered if, when Mom looked into her own dreams at the future of her only son, she also saw the great black wall of nothing that was just a little way down the road.

Jack knew that he could never put any of this into words. He was a very smart twelve-year-old, but this was something for philosophers. No one of that profession lived on their farm.

The moment, which was only a heartbeat long, stretched too far and broke. The brimming tears fell down Mom's cheeks, and she turned back to Jill. Back to the child who maybe still had a future. Back to the child she could fight for.

Jack was completely okay with that.

He looked at his sister, at those crimson eyes. They were so alien that he could not find *her* in there. Then Jill gave him a small smile. A smile he knew so well. The smile that said, *This isn't so bad.* The smile they sometimes shared when they were both in trouble and getting yelled at rather than having their computers and Xboxes taken away.

Then her eyes drifted shut; the smile lost its scaffolding and collapsed into a meaningless, slack-mouthed nothing.

There was an immediate panic as Mom and Dad both tried to take her pulse at the same time. Dad ignored the black ichor on her face and arm as he bent close to press his ear to her chest. Time froze around him, and then he let out a breath with a sharp burst of relief.

"She's breathing. Christ, she's still breathing. I think she just passed out. Blood loss, I guess."

"She could be going into shock," said Roger, and Dad shot him a withering look. But it was too late, Mom was already being hammered by panic.

"Get some blankets," she snapped. "We'll bundle her up and take the truck."

"No," said Roger, "like I said, we tried to take her to Wolverton ER, but they had it blocked off."

"Then we'll take her to Bordentown, or Fayetteville or any damn place, but we have to take her somewhere!"

"I'm just saying," Roger said, but his voice had been beaten down into something tiny and powerless by Mom's anger. He was her younger brother, and she'd always held the power in their family.

"Roger," she said, "you stay here with Jack and—"

"I want to go too," insisted Jack.

"No," barked Mom. "You'll stay right here with your uncle and—"

"But Uncle Rog is hurt too," he said. "He got bit and he has that black stuff too."

Mom's head swiveled sharply around, and she stared at Roger's arm. The lines around her mouth etched deeper. "Okay," she said. "Okay. Just don't touch that stuff. You hear me, Jack? Steve? Don't touch whatever that black stuff is. We don't know what's in it."

"Honey, I don't think we can make it to the highway," said Dad. "When we came up River Road, the water was half-way up the wheels. It'll be worse now."

"Then we'll go across the fields, goddamn it!" snarled Mom.

"On the TV, earlier," interrupted Jack, "they said that the National Guard was coming in to help because of the flooding and all. Won't they be near the river? Down by the levee?"

Dad nodded. "That's right. They'll be sandbagging along the roads. I'm surprised we didn't see them on the way here."

"Maybe they're the ones who blocked the hospital," said Roger. "Maybe they took it over, made it some kind of emergency station."

"Good, good . . . that's our plan. We find the Guard, and they'll help us get Jill to a—"

But that was as far as Dad got.

Lightning flashed as white-hot as the sun, and in the same second there was a crack of thunder that was the loudest sound Jack had ever heard.

All the lights went out and the house was plunged into total darkness.

7

Dad's voice spoke from the darkness. "That was the transformer up on the access road."

"Sounded like a direct hit," agreed Roger.

There was a scrape and a puff of sulfur, and then Mom's face emerged from the darkness in a small pool of match-light. She bent and lit a candle and then another. In the glow she fished for the Coleman, lit that, and the room was bright again.

"We have to go," she said.

Dad was already moving. He picked up several heavy blankets from the stack Mom had laid by and used them to wrap Jill. He was as gentle as he could be, but he moved fast and he made sure to stay away from the black muck on her face and arm. But he did not head immediately for the door.

"Stay here," he said, and crossed swiftly to the farm office. Jack trailed along and watched his father fish in his pocket for keys, fumble one out, and unlock a heavy oak cabinet mounted to the wall. A second key unlocked a restraining bar, and then Dad was pulling guns out of racks. Two shotguns and three pistols. He caught Jack watching him, and his face hardened. "It's pretty wild out there, Jackie."

"Why? What's going on, Dad?"

Dad paused for a moment, breathed in and out through his nose, then opened a box of shotgun shells and began feeding buckshot cartridges into the guns.

"I don't know what's going on, kiddo."

It was the first time Jack could ever remember his father admitting that he had no answers. Dad knew everything. Dad was Dad.

Dad stood the shotguns against the wall and loaded the pistols. He had two nine-millimeter Glocks. Jack knew a lot about guns. From living on the farm, from stories of the army his dad and uncle told. From the things Aunt Linda used to talk about when she was home on leave. Jack and Jill had both been taught to shoot and how to handle a gun safely. This was farm country, and that was part of the life.

And Jack had logged a lot of hours on Medal of Honor and other first-person-shooter games. In the virtual worlds he was a healthy, powerful, terrorist-killing engine of pure destruction.

Cancer wasn't a factor in video games.

The third pistol was a thirty-two-caliber Smith & Wesson. Mom's gun, for times when Dad and Uncle Roger were away for a couple of days. Their farm was big and it was remote. If trouble came, you had to handle it on your own. That's what Dad always said.

Except now.

This trouble was too big. Too bad.

This was Jill, and she was hurt and maybe sick, too.

"Is Jill going to be okay?" asked Jack.

Dad stuffed extra shells in his pockets and locked the cabinet.

"Sure," he said.

Jack nodded, accepting the lie because it was the only answer his father could possibly give.

He trailed Dad back into the living room. Uncle Roger had Jill in his arms, and she was so thoroughly wrapped in blankets that it looked like he was carrying laundry. Mom saw the guns in Dad's hands and her eyes flared for a moment; then Jack saw her mouth tighten into a hard line. He'd seen that expression before. Once, four years ago, when a vagrant wandered onto the farm and sat on a stump watching Jill and Jack as they played in their rubber pool. Mom had come out onto the porch with a baseball bat in her hand and that look on her face. She didn't actually have to say anything, but the vagrant went hustling along the road and never came back.

The other time was when she went after Tony Magruder, a brute of a kid who'd been left back twice and loomed over the other sixth graders like a Neanderthal. Tony was making fun of Jack because he was so skinny and pantsed him in the school yard. Jill had gone after him—with her own version of that expression—and Tony had tried to pants her, too. Jack had managed to pull his pants up and drag Jill back into the school. They didn't tell Mom about it, but she found out somehow, and the next afternoon she showed up as everyone was getting out after last bell. Mom marched right up to Nick Magruder, who had come to pick up his son, and she read him the riot act. She accused his son of being a pervert and a retard and a lot of other things. Mr. Magruder never managed to get a word in edgewise, and when Mom threatened to have Tony arrested for assault and battery, the man grabbed his son and smacked him half-unconscious, then shoved him into their truck. Jack never saw Tony again, but he heard that the boy was going to a special school over in Bordentown.

Jack kind of felt bad for Tony, because he didn't like to see any kid get his ass kicked. Even a total jerkoff like Tony. On the other hand, Tony had almost hurt Jill, so maybe he got off light. From the look on Mom's face, she wanted to do more than smack the smile off his face.

That face was set against whatever was going on now. Whatever had hurt Jill. Whatever might be in the way of getting her to a hospital.

Despite the fear that gnawed at him, seeing that face made Jack feel ten feet tall. His mother was tougher than anyone, even the school bully and his dad. *And* she had a gun. So did Dad and Uncle Roger.

Jack almost smiled.

Almost.

He remembered the look in Jill's eyes. The color of her eyes.

No smile was able to take hold on his features as he pulled on his raincoat and boots and followed his family out into the dark and the storm.

8

They made it all the way to the truck.

That was it.

9

The wind tried to rip the door out of Dad's hand as he pushed it open; it drove the rain so hard that it came sideways across the porch and hammered them like buckshot. Thunder shattered the yard like an artillery barrage and lightning flashed in every direction, knocking shadows all over the place.

Jack had to hunch into his coat and grab onto Dad's belt to keep from being blasted back into the house. The air was thick and wet, and he started to cough before he was three steps onto the porch. His chest hitched, and there was a gassy rasp in the back of his throat as he fought to breathe. Part of it was the insanity of the storm, which was worse than anything Jack had ever experienced. Worse than it looked on TV. Part of it was that there simply wasn't much of him. Even with the few pounds he'd put on since he went into remission, he was a stick figure in baggy pajamas. His boots were big and clunky, and he half walked out of them with every step.

Mom was up with Roger, running as fast as she could despite the wind, forcing her way through it to get to the truck and open the doors. Roger staggered as if Jill was a burden, but it was just the wind, trying to bully him the way Tony Magruder had bullied Jill.

The whole yard was moving. It was a flowing, swirling pond that lapped up against the second porch step. Jack stared at it, entranced for a moment, and in that moment the pond seemed to rear up in front of him and become that big black wall of nothing that he saw so often in his dreams.

"Did the levee break?" he yelled. He had to yell it twice before Dad answered.

"No," Dad shouted back. "This is ground runoff. It's coming from the fields. If the levee broke, it'd come at us from River Road. We're okay. We'll be okay. The truck can handle this."

There was more doubt than conviction in Dad's words, though.

Together they fought their way off the porch and across five yards of open driveway to the truck.

Lightning flashed again, and something moved in front of Jack. Between Mom and the truck. It was there and gone.

"Mom!" Jack called, but the wind stole his cry and drowned it in the rain.

She reached for the door handle, and in the next flash of lightning Jack saw Jill's slender arm reach out from the bundle of blankets as if to touch Mom's face. Mom paused and looked at her hand, and in the white glow of the lightning Jack saw Mom smile and saw her lips move as she said something to Jill.

Then something came out of the rain and grabbed Mom.

Hands, white as wax, reached out of the shadows beside the truck and grabbed Mom's hair and her face and tore her out of Jack's sight. It was so *fast*, so abrupt that Mom was there and then she was gone.

Just . . . gone.

Jack screamed.

Dad must have seen it too. He yelled, and then there was a different kind of thunder as the black mouth of his shotgun blasted yellow fire into the darkness.

There was lightning almost every second, and in the spaces between each flash everything in the yard seemed to shift and change. It was like a strobe light, like the kind they had at the Halloween hayride. Weird slices of images, and all of it happening too fast and too close.

Uncle Roger began to turn, Jill held tight in his arms.

Figures, pale faced but streaked with mud. Moving like chess pieces. Suddenly closer. Closer still. More and more of them.

Dad firing right.

Firing left.

Firing and firing.

Mom screaming.

Jack heard that. A single fragment of a piercing shriek, shrill as a crow, that stabbed up into the night.

Then Roger was gone.

Jill with him.

"No!" cried Jack as he sloshed forward into the yard.

"Stay back!" screamed his father.

Not yelled. Screamed.

More shots.

Then nothing as Dad pulled the shotgun trigger and nothing happened.

The pale figures moved and moved. It was hard to see them take their steps, but with each flash of lightning they were closer.

Always closer.

All around.

Dad screaming.

Roger screaming.

And . . . Jill.

Jill screaming.

Jack was running without remembering wanting to, or starting to. His boots splashed down hard, and water geysered up around him. The mud tried to snatch his boots off his feet. Tried and then did, and suddenly he was running in bare feet. Moving faster, but the cold was like knife blades on his skin.

Something stepped out of shadows and rainfall right in front of him. A man Jack had never seen before. Wearing a business suit that was torn to rags, revealing a naked chest and . . .

. . . and nothing. Below the man's chest was a gaping hole. No stomach. No skin. Nothing. In the flickering light, Jack could see dripping strings of meat and . . .

. . . and . . .

. . . was that the man's *spine*?

That was stupid. That was impossible.

The man reached for him.

There was a blur of movement and a smashed-melon crunch and then the man was falling away and Dad was there, holding the shotgun like a club. His eyes were completely wild.

"Jack—for God's sake, get back into the house."

Jack tried to say something, to ask one of the questions that burned like embers in his mind. Simple questions. Like, what was happening? Why did nothing make sense?

Where was Mom?

Where was Jill?

But Jack's mouth would not work.

Another figure came out of the rain. Mrs. Suzuki, the lady who owned the soy farm next door. She came over for Sunday dinners almost every week. Mrs. Suzuki was all naked.

Naked.

Jack had only ever seen naked people on the Internet, at sites where he wasn't allowed to go. Sites that Mom thought she'd blocked.

But Mrs. Suzuki was naked. Not a stitch on her.

She wasn't built like any of the women on the Internet. She wasn't sexy.

She wasn't whole.

There were pieces of her missing. Big chunks of her arms and stomach and face. Mrs. Suzuki had black blood dripping from between her lips, and her eyes were as empty as holes.

She opened her mouth and spoke to him.

Not in words.

She uttered a moan of endless, shapeless need. Of hunger.

It was the moan Jack knew so well. It was the same sound Toby had made; the same sound that he knew he would make when the cancer pushed him all the way into the path of the rolling, endless dark.

The moan rose from Mrs. Suzuki's mouth and joined with the moans of all the other staggering figures. All of them, making the same sound.

Then Mrs. Suzuki's teeth snapped together with a *clack* of porcelain.

Jack tried to scream, but his voice was hiding somewhere and he couldn't find it.

Dad swung the shotgun at her, and her face seemed to

come apart. Pieces of something hit Jack in the chest, and he looked down to see teeth stuck to his raincoat by gobs of black stuff.

He thought something silly. He knew it was silly, but he thought it anyway because it was the only thought that would fit into his head.

But how will she eat her Sunday dinner without teeth?

He turned to see Dad struggling with two figures whose faces were as white as milk except for their dark eyes and dark mouths. One was a guy who worked for Mrs. Suzuki. José. Jack didn't know his last name. José something. The other was a big red-haired guy in a military uniform. Jack knew all the uniforms. This was a National Guard uniform. He had corporal's stripes on his arms. But he only had one arm. The other sleeve whipped and popped in the wind, but there was nothing in it.

Dad was slipping in the mud. He fell back against the rear fender of the Durango. The shotgun slipped from his hands and was swallowed up by the groundwater.

The groundwater.

The cold, cold groundwater.

Jack looked numbly down at where his legs vanished into the swirling water. It eddied around his shins, just below his knees. He couldn't feel his feet anymore.

Be careful, Mom said from the warmth of his memories, *or you'll catch your death.*

Catch your death.

Jack thought about that as Dad struggled with the two white-faced people. The wind pushed Jack around, made him sway like a stalk of green corn.

He saw Dad let go of one of the people so he could grab for the pistol tucked into his waistband.

No, Dad, thought Jack. *Don't do that. They'll get you if you do that.*

Dad grabbed the pistol, brought it up, jammed the barrel under José's chin. Fired. José's hair seemed to jump off his head and then he was falling, his fingers going instantly slack.

But the soldier.

He darted his head forward and clamped his teeth on Dad's wrist. On the gun wrist.

Dad screamed again. The pistol fired again, but the bullet went all the way up into the storm and disappeared.

Jack was utterly unable to move. Pale figures continued to come lumbering out of the rain. They came toward him, reached for him . . .

. . . but not one of them touched him.

Not one.

And there were so many.

Dad was surrounded now. He screamed and screamed, and fired his pistol. Three of the figures fell. Four. Two got back up again, the holes in their chests leaking black blood. The other two dropped backward with parts of their heads missing.

Aim for the head, Dad, thought Jack. *It's what they do in the video games.*

Dad never played those games. He aimed center mass and fired. Fired.

And then the white-faced people dragged him down into the frothing water.

Jack knew that he should do something. At the same time,

and with the kind of mature clarity that came with dying at his age, he knew that he was in shock. Held in place by it. Probably going to be killed by it. If not by these . . . whatever they were . . . then by the vicious cold that was chewing its way up his spindly legs.

He could not move if he was on fire, he knew that. He was going to stand there and watch the world go all the way crazy. Maybe this was the black wall of nothing that he imagined. This . . .

What was it?

A plague? Or what did they call it? Mass hysteria?

No. People didn't eat each other during riots. Not even soccer riots.

This was different.

This was monster stuff.

This was stuff from TV and movies and video games.

Only the special effects didn't look as good. The blood wasn't bright enough. The wounds didn't look as disgusting. It was always better on TV.

Jack knew that his thoughts were crazy.

I'm in shock, duh.

He almost smiled.

And then he heard Jill.

Screaming.

10

Jack ran.

He went from frozen immobility to full-tilt run so fast

that he felt like he melted out of the moment and reappeared somewhere else. It was surreal. That was a word he knew from books he'd real. Surreal. Not entirely real.

That fit everything that was happening.

His feet were so cold it was like running on knives. He ran into the teeth of the wind as the white-faced people shambled and splashed toward him and then turned away with grunts of disgust.

I'm not what they want, he thought.

He knew that was true, and he thought he knew why.

It made him run faster.

He slogged around the end of the Durango and tripped on something lying half-submerged by the rear wheel.

Something that twitched and jerked as white faces buried their mouths in it and pulled with bloody teeth. Pulled and wrenched, like dogs fighting over a beef bone.

Only it wasn't beef.

The bone that gleamed white in the lightning flash belonged to Uncle Roger. Bone was nearly all that was left of him as figures staggered away, clutching red lumps to their mouths.

Jack gagged and then vomited into the wind. The wind slapped his face with all the Cheerios he'd eaten that day. He didn't care. Jill wouldn't care.

Jill screamed again and Jack skidded to a stop, turning, confused. The sound of her scream no longer came from the far side of the truck. It sounded closer than that, but it was a gurgling scream.

He cupped his hands around his mouth and screamed her name into the howling storm.

A hand closed around his ankle.

Under the water.

From under the back of the truck.

Jack screamed, inarticulate and filled with panic as he tried to jerk his leg away. The hand holding him had no strength, and his ankle popped free and Jack staggered back and then fell flat on his ass in the frigid water. It splashed up inside his raincoat and soaked every inch of him. Three of the white-faced things turned to glare at him, but their snarls of anger flickered and went out as they found nothing worth hunting.

"Jack—?"

Her voice seemed to come out of nowhere. Still wet and gurgling, drowned by rain and blown thin by the wind.

But so close.

Jack stared at the water that smacked against the truck. At the pale, thin, grasping hand that opened and closed on nothing but rainwater.

"Jack?"

"Jill!" he cried, and Jack struggled onto his knees and began slapping at the water, pawing at it as if he could dig a hole in it. He bent and saw a narrow gap between the surface of the water and the greasy metal undersides of the truck. He saw two eyes, there and gone again in the lightning bursts. Dark eyes that he knew would be red.

"Jill!" he croaked at the same moment that she cried, "Jack!"

He grabbed her hands and pulled.

The mud and the surging water wanted to keep her, but not as much as he needed to pull her out. She came loose with a *glop!* They fell back together, sinking into the water, taking mouthfuls of it, choking, coughing, sputtering, gagging it out as they helped each other sit up.

The white things came toward them. Drawn to the splashing or drawn to the fever that burned in Jill's body. Jack could feel it from where he touched her. It was as if there was a coal furnace burning bright under her skin. Even with all this cold rain and runoff, she was hot. Steam curled up from her.

None curled up from Jack. His body felt even more shrunken than usual. Thinner, drawn into itself to kindle the last sparks of what he had left. He moaned in pain as he tried to stand. The creatures surrounding him moaned too. Their cries sounded no different from his.

He forced himself to stand and wrapped an arm around Jill.

"Run!" he cried.

They cut between two of the figures, and the things turned awkwardly, clutching at them with dead fingers, but Jack and Jill ducked and slipped past. The porch was close, but the water made it hard to run. The creatures with the white faces were clumsier and slower, and that helped.

Thunder battered the farm, deafening Jack and Jill as they collapsed onto the stairs and crawled like bugs onto the plank floor. The front door was wide open, the glow from the Coleman lantern showing the way.

"Jack," Jill mumbled, slurring his name. "I feel sick."

The monsters in the rain kept coming, and Jack realized that they had ignored him time and again. These creatures were not chasing him now. They were coming for Jill. They wanted her.

Her. Not him.

Why?

Because they want life.

That's why they went after Mom and Dad and Uncle Roger.

That's why they wanted Jill.

Not him.

He wasn't sure how or why he knew that, but he was absolutely certain of it. The need for life was threaded through that awful moan. Toby had wanted more life. He wanted to be alive, but he'd reached the point where he was more dead than alive. Sliding down, down, down.

I'm already dead.

Jill crawled so slowly that she was barely halfway across the porch by the time one of *them* tottered to the top step. Jack felt it before he turned and looked. Water dripped down from its body onto the backs of his legs.

The thing moaned.

Jack looked up at the terrible, terrible face.

"Mom . . . ?" he whispered.

Torn and ragged, things missing from her face and neck, red and black blood gurgling over her lips and down her chin. Bone-white hands reaching.

Past him.

Ignoring him.

Reaching for Jill.

"No," said Jack. He wanted to scream the word, to shout

the kind of defiance that would prove that he was still alive, that he was still to be acknowledged. But all he could manage was a thin, breathless rasp of a word. Mom did not hear it. No one did. There was too much of everything else for it to be heard.

Jill didn't hear it.

Jill turned at the sound of the moan from the thing that took graceless steps toward her. Jill's glazed red eyes flared wide, and she screamed the same word.

"NO!"

Jill, sick as she was, screamed that word with all the heat and fear and sickness and life that was boiling inside her. It was louder than the rain and the thunder. Louder than the hungry moan that came from Mom's throat.

There was no reaction on Mom's face. Her mouth opened and closed like a fish.

No, not like a fish. Like someone practicing the act of eating a meal that was almost hers.

There was very little of Jack left, but he forced himself once more to get to his feet. To stand. To stagger over to Jill, to catch her under the armpits, to pull, to drag. Jill thrashed against him, against what she saw on the porch.

She punched Jack and scratched him. Tears like hot acid fell on Jack's face and throat.

He pulled her into the house. As he did so, he lost his grip, and Jill fell past him into the living room.

Jack stood in the doorway for a moment, chest heaving, staring with bleak eyes at Mom. And then past her to the other figures who were slogging through the mud and water toward the house. At the rain hammering on the useless truck. At the farm road that led away toward the River Road. When the lightning flashed, he could see all the way past the levee to the river, which was a great, black, swollen thing.

Tears, as cold as Jill's were hot, cut channels down his face. Mom reached out.

Her hands brushed his face as she tried to reach past him.

A sob as painful as a punch broke in Jack's chest as he slammed the door.

11

He turned and fell back against it, then slid all the way down to the floor.

Jill lay on her side, weeping into her palms.

Outside the storm raged, mocking them both with its power. Its life.

"Jill," said Jack softly.

The house creaked in the wind, each timber moaning its pain and weariness. The window glass trembled in the casements. Even the good china on the dining room breakfront racks rattled nervously as if aware of their own fragility.

Jack heard all this.

Jill crawled over to him and collapsed against him, burying her face against his chest. Her grief was so big that it, too, was voiceless. Her body shook and her tears fell on him like rain. Jack wrapped his arms around her and pulled her close.

He was so cold that her heat was the only warmth in his world.

Behind them there was a heavy thud on the door.

Soft and lazy, but heavy, like the fist of a sleepy drunk.

However, Jack knew that it was no drunk. He knew exactly who and what was pounding on the door. A few moments later there were other thuds. On the side windows and the back door. On the walls. At first just a few fists, then more.

Jill raised her head and looked up at him.

"I'm cold," she said, even though she was hot. Jack nodded; he understood fevers. Her eyes were like red coals.

"I'll keep you warm," he said, huddling closer to her.

"W-what's happening?" she asked. "Mom . . . ?"

He didn't answer. He rested the back of his head against the door, feeling the shocks and vibrations of each soft thud shudder through him. The cold was everywhere now. He could not feel his legs or his hands. He shivered as badly as she did, and all around them the storm raged and the dead beat on the house. He listened to his own heartbeat. It fluttered and twitched. Beneath his skin and in his veins and in his bones, the cancer screamed as it devoured the last of his heat.

He looked down at Jill. The bite on her arm was almost colorless, but radiating out from it were black lines that ran like tattoos of vines up her arm. More of the black lines were etched on her throat and along the sides of her face. Black goo oozed from two or three smaller bites that Jack hadn't seen before. Were they from what had happened at the school, or from just now? No way to tell. The rain had washed away all the red, leaving wounds that opened obscenely and in which white grubs wriggled in the black wetness.

Her heart beat like the wings of a hummingbird. Too fast, too light.

Outside, Mom and the others moaned for them.

"Jack," Jill said, and her voice was even smaller, farther away.

"Yeah?"

"Remember when you were in the hospital in January?"

"Yeah."

"You . . . you told me about your dream?" She still spoke in the dazed voice of a dreamer.

"Which dream?" he asked, though he thought he already knew.

"The one about . . . the big wave. The black wave."

"The black nothing," he corrected. "Yeah, I remember."

She sniffed, but it didn't stop the tears from falling. "Is . . . is that what this is?"

Jack kissed her cheek. As they sat there, her skin had begun to change, the intense heat gradually giving way to a clammy coldness. Outside, the pounding, the moans, the rain, the wind, the thunder—it was all continuous.

"Yeah," he said quietly, "I think so."

They listened to the noise, and Jack felt himself getting smaller inside his own body.

"Will it hurt?" she asked.

Jack had to think about that. He didn't want to lie, but he wasn't sure of the truth.

The roar of noise was fading. Not getting smaller, but each separate sound was being consumed by a wordless moan that was greater than the sum of its parts.

"No," he said, "it won't hurt."

Jill's eyes drifted shut, and there was just the faintest trace of a smile on her lips. There was no reason for it to be there, but it was there.

He held her until all the warmth was gone from her. He listened for the hummingbird flutter of her heart and heard nothing.

He touched his face. His tears had stopped with her heart. *That's okay,* he thought. *That's how it should be.*

Then Jack laid Jill down on the floor and stood up.

The moan of the darkness outside was so big now. Massive. Huge.

He bent close and peered out through the peephole.

The pounding on the door stopped. Mom and the others outside began to turn, one after the other, looking away from the house. Looking out into the yard.

Jack took a breath.

He opened the door.

12

The lightning and the spill of light from the lantern showed him the porch and the yard, the car and the road. There were at least fifty of the white-faced people there. None of them looked at him. Mom was right there, but she had her back to him. He saw what was left of Roger twitching in the water so he could see past the truck. He saw Dad rise awkwardly to his feet, his face gone but the pistol still dangling from his finger.

All of them were turned away, looking past the abandoned truck, facing the farm road.

Jack stood over Jill's body and watched as the wall of water from the shattered levee came surging up the road toward the house. It was so beautiful.

A big, black wall of nothing.

Jack looked at his mother, his father, his uncle, and then down at Jill. Her cold hand twitched. And twitched again.

He wouldn't be going into the dark without them.

The dark was going to take them all.

Jack smiled.

FROM NIX'S JOURNAL

ON DYING
(BEFORE *ROT & RUIN*)

Someone I know died today.

A kid. A girl.

Jasmine Patel. We called her Jazz.

Jazz.

She was a year older than me. A tenth grader.

We weren't friends. I hardly knew her.

Okay, sure, I mean we went to the same school, and there aren't all that many of us. A hundred kids in each grade. You see the same faces in school, on the playground, around town. You bump into people at the New Year's party and the harvest fair and all that. You say hello if you meet them at Lafferty's Store when you go in to buy pop. Or maybe you're both in the same line on the day the new Zombie Cards come out. You say hi if you pass on the street.

But that's it sometimes. You know them but you don't _know_ them.

You're not friends exactly.

Friendly, or maybe just polite. There's probably a difference between those two things.

But I didn't really know Jazz that much.

I always knew her, of course. She was always here in town. She was always a year ahead of me in school. She always was.

And now she's not.

It happened this morning.

We were in the playground on a free period. I was there with Benny and Chong, and we were waiting on Morgie, who volunteered to go and get us a big bunch of grapes from the cafeteria. We were in our usual spot, on the edge of the softball diamond. The Gorman twins were tossing an old Frisbee that was patched with duct tape, and our history teacher, Mr. West-Mensch, was playing basketball with some of the juniors and seniors. It wasn't too sunny, and there were a lot of big clouds up in the blue sky. We were trying to decide what they looked like.

"See that one there?" said Benny. He was lying on the bleachers with his head on my shoes, pointing up to a cloud directly over us. "That's a parrot."

"You've never seen a parrot," said Chong.

"Yes, I have. There's a picture of one in the art room."

Chong made that face he makes when he doesn't want to admit he's wrong but has to. "Fair enough. But that cloud doesn't look like a parrot."

"Yes, it does."

"More like a macaw."

"Oh, shut up," said Benny.

I pointed to a little cloud over the trees. "It's a bunny."

They both looked.

"How come every cloud looks like a bunny to you?" asked Benny.

"No, they don't," I said.

He pointed to another one. "Okay, then what does that look like?"

I didn't want to answer, because it really looked like a bunny too. Which is not my fault. I don't make the clouds. I can't help it if some of them look like bunnies. That's just Benny being ridiculous.

That's when we heard the scream.

I read once that sometimes people used to hear screams and pretend they didn't. Really. They could be walking down the street in one of those old big cities where millions of people used to live, and they'd hear a scream or maybe actually <u>see</u> someone screaming, and they would just walk on by. Mom says it's because they didn't want to get involved, but she can't be right. How could someone not want to get involved if someone was that hurt or scared, or if they were in trouble? I mean . . . who would _do_ that?

So when we heard the scream, we all looked around. We all got up right away. There are a lot of things a scream might mean, but as far as I know, none of them are good.

That's when we saw Jazz Patel.

She was walking really weird. Half running, half stumbling, and she kept slapping herself. Slapping her face and arms.

And she kept screaming.

We all ran. Everyone did.

Everyone in the school yard.

When someone's in trouble, you have to do something. You have to find out what's happening.

I heard someone say it before we even reached her.

"Fire ants! Fire ants!"

That's when we saw it. Saw them.

Jazz was covered with them. Hundreds of tiny red ants. I could see the bites on her arms and her face. Dozens and dozens of bites.

We could all see what those bites were doing to her.

She was swelling up.

"god," said someone, "she's having a fit."

Chong knew the word for it. Chong always knows the word. "Anaphylaxis."

An allergic reaction.

Most kids aren't allergic to fire-ant bites. It's the same with bee stings and tarantula bites. But you never know until you get bitten.

Mr. West-Mensch came pushing through

the crowd and told us all to get back.
He picked Jazz up and ran with her—
actually ran—across the school yard
and inside the school. A bunch of kids
followed. Her friends, mostly. And some
of the kinds of kids who need to see stuff
like this.

We didn't. Chong, Benny, and I stood
there. Morgie came up holding the grapes
in a pouch he'd made by pulling out
the bottom of his T-shirt. He stared at
Mr. West-Mensch as he took Jazz away.
Morgie's mouth hung open.

"Jazz—?" he asked.

We told him what happened.

Morgie looked sick. "She looked really
bad."

We didn't say anything because it seemed
mean somehow to say it. But we thought
it. Jazz looked really, really bad. Like
she could hardly breathe.

"My cousin DeeDee used to be allergic to
peanuts," he said. Again, none of us said
anything. We all remembered DeeDee.

She'd been a house painter and sometimes did face painting at the fair.

That was then.

DeeDee ate something that she didn't know had peanuts in it. Only a little bit, too, from what everyone said. She ate it and she had anaphylaxis too.

That was a bad night. I didn't see it. Neither did Benny or Chong, but we all knew that Morgie had.

Sometimes Morgie goes and puts flowers on her grave. He was close with DeeDee. He loved her. And for a long time he hated his dad because of what had to be done.

The dead don't stay dead. We all know that. Everyone knows that.

Ever since First Night, anyone who dies, no matter how they die, comes back.

We make jokes about it. We call it "zomming out." They're bad jokes, but sometimes that's the only thing you have to keep from screaming.

Morgie's dad had to use a sliver on DeeDee.

A sliver.

It sounds like something nice. A sliver of cheese. A sliver of turkey on Thanksgiving. A sliver of chocolate when you get an A on a test.

Not the same thing.

Slivers are little pieces of metal. Flat on one end for pushing. Sharp on the other end. You have to stick them in the back of the neck, right where the spine enters the skull. We all learn about it in school. We all have to practice with slivers on cantaloupes and on dummy zoms made from straw.

Everyone in town—all the adults, anyway—carries at least one sliver.

Morgie's dad had to use his. Morgie understood. I mean, he's a little slow sometimes, but he's not stupid. He understood. But just because you understand something doesn't mean you can deal with it.

For a long time Morgie couldn't deal. He treated his dad like he'd done something bad to DeeDee. Like he'd <u>hurt</u> her.

It was a while before they could even talk about it.

Then one day Morgie sat on a rock down by the creek and cried harder than I ever saw anyone cry. He cried so hard I was scared for him. He kept punching his thigh, over and over again. Sometimes he punched himself in the side of the head. And cried. I tried to help him, but he screamed at me so loud that I got scared.

So . . . I went and told his dad.

I don't know what happened exactly. Morgie's dad went running down to the creek and told us to stay away. He and Morgie were down there for a long time. A couple of hours.

Morgie didn't go to school for two days, and his dad didn't go to work. Tom said that he saw them down at the creek again. Fishing.

That was a couple of years ago.

The thing with Jazz was today.

We're all taught what to do with a fire-
ant bite. You have to elevate the spot
where the bite was, then wash the area
to reduce the risk of infection. Then you
place a cool compress on it. As soon as you
can, take an antihistamine.

We even have some old epinephrine pens
one of the traders found in a hospital.
They used one on Jazz.

It didn't work.

She went into convulsions.

And then she died.

Just like that.

No long disease. Not the flu. No zom bite.

Ants.

Little red ants.

Ordinary stuff.

When you live in a world where there

are seven billion zombies, you think about
death coming for you with hands and
teeth.

Not ant bites.

Somehow it feels worse.

They sent us home early from school. No
one was allowed in the nurse's office
after they brought Jazz in. Just teachers.

Teachers all carry slivers.

I barely even knew her, and I'm not
really sure I liked her all that much.

But I can't stop crying.

The Valley
of the Shadow

Coldwater Creek, California

(On First Night, fourteen years before *Rot & Ruin*)

1
Hannahlily

Hannahlily Bryce was pretty sure that Tucker Norton was it.

The actual *it*. As in *the* one.

If she had made him from parts she special-ordered, he could not have been more perfect. Six feet tall with straw-colored hair, perfect teeth, and eyes that were a stormy swirl of blue and gray. Like Hannahlily and unlike a lot of other farm kids, Tucker took a good tan that lasted well into the winter. And like her, he was fit. They loved to run together down the country lanes in Coldwater Creek. They rode horses together in the state forest. And they spent a lot of their time laughing.

He was everything her last boyfriend, Kyle Hanrady, wasn't. Actually, her last three boyfriends combined couldn't stack up to Tucker. So as far as she was concerned, he really was it.

She wanted to tell him that. Hannahlily wanted to tell Tucker that she loved him.

But . . .

After Kyle, Hannahlily had become very cautious. Kyle had been good-looking and all, and he had a bit of the backcountry bad-boy vibe that Hannahlily knew she was a sucker for. But Kyle was also a bit grabby and seemed to have a difficult time grasping the concept of "no."

Tucker was a gentleman. Not that he was unromantic, but he respected boundaries. As far as Hannahlily could tell, he was the last of that breed, and she didn't want to let him get off the reservation. No way, José.

Today was going to be a special day for them. Romantic and dangerous, and Mother Nature was cooperating. The storm was huge, and everyone in town had been going nuts about it. How could they not? The TV weathermen were all but predicting the end of the world with this thing; and storms like this were so rare in central California. Hannahlily figured school would close early and everything would get a little confused after that. She told her mom that she was going to go to her friend Amber's place if they let them out early. Amber lived near the school, and her house was on high ground. Hannahlily had ridden out a couple of snowstorms there already, and her mother was cool with the arrangement. Amber, of course, was in on everything from the jump. She could lie like a politician, and she was so sweet-natured that everyone always believed her.

Tucker lived with a father who worked two jobs and a mother who was always drunk. Hannahlily knew that sadness was part of what made Tucker so sensitive, and it added a nice layer to his brooding nature. Hannahlily liked brooding guys, especially if they looked like Tucker. She didn't like that quality about herself, but she was pretty sure she'd date a serial killer if he looked like Tucker. You could crack walnuts on those abs.

The plan was to go to school, swipe their student IDs, wait until the storm emergency got rolling, and then duck out while everyone was heading for the buses. Tucker's truck could slog through any amount of mud. His uncle Slim had a farm at the edge of town, and Slim was currently in the VA hospital for lung cancer. She felt bad for him, but at the same time, it left the farm empty.

The farm, and the farmhouse.

Outside, the storm hooted and howled and pounded away at the sprawling old house. Shutters banged and timbers creaked. Inside, there was a noisy fire burning brightly in the stone hearth. Pine logs popped and shifted. Firelight glinted on the tall glasses of sweet tea. And in Tucker's eyes when he smiled at her.

They were wrapped in a huge fleece with a pattern of autumn leaves, pinecones, and acorns. They were still fully clothed, but the option to change that was on the table. Hannahlily's iPod was playing a moody mix of the kind of slow-groove R & B they played on late-night radio. The iPod and speakers were on batteries now that the power was out.

"Listen to that wind," she said, snuggling close.

"Fierce," he agreed. "I like it, though." He took a lock of her long brunette hair between his fingers, smelled it, smiled, and kissed it.

Hannahlily closed her eyes and smiled. This was exactly the moment she'd painted in her mind. Real romance. Not just grunting and kissing and trying to keep Kyle's twenty-five hands from pawing her.

Tucker was gentle, and even when they were this close and this alone, it was clear that he respected her. Boundaries meant something to him. Not that he wasn't standing right there at the edge of the safe zone, but he was waiting with true respect and patience for a signal to cross the line.

Neither of them were in too much of a hurry for that moment. Waiting, drawing it out, taking time somehow made it sweeter. It made it nicer.

So they sat together, her head on his chest, listening to the storm.

The warmth of the blanket, the calm patience of Tucker, and the crackling fire were all pulling her gently down into a semi-sleep.

Three rooms away, unheard by either of the young lovers, the back door opened. The sound was smaller than the groans of the old house and the moans of the line of slow, shambling, hungry intruders.

2

The Bride

The woman in the wedding gown shuffled forward, her dirty white shoes scuffing on the back porch floorboards of the old house. She had lived all her life in Coldwater Creek and had planned to live out the rest of it here on the fringes of Yosemite Park. She wanted to grow old and die here.

That had already been accomplished. Not the growing old part. Just the dying. It hadn't happened in the way she had imagined through girlhood and young womanhood, through high school, college, and her first years as an apprentice ranger in the big national park.

She had expected to be married that afternoon to another ranger, a big, bearded, gentle man named David.

All their friends and family and coworkers were there at the chapel waiting for them.

Then the world tilted enough to let everything that mattered slide off the edge. Her dreams and hopes, her expectations.

Her plans.

Her life.

The last memory she'd had before the plague took her was of David standing over her, eyes streaming tears, body streaked with blood that was not his. Nor hers. A big wooden cross in his hands, raised above him, poised to smash down.

Ready to kill her.

To end her.

As he had ended others as the madness swept through the congregants and guests and sanity devoured the world.

But as the darkness closed around the bride's mind, David had paused on the very brink of commission. Horror and grief and shock and pain and ten thousand other emotions warred on his face.

It was clear that he had wanted to kill her, needed to. Had to.

This was the plague, and it took only a few moments for anyone to understand its rules. The infected bite people. The bitten die. The dead rise. The cycle continues until no one's left alive. They'd all heard the news stories about this, but those stories were all back East. In Pittsburgh and Philadelphia. In New York and Atlanta.

Not here.

Not in California.

Not in Coldwater Creek.

Not in this little church.

Not today.

Not now.

Not . . .

God.

David had knocked her down after she'd bitten her own mother. After she'd bitten David's sister.

He'd struck her once with the heavy cross.

Now he was poised to finish it. To finish her.

David. The last man standing.

David, who had once wanted to be a minister, who'd almost taken a scholarship to a seminary. David, who was the gentlest person she'd ever known.

In that moment he had been every bit as much a monster as the dead who thrashed and moaned around him. The cross raised in his strong hands. The need to end her and this madness written on his face.

She wanted to tell him to do it.

She tried.

She begged him to end her life. No—to end what *this* was. Whatever this was.

Un-life.

She screamed her plea to him.

She was sure of it.

But all that came out of her mouth, all that she could hear, was her voice making a strange, long, low, unutterably desperate moan of bottomless hunger.

That wasn't what stopped him. The moan was no different from the ravenous cries rising from every dead throat in the chapel. If it had been only that, then even David would have brought the cross down and ended her life. Ended her pain. That was how he would see it, she was certain.

Helping her. Not killing her.

After all, she was already dead.

No.

What stopped David was something else. Something he saw. Something she saw him *see*. Something so . . . so terrible.

He looked into her eyes.

And saw *her*.

Dead, but not gone.

Destroyed, but not chased out of the ruin of her body.

There.

Still there.

Trapped inside the cage of her own stolen flesh. A prisoner who was still chained to the input of all five senses. She could see everything, smell the blood, taste the black poison of whatever lived within the plague, felt the deadness of the dying heart in her chest, and heard David's voice.

"Please," he said. It was not a plea to have her do something or to get something, or even for help.

Please.

It was a prayer to whatever fractured power still ran the universe, that what he saw in her eyes was a lie.

Only a lie.

But the bride knew that it was not a lie. She was still in there. Her body was not her own, would never again be hers to control. And yet she was still in there. Lost. Trapped.

Aware.

And David saw that. He knew it.

If the world had not already been falling apart, that's when it would have collapsed.

They had been married for less than a minute when the driver of the limo had come blundering in, collapsing against the last row of people. Already bitten, already bleeding.

One minute.

David was her husband, and she was his wife. His bride.

He looked into her dead eyes and saw something, saw the truth that maybe no one else knew. He saw it because it was like him to see those kinds of things. He was always the type who got to know people on a deep level.

It was what made people love him. And trust him.

It was what broke his heart for the second time in minutes. It was what made him drop the cross and stagger back, clamping a hand to his mouth to stifle the scream that he so badly needed to let loose. It was what kept him from killing her.

And it was what drove him from the chapel, the scream finally breaking from him as he burst out into the sunlight of his first day in hell.

Now the bride went where her body went. She fought with it. So hard, so hard. Trying to wrest back one single bit of control. A finger, a step, a turn of the head.

But it was like being buckled into a runaway car. All she could do was experience the horror.

Every moment.

Every hour.

Every bite.

3
Hannahlily

They kissed for so long that her lips hurt.

It was a good hurt.

Tucker could be as forceful as their shared passion permitted; but mostly he was gentle. Talented. Considerate.

Perfect.

The night and the storm had wrapped themselves around the house, but the old timbers kept them safe; and the fire and their closeness kept them warm. Hannahlily kept waiting for the moment when Tucker would make the inevitable guy move. At first she thought that was what she wanted, that if it was what *he* wanted, she would agree.

As the night moved slowly into the depth of the storm, she began dreading it.

The change was subtle.

Never once before in her life had she wanted anyone as much as she wanted Tucker. He was it. All of it. Everything on her checklist. Everything she knew she would ever want. A dream factory.

Which made her begin to wonder if she was simply being stupid.

Was that it? Was she being a girl? No, that was wrong. It really wasn't a girl thing, and her female pride raised its head and shook off that kind of thinking.

No.

This wasn't really about her being female. This was about her wondering if she was mature enough to evaluate

Tucker. To read him and make the right guesses about who he really was.

Hannahlily wasn't even entirely sure that was an age thing. Her aunt Sis was no judge of men. And both of her brothers, Johnny and Al, were fools for any kind of woman, no matter how badly they were treated. Aunt Sis was thirty-two, and her siblings were forty and forty-four.

No. Maybe it was a human thing.

Tucker appeared to be everything that was right about guys. Decent, honest, gorgeous, patient, respectful.

But at the same time she knew—with no possibility of error—that he wanted her. That he wanted to sleep with her.

The question was whether he wanted to hook up with her or make love to her.

For Hannahlily that was the big difference. Every other boy she'd ever dated might as well have had '"hookup" tattooed on their foreheads. Tucker didn't seem to be like that, but why not?

Was it something about her?

Was it something about him?

Could a guy—especially a seventeen-year-old guy— actually have enough self- control and respect to be able to control his urges?

That sounded as likely as pink unicorns traipsing through the yard.

Maybe less likely.

Guys, after all, were guys. Hannahlily had learned all about the biology of it in health class. The sex drive was a hardwired biochemical impulse to procreate. It was tied to the lizard brain's basic species survival drive. And guys got reinforcement about sexual conquests in everything from rap songs to commercials for Ford pickup trucks. Her aunt Sis said that even the most civilized man was only a grunt and a short step away from a Neanderthal, especially when they thought they could get some action from a female.

So what was Tucker's deal?

They held each other, and they kissed, and they touched, but they kept their clothes on, and things never got past a certain point.

Hannahlily was grateful.

Hannahlily was also mildly annoyed.

Didn't he *like* her?

Didn't he love her?

What was wrong with him?

What was—?

There was a sound.

And they both froze.

"What was that?" she said, her voice thin and breathless.

He raised his head and listened. "What was what?"

"I heard something."

She saw the brightness of his smile in the firelight. "The whole place sounds like it's about to fall down."

They listened. The wind was a banshee shriek. The bones of the old house creaked and complained. Water dripped somewhere inside.

"It's just the storm," he said.

"No, I *heard* something."

"Hey," he said gently, brushing hair from her face with a gentle sweep of his fingers, "it's okay. We're good here. It's just the—"

He stopped.

She didn't have to ask why.

They both heard it.

It wasn't the creak of old timbers. It wasn't the banging of loose shutters or the rattle of glass in loose panes.

It was a different kind of sound. The kind of sound houses don't make unless they're haunted houses in horror movies.

It was a human sound.

A moan.

Low, but not sneaky.

No, whatever made that sound was not some imp trying to hide. This wasn't a poltergeist. This was something else.

An empty sound. Mostly empty. Not a voice calling out. Nothing like that. This wasn't someone trying to warn the lovers that someone was about to enter their firelit nest.

No.

This was a moan.

And in its near emptiness it was directed in no particular direction. Yet it filled the house with meaning.

Without words, without articulation, it spoke of a need greater than anything Hannahlily had ever felt. Greater than Tucker felt. Greater than the need that had brought them here. More insistent than the needs that locked them together in their secret and private darkness.

It was a hungry moan.

And it came from the other side of the kitchen door.

4

The Bride

There was a muscular pickup truck parked by the back door, and the downstairs front windows of the old house glowed with the golden light of a fireplace. The bride did not even glance at it as she approached the house and went to the back door. A dozen others followed her from the wedding along with six more who had begun walking with her along the rain-swept roads. Strangers, but now part of something.

A family?

A horde?

A swarm?

The bride did not know which word fit. Maybe there was no word in the dictionary that explained this.

Her hand reached out to turn the doorknob, but it was a clumsy motion, and even as she did it, the woman inside could feel herself drifting backward from the action as if the one had nothing to do with the other. A reflex action, but not any choice of hers.

The kitchen door opened and her body went inside, taking her consciousness with it. As if whatever was about to happen in the old house required a witness.

The kitchen was dark, but light came from under the door. Warm light that moved and flowed. Firelight, not lamplight.

The body—the bride no longer considered it hers—stopped for a moment as if confused by this light. Or by the second door. Whatever reflex had allowed it to turn one doorknob was already fading, as if there were only a little rational thought or motor memory left and it was already draining away. Besides, there was no knob here. Only the flat wood and decorative trim of the door.

As wind blew in from the open doorway to the outside, it brushed against the inner door and made it sway. As if the door wanted to open and was trembling with anticipation.

The bride moved forward as the other wedding guests and the roadside strangers crowded in behind her. They milled, pushing forward. Pushing her forward.

Beyond the door there were voices.

Two.

Male and female. Young. Whispering.

"It's okay," said a boy's voice. "We're good here. It's just the—"

He stopped speaking as the hand that the bride had once owned reached out and pushed on the door.

The door opened at her touch.

She moved into the next room. A big room that was part dining room and part den. A fire crackled in the stone hearth. And on the floor, wrapped in a thick blanket, with hair and clothes tousled and faces flushed, were the owners of those voices.

A pretty girl.

A handsome boy.

Just the two of them, caught in a moment of shock that had not yet turned to horror.

It would, though.

The bride knew that much.

Horror was what she had brought to this house. It was

the only gift she had received at her wedding, and it was all she was allowed to share.

Horror, and all that the horror promised.

Every dark thing.

She spoke that horror in a voice of hunger and of need. The others behind her raised their voices in chorus.

She led the silent procession from the kitchen into the den.

The silence was torn out of the moment as screams filled the air.

5

Hannahlily

The shocked silence that gripped Hannahlily Bryce exploded into a shriek of absolute horror. There were people all around her. Strangers. Muddy and bloody and wrong. White faces with red mouths and black eyes. Plucking at the blanket and at her clothes, her hair, her skin.

"Tucker!"

But Tucker was frozen into the moment for one heartbeat longer than her. One heartbeat too long, his whole body locked into rigid stupefaction. His mouth worked as he tried to say something, ask something that would make sense of this; and the movement mirrored the movements of the hungry mouths around him.

Time suddenly seemed to slow down for Hannahlily. She saw the creatures huddled around her, she saw Tucker—muscular, powerful, capable, and totally frozen in fear—and she glimpsed the impossible future. Blood and pain and death. She didn't even know how she understood the nature of this attack. It wasn't a gang beating. This was death of a different kind, a nightmare kind. She saw the red mouths and she knew that.

We're dead.

The thought was as clear in her mind as if she had spent hours contemplating this very incident.

And then suddenly time jumped back to normal as the mouths descended toward her flesh.

Hannahlily screamed as loud as she could, shoved Tucker away from her, rolled backward onto her shoulders and kicked upward at the creatures. She was slender, but she was strong. Cheerleading, gymnastics, dance. Fear. Her legs shot upward and her bare feet caught two of them under the chins. One foot sent a man with wire-frame glasses flying backward; the other caught the jaw of a woman with frizzy brown hair, and at that angle the woman's head spun on the neck and there was a huge, wet *crack!*

As the woman fell backward, Hannahlily was moving. She bashed aside the white hands and scrambled toward Tucker, shoving and punching him until he suddenly snapped out of his stupor.

"God!" he yelled, and then he was on his feet, pulling Hannahlily up. Tucker punched one of the things in the face, smashing its nose with an overhand right that would have put most strong men down on their knees. The creature, a National Guardsman in the remains of a hazmat suit, merely staggered back from the force of the blow.

Two more of the things flung themselves at Tucker, and he went crazy on them. He was fast and powerful, kicking, head-butting, using every trick he'd learned in boxing and mixed martial arts, and he hit everything he tried to hit.

It just did no good.

"Run!" screamed Hannahlily. She grabbed the back of Tucker's sweater and yanked him away from the grasping, biting, scratching knot of attackers. He stumbled backward and almost fell, but she pulled him back to his feet. Then he turned and shoved her, and they were running through the dining room into the kitchen and out through the open back door.

"The truck . . . the truck . . . the truck!" he bellowed, but Hannahlily was already heading for it at a pace that outstripped his. They ran around the house to where the truck was parked. The strange, hungry, moaning creatures staggered behind. Some chased them all the way to the truck, others seemed to become distracted by the storm and stumbled out into the fields or onto the road.

Then they were inside the truck. The keys were in the ignition. Out here, this deep in farm country, the keys were always in the ignition, and the big engine roared to life as if it, too, were startled into a desperate frenzy. The white figures were in the yard now, coming around the house toward the truck, but Tucker gave the truck as much gas as it would take. The back wheels spun for a moment, kicking up huge arcs of mud that splattered the figures and the side of the house; then the truck found purchase, and it shot forward toward the road.

A figure stood in the way, and it, more than all the others, seemed to be conjured from some bizarre fantasy of madness.

It was a woman in a pretty white bridal gown. Her mouth was open to scream her ugly need at Hannahlily; her hands reached out and clawed the air as if she could tear the young couple from the truck.

Tucker bellowed something incoherent and hit the gas as he steered right toward her. Then Hannahlily did something that she could never thereafter explain to herself. She grabbed the wheel and shoved it the other way, fighting Tucker's strength to turn the pickup. The bride loomed in the headlights, but the truck swerved and only the rear fender brushed the bride. It was enough to lift her, to fling her into the teeth of the storm, to drop her in a muddy puddle.

But as the pickup roared down the road, Hannahlily turned and looked through the rear window, and in a flash of lightning saw the bride get slowly and shakily to her feet.

Tucker was yelling as the house dwindled behind them. "God . . . oh God . . . oh God! What's happening? What were they?"

The truck punched a hole through the night, found the main road, and rocketed along it toward town.

Hannahlily heard a voice praying. It took her a moment to realize that it was her voice. Praying. Begging God and Mary and the saints. Using fragments of prayers she'd learned in Sunday school. Old stuff. She hadn't been to church at all except for Christmas Eve with her folks. But as her awareness caught up with the prayers, she realized that in that moment those prayers were meant. They were meant with every last bit of who she was.

God. Please.

Please.

She remembered the crazy news stories and quickly turned on the radio.

The music stations played music.

The news, though.

The guy who read the news . . .

He was crying. Screaming and crying.

On the radio.

They drove all the way to the edge of town before they saw the first explosions. Then they stopped on a hill, and Tucker put the pickup into park. They sat together and watched.

The road down from the hilltop was clogged with cars. So was the one rising from the burning town.

Their town.

Even with storming winds blowing, there were helicopters in the air.

Hannahlily and Tucker watched in stunned silence. Their mouths slack but their minds screaming. Even in the absence of all information, they both knew that what they had just escaped were not people. Not anymore. They were *things*. Creatures.

Tucker was shaking his head in denial of everything. His eyes were fever bright as he cut looks at her. "Are you okay?" he asked. "Are you hurt?"

She shook her head. "I'm . . . I'm . . . no . . . no, I'm okay."

"Thank God," he said. He gripped the wheel and drove into the night, heading for the road back into town. When Hannahlily reached out to squeeze his arm, he yelped in pain.

"What's wrong?"

"I don't know," he said with a wince. "I think one of those crazoids . . . *bit* me."

Hannahlily stared at him in the dark cab of the truck.

"It's not bad," he added quickly. "Don't worry. I'll be fine."

Hannahlily continued to stare. Just as she had known on an instinctive level that the things that had attacked her were not quite people, she knew with equal certainty that neither of them was going to be fine.

Ever again.

FROM NIX'S JOURNAL

ON LOVE
(BEFORE *ROT & RUIN*)

I don't understand love.

I don't think anyone does.

I know, big surprise, right? Insight of the century.

The whole thing is so weird, though. So hard to make any sense of. Especially in the world as it is.

Before First Night, love was all about meeting the right person, getting together, building something important, and then making a life worth living. Family and kids and all that. At least that's how it seems from everything I ever read. People find each other and they try to live happily ever after.

The thing is . . . what does that even mean?

How can there be an "ever after" if the world ended? Doesn't that mean love ended too?

Doesn't it mean that there's no point to love? If there's no future, why fall in love? Why get married? Why have kids? Why hope?

Is this even real love? Without hope for the future, are we just going through the motions? Is love in what's left of the world just a habit? Or some kind of biological thing that's only chemicals in our heads reacting? Is it only our minds trying to make sense of animals who follow an instinct to continue to breed? In science class they told us about the "inherent need to perpetuate the species."

Is that all love is?

Is that all it ever was?

I hope not.

I really hope not.

A Christmas Feast

The First Winter After First Night

(Thirteen and a half years before *Rot & Ruin*)

1

The living moved like ghosts through the fog.

The dead waited in the swirling mist.

There were screams in the air. A few shouts and gunshots.

And the moans.

Always the moans.

Long, and low, and plaintive. Uttered by mouths that hung slack, rising from chests that drew breath only to moan—never again to breathe. The moans spoke of a hunger so old, so deep, so endless that nothing, not even the red gluttony of a screaming feast, could satisfy it.

The hunger existed.

Like *they* existed.

Without purpose and without end.

The mists were as thick as milk, white, featureless, hiding everything until far too late. Figures moved through the fog.

And the dead waited for them.

2

The man and the boy heard those moans and huddled together, biting the rags they wore as scarves to keep from screaming.

They were beyond tired. Beyond weary.

Both of them were thin as scarecrows. Barely enough meat on them to allow their bodies to shiver. Clothing was torn, patched with duct tape and rope.

Most of the time the man carried the boy. Sometimes—like now—he was too weak, too starved to manage it. The boy stumbled behind him, clutching his hand, too weary to cry. That was when they moved the slowest. That was when they were the most vulnerable.

The boy, Mason, was six. A lean phantom of the chubby child he'd been when they'd run away in August. It was only four months, but weight had fallen from them like leaves from an autumn tree. There were dead things out there that had more flesh on their bones.

The man—Mason's older brother, Dan—stuffed the boy's clothes with wadded-up pieces of old newspaper. It helped some, trapping little bits of warmth.

Dan wore three sets of long johns, and he still looked skinny.

"I'm hungry . . . ," said Mason. Not for the first time. Or the hundredth.

"I know," said Dan.

"I'm *tired!*"

"I know."

"I want my mommy!"

The man squeezed his eyes shut, but the tears found their way out anyway. "I know," he whispered. "Me too."

3

Almost the worst thing for Dan was how much he envied the dead.

They were always hungry, sure, same as him and Mason. Hunger was everywhere. But the dead didn't seem to mind it. They never wept for the want of food. They hunted, sure. That's all they did. But once Dan and Mason had slept in a church tower, and all day Dan watched the dead ones walk around or stand or sometimes kill and eat. When they feasted, they did it like dogs. Like jackals. They tore people apart and consumed everything as fast as they could. Like they were starving. As Dan and Mason were starving.

But when there was no meat, when there was no one to kill, they just . . . *were*. They didn't fall down from hunger. They didn't scream with the pain of needing food.

They just kept being. . . .

Being what?

What were they?

The newspapers threw a lot of words around before it all went silent. Walkers. Rooters. Flesh-eaters. Ghouls.

Zombies.

Them.

Whatever they were, they never seemed to actually mind being hungry.

Like they never minded the cold. Or the rain. Or the wind.

They just were.

Dan hated the thought of envying them.

He hated himself for feeling that envy.
He hated himself.
He hated.
And he hungered.

4

They'd left the highway four hours ago.

That was the route most of the refugees had used, even though none of the cars worked anymore. Something had happened to them. There had been big explosions, high up and far away, and all the cars died. Cell phones, too. Everything electric.

The two of them had been following a highway for days. The highways were straight routes. The cars offered some protection when the dead found them. You could hide in cars. At least for a while. Some of the dead could pick up rocks and smash the glass. If you were still, if you were quiet, you could wait out the night, and in the stillness of the morning you could steal away.

But then there was a spot where hundreds and hundreds of the dead crowded the road. Everyone ran. Dan tossed Mason over the guardrail into the thick grass, leaped the rail himself with half a second to spare, scooped up his brother, and ran.

And ran.

And ran.

The people who ran down into the valleys didn't make it. There were rumors about that. It was worse in the lowlands.

When the dead weren't following prey, they followed the path of least resistance. They crowded the lowlands because gravity pulled with subtle insistence on stumbling feet. Fewer of them fought that pull to walk uphill. Not unless there was meat to find. A handful of travelers out scavenging shared this new lore with Dan. When the highways became impossible, Dan took his brother up the slopes, into the foothills of the mountains.

At first there were just as many of the dead. Hungry, tireless. Awful.

But soon there were fewer. The higher they climbed, the fewer there were.

Fewer.

Never none.

They passed places where people had fought and died. Some of them were still there, but these were not the staggering dead. These bodies had terrible head wounds. Gunshots, blows from blunt weapons.

"Don't look at them," Dan warned his brother.

But the boy looked. Of course he looked. His eyes were filled with . . .

Nothing.

Mason had been too young to understand much of what was happening when the plague swept out of the TV news and into their lives. Since then there had been no chance to give him a sense of what the world was like. What the world should have been like. Horror was everyday. Horror was everywhere. So how could his brother, how could little Mason, have any understanding of how bad things were? For him—for both of them—every moment was built around moving forward, staying safe, scavenging food, finding water. Finding warmth.

Beyond where the bodies lay, a small lane spurred off from the main road. A wrecked car blocked the entrance, but when Dan leaned over the crumpled hood, he saw that the lane was clear.

Dan nodded, accepting it as a gift. Believing it to be so.

He picked Mason up, kissed him on the forehead, set him down on the hood of the car, and pushed him gently to the other side. Then he climbed up and over to help him down onto the ground again. A signpost wrapped in withered creeper vines read SULLIVAN LANE.

He didn't know where it went, but any road was good as long as it wasn't the one they were on. Besides, the lane was lined on both sides by heavy pine trees that blocked the fierce winds. Without those winds, the temperature was bearable. The snow was piled in long drifts against the trees, but the center of the lane was barely dusted.

"Come on," he said again. Mason tried to walk, and he made it for a quarter mile before his stumbling feet failed. Dan scooped him up before he could fall, and though his own strength was flagging, he carried his brother into the wintry night.

Snow fell the way snow does. Soft, quiet, quilting the world with whiteness, hiding the truth of what lay beneath. It dampened down the sounds from farther down the road. The moans. The cries. The gunfire. All of it was distant anyway, and the snow shushed it to silence.

It was powdery and dry, and it blew slow drifts across the road. The air was frigid and the temperature was dropping. Rags and newspaper were not enough.

Dan saw the uneven lumps in the road ahead and knew what they were. A fight that had ended the way these fights do.

Badly.

He kept going, though. What else was there to do? Keep moving or lie down here and wait for either the teeth of the wind or the teeth of the dead to do their work.

The only grace, and it was small, was that the wind blew at his back rather than in his face. It pushed him, ever so subtly, uphill.

So it was uphill he walked, clutching his brother in his arms, feeling the ten tons of the little boy turn to twenty tons, to thirty. Dan never once let go, though. No, sir, he did not do that.

Hours passed. The night deepened with the snow.

Dan tried not to count the bodies in the snow. He knew that was the kind of thing a madman would do. Counting the dead as a way of passing the time. That wasn't right.

Then after a time he realized that there were no more dead to count. The road stretched ahead, pale despite the darkness of night. Smooth and unbroken.

Dan stopped for a moment and set Mason down. The kid was out on his feet and he sagged against Dan, leaning on his thighs, fingers hooked into his pants pockets, eyes closed.

"It's okay," whispered Dan, smoothing the boy's matted hair. "We're safe."

Saying that was dangerous. Believing it was dangerous.

So dangerous.

There was hope in that concept, and hope was like a back-stabbing friend. You could trust it sometimes, and then it would turn and drive its blade deep.

They had to be careful. They had to learn to live without

trust. To live without assumption or expectation.

To live without.

That made the road so hard, so long, so lonely. And the man and his little brother were too far gone to be company to each other.

Dan never stopped watching. He never let his attention slacken.

"I'm cold," said Mason, and the way he said it jolted Dan. It was in a sleepy, dreamy, resigned voice.

Dan knelt, feeling his brother's face and fingers. They were like ice. The temperature was plummeting, and the fog was turning to crystals in the air. It was so humid he knew that it would start snowing soon.

Panic flared in his chest. He rubbed Mason's cheeks and arms, trying to coax the circulation, fighting to keep alive the spark of heat in the boy's limbs. He took Mason's icy fingers and put them in his own mouth, breathing his own heat onto them.

Mason's eyelids fluttered, but his eyes didn't open.

"Please," begged Dan, feeling tears break from his eyes and run like boiling water down his cheeks. "Please. God . . . please."

He was aware, as everyone was aware, that prayers were not being answered anymore. If they ever had been. While on the road, Dan had a lot of time to think about all the desperate and needy ones who had begged for God's mercy in times of war and famine, in wretched hospitals and on sinking ships. If there was a plan in God's mercy, or his lack of mercy, Dan couldn't see it. He still believed, but the structure of his belief had collapsed with the world. Those nights hiding in a church had not restored his confidence that grace would be afforded to him. He was pretty sure he didn't deserve any anyway.

But Mason was a kid.

Six years old.

Dan did not believe in the concept of original sin. That seemed like bullcrap to him. Sin was earned. Babies don't have any. They can't, or God is a jerk. Dan didn't think God was a jerk. Merciless, maybe, but not an actual malicious jerk.

So where was mercy?

Where, in the endless dark of this night, was his grace?

"Please," he prayed as he tried to rub life back into his brother's flesh. "Please."

5

"Danny—?"

Mason's voice was so pale, so empty.

But it was there.

The dead don't speak. They can't.

Only the living can do that.

Dan hugged his brother to him. He pulled the ends of his coat around the boy. Maybe together their heat would be enough.

Maybe.

Sobbing, Dan picked Mason up and squinted into the darkness. The snow clouds must have been thinner than he thought, because he could see light. Moonlight? Was it a full moon? Or a gibbous moon?

He didn't know. He'd come to learn the phases of the moon during his months on the run, but it had been cloudy for days.

Still, there was light.

Cold and . . .

Yellow.

Yellow?

Dan frowned at it. Moonlight was white. Moonlight on snow was blue.

This was yellow.

And it was wrong. It seemed to reach up to paint the undersides of the trees. It wasn't coming down from the clouds.

Yellow light.

Not sunlight yellow. There were hours of darkness left to go.

Yellow.

Like . . .

He was running before he knew it.

Aching, weary legs pumped as if he'd been resting for hours. He could feel his heart hammering inside his chest. Like fists beating on a door.

Like hope pounding to be let out of Pandora's box.

The road snaked and whipsawed as it climbed the mountain. There were houses on either side. Doors smashed open or boarded up. Blood streaks and spatters. Bullet holes. Nowhere he dared go.

The light was ahead. Up the hill. Near the top.

No.

At the top.

His legs were trembling so badly that he knew he couldn't

go on much more. He needed to set Mason down. He needed to rest.

But not out here in the cold. In the snow.

Not in any of those houses where death had come calling.

The light was stronger.

Closer.

Brighter.

Dan rounded another bend. Another. Another.

And then there was a long space of nothing. Just trees and empty fields on either side of the road. The snow was unbroken up here. Nothing and no one had come this way in hours.

There was a huge stand of old trees. Oaks and pines and maples. So heavy they blocked the view of the top of the hill.

But through them . . .

Through them.

The yellow light.

He could see it shining on the snow, glimmering on each snowflake.

So close.

"Hold on," he whispered to Mason, but the boy did not respond. He was limp in Dan's arms. "Hold on."

Dan kept going along the road, up the road, to wherever this road led. If it led to a pack of the dead, then he knew he would drop to his knees and try to hide Mason with his own body. Or maybe he'd just smother the boy. Choke him out and leave him to come back as one of them. They never wept for hunger.

If that happened, maybe he could find a way to kill himself, too. It would be better to go wandering with Mason than to let the boy go on alone.

Dan knew that this was a crazy thought. It was nuts.

He was nuts.

Of course he was. How could he not be? The world had ended. Humanity fell, the dead rose. None of that was sane.

Not one bit of it.

Dan kept going, ignoring the pain in his thighs and calves.

Chasing the light.

Chasing hope.

Ready to give in if hope was as false as everything else. Expecting it to be that way. Why should hope be any different?

The road curved around the big stand of trees.

Around.

Around.

And . . .

"God . . . ," whispered Dan.

He nearly dropped Mason.

The light.

The light.

The light.

Oh God, the light.

6

The door to the house stood open.

Light spilled out onto the snow, into the night.

Yellow.

Golden.

Real.

Dan felt a pain in his heart, and for a moment he thought this was all a cheat, that his heart was going to burst right there, fifty feet from the front door of this house. This cottage in the woods.

This.

Home.

"Please," he said again, this time not to God but to his own body. To his legs.

Forty feet.

Mason had not moved in a long time.

Thirty feet.

Wind blew past him and whipped snow into the open doorway.

Twenty feet.

His brother felt like a block of ice in his arms.

"Please . . . please . . ."

Ten feet.

When he reached the doorway, his questing left foot stepped down but the ankle and knee had no more to give. He fell forward and down. He tried to hold on to Mason.

Tried.

But his brother fell from his hands, landed, slid inside the house.

Dan fell on his face. On a thin carpet of snow over a thick carpet of soft fibers.

He felt toward the light, but he landed in darkness.

7

Dan opened his eyes and saw the wrong thing.

Not snow.

He saw a pillow.

On a carpet.

A pillow under his head, on the carpet.

It made no sense.

His mind struggled to understand it while his body struggled to wake up. There was pain everywhere. In the legs that had walked for so many miles. In the arms that had held Mason for so long. For too long. His biceps and forearms felt stretched. His fingers were like rusted hinges.

He could understand the pain.

Not the pillow.

He couldn't understand the pillow.

"Danny—?"

Dan's head whipped sideways, and there was a face. Inches away.

Mason.

Not frozen.

Not dead.

Not undead.

Mason.

Covered in dirt and dried snot and . . .

And . . . ?

Gravy?

It glistened on the boy's cheeks and chin.

Mason was smiling.

Smiling?

Dan could not remember the last time his brother had smiled. He would have bet that Mason couldn't do that anymore. That Dan himself couldn't. That smiles had died out with most of the people. With all the people they'd ever known. Mom and Dad. Janie. Uncle Jimmy and Aunt Sally.

No more smiles.

Except that Mason was smiling.

"Mason?" he said. It came out as a croak.

Dan shifted, tried to roll onto his side. That's when he realized that there was a blanket over him. No, a quilt. Thick and brightly colored. A quilt over him, a pillow under his face. And no wind.

The door was closed.

And Mason was eating something covered with rich brown gravy.

There was light in Mason's eyes.

Actual light.

It took a long time for Dan to sit up. Years. It was like jacking up one of the great pyramids. Slow, requiring so much strength, so much engineering. Just to sit up.

He sagged back against the wall. They were in an entrance foyer. Eight feet long. Umbrella stand with two umbrellas, a hiking stick, and a yellow plastic Wiffle bat. Pictures on the wall. Seascape on one side. The kind you get at Ikea. Comes already framed. Smaller pictures on the other side. One big family portrait, lots of small individual pictures. Husband and wife, kids. Grandparents. A smiling dog with a lolling tongue. Dad was black, mom looked white. Kids were in assorted shades of coffee with and without cream. Grandfather—clearly hers, not his—with a heavy beard shot through with gray, and kind eyes. Dog was a chocolate Lab. Everyone looked happy.

"Is anyone here?" Dan asked.

Mason shook his head.

"No one?"

"Just Santa Claus," said the boy.

Dan said, "What?"

8

Mason showed him.

He helped Dan up. Another feat of engineering. The floor canted and rippled, the room spun on its gimbals. Settled slowly. Became steady after a lot of crooked moments.

"In here," said Mason.

He pulled on Dan's hand. The kid's fingers were still cold. Still too cold.

But there was warmth here. Heat.

When Dan staggered after his brother into the living room, he saw why. There was a fire in the fireplace. Nearly out, but still burning. There were candles standing in piles of melted wax. There was a Coleman camp lantern. Lots of light. More warmth than Dan had felt in . . .

In too long a time to remember.

He shivered as if his body was reluctant to release the cold stored in his cells.

Dan didn't care about that. He didn't even remember the cold. He barely registered the candle and lantern light.

Instead he looked at something in the corner and something in the adjoining room. His eyes—his whole head—kept moving back and forth between these things. Seeing them. Not believing them. Not understanding them.

In the corner of the room, dominating that whole part of the living room, standing eight feet high, was a Christmas tree. Covered in brightly twinkling multicolored LED lights. A battery stood on a small vase pedestal, wires running over and up into the tree, powering the lights.

The lights.

Christmas lights.

The tree was full and fresh, the pine scent perfuming the air, mingling with the burning logs. A living smell, even from burning wood and cut-down tree. It smelled alive. The lights looked alive. And around the base of the tree was a mountain range of presents. Carefully wrapped in bright paper with delicately tied bows.

Dozens of them.

Through the archway, in the dining room, was a table set for seven people. Forks and knives, linen napkins in a poinsettia pattern. Sparkling stemware. Silver plates and bowls and tureens.

All of them filled with food.

All of them.

Mounds of mashed potatoes and candied yams. Green beans smothered in baked almonds. Broccoli and cauliflower decorated with thin twists of red and green peppers. Bowls of peas and corn. A basket with one flap of a holly-patterned cloth peeled back to reveal the curves of honey-brown rolls. And in the center of the table, rising above everything else, was a whole roast turkey. A big one. Golden skin except where one part of the breast had been torn away by greedy little hands, and there it was pure white.

Dan almost fell down.

He wanted to, maybe should have.

This was unreal, after all. This couldn't be here. Christmas was extinct. Christmas had died along with every other holiday. Christmas Day meant nothing more than any other day. There were a lot of days, and none of them were special anymore. They all ended with hunger and darkness, except the ones that ended in death.

Except . . .

Dan squeezed his eyes shut and took a breath so that he would be braced for the reality of an empty room and a bare table when he opened them again.

He opened them again.

The table was still there.

The food was still there.

"Santa brought us Christmas dinner," said Mason. His voice was far too reasonable and normal. It jolted Dan, who turned and looked at his brother.

"What?"

"Santa did this," said Mason. He wiped at the gravy on his cheeks, then licked the back of his hand. "It's not cold yet."

"Santa?"

"Sure. I saw him. Santa was here."

"What?"

"Santa. He was here."

"Here?"

Mason pointed toward the kitchen. "I saw him out in the yard. He had his red suit and white beard. It was Santa."

There was no hysteria in Mason's voice. There should have been. How could there not be?

Dan felt his heart begin to hammer again. "Show me."

Mason took his hand again and led him through the dining room and into the kitchen and up to the back door. Light from a second Coleman lantern threw pale window squares onto the snow-covered lawn.

There was a man in the yard.

The man had a white beard.

He wore a red suit.

Dan moved closer to the window and studied the figure.

Then he stepped back. Slowly. Making absolutely sure not to make any sudden moves. He very carefully, very quietly found the dial on the lantern and turned down the gas until the kitchen was plunged into darkness.

Darkness was safe.

"Why'd you do that?" asked Mason. "Now we can't see Santa."

Dan said nothing.

Out in the yard, the figure turned toward the house.

The beard was white. Sure. Except where it was red. There was snow on the red, so it was a layered effect. Hiding the truth. Changing the truth.

His shirt had probably been red to start with. A checked flannel shirt. Redder now by far. A belly. What someone might have called a comfortable belly. You say that about old guys with paunches. Mostly bald head, a fringe of white.

Red and white.

Fat.

Not jolly.

"Go back into the other room," said Dan.

"But . . . Santa . . . ," said Mason, not budging.

Santa. God.

Dan wondered who it was out there. Father? Grandfather? Or another survivor? Maybe a neighbor from one of the other houses. Maybe coming over to share the world's last Christmas dinner. Maybe someone who had helped gather enough supplies to make it special. To give the family one perfect night. If so, what had happened? Why had everyone gone out? Did they want to take a Christmas picture in the snow? Did someone have an old Polaroid camera? Or a digital camera that they kept charged somehow? Had they been crazy enough—or felt safe enough—to go out and watch the snow? Had they sung a carol as the snow fell and thought that the dead were too far away to hear? Or that the storm would muffle their voices?

Something had happened, though. Something made them all go outside and leave hot food on the table. Their coats were gone. Their boots. They'd dressed for it, but they couldn't have meant to be out there long.

Except . . .

There were footprints out in the snow, but if there was blood, the snow hid it. If there were bodies, they'd wandered off.

Except this one old man.

Except Mason's Santa.

God Almighty.

He looked at his brother, at the unfiltered joy on a face that Dan thought had forgotten how to smile.

The truth is no blessing, he thought. *The truth is no gift.*

He knew he had to do this right. If he did it wrong, Mason would probably cry. He didn't cry out loud much—even as young as he was, Mason had learned the rules. But this was different. The dinner, the presents. The man in red and white. Mason sounded strange as it was. Dan couldn't risk dragging him back out into the cold. Not the cold outside, but the cold of the real world. It might break him. The kid was already cracked.

So, he knew, was he.

If Mason started crying, or worse, screaming, Dan knew that he would too.

So he said the kind of thing you'd say if the world wasn't broken.

"Shh," he said softly. "Don't let Santa know you can see him. He has to do everything in secret. That's how it's done. It has to be in secret or the magic won't work."

That kind of thing made sense to a six-year-old.

It damn near sounded reasonable to Dan.

Things had to be done in secret, or the magic wouldn't work.

Survival was a kind of magic. At least it was these days.

He backed up very slowly. Without haste. Haste meant panic. He didn't want that to be the message of his body language. He backed into Mason and gently pushed his brother out of the kitchen. Dan took the lantern with him.

Then he stopped, thinking it another step past the moment.

"Stay here," he said. He reentered the kitchen. The back door was closed. It had a bar across it. There were shutters mounted inside the windows. Dan closed the shutters very slowly. They were heavy. Solid panels of wood that had been reinforced with strips of metal. The work was good. Someone knew what they were doing. The shutters completely blocked the windows. There was another shutter for the kitchen door.

He shut that, too. Thick cotter pins hung on lengths of airline cable. Dan slotted them into place and felt his heart begin to beat normally.

He went out to the dining room. Mason was scooping handfuls of corn and peas into his mouth.

"Eat slow or you'll get sick," said Dan.

The boy nodded. He didn't have the strength to eat fast.

Dan's stomach churned. He wanted to eat. Needed to. Had to.

But he didn't. Not yet.

Instead he went through the house and made sure all the shutters were pinned in place. He pulled the drapes over them to block out any stray splinters of light. The front door had brackets for heavy cross-grain timbers, and he hefted them into place. Oak. Heavy. Safe.

Then he took the lantern and went upstairs.

More candles. Sleeping bags. Stacks of boxed goods. Food. Medical supplies.

Guns.

Guns.

Jesus Christ.

Guns and ammunition.

Hundreds of gallons of water in one, two-and-a-half, and five-gallon bottles. Cases of soda. Cartons of powdered milk.

Dan was crying by the time he finished checking the rooms.

There were beds for nine people. All the beds had been slept in.

But there was nobody home.

Nobody.

It made no sense.

Why would they leave this place?

They'd found a way to keep themselves going. They'd found food and clothing and everything they'd need. There was enough to keep them safe for months. Maybe for years.

They'd even cut down and decorated a tree. Wrapped presents.

Cooked a feast.

So where were they?

Why had they left?

He thought of the man in the yard. Granddad.

Okay, so the old man had died. But there was no blood inside the house. No sign of violence. Nothing to indicate that the man had died and reanimated in here. No evidence that he'd attacked and killed his own children and grandchildren.

He was outside.

And where were they?

Dan stood at the top of the stairs. He held a shotgun to his chest tighter than if it was a talisman. Tighter than if it was Jesus on the cross.

"Dan—?" called Mason.

"Shh!" hissed Dan as he leaned down the stairs.

"Come on. It's getting cold."

Not the house.

The food.

Dan came downstairs.

He pulled out a chair for Mason. He sat in the one next to him.

"Is it Christmas?" asked the boy.

"I—I guess so."

"Do we get to open presents?"

Dan glanced at the presents. There were so many of them. Surely some would have to be appropriate for a little boy. Maybe socks. Maybe a toy. What did it matter when you had nothing at all?

"Sure," he said. "In the morning. Presents are for Christmas morning."

He reached for the carving knife and fork.

Mason looked at him, his eyes wide and filled with light. "Don't we have to say grace first?"

Dan wiped at the tears in his eyes. He bent and kissed Mason on the top of the head.

"Yeah," he said. "I guess we do."

They said grace. It surprised Dan that he could remember how to say thanks.

The words came.

Slowly, in shuffling steps through his mind. But they came.

He said grace.

They said amen.

Outside the wind howled and the snow fell. Outside there were moans on the wind.

Inside it was warm.

Inside it was Christmas.

Dan stuck the tines of the fork in to steady the turkey and to steady his own trembling hands. Then he began carving.

FROM NIX'S JOURNAL

ON SURVIVING

(BEFORE *ROT & RUIN*)

Everyone always talks a lot about
survival.

I'm not sure I understand what that
means, though.

We survived First Night. When the plague
started and the dead began attacking
the living, some people survived. Thirty
thousand people, as far as we know. Tom
thinks there's probably more, though.
Other towns like Mountainside, Haven,
and the other seven. Maybe too far away
for us to have heard anything about
them. Maybe in other countries. As Mom
always says, "It's a big world."

She's right. It's really big.

There used to be seven billion people on

Earth. Could all of them have really died?

Chong and I talk about this a lot. He's like me—he doesn't believe that we're the only ones left. He says it's "statistically improbable." He says that natural barriers like rivers, canyons, deserts, mountains, and stuff would have given people a chance to escape or defend themselves. I think so too. But I also think that there are places that were built to be defended. Castles, military bases, underground bunkers, high-security places. Mr. Lafferty at the store says that there are hundreds of secret installations, and thousands of bases around the world. He thinks that maybe there are millions of people still alive.

But everyone's cut off.

How will we ever find them?

How will they ever find us?

PART TWO
THE DYING YEARS

The Light That Never Goes Out.

First Night
Memories

1

Pastor Kellogg

(On First Night, fourteen years before Rot & Ruin*)*

It rained the night the world ended.

A hard, bitter, soaking rain, as if God and all his angels were weeping. Fanciful, sure, but to John Kellogg, pastor of the Pittsburgh Three Rivers Church, it seemed likely that heaven should mourn the end of all those years of living, of building, of crafting laws and striving to refine the humanity of the race. The whole process, from dropping out of the trees to the mapping of the human genome, should have amounted to something more substantial, something not so easily smashed flat and brushed away.

But it didn't, and the steady rain felt like tears to him. God's tears.

It was a strangely religious moment for a man who had been gradually losing his faith, year after grinding year. Caring for the homeless. Running shelters for abused women and runaways. Watching people drop out, one by one, from the twelve-step meetings held in the church basement. Trying to comfort mothers of sons killed in deserts half a world away for reasons even the politicians couldn't quite agree on.

That morning John Kellogg had argued with his wife

about it. He told her that he just couldn't do it anymore, that whatever spiritual reservoir he'd once possessed was now used up. Molly had a simpler faith, one whose unshakable nature Kellogg had always envied.

"Give it another year," she said. "Go talk to the bishop. Get some help before you throw away everything you've worked for."

It had been a troubling conversation. Their son, Matthew, did not believe in anything. Or said that he didn't. He'd sat at the breakfast table, head bowed over his Cheerios, and took no sides. Matthew thought it was all silly. Religion, spirituality, the whole works. On the other hand, he was too smart to risk siding with his father on this one. Not against Mom's iron will.

That was this morning.

Now Pastor John Kellogg sat in his office behind the church and watched the falling rain through the open window. Behind the noise of the storm, threaded through the steady hum of the downpour and the detonations of thunder, he could hear the gunfire.

And the screams.

Kellogg looked out at the rain, silver droplets flickering downward against the purple-black sky, and as the heavens wept he continued to slowly, methodically, and carefully sharpen his knives. They were kitchen knives, but they were all he had. Kellogg did not own a gun and had never even handled one. He loved to cook, though, so knives were more comfortable in his hands. Or . . . had been more comfortable. Comfort of every kind, he judged, was over. He took his time, even as time melted away in the storm.

He tried not to listen to the sounds coming from inside the church. There were no more screams. Those had faded a long time ago. Now it was just moans. Low and constant and hungry. And the slow shuffle of clumsy feet.

He ran the edges of the knives along the whetstone. Kellogg was not really sure if the knives would work. He'd had to use a golf club earlier. That was terrible. Loud and messy and awful. Maybe the knives would be quicker and cleaner—for everyone.

Kellogg was careful with the whetstone, needing to get it right.

Because it was almost time to start the killing.

The moans were constant. And there was a dull, slack pounding on the door. Limp hands beating on the wood.

Whose hands?

Mrs. Kulp, the choir director?

Molly?

Matthew?

"God help me," whispered Pastor Kellogg.

The only answer he heard, though, were the moans.

2

Fluffy McTeague
(Six months after First Night)

He wasn't who he'd been.

He was certain of that.

The person he'd been, he was absolutely certain, had died back there in San Francisco.

That person had been too weak to survive.

That person would never have made the kinds of choices or done the kinds of things he'd done.

No.

When the dead rose, Ferdinand McTeague was still a good man. He was a good husband to Alex; a good father to their adopted sons, Quinn and Taye; a good manager at the hotel; a good employee of the corporation that owned the hotel; a good member of the community, the PTA, the condominium homeowners' association; a good supporter of human rights, animal rights, and sustainable energy; a good son to his parents; a good brother to his sister, Claire.

That's what he had been.

Good.

As he stood in the road and watched San Francisco burn, he wondered what "good" meant.

The fires reached upward with fingers of yellow and orange and red and clawed at the ceiling of clouds. Those clouds glowed as if they were about to burst into flame too.

From here, from this vantage point, Ferdinand could not hear the screams. Or the moans. All he could hear was a long, loud, sustained roar as tens of thousands of buildings and homes burned. He could not see the dead—or the living, if there had been any left before he began setting his fires. But he could imagine those souls flickering upward inside the flames, escaping through the clouds into heaven.

He leaned against the fender of an abandoned car. Electromagnetic pulses from the nukes that had wiped out most of the big cities had killed all the cars. Somehow San Francisco hadn't been nuked, but the EMPs still turned off all the power.

That had made it harder to escape. The lack of power, of lights, of vehicles had probably killed more people than the plague itself. One of the last official statements had been some nonsense about using nuclear weapons to wipe out the main areas of infection. That hadn't worked, and any bloody fool could have told the bozos in Washington it was a stupid plan. All it did was make sure the people had no way to flee. It turned off every light but the one that more or less said "Open Buffet—All You Can Eat."

The smoke from the fire was being pushed around by the wind, and some of it was beginning to come in his direction.

He moved away, allowing himself to be chased into the darkness by the sooty evidence of his crime.

He was sure that there had to be some living people down there.

Had to be. Surviving, as he had survived for so long.

Now . . .

No.

Now San Francisco was going to burn to the ground. No engines would come, no burly firefighters would douse the conflagration. It would all burn.

Maybe it would spread, too.

Ferdinand had left trails of gasoline across the Golden Gate to coax the fires.

He wanted it all to burn.

That was the point.

Nukes didn't kill the infection.

Fire always did.

It was just that there hadn't been enough fire.

Now maybe there would be.

Fire purifies. They even set controlled fires on farm fields to restore and refresh the land.

Maybe it would do that here, too.

He hoped so.

He wiped at the tears in his eyes. Ferdinand was not in the habit of lying to himself. He never had. He didn't try to convince himself that those tears were from the smoke.

No.

Down there, somewhere within those towering walls of flame, were Alex, and the boys, and his parents.

His sister, too.

All of them.

Or . . . the versions of them that had been left to haunt him once they'd contracted the plague. The versions of them that had attacked one another. The versions that had tried to kill him before he'd overpowered them and locked them in rooms.

Now they were burning.

Burning.

Fire purifies.

It ends.

It releases.

As he walked away, he wept.

He walked all night and well into the morning. He outwalked the smoke. He wondered how far he would have to go to outwalk the memories.

He was sure that there was no number for it.

As he walked—that day and over the many days that followed—he wondered who he was now. He was no longer the quiet, gentle, mildly funny and always agreeable hotel manager he had been for eleven years. He was no longer that good man. He was no longer a husband, son, father, or brother.

He had burned everyone he ever loved.

A good man did not do that kind of thing.

A good man does not slaughter his way out of town and then light a blaze that threatens to burn down heaven itself.

No.

He was not that good man anymore.

So who was he?

It was a question he could not answer.

Not yet.

He walked on, heading south and east. Toward the center of the state, toward the mountains. Maybe he could find somewhere where he could be a good man again.

Maybe.

But where?

3

Tom Imura

(Five months after First Night)

Tom heard the sounds of killing long before he smelled the blood.

He knew that this was killing and not just fighting. The screams told him that much. Men didn't scream like that unless they were dying.

The woods were dark, and he knew how to move through them without making a sound. His older brother, Sam, had taught him that. Sam, who was almost twenty years older than

Tom, had been a top special forces soldier, and he'd taught Tom a lot of useful skills. Tom, a change-of-life baby for their mother, had idolized Sam and hung on every word, paid close attention to every lesson. He wanted to *be* Sam.

As he crept through the forest toward the fight, Tom wondered for the millionth time where Sam was. There had been one desperate phone call from his brother on the night it all fell apart. Sam had warned him to take care of the family.

After that, nothing.

Not a word.

Tom was sure that if Sam were alive, he would have found a way to make it home. But First Night was five months ago. The world had ended. Sam had never come home.

The sounds were close now, and Tom slowed as he approached the wall of trees, beyond which was a clearing. He left his sword sheathed and his gun holstered. He wasn't coming to join the fight. Not yet. Tom had already learned hard lessons about assuming that every fight was a human defending against the living dead.

Most of the fights he'd seen over the last few weeks had been a lot different from that. Worse, in some ways.

He eased down into the black shadows beneath a twisted willow and watched with amazed eyes at what was happening.

The clearing was actually the backyard of a substantial house. There was a jungle-gym play set and an inground pool. The play set looked brand-new, like it had never been shared by laughing children. The pool, though, was a soup of polluted water, decaying leaves, and corpses.

Some of the corpses looked like they'd been floating in that muck for weeks.

Three of them, however, were horribly fresh.

There were five other corpses—two zombie and three human—sprawled on the grass. One of the humans was missing most of his head. The other two had multiple cuts to their faces, throats, and bodies. One of these was already twitching, a sure sign that he was about to reanimate.

On the grassy, overgrown back lawn, a fight was raging among six living people.

Five of the men were dressed in biker leather. They were filthy, bearded, and brutal-looking. They had a variety of weapons in their hands—pipe clubs, lengths of chain, and various deadly hunting knives.

The sixth was a big man dressed in loose black military pants, a black tank top, and combat boots. His hair was short and blond and shot through with gray. He looked to be north of forty, but he moved with the oiled grace of a much younger man. He had a short-bladed folding knife in his right hand, the blade barely three and a half inches long.

That blade, though, and the hand that held it, were covered in blood.

The man grinned as he moved, shifting constantly to keep the five men from closing around him. Tom approved. It was a solid martial arts tactic.

One of the bikers faked left and rushed right with a sweep of his chain to try to knock the knife out of the man's hand.

It was a very fast attack.

Tom, who was fast himself, and who was a trained observer, did not see what happened. There was a blur of movement, a flash of silver, and the biker was sagging to his knees, his chain forgotten, clamping hands to his throat.

It had happened so *fast*.

Impossibly fast. No one could move like that.

But he was wrong.

The big man with the knife lunged at the man on the outside of the remaining four, knocked aside a gloved fist holding a butcher knife, and delivered four cuts that were too quick to follow. The biker howled in agony and fell, propelled by a palm-strike to his temple. He crashed into a third man and dragged him down.

The other bikers rushed the man, and as he danced backward, his heel skidded on a patch of blood-soaked grass. He fell, and they piled on him.

Tom found himself moving. It wasn't a planned thing, because he really didn't know who the good guy was in this fight. It could as easily have been two groups of cannibal scavengers as a bunch of survivors trying to punish someone who'd stolen their supplies.

His instincts wrote a different scenario, though.

There was something about the big blond man that spoke of courage and maybe even nobility. He didn't have the cannibal craziness in his eyes. Nor did he look underfed and desperate enough to try to rob a gang.

No. These bikers had probably targeted him.

Bad move for most of them.

Tom broke from the cover of the trees and launched himself into a jumping kick that smashed into one of the two men. He flopped over sideways and Tom landed next to him, stumbled, caught his balance, and whipped out his sword. The biker had time for one word.

"Don't—!"

Then sword moved through the air and through flesh and the biker's voice was still forever.

The shock of the cut trembled up Tom's arm. The shock of having killed someone shuddered inside his chest. It was not the first time he'd had to do it, but it was not something that got easier. If anything, it was getting harder. Requiring more of him. Or perhaps cutting more of him away.

He wheeled around in time to see the big man toss the corpse of the fifth biker aside. The man's neck was twisted in an ugly way.

The man got up with fluid grace and stared at Tom for one long second, and in that moment Tom was sure this man was taking full and accurate stock of him, his weapons, and maybe even his level of skill.

The man reversed the knife in his hand and cocked his arm. "Better duck," he said.

Tom heard a soft sound behind him and he ducked, pivoted, and slashed, knowing that it was the third man, the one who'd been knocked down by the second man who'd been killed. He flicked his sword out, and it struck in the same instant as the knife thrown by the big blond man.

The last of the bikers stared at them in disbelief. He dropped the big meat cleaver he held, tried to speak past the steel stricture in his throat, failed, and fell face-forward onto the grass.

Tom got to his feet and backed a few paces away. He kept his sword in his hands, wary of the blond man now that it was just the two of them.

"Are there more of them?" he asked.

The blond man took a folded kitchen towel from his

pocket and began sponging blood off his arms. "There were."

"What?"

There was a sound—soft and strange—and Tom whirled to see a massive dog standing in the open doorway at the back of the house. He was a brute. A mix of white shepherd and Irish wolfhound. And he was covered with leather armor into which spikes and knife blades had been fastened. The spikes and the dog's muzzle were bright with fresh blood.

The dog began walking across the yard, circling wide to stay out of range of Tom's sword. He didn't go over to the blond man, but instead stopped at a useful angle if the two of them planned a flanking maneuver on Tom. It was evidence of how well this dog had been trained.

"How many?" asked the man, and the dog answered with three sharp barks.

"Did—" began Tom, "did he just . . . answer you?"

"Sure," said the blond man. "Why not?"

"He's just a dog. . . ."

"First off, his name is Baskerville, and he's not just a dog. He's a combat dog, and the son and grandson of combat dogs. And, second, it's a simple response. It's not like he recited *Candide*."

"Um . . ."

The blond man looked him up and down. "You're the one they call Fast Tommy."

"What?"

"That's you, isn't it? Japanese guy with a *katana*. Sometimes seen with a little kid. You're part of that group in the mountains by the reservoir, right? What are they calling that place now? Mountainside?"

"How do you know that?"

"Word gets around," said the man. "But you're Fast Tommy."

"No one calls me that."

"Pretty sure everyone calls you that, son. Maybe not to your face. But let's face it, the world's getting pretty damned empty. How many Japanese guys with swords are there going to be running around in central California?"

Tom said nothing. In truth he had heard that nickname, but he disliked nicknames. That one was only marginally better than another he'd heard.

Tom the Killer.

That was a horrible nickname that had been hung on him after he had a run-in with a group of cannibals. He tried to shake it, but nicknames are like gum. They stick to you.

"Who are you?" he asked. He'd searched his memory for any stories of a man like this but came up empty.

The man smiled. He had a good smile, but it did not go very deep. It was surface and it was cold. "Captain Joe Ledger," he said.

Neither man offered to shake hands.

"Captain of what?"

"Army Rangers, once upon a time. Though, to be precise, I was a sergeant in the army. Then a detective with the Baltimore police."

"That where you got the rank?"

"No. I ran with a Special Ops crew for a while. The Department of Military Sciences."

"Never heard of them."

"You wouldn't have. Covert. Very specialized. We hunted terrorists who had exotic bioweapons."

Tom looked around at the empty world. "Guess you missed one. If that's what this was."

"This was something else," said Ledger. "Still working out exactly what, but it didn't come at us as a terrorist thing. If so . . . then maybe my team would have been on the clock. As it was . . ."

He spread his hands.

It left a lot unsaid, but it also said much. There was deep grief behind that false smile. And maybe some shame, too. This man had not been able to prevent this. Maybe no one could have, but it could not be easy for a man of this kind to abide the loss of everything if it was his job to prevent it. He wondered how the man stayed sane.

Or if he was even sane at all.

A moan made him turn, and he saw two of the bikers struggling to get to their feet. Their eyes were vacant of everything, but there was clear need in the moans they uttered.

"Would you mind?" asked Ledger. "I've got to sit my butt down. I'm way too old for this crap."

He limped over and sat on a swing in the yard. Tom stared at him, and then at Baskerville, who went over and sat next to him.

There were three zombies now, and another who was beginning to stir.

This is a test, he thought. *He wants to see if I understand how this all works.*

Tom nodded to himself, then raised his sword and did what had to be done.

"Three more in the house," said Ledger. "Baskerville

cripples them, but he's not allowed to bite. Don't want him to get sick on zombie muck."

Without saying a word, Tom went into the house. The three zoms there had been ruined by the dog and its spiked armor. They could never have risen, but he could not abide leaving them here to suffer. Or to endure. Whichever word worked for the things they had become. He ended them.

As he walked out into the yard, the soldier was swinging slowly back and forth, watching a flock of starlings fly from tree to tree. He didn't turn to watch Tom approach.

"It's quiet now," he said.

Tom said nothing. He cleaned his sword and resheathed it.

"That's what I call it when we kill those zoms," continued Ledger. "It's how I think of it. They've been 'quieted.'"

Tom thought about the word and nodded to himself. It was a good word for a bad thing. It was a word that changed the meaning of the act of killing.

"Sit," said Ledger, waving him to the second swing.

After a moment, Tom sat.

"Thanks for the assist," said Ledger.

"Not sure you needed one."

Ledger smiled and shrugged. "Thanks anyway."

They watched the birds. Ledger fished in a pocket and produced two energy bars and handed one to Tom. It was like being given a pot of gold. He tore it open and ate it greedily. Then he shared his canteen with Ledger. The dog came and lay like a sphinx on the grass between them.

"Tell me your story," said Ledger, and Tom did so. Ledger then shared his, or at least an abbreviated version of his. Each story was grown from a seed of heartbreak and loss.

After they were done, they said nothing for five whole minutes.

Then Tom asked, "Who are these guys and why did we just kill them?"

"Ah," said Ledger. "Call it us doing a much-needed public service."

"What's that mean?"

"It means that these boys are part of what is quickly becoming a real problem, and as you have probably noticed, we don't need any more problems. Seven billion hungry corpses will pretty much fill my quota for crap I do not need. But the skull-riders are something new."

"Skull-riders?"

"I know. Couldn't be more of a cartoon name. If you go over and examine them, you'll see that they all have some kind of skull tattoo."

Tom shook his head. "I'll take your word for it. Who and what are they?"

"Most of them were pretty ordinary. Some were even bikers, but not all of them. For the most part they're predators who have found a cause. Something that motivates them, unites them, and inspires them."

"Which is?"

"They capture kids. Boys and girls. Some young men and women, too. They have camps. Do you really need to know what goes *on* in those camps?"

Tom wanted to vomit. "You know this for a fact?"

"I do. I've closed down a couple of those camps."

"Alone?"

Ledger shook his head. "I reconnected with a couple of

my guys from the DMS. That's a story in itself. And I'm always scouting for new talent. I want to form a kind of informal law out here. More law enforcement than anything else."

"Are you serious?"

"As a heart attack. I never cared much for bullies or any other kind of predator. Didn't tolerate them much before the Fall, and I can't say I've got the warm fuzzies for them now. Maybe less so now. The skull-riders are a bad, bad bunch. I've decided to make them my new hobby."

"How many are there?"

"Not counting this pack of morons?" Ledger said, nodding to the bodies. "Maybe twenty-six, twenty-seven packs ranging from four to twenty riders."

"And it's you and a couple of other guys?"

"So far."

"You're nuts."

"Been told that."

"How many have you . . . ? You know?"

"Counting these guys, my boys have taken out fifty-seven. Men and women. I don't cut breaks for gender when it comes to this stuff. Besides, one of the pack leaders is a woman. Mama Rat. Charming lady, from what I've heard. She and a few other packs have been working their way toward San Jose, which is where I'm heading. Figured Baskerville and I would have us some fun. And . . . I'm also looking for his brother. Damn dog got lost during a running fight, and I met someone who said they saw a dog that fits the description on the outskirts of San Jose. So . . . that's where I'm heading."

He turned and looked at Tom.

"What?" asked Tom.

"I . . . don't suppose you'd like to join me?"

"I can't. My little brother's in Mountainside and—"

"So why are you out here, then?"

Tom took a moment on that. "Looking."

"Looking for what?"

"There's only a few hundred people in town. And maybe twice that many in a second town just north of us. That's not enough. If we're going to come back from this, we need everyone we can."

"Five thousand minimum," said Ledger, nodding. "That's the standard model for rebuilding the gene pool."

"We're nowhere near that."

Ledger nodded. "Let me put it this way, then. If the skull-riders are sending multiple packs to San Jose, what do you think they expect to find? I mean, it's a very specific target. Don't you think there have to be at least some reliable rumors about survivors?"

Tom said nothing.

"That's what I think," said Ledger. "And since I've got nothing better to do than try to do what I can—which is a passive way of saying it's a moral imperative, just in case you weren't following—I'm going to follow every lead I can. Every rumor I can. Every chance I can. Do I have to explain why?"

Tom stood up and walked a few paces away, his hands thrust into his back pockets.

"My brother . . . ," he began, then stopped.

"Your brother needs a world to inherit," said Ledger gently.

The birds still filled the air, moving from tree to tree to tree.

"I . . . ," Tom said, then stopped again, shaking his head. Then he sighed and turned. "Okay."

Ledger stood up.

"Just for a little while, though," said Tom. "I don't want to be away from Benny for too long."

Ledger offered his hand. "Welcome to the war," he said.

After only a slight pause, Tom took the offered hand.

4

Benny and Chong
(A few weeks before Rot & Ruin)

"Happy birthday," said Chong, and handed Benny a small parcel wrapped in brown paper and tied with twine.

Benny grinned. "Hey, thanks, dude!"

They sat in the shade of Benny's porch with cold glasses of iced tea and the crumbling debris of Mrs. Riley's corn-and-walnut muffins. Overhead the summer sun was a fireball, but there was a breeze off the reservoir that was damp and cool.

"How's it feel to be fifteen?" asked Chong, who would pass the same milestone in ten days.

"Same as being fourteen, eleven months, and thirty days."

"What I figured," Chong said. "We have to get jobs."

"Yeah."

They both sighed. The town regulations were inflexible. All teens had to get a job within two months of turning fifteen or they'd have their rations cut by half. Chong was no more enthusiastic about it than Benny. Fifteen had always seemed a million years off.

"I'm probably going to get a job at Lafferty's," said Benny. "Work inside. All the pop I can drink."

"Lafferty's isn't hiring. I asked."

"Oh. Crap."

"What about that erosion artist?" asked Chong. "You can draw pretty good. Bounty hunters always need good erosion portraits."

It was true. Erosion portraits were a solid business. Artists painted pictures of how people might look if they'd been zommed out. Bounty hunters used the portraits to try to find the zom in question and put them down. Tom called it "giving closure," but Benny thought that was a sissy way to phrase it. Charlie Pink-eye and his buddy, the Motor City Hammer, had cooler names for it. Bag-and-tag jobs. Shutdowns. Drops. Things like that.

"Maybe," Benny said uncertainly. "Could be fun. Could be boring."

"Better than shoveling horse poop at the stables."

"Good point."

They sipped their tea.

"Open it," prompted Chong, changing the subject.

Benny grinned and tackled the knots. Just to be devious, Chong had tied a series of bizarre sailor's knots in the twine. Stuff they'd learned in the Scouts. It took Benny five minutes to solve them, and he stuffed the twine down the back of Chong's shirt. Then he unwrapped the parcel paper to reveal six packs of brand-new Zombie Cards.

"*Dude!*" cried Benny, grinning hard enough to sprain his face.

"I get your doubles," warned Chong.

"Yeah, yeah . . . *dude*! This is soooo cool."

Benny tore open the first pack and immediately struck gold. The very first card was of a man with a scarred and ugly face, short dark hair, and pistol butts sticking out of every pocket.

"Niiiiice!" said Chong. "Read the back."

Benny flipped the card over and read the text:

> The Bounty Hunters #95: "The Motor City Hammer." The Hammer is half of the most famous and successful team of bounty hunters to work the Ruin since First Night. With his partner, Charlie Matthias, the Hammer has racked up more confirmed kills than anyone; and he's rumored to have amassed a fortune from all the heads he's taken!

Benny turned and gave Chong a high five. "Oh, man, I have soooo wanted this card. Now I have both Charlie *and* the Hammer."

Chong was grinning too. "Just remember, I get the doubles."

"Yeah, cool, no problem."

They stared at the card for a long time. The Motor City Hammer was so dangerous, so tough, so *everything* that Benny wanted to be. Not like Tom. Nothing like Tom, even if they both did the same thing. It made Benny laugh to think that Tom considered himself a bounty hunter. As if he could ever be as tough or cool as the Hammer. What a joke. Tom the Coward couldn't hold a candle to the Hammer. Or Charlie.

Never in a million years.

Benny turned over the next card, which was a double he already had, and he handed it to Chong. The Bride of Coldwater Creek. One of the most famous of the zoms still active in the Ruin outside town. He flipped over the next card, and the next, thinking about Charlie and the Hammer.

How insanely outstanding would it be to get a job with them? To apprentice with the toughest bounty hunters in the entire Ruin?

Benny kept grinning and nodding to himself.

Yeah, he thought, *that's what I'm going to do. I'm going to be exactly like them.*

FROM NIX'S JOURNAL

ON BEING A HERO
(AFTER THE EVENTS OF *ROT & RUIN*)

The other day, when we were all at Chong's house for dinner after training with Tom, Mrs. Chong said something strange. It was at the beginning of dinner, during grace. Only, instead of a regular grace prayer for food and abundance and all, she said this:

"Lord, thank you for the blessing of these young heroes. Thank you for letting us know that honor has not vanished from our green Earth. Thank you for restoring hope to those who need it."

I guess it was meant as a compliment, because before dinner she and Mr. Chong bullied Tom and Benny into telling the whole story—again—of how they rescued me from Charlie Pink-eye, how we met Lilah, and how the bunch of us took back the kids Charlie's gang was taking to Gameland.

So, sure, she was trying to be nice, but it felt really weird. No one said much of anything all the way through dinner. Except for when Benny asked Chong to pass the mashed potatoes, I don't think anyone said two words until Mr. Chong cut the apple pie Tom brought.

I know I couldn't speak at all. My face burned all night. And Benny didn't look at anyone. Only Lilah seemed unaffected by it, but she didn't say much because she never says much.

Over pie, Mrs. Chong tried to apologize, but I don't think she really understood what there was to apologize for. She'd been trying to be nice.

Here's the thing about that, though. Okay, so we rescued those kids, and that's pretty great. And we stopped Charlie and the Hammer from kidnapping more kids to take to Gameland, and that's cool too.

But what Mrs. Chong doesn't really get is how we did all that. I mean, she doesn't understand what we had to do that night.

She thinks we were all being heroes.

We weren't.

We were being killers.

That's the thing nobody gets.

Maybe I don't even understand it. Sometimes in order to be a hero, you have to do some really terrible things. Maybe that's why guys like Tom, who really is a hero, hate being called one.

It reminds him of the things he's had to do.

I know that I don't consider myself a hero. I never will.

I killed people that night.

Bad guys, sure, but people.

How can I possibly want to cheer about that?

How could anyone?

Overdue Books

(One year after First Night;
thirteen years before *Rot & Ruin*)

Kamiakin High School
Washington State

The poster on the wall read:

KNOWLEDGE IS POWER.
BOOKS CONTAIN KNOWLEDGE.
READ.
BECOME POWERFUL.

Walker paused to read it every time he came into the library.

Even when he was dog-tired.

Even when he was covered in black gore from killing zoms.

It was because of those words, and the truth behind them, that Walker was still alive. Him and Keaton and their dog, Dewey. Not that the dog could read it, but the boys had saved the dog's life with animal first aid they'd found in a book.

They lived according to those words, and month after month, year after year, they survived.

The others?

Well . . . some folks are so darn stubborn that they get in the way of their own best interests. They *can* learn, the knowledge is there, but they won't stop long enough to learn something new. Or they refuse to admit that what they do know is either faulty, outdated, or wrong.

Like that guy, Smithwick, who crashed here at the library last year.

Smithwick was a loner trying to make his way in a destroyed world, surviving by the skin of his teeth, always on the edge of starvation. The boys brought him in, fed him, and treated the man's injuries. After a week, when Smithwick was able to talk, he described the hardships he'd encountered in the great Rot and Ruin. The boys brought him stacks of books to read. Books on survival skills, on foraging for food, on hunting, on first aid, even a book on which edible plants offered the best nutrition.

Smithwick leafed through the books but never read them. Not one.

"I already know what I need to know," he said.

"Are you kidding?" asked Keaton. "You were half-dead when we found you."

"I was doing just fine," the man insisted, then waved his hands at the towering stacks of books that filled nearly every inch of what had once been a school library. "These books didn't save the world, did they?"

Keaton wanted to argue, but Walker gave a discreet shake of his head. A *don't bother* thing. They'd met too many people like this. The kind who would defend a bad choice simply because it was *his* choice. The boys figured it was a kind of teenage oppositional defiant disorder that fueled adult narcissistic behavior in someone suffering from PTSD. Or possibly a simple maladaptive coping method. Something like that.

There were a lot of books on psychology in the library. They read everything they could about trauma and damage.

And loss.

The boys were survivors who'd been born into a ruined world. Everyone they'd ever met was damaged. They knew that they were damaged too. It was the way of this world.

The difference was that Keaton and Walker accepted it.

Explored it.

Worked on it.

Individually and as friends.

They didn't leave it to fester like a wound of the soul. Understanding it helped them through the dark days after the last of the adults died off. Despair was the real enemy. Knowledge was their weapon. It helped them have the optimism to keep going.

Smithwick was a lost cause.

They tried.

But . . .

Walker and Keaton sat on the roof of the Kamiakin High School Library, drinking cups of rainwater they'd caught in plastic bags, eating chicken they'd raised and roasted. Dewey, their blue heeler, lay sprawled between them, chewing his way through a mound of scraps. The dog had rings around his eyes that looked like glasses, and that seemed appropriate for a library.

Down below, the living dead milled in the hundreds.

Lost souls.

They weren't even evil. They just . . . *were*.

Smithwick wandered in a slow circle directly below them, his flesh faded to gray and withered to a leathery toughness. Both boys wished he would leave, wander away, go elsewhere. But the dead didn't wander off unless they were following prey. Otherwise, they stayed where they were. Some of the zoms stood still as statues, their limbs wrapped in creeper vines.

Keaton picked up the book he'd been reading and opened it. *I Am Legend*, a postapocalyptic tale, which seemed appropriate to Keaton. Vampires, though; not zombies. Even so, it featured a hero who was very practical when managing his own survival. Keaton liked that. Emotions were good, and even random craziness, but survival depended on smarts, on common sense, and on applying knowledge. Keaton had read over three hundred books about surviving the end of the world. Some were very helpful. Some were silly. Some merely entertaining. There were even some written as instruction manuals for what to do in the event of a global disaster.

Of course, none of those books had accurately predicted a zombie apocalypse, but that was to be expected. After all, zombies. Who knew?

Beside him, Walker was reading a book on handcrafting body armor.

Walker had built five separate generations of body armor so far. The two of them could stroll through a sea of zoms without getting bitten. Walker was always looking for improvements. Better mobility, lighter weight.

Below them the dead moaned. Keaton could swear he could hear the high, reedy sound of Smithwick's voice. Sad.

Suddenly the zombies stopped moaning.

They froze for a moment, and then they began turning toward the east, raising their heads, staring with dead eyes at the empty sky. Keaton and Walker stared too.

"What the—" began Walker, but his voice trailed off.

"It's coming back," gasped Keaton.

They looked at each other for a moment; then both of them burst into huge grins. They jumped up from their chairs and ran across the roof, laughing with excitement.

They'd prepared for this.

Researched it.

Done everything by the book. Step by step.

Keaton dug a pack of all-weather matches from his pocket and thrust the flame into a small pile of rags soaked in combustible chemicals. The rags caught at once, and bright fire raced along the lines they'd laid out in fireproof troughs of crushed stone. Walker crouched behind an old dry-erase board mounted on a hinged frame and tilted the board upward so that the row upon row of old cell phones were angled just so. Sunlight flashed from the metallic mirrorlike material that had once been hidden behind each tiny screen.

The lines of fire and the reflective screens each spelled out words.

ALIVE INSIDE was written in fiery letters.

UNINFECTED shone with mirror brightness.

Keaton grabbed a pair of bright-orange signal flags and tossed them to Walker. Then he jogged over to the corner of the wall, where they'd mounted a heavy hand-crank alarm they'd scavenged from a fire station. Keaton began cranking the handle, and a wail burst from the bell-shaped mouth of the siren, louder than any sound in their quiet world.

Walker began flapping the signal flags. Spelling out words.

S.O.S.
ALIVE INSIDE.
LAND HERE.

Dewey barked and barked.

The noise in the air changed.

Instead of a drone that crossed their horizon line, it suddenly changed. Became louder.

Came closer.

Below, the dead moaned louder, agitated by the siren and the thrum of the thing in the air. They reached for it.

They tried in vain to grab for the big helicopter.

Keaton cranked the siren; Walker signaled and signaled.

The helicopter came closer and closer until the rotor wash whipped away the smoke from their fire and blew out the flames.

Keaton stopped cranking.

Walker lowered his flags.

Dewey's tail whipped back and forth.

The helicopter hung there in the air. Something they'd only ever seen on the edges of their world. Something that belonged to the old world. Something they'd read about in books. Now, here.

Drawn to them by their signals.

Pulled by their wills and through the things they'd read about.

Survival skills included how to signal for help.

The boys stood there, waving with their hands now.

Grinning.

Laughing.

Tears rolling down their cheeks.

The side door of the helicopter opened, and a man dressed in military camouflage fatigues stared out at them. Even from fifty yards away they could see the surprise on his face as he looked at them, and at the apparatus they'd constructed on the roof.

Then a slow smile formed on the soldier's face.

He gave them a thumbs-up.

Then held up his hands, fingers splayed, pulsing them three times.

Wait. Thirty minutes.

The helicopter rose, climbing and turning. Looking for someplace to land.

Keaton and Walker watched it go.

Then they turned and glanced at the open roof door.

Keaton grinned. "How many books do you think they'll let us take?"

Walker gave him a devious smile. "Let's find out."

They rushed inside to make their selections.

Below them, all around them, the mindless dead moaned for something they could never have.

FROM NIX'S JOURNAL

ON KNOWLEDGE
(BEFORE *DUST & DECAY*)

We trained with Tom every single day.

Most of the people in town made jokes about us being samurai, and they thought that all that meant was we trained with swords.

If they only knew.

Tom never bothered to correct people about it. I guess we didn't either.

But the truth was that we learned a lot more than how to use wooden swords. More than how to do kicks and punches and combat stuff.

A lot more.

Tom told us one afternoon that "knowledge

is power." I know that everyone says that, that it's an old saying. The reason I'm writing it down now, though, is because I think I finally understand it.

See, Tom taught us all sorts of stuff. He taught us how to hunt and stalk; how to track and how to confuse someone if they're tracking us. He taught us about plants we might find out in the Ruin—the ones you can eat, the poisonous ones, the ones that can be used for first aid. He taught us about how to read the landscape like a book. He said that nature was always trying to tell us something, and all we had to do was slow down, stop for a moment, and pay attention. He taught us how to listen to the wind and the things it says when it moves through different kinds of trees and through the summer grass and over rocks.

He made us read books on anatomy. Factoid: It takes eight and a half pounds of pressure per square inch to break the adult male elbow. Kind of cool, kind of disgusting.

We learned a lot of stuff like that.

We also learned how to use spiderwebs to fight infection, how to make shoes out of tree bark and leaves, how to walk so quietly that we could come right up to a deer and pet it without spooking it.

He taught us to always leave the forest the way we found it.

He gave us reading lists of stuff that had no connection to fighting. Poems and plays and essays about what it means to be a human being. We spent one afternoon just mixing colors from pigments we collected in the forest.

It was Morgie who finally asked him why we were learning all that crap (his word choice!) instead of just training to fight. Benny got all tense, because I guess he thought Tom was going to get mad, but Tom didn't.

Tom asked a question that really surprised us. The answer made me cry, though not right then. Later, when I was alone.

Tom asked Morgie, "Why are you training to be a samurai? What's the point?"

Morgie got all defensive, the way he does, and said that we were training to fight zoms and to stop people like Charlie and the Hammer.

Tom kept pushing him. He said that wasn't enough of an answer. He asked us all what we were fighting _for_. "What," he asked, "is the purpose of a samurai?"

That seemed like an easy answer. Benny said, "'Samurai' means 'to serve.'"

Tom nodded and said that was a definition, but not an answer. Who did we serve, and _what_ did we serve?

It kind of caught us all off guard. We didn't know how to answer.

After we all kept saying the wrong things, it was Chong who figured it out.

He said, "People think that learning to be a samurai means learning to fight and kill."

Tom smiled and said, "But . . . ?"

"But we're not learning how to kill,"

Chong continued. "We're learning how to be alive."

Benny was nodding as he said it, and I think even Morgie got it.

Dead & Gone

(Five years before *Flesh & Bone*)

1

Sometimes survival is a feast. Sometimes it's rainwater in a ditch and a bug.

The girl knew both kinds, and all the kinds in between.

Out here, you had to learn every kind of survival or you stopped learning. Stopped talking. Stopped breathing.

The hunger, though—that never goes away.

Not while you're alive.

Not after you're dead.

2

The girl fled across the desert.

She had bloodstains on her hands and on her clothes. She was certain that those stains were on her heart as well. On her soul.

As she ran, the girl prayed that they would not find her, that they would stop looking.

But they would never stop looking. Never.

Not as long as her mother wanted her dead.

Somewhere, out beyond the heat shimmers that hovered over the sandy horizon, killers were tracking her. Reapers of her mother's Night Church.

They would never stop because they believed—truly

believed—that tracking her down was their holy purpose. She was the sinner, the pariah. The monster that they hunted in order to rid the world of a dreadful impurity.

The reapers.

With knives and axes and bladed farm tools they hunted her. Wanting to find her. Craving her death.

And so many of them were her friends.

From them, and from who she had once been, the girl tried to hide herself in the vastness of a cruel desert.

3

She was hungry.

It was that deep hunger, the kind that made her sharp and quick for hours. A belly-taut ache that can't be outrun.

When she was that hungry, she couldn't be lazy. She couldn't climb a tree and lash herself to a thick limb and let the day shamble past.

No, this kind of hunger made her go hunting. It shook her loose from the crushing depression she'd felt since leaving the Night Church.

Before she left, she checked her weapons—the fighting knife she'd carried since she was seven years old, the strangle wire, the throwing spikes, the sling with its bag of sharp stones. She looped the coil of rope across her body.

Her home for the last three days had once been something called a FunMart. She had no idea what that was. It had shelves like a lot of the stores she'd seen, but there was nothing on them. The floor was littered with the torn wrappers of bread loaves and cracker boxes, but everything of value had been scavenged by refugees over the last twelve years, and any forgotten crumbs had been devoured by insects and animals. But the place was dry, and it got her out of the desert heat.

Now it was time to leave. She knew that she wouldn't be coming back here. The reapers were still out there somewhere. Maybe weeks behind her, maybe much closer. She had only stayed this long at the FunMart because of the gripes—a terrible storm that had raged in her intestines after eating a piece of questionable food. That lizard she'd caught and cooked must have been sick, or it had carried some kind of toxin. For two whole days her stomach felt like it was filled with razor blades and acid. She threw up everything she ate, which was also a terrible waste of food. Nothing of value went into her system. No proteins or fats or useful calories. No nutrients.

When the gripes passed, the girl was left weak and trembling. If even the weakest reaper came at her, she could not have defended herself.

The desert offered no obvious comfort. Food had to be caught, and there was very little water. So survival required movement. Hunger demanded it.

Even so, she lingered at the door of the FunMart.

The girl did not have a home. Not anymore. And the home she used to have was not a place she could return to. No way. To the people she left behind she was a disgrace, a lost soul.

A monster.

Places like this empty shell of a FunMart offered no real protection; it was not a home in any genuine way. It was a place to be sick, and if she stayed longer, it would be the place where she died. The reapers were coming. She did not know when they would find her, only that they would.

Beyond the door was the road that stretched through the endless desert. Beyond the door was the truth. The loneliness. The fear.

The hunger.

The hunger called to her. It yelled. It shrieked.

So she had to leave.

Not soon.

Now.

Get your skinny butt in gear, girl, scolded her inner voice. *No handsome prince is going to stroll out of a fairy tale and serve you a hot breakfast of eggs and grits.*

"Shut up," she told herself. Her voice sounded dusty and far older than her fifteen years.

She could see a faintness of green down the road. Sparse woods that had once been vast groves of fruit trees set, improbably, on the edge of the Nevada desert. Patches of scrub pine and weathered creosote bushes were thriving there now as the orchard died. The ghosts of the fruit trees stood like pale sticks. She reckoned that the water pumping stations were dead. All these years of blowing sand and dust had frozen the gears in the rows of tall, white wind turbines. Now they stood above the orchard, silent as clouds, offering the lie of power in a powerless world.

Beyond the forest was a town. It said so on the map she had.

A place called Red Pass, which looked to be have been built into the cleft of a long ridge of low mountains.

Red Pass. The name meant nothing to her, but the fact that it was a town meant that there might be some vittles.

Old canned stuff. Maybe some gardens with enough life for wild carrots and potatoes to still be growing. She knew that birds lived in some of the old towns. Even a scrawny pigeon was roast breast for dinner and a day's worth of soup from the rest. And where there was one pigeon, there would be two.

The town was where she had to go.

Ten miles under the August sun.

It had to be done during the day, though. At night she would not be able to see, or hunt, or defend. And they did not need the light to find her.

They.

The gray people. The wanderers.

The hungry ghosts.

She knew they were not really ghosts. That was just something her father used to call them. Hungry ghosts.

They were also in the towns.

They were always in the towns.

It's where they'd lived. It's where they'd died.

It's where they waited.

And she, hungry and desperate, had no choice but to leave her empty little place of safety and journey into the places of the dead.

Hunger demanded it.

4

"Sister Margaret!"

The words tore her out of a daydream of food and dragged her into horror.

The girl spun around and crouched.

There were three of them. Two men and a woman. They rose from the desert, shedding the sand-colored cloaks that had allowed them to hide and wait until she stumbled right into their trap.

Now you walked into it, girl, said her inner voice. *You done gone and stepped right into a snake pit and no mistake.*

They were dressed all in black, with red streamers tied to their ankles and wrists. Stylized angel wings were embroidered on their chests. Their heads had been shaved and comprehensively tattooed with complex images of tangled vines and flowers.

Just like hers.

It was a requirement of everyone in the Night Church. A permanent mark that could not be removed. It was supposed to prove an unbreakable attachment to the god of that faith.

Now it was the only thing that made the girl look like she was connected to them. She did not wear the dark clothes and red streamers and angel wings. She wore ratty jeans, stolen sneakers, and a leather vest buttoned up over her bare skin. She had no other clothes, and she would rather die than wear the clothes of a reaper.

Never again.

The reapers approached, smiling the way they're taught to do. Smiles of false welcome, of false acceptance.

There was no trace of real acceptance in the Night Church. You were collected by them, you belonged to them, but there was no approval of who you were.

"Sister Margaret," said the taller of the two men as he walked toward her. He held a broad-blade machete in one muscular fist, carrying it casually with the tip pointed toward the ground. "Praise be to the darkness that we found you."

"Stop right there, Jason," warned the girl. "Y'all turn around and be on your way."

They continued to smile at her. The shorter man had a hunter's hatchet tucked through his belt. Sunlight gleamed along the wicked edge as he drew it.

"We bring love and greetings from your mother, Sister Marg—"

"Don't call me that," snapped the girl. "That's not my name no more."

"What name do you want us to use, sister?" asked the woman. She was young, no more than three years older than the girl. Maybe eighteen, but already there were combat scars on her face, and her eyes were ablaze with righteous anger.

"I don't have a name no more, Connie," said the girl. "I left all that behind when I left the church."

"That's not true, little sister. Your mother sent us to bring you home, to bring you back into the peace and love of the Night Church."

"I know you, Connie. You don't open your mouth 'cept when a lie needs to come out."

Sister Connie's smile flickered, and her eyes went cold. "And you can't help but carve more sins onto your own soul."

Sister Connie drew her blade—a slender double-edged antique dagger that had been looted from a museum in Omaha. The girl had been there when Connie had found the weapon four years ago. Six families had been living in the museum, and they had refused to join the Night Church. The reapers had cut through them like scythes through ripe wheat.

The girl, only eleven at the time, had killed too. It had not been the first time she'd ended the day bathed in innocent blood.

The memory burned in her mind as she saw that knife in Sister Connie's hand.

"C'mon, Sister Connie," said the shorter man, "it's too hot to stand here and play games with this brat."

"Hush, Brother Griff," said the young woman. "We were told to give our little sister here a chance to recant her wicked ways and come back to the church."

The girl laughed. A single, short bark of harsh derision.

"Come back? What kind of sun damage have y'all had on what little brains ye got that my 'coming back' was even a possibility? Mom doesn't want me back and we all know it. She wants me dead and left to the vultures. Anything any of y'all say different would be a goll-durn lie."

Jason, Griff, and Connie stared at her with a variety of emotions playing on their faces. Anger at her sass, shock at the bald intensity of her words, confirmation of their private thoughts, and something else. A cruel delight that the girl knew only too well. The anticipation of wetting those blades as they opened red mouths in her flesh and sent her screaming into the eternal darkness.

None of them answered her, though.

The girl said, "Y'all don't have to do this. We can all just walk away."

The three reapers began to spread out, forming a loose half circle around her, hands flexing to find the perfect grip on each weapon.

The girl sighed. It was so heavy a sigh that it felt like a

piece of her heart was being pulled out of her chest and flung into the wind.

"I tried," she said, though even she wasn't sure to whom those words were directed. "Dang if I didn't at least try."

She drew her knife.

They moved first. They moved with lightning speed.

Perhaps in their excitement they had forgotten just who it was they'd been sent to find. There were three of them. They were all older than the girl, larger and stronger than the girl, better armed than the girl.

It should have ended there.

Brother Jason lunged first, raising his arm and chopping down with the big machete. The blade cut through the air where a girl-shape had been a millisecond before. Jason's swing was so heavy, backed by all of his weight and muscle, that the blade chopped deeply into the highway blacktop, sending shock waves up his arm.

The girl spun away from the blow, twirling like a top but staying so close she could feel the wind as Jason's weapon whistled past. She continued her spin and flashed her arm out, silver glinting in her hand, and then the dry air was seeded with red.

Jason made a confused gagging sound that was more surprise than pain as he dropped his knife and clutched his throat. A throat that was no longer constructed for breathing.

"Get her!" screeched Sister Connie, and thrust out with her knife. But the girl darted away, ducked under the swing of Brother Griff's hatchet, slashed him across the top of one thigh, and then shoved him toward Connie.

Griff tried to keep his balance; Connie tried to jerk her knife back.

Griff suddenly screeched like a gaffed rabbit and dropped to his knees. The movement tore the knife from Connie's fingers. She stared in horror as blood bubbled from between Griff's lips.

"No . . . ," he said, his voice thick and wet.

But the moment said yes, and he fell.

That left Connie standing there, her hands empty, her companions down, and all of it happening so fast.

They stood there, face to face no more than six feet apart. The wind blew past them, making the streamers on Connie's clothes snap and pop.

Connie tried to say something, tried to frame a comment that would make sense of the moment. "I—" was all she managed before the girl cut her off.

"Run," said the girl, her voice raw and ugly.

Connie stared at her. "W-what . . . ?"

"Run," the girl repeated. *"Run!"*

Connie stood there, blank-faced and unsure of what was happening. An easy and certain kill had somehow become a disaster.

"Griff and Jason were good fighters. Not y'all, Connie. Y'all were never no good," the girl said quietly. "But me? Heck, I was taught every dirty trick there is by Saint John of the Knife."

Connie paled. She knew all about the girl's training and her level of skill, but hearing of it again and seeing the proof of it demonstrated in the silent bodies of Griff and Jason chilled her to the bone. Her lips quivered with sudden fear.

"No . . . ," she said. "Don't."

"Run away," said the girl who was no longer Sister Margaret. Her arms were red to the elbows with bright blood. "Run away and tell my mother not to send any more of her killers after me. Tell her to leave me alone. Tell her to forget I exist. Tell her I died out here."

"I . . . can't . . ."

"You better."

"I—"

Connie's protest was interrupted by a low groan. She looked down to see that Griff's eyes were open. His dead eyes.

His dead mouth opened too, rubbery lips pulling back from bloody teeth as he uttered that deep, terrible moan of awakening hunger. He reached for Connie with twitching fingers.

Connie gave a shrill cry of horror and sprang back.

Right into Jason.

He wrapped his big arms around her and dragged her back.

Connie fought against him, driving her elbow into his stomach, head butting him with the back of her skull, stamping on his feet, and all the while trying to free an arm so that she could wave the red cloth ribbon under his nose. He snapped at her, trying to bite her hand, trying to bite her face.

The girl knew about those ribbons. The reapers soaked them every few days in a noxious chemical mixture that made the gray people react the same way they did around other dead. When the chemical was strong, the dead totally ignored the reapers.

"How long since you dipped your streamers, Connie?" she asked.

Connie's face, already pale, went whiter still.

She screamed. Loud and terrible.

And then the girl was moving. She lunged in and slammed the steel pommel of her knife against the dead reaper's temple, knocking his head sideways. That loosened his hold, and the girl grabbed the shoulder of Connie's shirt and gave her a single violent pull. Connie staggered three awkward steps backward, then fell over Griff, who was trying to get to his feet.

The girl ducked low and slashed Jason's ankles, cutting the tendons. Even though the man was past feeling pain, his skeleton still needed those tendons in order to stand. Jason toppled into the dust.

Connie was still screaming, but now her horror was directed at Griff, who crawled toward her, teeth bared, fingers scrabbling for purchase on her trouser cuffs. In her panic and confusion Connie had lost herself completely, forgetting everything she'd learned, everything that had helped her survive this long since the Fall.

The girl knew that Connie was going to die.

She almost let her die.

Almost.

Instead, with a sigh of disgust, the girl jumped forward and kicked Griff in the side of the head with the flat of her foot. It toppled the dead man onto his side. Connie stopped moving and stared.

The girl walked up behind Griff, used another kick to knock him flat on his stomach, crouched, and drove the point of her knife into the cleft formed by the bottom notch of the skull and the upper part of the spine. The brain stem. The knife slid in without effort, and Griff instantly went still. No death twitch, no transition. Living death, and then the forever kind of death.

Jason was eight feet away, crawling toward them.

The girl looked at him, then turned to stare down at Connie.

"I told you before and this'll be the last time," said the girl. "Run away. Tell my mother and Saint John and all the others to leave me alone."

"They won't. You've sinned against the church and against your mother. The reapers will never stop. You belong with us. You belong to the church, heart and soul, flesh and bone. You know that, Sister Mar—"

The girl moved like lightning and crouched over the reaper, the bloody tip of her knife pricking the softness under Connie's chin.

"Call me that again and I'll butcher you like a hog and leave you to bleed out here. I'll leave you to Jason and the flies and the scorpions. Y'all think I'm joshing you?"

Connie shook her head.

The girl leaned closer. "Tell them, Connie. Tell them to leave me be."

A tear broke from the corner of the reaper's eye. "They *won't*. The reapers will never stop. You *know* that. You know that they'll never stop looking for you. And they *will* find you and they will kill you. You belong to the Night Church. You belong with us."

"I don't belong to anybody!" snarled the girl. "Why can't you get that through your head? I don't belong to the church or to

my mother or Saint John or anybody. Leave me alone."

Jason was inches away now. The girl pivoted away from Connie, knocked Jason flat, and ended him the way she had ended Griff. A single thrust delivered with the cold precision of a perfect killer.

Exactly the way she had killed before. Exactly the way she had ended the lives of countless gray people. And countless living people.

The girl stood up and backed away from the living reaper and the two dead men.

"Y'all just used up whatever bit of mercy I had left," she said. "Don't let me see you again."

With that she turned and walked away.

She didn't look back. Didn't watch to see if Connie got up and grabbed a weapon.

She offered her unguarded back to the reaper.

The girl left a trail of broken minutes behind her. She was halfway to the horizon line when the first sobs broke in her chest.

5

That night she caught a small turtle and ate it.

And threw it up.

She curled up in the backseat of a highway patrol car that was pocked with bullet holes and surrounded by bones. As night collapsed around her, she used spit and a piece of cloth to try to wipe the blood from her hands and arms. It left a brown stain.

She cried all night and finally fell into a weary slumber before dawn.

The hunger screamed at her until she woke up.

6

As she staggered through the morning, she daydreamed of cool trees and running water. Of leaping fish and bushes heavy with ripe berries.

Way off in the distance she heard a roar, and she stopped, whipping out her knife.

It was a cat, a big one.

Las Vegas was less than forty miles from where she stood. Las Vegas used to have those shows with the white tigers and golden lions. There was a zoo behind one of the casinos, with jungle predators of all kinds. When her father was still alive, back when it was just the two of them traveling through the wasteland looking for shelter, they had gone past the old gambling town. They met a half-crazed man who described the terrors of Vegas: the dead constantly at war with tigers and lions for control of the hunting grounds, and the people who tried to survive there.

The crazed man's stories were all past tense.

Nobody lived in Las Vegas anymore, and the cats—like the dead—had gone into the desert to find fresh meat.

That roar came from way over in the tumble of red rocks to her left. The big cats made that terrible shriek when they'd killed something. It's part triumph and part warning—I killed this and I'll defend my meat.

That kitty cat is too durn big and mean, she thought. *You don't want no truck with it, do you, girl?*

She often talked to herself as if she were an adult scolding a child. Like there were two of her. It took the edge off being so completely alone.

The girl hurried along the road, wanting no part of whatever red drama was happening behind those rocks. She was hungry, but her hunger had not yet driven her crazy enough to want to fight eight hundred pounds of muscle and claws. She was fifteen, and prolonged hunger had leaned her down to ninety pounds. All that was left of her was bone, hard muscle, and pain.

The road ahead was clear for half a mile before it curved around a big, white piece of junk. The girl thought it was an overturned tractor trailer—they always held the promise of some item left behind after scavengers had come through like locusts. But as she approached, she realized that it wasn't a truck at all. It was too big.

She hurried to see what it was.

The closer she got, the more she realized that it was massive. Much bigger than she'd thought. The thing had to be well over two hundred feet long with wings nearly as wide. It had once been snow white with a broad sky-blue line that covered the cockpit and ran all the way to the towering tail. But there had been a fire, probably on impact. Much of the white and blue paint was soot-blackened, and in places it had burned completely away to reveal the silvery glint of steel. Rusted now, and pitted by endless blowing sand.

Words had been painted in black along the sides: THE UNITED STATES OF AMERICA.

And on the shattered tail there was a number: 28000.

The girl knew about jets, of course. Everybody knew about them. There were airports full of them. The bones of all kinds of aircraft littered the landscape. The girl had even spent two nights camped out in the shell of a Black Hawk helicopter.

But she'd never seen one this big. Not up close.

The four big engines lay half-buried in the sand, torn away by the impact. Behind the jet was a deep trench cut like a rough scar into the landscape and all the way across the blacktop. The jet had spent a long time grinding to a halt, and now it lay still and silent, its engines cold, the windows shattered and filled with shadows.

The jet presented a tricky choice. There could be bottled water, cans of soft drinks, plastic bags of stuff like nuts and crackers. Things that had enough preservatives in them to last. Not good food, but a far mile down the road from no food.

The doors were shut, and the windows were too small to climb through, and it would take some doing to climb up onto the nose of the craft and enter that way. On the up side, it didn't look like anyone else had been inside the jet, which was odd because it was right there, big as anything. On the downside, if the doors were all closed, then what had happened to the people on board? Had they managed to climb out? If so, how?

If not . . . were they still there?

A jet this size had to have carried a lot of people.

All of them could be dead.

And waiting.

"No," she said. Her voice sounded as dry as the desert wind.

She stared up longingly at the plane.

If it was empty, then it was high and safe, and out of the wind. It could answer all of her needs. It could be a kind of home.

The wind whipped past her, lashing her cheeks with coarse sand. It stung her scalp. She closed her eyes for a moment, wrestling with herself about this choice.

There was the choice she wanted to believe in, and there was the sensible choice.

You'd have to be dumber than a coal bucket to go up yonder.

"No," she said again.

With a reluctance so great that it felt like grief, the girl turned away from the jet, dragging her eyes from those smashed-out cockpit windows, turning her whole body with an effort of will. She walked slowly around the jet, studying it from every side, marveling that such a massive thing ever could have flown.

She looked into the desert that ran alongside the road. Far, far in the distance she saw some shapes moving. People. At least a dozen of them, maybe more. She faded into the shadows of the plane and watched them, squinting to try to decide what she was seeing. Were they the gray people? Sometimes they moved in bunches, a small mass of them triggered into movement by passing prey.

There was a flash of sunlight on metal.

No.

Not the dead.

Reapers.

She cupped her hands around her eyes and studied the group, counting the shapes, counting the flashes of sunlight on sharpened steel.

Twenty of them? Twenty-one.

Too many.

There was one shape that walked in front of the others, and it was his weapon that most often caught the sunlight. Even though she was too far away to see him clearly, she thought she knew who this was. Brother Andrew. One of the most senior of the reapers. A bull of a man who carried a two-handed scythe.

"No," she murmured. "Go away."

In time, they did. But they were heading in the same direction she was, northwest, their course paralleling the road. They were miles away, though, following a second-ary road. Perhaps they thought she was on that road, that she would take the road less traveled in hopes of eluding pursuit.

The girl crouched in the shadows until Brother Andrew's party was gone, reduced first to tiny dots and then entirely lost to distance and heat shimmer.

Then she stood and stretched her muscles, trying to ignore the ache in her belly. The girl took a steadying breath and began to walk. She cast a single look over her shoulder, and what she saw made her pause within a few steps.

A turkey buzzard sat on the jet's broken wing. Its dark wings were threadbare and in disarray, its wattled red throat was thin, and its eyes looked totally dead. For a horrible moment the girl thought that the vulture *was* dead, that it had somehow caught the plague that had cut like a reaper's scythe through all of humanity. But then it made a small, plaintive caw.

It wasn't dead. It was starving.

Like her.

The thought absolutely chilled her and nearly took the heart out of her. If something like this carrion bird—a creature that would eat anything it found—was starving out here, then what hope was there for her?

She turned away from the sight of it.

"No," she said one more time. She tried to say it with anger, with determination, with purpose.

It sounded like a cry.

The girl hurried away, pushed by fear, pulled by hunger.

7

That night she slept in the back bay of a wrecked Ford Explorer. She had to pull bones out of the front seats. Driver and passenger had bullet holes in their skulls. Someone who knew his business had sent them into the darkness. As she pulled them onto the road—a man in a suit, a woman in the sun-faded rags of a flower-patterned dress—the girl said a little prayer for them. She hoped they had been good people. She hoped they hadn't suffered much.

Before she climbed into the car to sleep, she walked out among the rough desert brush to see about setting some simple snares. If she did it right, and if she had any luck, maybe she could catch a chipmunk, a gecko, an antelope squirrel, or even a weasel.

She'd eaten worse.

Recently.

The memory of the lizard and the turtle made her stomach churn.

Stop your grousing. . . . You'll eat what you catch, or you'll starve and die.

She walked around the area for a while until she found a small game run that showed use by several species. The prints were not as distinct as they would have been on a game trail, but she was experienced enough to determine that the prints were recent. She followed the run until it intersected another, equally as small. The runs led toward the open desert, and in the faded twilight she could see a thick stand of Joshua trees. There must be water down there. Not a lot, or there would be heavier game sign, but enough for these runs to become well traveled by small animals.

The girl backtracked a hundred feet and washed her hands with sand to remove any trace of her skin oils. Only then did she pick up the materials she would use to make the traps. Humans were predators, and their scents scared off most animals.

She dug a pit and carried the fresh dirt out into the desert. Fresh dirt—or any sign of disturbance—warned prey away. When she gathered sticks, she used only those that had fallen and dried out. Freshly cut sticks bled sap, and that carried a smell that warned prey of a disturbance. The girl made sure that she did nothing that would alarm the animals.

One good way to remove human scent was to coat the trap with mud from an area with plenty of rotting vegetation, but in the desert, in the failing light, she did not have the time to find it. She used the last of the light to rig a whip snare that would lash out and kill her prey. It would only work on something small, but it was all she could manage.

She built three traps before the light and her strength failed.

Then she erased all signs of her presence, hoping that she did it so well that in the morning there would be something to eat.

She had a few slivers of hope left. Enough for tonight.

Then she rigged a few pieces of plastic that she carried with her, stretching them off the ground on sticks, setting them where the shade would be in the morning. With luck, condensation would give her at least a mouthful of dew.

As the sun set, the desert turned from a furnace to a freezer. Sand does not hold heat for long, and soon the girl was shivering. Last week she had owned a bedroll and a blanket, but they had become infested with fire ants, and while she was trying to smoke the pests out of the cloth, a sudden wind sent sparks flying into the material. She had been seventy yards away, washing her other clothes in a thin steam. By the time she ran back and stamped out the fire, her bedding was ruined.

Now she stood by the open door of the car looking at the skeletons wearing ancient clothes. The material was thin and weathered and would offer only a little warmth. It was also wrapped around the bones of dead people.

The girl took the clothes.

It was the kind of night her father used to call a "three-dog night." The kind where everyone, human and animal, crowded together for warmth. She thought about the dog she'd had years ago. *Willyhog*. He had been caught in a blind alley by four of the gray people. Dad had tried to rescue him, but he was never a fighter, and the girl had been too young to do much good. Dad dragged her away while Willyhog's screams tore holes in her soul.

She wished that he were still alive, still with her. The two of them would be something. Willyhog could find the shadow of food on a dark night, and no mistake. He had been a bluetick coonhound, and she'd loved him more than anything.

She crawled into the car and closed the door, wincing at the banshee squeak of the old hinges, and huddled in the back. She pulled the dusty old clothes over herself and tried not to notice the chattering of her teeth.

The sun was gone now, and soon the sky was littered with billions of stars. So cold and so distant. But so pretty.

For all that "pretty" mattered to her.

It used to mean something. It used to mean a lot. Now she found it hard to even remember what it was about it that had mattered. She would give all the stars in the sky, and every golden dawn, and all the birds that ever sang a pretty song for a thick steak and a plate of vegetables.

She wondered if she would kill for that.

It troubled her that with each day it was getting harder and harder to decide that she would not.

As starlight painted the landscape in blue-white light, the girl prayed to whoever was listening that tomorrow there would be food.

She did not expect her prayers to be answered. Not because of any lack of faith—the girl did believe that there was something up there or out there or somewhere—but she no longer knew what that was. Her mother and the others in the Night Church had drummed one vision of god into her head, but it was a brutal, harsh, and ugly thing. A faith born when the world died, one that flourished as more and more people died. For years she had been a part of that. For years she had belonged to that.

That time had passed.

Now she was a part of nothing. She belonged to nothing. Now she was alone.

No, the girl believed that the heat of the day and the cold of the night, the deep hunger and the awful loneliness, the pain and the shame, were all forms of punishment.

As she did every night since she ran away from the Night Church, she murmured these words right at the point where sleep began pulling her down.

"I'm sorry for the pain I caused, the blood I spilled, and the lives I destroyed. With all my heart and soul, I'm sorry."

Then the ragged claws of sleep dragged her down into dreams of hunger and dying.

8

In the morning something impossible happened.

9

The girl rose with the first light of dawn, her hunter's mind alert to the touch of sunlight on the smoked-glass windows of the dead SUV. She woke quickly, her senses sharpened by months of surviving on her own.

Slowly and cautiously she looked out of each of the

windows, looking for predators, alive or dead.

Looking for reapers.

The desert was empty and vast.

She opened the door of the SUV and moved outside and away from the vehicle, running low and fast and then turning to look back. It was a trick she had learned the hard way. Sometimes predators waited on top of a vehicle. And sometimes there were blind spots when you were inside. From a distance she could see all around the car.

There was no one and nothing. No sign of Sister Connie or Brother Andrew or anyone from the Night Church.

She crept back and examined the plastic she had set up the night before, and for the first time in days she smiled. The center of each sheet of plastic was bellied down, heavy with dew. The girl fetched her canteen and carefully poured the water into it. The combined water filled her canteen nearly to the top. She licked the last drops off the sheeting and carefully folded it and stowed it in her pack. Then she went to check the traps.

From a distance she could tell that all three of the traps had been sprung, and her heart leaped in her chest. She broke into a run, eager to see what kind of meat the night had brought to her.

Almost immediately she slowed from a run to a fast walk to a sudden stillness. She tore the slingshot from her pocket, loaded it with a sharp stone, and wheeled around, looking for an enemy.

For a trickster.

For answers.

Was this some strange and subtle trap set by Brother Andrew?

The desert seemed totally empty.

She turned back to the snares.

What in the sam hill is going on? she demanded, not sure if she thought it or shouted it.

In the center of each one, standing perfectly erect, glinting in the morning sunlight, was an aluminum can.

Not the empty, rusted cans that were everywhere, discarded years ago by scavengers. These cans were not rusted. And they were not empty.

The girl approached the closest one very cautiously, ready to counterattack if her own snares were baited to catch her. She saw no trip wires, no sticks bent back under pressure. The ground did not look like it had been excavated to dig a pit and then covered over.

The can was still there. A square can. Blue, with an illustration of some kind on it.

She crept closer, and in her belly hunger warred with caution. Hunger became a white-hot screaming thing.

When she was five feet away she could read the label of the can. She mouthed the word.

"Spam."

She knew what that was. Meat in a can. It was old, but the can was not puffy with expanding gasses the way they got when the contents were spoiled. Cans like that were filled with deadly bacteria.

This can looked fine.

She left it there and moved over to the second snare.

That can was round, tall, also blue. It said: DOLE PINEAPPLE CHUNKS—100% PINEAPPLE JUICE.

The third can was red. GOYA KIDNEY BEANS IN SAUCE.

She looked around.

Nothing.

She made a circle around the traps, going out as far as a mile.

Nothing.

No footprints. No sign.

Just three cans. Meat, fruit, beans.

If she was smart, if she was careful, she could live on that for a week. Maybe more. The beans and the meat were both protein.

The girl straightened and eased the tension on the slingshot.

"Who are you?" she yelled. "Where are you?"

The wind answered with a whisper of sand across the landscape.

She grabbed the cans and ran back to the Explorer.

She was laughing.

She was weeping.

She wasn't going to die today.

10

It was so hard to resist the temptation to open all three cans and have a feast, but that would be a bad choice. She gave it some thought, forcing herself to work it through before she took any action. That caution had kept her alive until now.

The meat would keep as long as the can stayed sealed and out of direct sunlight. To open it now, in this heat, without any means of keeping it cold, would mean that she would have to eat it within a day or so before it spoiled. The fruit, as much fun as it would be to taste something cool and sweet, had no protein.

The beans were the smarter choice. She could eat them throughout the day, and they would keep her going as she continued on toward the town.

It would mean leaving this place, and leaving whoever had left the food for her.

She half believed that it was one of the loners. There were a few of them even out here in the desert—people who could not abide company, who preferred the absolute stillness of a world on the brink of death. Most of the loners were crazy, and a lot of them were downright murderous. There were so many tales—not all of them tall—about loners who trapped unwary wanderers and killed them. Sometimes in order to loot their supplies. Sometimes to enforce their own isolation. And, if some of the tales were to be believed, because a lone traveler was a handy source of food.

It hurt the girl's mind to think that anyone would turn to cannibalism in a world where everyone who died had been reborn as a flesh-eating monster. But the stories were there, and many of them were told by people who weren't prone to exaggeration. That made them all the more frightening. These weren't scary stories told in the dark to frighten children. These were firsthand accounts by hardened travelers who had nothing to gain by making up such tales.

Avoiding loners was a smart habit of anyone who traveled the wastelands.

And yet leaving her three cans of vittles was not an act of cruelty or hostility. Not unless the cans were tampered with or poisoned, and the girl had examined every inch of them under the stark light of the morning sun. No pinholes, no evidence that the cans had been opened and somehow resealed.

No, someone had given her the cans as an act of charity.

After weighing it all out and eliminating the risks, she took the can opener from her pack and carefully worked its sharp hook around the edge of the can of beans. She did it slowly, with great control, making sure not to spill a single drop of the sauce.

She set the lid aside and looked at the nutrition information on the can. High in protein, low in sodium. The first was a good thing; the latter wasn't. Not in the desert, where the heat leached water from the body. Sodium helped retain water. Lots of iron, though, and she needed that.

Sitting in the shade of the Explorer she ate half the beans. Taking her time, chewing them one at a time, almost weeping from the wonderful taste. Licking the sauce from her fingers.

It took an incredible amount of willpower not to eat the whole can. Once she started, her mind conjured a hundred reasons why she should continue on and clean out every last bean, every last drop of rich red sauce.

"Don't be a hog," she told herself, speaking the words out loud. "Like as not we'll be wanting those beans afore long."

Her scolding voice sounded just a bit like her father's, and that made her smile as she wrapped the can in the plastic she'd used to gather morning dew. It went into her pack along with the other cans.

She could already feel the effect of the food. When she pulled herself to her feet, there was strength in her legs. When she took a breath, she could feel her lungs fill all the way.

"I'm obliged to you," she said aloud, but her voice didn't seem to carry very far, so she used her finger to write a thank-you in the grime on the Explorer's broad windshield.

Then she addressed the road that lay before her. She knew that she had a piece of work ahead of her. Today already held the promise of being hotter than yesterday. Hot enough to make rock soup, as her father used to say. The town was at least six miles ahead.

Now, though, she was sure she could make it.

She dug a scarf out of her backpack and tied it over her tattooed scalp.

Don't want to boil what brains you got left, girl, she told herself.

Then she stepped out of the shade of the SUV and onto the road.

For the first four miles there was nothing but road and a few smashed cars on the shoulder, but none that held any surprises. She found a lot of bones along the way—mostly animal bones—but there were human skulls and rib cages mixed in. No way to tell how they died, but out here there was no shortage of things that would pick a juicy bone clean in no time. When she squinted and looked up into the sky, she saw a single vulture drifting on the thermals, maybe two thousand feet up. Was it the same starved buzzard who'd watched her from the wing of the plane?

"Not today, you ugly varmint," she said.

The buzzard, pretending indifference to her, continued to circle above the road she walked.

Then the girl saw the tank.

It sat askew in the middle of a steel bridge that spanned a dry riverbed. The tank was massive, with a hull that was easily twenty-five feet long and a dozen feet wide, and it had been slewed around to completely block the two-lane bridge. The long cannon barrel pointed away from her, as did a heavy-caliber machine gun. The tank and the ground around it were littered with hundreds of empty shell casings that were pitted and rusted.

The tank was monstrous and looked like it was powerful enough to win any battle. And yet here it stood, empty, its sides stained with old smears that were probably once bright red.

She either had to climb over the tank or go down into the riverbed. The sides of the riverbank were very steep, though, and it would take a lot of sweaty effort under the pitiless sun to make that detour.

She walked sideways down the edge of the riverbank to see around the tank.

On the other side was a long line of wrecked cars and trucks, stretching off into the heat haze. Beyond them, she could see the purple silhouettes of buildings.

The town she'd seen on the map.

Nothing moved, though. No gray people. No reapers.

Nothing that she could see.

This was different from the jet; it wasn't an enclosed,

darkened death trap of a metal shell. If she got into trouble she had a fallback plan. She could run.

So, she climbed.

There were all sorts of metal fittings that were useful as handholds. It was hot, though. The first touch burned her fingers, and she whipped them away.

Well, I guess you ain't the sharpest knife in the drawer, are you, girl?

There were pieces of cloth in her pack, and she dug them out and wrapped each of her hands. Burned hands were blunt survival tools, and she couldn't allow that.

With her makeshift mittens in place, she grabbed a handhold on the tank and began to clamber upward. The tank was easy to scale, and once she was atop the big turret she paused. The machine gun was belt-fed, and there were still a dozen unfired rounds. The weapon was smeared with the dusty brown residue of old blood, and when she turned to examine the curved metal hatch that led down into the tank, there was a clear handprint. The gunner must have been badly hurt, perhaps bitten, when he'd deserted his gun and tried to escape.

She heard a faint moan.

That ain't the wind, she thought.

The girl pulled her knife and froze, then tilted her head to try to locate the sound.

At first she thought it was behind her, but the road she'd walked was completely empty. Then she heard a faint rasping sound.

No, not rasping.

Scratching.

And then another soft moan.

It sounded so close, and yet there was no movement anywhere.

That's when she realized where the sound was coming from.

The plaintive moan and the feeble scratches were *below* her.

The girl turned and looked at the hatch once more. The handprint was partially obscured by the closed lid, and she understood. The wounded, dying gunner had crawled back inside the tank and pulled the hatch shut. Down there in the darkness his wounds had killed him, and the plague that lived in everyone had brought him back.

"*Gawd!*" she gasped.

Revulsion filled her, and she gagged at the thought of that soldier, trapped in the iron kettle of the tank, cooked by a dozen summers of Nevada heat, kept alive by the plague. Below that hatch was some blackened nightmare thing, its nails scratching at the underside of the hatch, its hungers awakened by her presence on the turret, its mind consumed by disease and filled only with a need that could never be satisfied, not even if it somehow managed to feast on her. The hungry ghosts of this old world could never eat enough, never feed enough to assuage their monstrous appetites.

She backed sharply away from the hatch, fighting down the urge to throw up.

The horror of it was so great that she missed her footing and tumbled backward, twisting as she pitched off the tank and onto the unforgiving blacktop.

The girl had just enough time to turn her body, to position herself for the impact, as she had been taught in the Night Church. She landed hard, and the jolt drove all the air from her lungs, but nothing broke. However, her blade went tinkling away under a parked car.

"Laws a mercy, girl. You are dumber than a coal bucket," she groaned.

For a long time she lay there, gasping for hot air, appalled at the image in her mind of that roasted creature scrabbling to escape its prison.

Pain washed through her in waves as she struggled to sit up. As she stood, the world took a lively sideways reel, and she had to slap her hands against the hood of the closest wrecked car for balance.

Screw your head on rightways round, she scolded herself.

She stayed there for a moment, waiting until the world stopped spinning. All she could see were cars that had been rammed into one another or blown to black skeletons by the tank. The scene was typical of many she'd seen, many that her father had interpreted for her. The cars were part of some mad exodus of refugees fleeing the growing armies of the dead. They probably thought that the vacant desert would be a haven, but this tank had been deployed to block the bridge. Maybe the soldiers thought that some of the people in the cars were already bitten, or that the fleeing civilians were smuggling out their dead or dying relatives. That sort of thing had happened a lot, she knew. Growing up, she'd heard countless tales about how people—crazed with fear and grief, confused by the collapse of their world—did insane things. One woman she knew, one of her mother's personal servants in the Night Church, confessed that she'd carried her own two dead children out of Houston in the trunk of her car. Even though they thrashed and pounded on the trunk after she knew that they were stone dead, the woman had brought them all the way to Wyoming before electromagnetic pulses from the nukes dropped by the army on the major cities killed her car. The woman said that it took four grown men to pull her away from her car so the right thing could be done for her children.

Everyone had stories like that.

Her dad had said that it explained a lot of why the plague had spread farther and faster than it should have.

We killed ourselves, Dad had said. *If we'd had a chance to adjust to what was happening, to study on it some, and to know which way to jump—why, then we might not have deviled it all up. But we panicked, and panic fair killed this world.*

And laziness is going to kill you, girl, snapped her inner voice. *You best collect your knife and your wits before you lose both.*

"Knife," she said aloud.

Moving carefully, she knelt down and fished under the nearest car for her knife, but it was too far away. So she stretched out on her stomach and half crawled into the darkness below, scrabbling at the weapon's leather-wrapped handle, coaxing it into the curl of her fingers.

A sound made her freeze.

Scuffing sounds.

At first she saw nothing, and for a broken moment she wondered if she was only imagining the sounds.

Laws a mercy, no . . .

The unmistakable sound of clumsy feet moving uncertainly along the blacktop.

Not merely one set of feet.

Many.

And then the moans.

11

She scrambled out from under the car and clawed her way up the side of the vehicle until she was on her feet. Her head still swam from the fall, but her legs didn't buckle.

Thanks for small mercies, she thought sourly.

She rose cautiously and peered over the hood of the car.

A dead child was right there. Ten feet away.

It might have been a little boy once. It was impossible to tell. There was so little of it left—just enough for the body to remain upright and the limbs to move. But clearly the hungry dead who killed him had feasted for far too long on the tiny body. A head that was more skull than face drooped on a ruined neck.

"Oh, you poor baby," she whispered.

But even a whisper was too much.

The child's head snapped up; the destroyed face turned toward her. All that was left of the ears were lumps of gristle, but somehow it heard her. Its shredded nose wrinkled like a dog sniffing the air.

The girl jerked back from the side of the car.

If the dead had been an adult, or even a child whose body was still mostly intact, she would have reacted differently. She knew that, even though it was too late to do anything about it.

The creature opened its lipless mouth and moaned at her.

It was a sound without form but one that was filled with meaning. A broken, bottomless cry of hunger.

Then the thing was moving toward her, colliding blindly

with the fender of the car, bouncing off, trying again, moving toward her smell, edging by some crude instinct toward the front of the vehicle. Coming for her.

She would have to flee or kill it.

Indecision rooted her to the spot, chained her to the moment.

Behind her was the tank and the long road back to the empty FunMart.

In front of her were the cars.

And the shapes that she could now see moving among them. They were as pale and dusty as the cars, shambling artlessly between the dead machines, bumping into one another, crunching over bones, spent shell casings, and ancient debris.

Move, move, MOVE, you fool girl!

As abruptly as if someone had snapped fingers in front of her eyes, the spell was broken and she was moving. She put one foot onto the bumper of the car, and just as the dead child rounded the headlight and reached for her, the girl climbed quickly onto the hood, up the windshield, and onto the roof.

She sheathed her knife, pulled her slingshot out of her pocket, and seated a stone in the pouch. This was no time for knife work. From up there she could see how bad it was. How many of *them* there were.

At least a hundred.

No . . . more. Probably two or three times that number. With every second more of them tottered out of the shadows cast by wrecks or stepped out through open doors of old cars, their joints popping with a disuse twelve years in the making. Clouds of dust fell from them, having gathered inches thick over time. The girl did not have to wonder why they were still here, or why some of them had not moved in all that time. Folks called them the gray wanderers, but the truth was that most of them did not wander at all. Once they reanimated they would follow prey, but if there was no prey to follow, they would do nothing, go nowhere. They had no imagination, no drive beyond the urge to devour the living. In the absence of life they would remain where they were while the sun chased the moon across the sky, year upon year.

The girl glanced at the desert that ran beside the road. She could run, but that was a temporary solution. The dead could see her more easily out in the open, and so could the reapers. She would be like a bug on a white sheet. Here among the cars she had cover, and she could climb over the vehicles far faster and more easily than they could. Neither choice was a perfect solution. Each held its own advantages and offered its own complications.

The ones closest to her moaned with their pitiful dry voices.

One, a tall man in the rags of a set of blue coveralls, lunged at her, but she crouched and spun, drawing the sling-shot tight and loosing a stone. It struck him in the forehead hard enough to snap his head backward and send him sprawling into the arms of the other dead. He struggled to grab her even as he fell beneath their relentless feet.

"*Move!*" she yelled, and the sound of her own voice was the whip that made her run to the end of the car and leap across the distance to the next one. She landed with a hard thump, her slight weight denting the hood, her thighs flexing to take the impact, arms pumping for balance. She ran and jumped, ran and jumped, as wax-white hands reached for her. Dry fingertips scraped along her calves as she leaped over their heads.

She fired stone after stone, knocking some of them back, knocking a few down, clearing a path. It was hard work, though, and with every step, every pull on the slingshot, every leap, her energy was flagging. And there were two miles of cars in front of her.

As she ran, she heard a strange mewling cry and realized with horror that she was making the sound. A whimper, like a whipped dog might make.

Shut your gob and run!

The next vehicle was a pickup truck, and she leaped high and hard to clear the outer edge of the bed. Her left foot made it with half an inch to spare, but her right was half an inch too low, and the girl suddenly pitched forward and down into the truck bed. It had a black rubber liner, but it felt like iron as she struck. She tried to tuck and roll, but she banged her shoulder against the far side.

Immediately gray arms reached over the metal bay toward her.

"No!" she shrieked, trying to shrink back from the withered flesh and clawing fingers. But they crowded around the truck, reaching, reaching.

Fireflies of pain danced in her eyes. Lying there on her back, she dug out stone after stone and fired her slingshot. One dead face rocked back, and then another spun away with a shattered jaw, and a third toppled backward with one eye suddenly blown dark by a stony missile. She fired eight stones, ten, fourteen . . .

She had to keep firing.

She didn't even have the chance to get up.

She dug into her pouch for another stone. And another . . .

Then her scrabbling fingers found only empty leather. The pouch was empty.

The girl flung the slingshot down, tore the knife from her sheath, and began chopping at the hands, cutting dry tendons, filling the air with fingers that twitched like white worms.

And all the time she screamed.

With a last desperate howl of mingled terror and rage, the girl swung her legs up and over her head and back-rolled to her feet with her spine hard against the rear window of the truck. The dead climbed up, scaling the truck by clambering over one another as they sought to tear her apart.

The girl crouched there, teeth bared in a feral snarl of final defiance, one hand balled into a fist, the other locked iron-tight around the knife, ready to fight all the way to her last screaming breath.

"Come on—*come ON!*" she bellowed.

And that was when the siren went off.

12

Every face turned, every set of eyes darted toward the sound, searching out the source of a high-pitched keening wail that rose impossibly loud above the road. The girl's head turned too.

There, on the gravel-strewn shoulder of the road, was a boy.

Not a dead boy.

This one was very much alive.

He was no more than ten, thin and dark-haired, with skin the color of chocolate. He wore faded blue jeans, sneakers—real pre-apocalypse sneakers—and a T-shirt with a full-color illustration of a grinning cartoon rat standing on a strange wheeled board. His head was shaved into a Mohawk that was dyed as blue as the sky above. The boy held a hand-crank firehouse siren, and he was working it with every bit of his strength, grinning from ear to ear while he did it.

The dead seemed to forget all about the scrawny girl-flesh they had been seconds away from devouring, and instead began shuffling toward the boy and his siren. When they were a dozen feet from him, he began walking backward, laughing as the dead followed him.

It was so . . . weird, so strange, so outside of all sense that the girl simply stood there, knife in hand, and stared slack jawed.

Then a voice behind her said, "I got to say, sister, you are a crazy riot of a fighter. Never seen anything like you before."

Her jaws snapped shut as she whirled, bringing up the knife in a slashing attack that would have gutted a grown buck, but the owner of the voice leaped nimbly out of the way. Another boy stood there.

"Whoa, little sister," he said with a laugh. "That's no way to treat friends."

She stared at him.

He was older than the little brown-skinned boy. Maybe sixteen, and even in the heat of her fury, the girl realized that he was *beautiful*. That was the word her mind grabbed at. The boy was very tall and lean, with finely sculpted muscles and a deep desert tan. He had lots of curly blond hair and eyes as blue as the younger boy's hair. White teeth flashed in an almost unbearably handsome face. He wore a pair of khaki shorts, a thin green tank top, and sneakers that looked brand new. Around his neck he wore a silver necklace from which hung an old-fashioned skeleton key.

Despite the boy's handsome face and white smile, she narrowed her eyes and snarled at him. "Y'all ain't my friends. Put your hands on me and I'll cut off some parts y'all don't want to lose."

He looked alarmed—but it was a comical alarm, heavily exaggerated. "Yeah, let's not go in that direction, okay?"

The boy took a small step toward her.

"I'm warning y'all. . . ."

"I know, but our door's open," he said, nodding past her. "I think it's time to hightail it."

The siren wound down, and the girl looked over her shoulder to see the laughing little boy turn and run away with more than a hundred of the gray people following. The little boy did not seem to be trying very hard to escape the dead, though, and the girl realized that he was staying close enough so they could smell him.

"That young'un's plain crazy in the head," she said.

"Gummi Bear?" said the older boy. "Yeah, he *is* that. Gummi Bear's always been a bit twitchy."

She turned back to him, the knife still clutched in her fist. "Gummi Bear? That's his name?"

"Uh-huh."

"And who are y'all?"

"Jolt," he said.

"Jolt?" She peered at him suspiciously. "That ain't a name; it's a verb."

He grinned. "And look at you with the actual school education."

"My daddy taught me to read and write. He was a doctor."

"Yeah, well my daddy taught me not to try and fight six hundred zees with a knife."

Zees. It was an expression she'd heard only once or twice. Zee for zombie. Most of the people she knew called the dead "gray people." Once or twice she had heard travelers call them "zoms." She liked "zees," though she didn't care to let this crazy boy know that.

There was a sound behind him, and one of the dead appeared beside the truck and made a grab for Jolt's ankle. But then the young man did something that appeared almost magical. He did what looked like a cartwheel, but he did it in midair, spinning his body off the truck and landing well beyond the creature. It was the smoothest acrobatic move the girl had ever seen, with the kind of apparent effortlessness that concealed highly trained muscles.

The zee swiped the empty air where he had been, and for a moment it looked totally blank. Then it sensed him and turned around to face its elusive prey.

"Yeah, I'm over here, Dusty," said Jolt.

"Dusty? You know his name?"

Jolt darted close to the dead man and slapped his chest, kicking up a cloud of brown dust. Then he spun away out of reach.

"They're all dusty. Dusty, Lumpy, Ugly, Slowpoke, Shambler . . . take your pick. Got to call 'em something."

The girl climbed out of the pickup and stood on the far side, with the whole truck between her and both boy and corpse.

Jolt hopped up onto the hood of a car as if he had springs under his shoes. The zee took another swipe at him, but Jolt dove into a handstand, ran up the windshield, and, once he was on the roof, flipped back to his feet. It was the strangest thing, like watching the bizarre antics of a character in a dream.

"I—" she began, but then she heard a scuff behind her, and she spun as a fat gray woman with bullet holes in her chest reached for her. Without thinking, the girl parried the grabbing arms and ducked low to slash the tendons on the creature's ankles. As it buckled down to its knees, the girl grabbed the zee's filthy hair, shoved its head forward, and drew back her arm for a knife-thrust that would have severed the brain stem and sent the monster into the final darkness of absolute death.

"No!" cried Jolt with unexpected force and passion.

The girl froze, looking over her shoulder as the boy leaped like a monkey from the hood of the car to the hood of the pickup and flipped down to the ground beside her. He shoved her knife arm away and pushed the zee in the other direction.

"What are you doing?"

They both yelled it at exactly the same time.

"There's no reason to hurt it," said Jolt, his smile gone.

"It was trying to bite me," she fired back.

"So what? You telling me that you can't get away from a fat old zee like her without killing her? I had you figured for a fighter with a little bit of skill. Guess not."

Her face felt like it was about to catch fire. "And I figured you for someone with a handful of wits under all that blond hair," she yelled back, "but I guess a handful isn't enough."

"Whoa, wait—didn't we just save your life? Or am I thinking about a totally different psycho bald chick?"

The girl slipped the knife into its sheath and then shoved the boy as hard as she could with both hands. If she expected him to fall she was disappointed. He took a single backward step but turned it into a pivot and bent his knees to slough off the force. As he straightened, he got right up into her face.

"Don't do that again," he said quietly. "We're trying to help."

"I didn't ask for your help."

"But you got it, so that song's sung."

The crippled zee was crawling toward them. The girl and Jolt looked down at her, and she truly did seem to be helpless and pathetic. Over by the shoulder of the road, the zees called by Gummi Bear's siren were shuffling back toward the cars.

Toward *them*.

"We can stay and argue," said Jolt, "or we can get the heck out of here."

He touched her shoulder to try to guide her away, but she shook him off. "Don't touch me."

"Okay," he said, "for the record, you touched me first. You shoved me."

"Didn't neither. Y'all touched *me* first when you swatted at my arm like it was a skeeter."

He considered. "Maybe. Doesn't matter. We can get out

of here, or we can rub steak sauce all over each other and go dancing with the lunch crowd."

"Why in tarnation do y'all talk like that?"

He smiled. "That question may be funnier than you know."

"I'm thinking of kicking you in a bad place."

Jolt held up his hands, palms outward in a "no trouble" gesture. "Okay, come on, let's not do this. Besides, it's going to get crowded again. We should go."

She looked at the approaching dead and then around at the densely packed cars. "Which way? Out into the desert?"

"Nope."

He took two running steps and leaped hands-first toward the closest car, then slapped his palms on the hood. In a demonstration of incredible flexibility and coordination, he shot his feet forward between his arms so that he cleared the other side feetfirst. Jolt landed on the far side, then jumped onto the bumper of a truck with his left foot, surged upward and leaped onto the hood of an adjoining car with his right foot, and flipped over out of sight. A moment later he appeared atop the roof of a Post Office truck two rows away. The girl had never seen anything like this acrobatic running. Jolt stopped, turned, and waved.

"What are you?" she said. "A monkey-boy?"

He grinned. "You coming or not?"

The ease with which he moved impressed her and annoyed her in equal measures. He made escape look easy . . . and fun. After all her weeks of struggle and hardship, clawing and scrabbling her way through every hour of every day, his obvious joy in running like an ape under the desert sun was . . .

Was *what?* She didn't know what to call it.

Was she offended? Intimidated?

Dazzled?

Get hold of your wits, you silly cow, she scolded herself.

She ground her teeth together, set her jaw, and leaped for the hood of the nearest car.

And made it with more grace and balance than she expected.

She ran up the car and launched herself across a six-foot gap between that one and the next, landed with only a moment's pinwheeling of arms, and repeated it until she nearly caught up to him. Then her foot slipped and she began to fall, but instead she pitched herself into a tight shoulder roll that whipped her across the ground so fast that she came out of it in a small leap that she used to hop up onto another car. Rolling and tumbling was something she'd always been good at, but the fall was an accident, and the save was more luck than style. Even so, she ended her jump dead center on the hood of the car.

Jolt broke into furious applause and hooted his appreciation. Clearly he thought the roll and leap were intentional. His smile was brighter than the sun.

"Wow—look at you," he said, nodding. "You're a real firecracker, girlie. You're a total riot, you know that?"

"Yeah," she said sourly—though she blushed as she said it. "I'm a riot."

As if in answer, the masses of the dead let out a chorus of hungry moans.

"Oops, c'mon, riot-girl, let's *burn.*"

With a laugh and no backward glance at all, Jolt spun and

leaped for the next car, and the next, and the next.

"All boys are crazy," she told herself. Nothing—not an inner voice or anything else in the world outside—attempted to contradict her.

13

What she really hated was that it was fun.

Running like the wind, jumping high over the reaching hands, dodging and twisting, pushing her body and reflexes to their limits while acting like no limits existed. Not for them, not here and now.

Before this, physical exertion was all built around combat training. Saint John and the others at the Night Church made all of the kids train. Fourteen hours a day. Hand to hand, with weapons, target practice, hunting and tracking, gymnastics, climbing, and all of it geared toward the single purpose of killing. Not that they called it that. "Sending people into the darkness"—that was how they phrased it in the Night Church. Back when she was Sister Margaret, the girl had been the best in every class. The fastest, the fiercest, the most lethal. Her mother demanded it, and Saint John pushed her relentlessly in order to make it happen. And she was the best. No doubt. A murder machine.

And now . . .

Now she ran free, ran laughing, just for the sheer joy of it.

It was the strangest thing she had ever done.

She was certain it was the most fun she had ever had.

The younger boy, the one with the burned face—Gummi

Bear—joined them, but he wasn't running free over the cars. He was on a bicycle. The girl had seen a lot of bicycles over the years. After the EMPs they were one of the few transportation machines that worked. This one was squat and tough-looking, not like the more slender touring bikes she'd seen. Gummi Bear pedaled his like a demon, and it tore along the edge of the road, kicking up a wall of dust and spitting chunks of gravel from under its fat tires.

"Look out!" she screamed as one of the gray people lunged at the boy from behind a toppled tour bus, but Gummi Bear laughed at her and did something that appeared to be completely mad. He slapped the bars and propelled his entire body off the bike, rising into the air as if pulled by strings. The bike rolled to one side of the zee, and the boy sailed over the creature's reaching hands and then dropped down into a fast, controlled run directly behind the monster. Gummi Bear then cut left, caught his bike before it fell, flipped himself back onto the seat and was pedaling fast again before the zee was finished grabbing empty air.

"Wooohooo!" yelled Jolt, pumping his fist into the air. He stood on the hood of a Lexus, laughing with pure delight. "You ever see a fox-hop like that, riot-girl?"

The girl said, "Umm . . . no?"

"You're darn right *no*. And I'll bet you a full bag of prime goods that Gummi Bear's going to be a full-out player before he's twelve."

"A player? What's that?"

Jolt didn't answer; he was too busy yelling compliments at Gummi Bear.

The boy suddenly lunged up, pulling the front end of

his bike completely off the road. He waggled the front wheel back and forth, landed with a dusty thump and was off, dodging and weaving on and off the road, slipping past zees with inches to spare.

Laughing.

All the time laughing.

It was all so crazy and so well done that, despite everything, the girl laughed too.

She turned and saw with a start that the town was much closer. Without realizing it she and Jolt had run more than half the distance to the cluster of buildings. It was incredible. The hunger, the aches, and weariness were still there—but at the moment her system was flooded with adrenaline and something else. She didn't dare call it by its name because "happiness" was such a rare and elusive thing she was afraid of chasing it away.

"Hey, Riot!" called Jolt. "You daydreaming?"

"That's not my name," she yelled back, but there was a laugh in her voice.

"Okay—what *is* your name?"

She had to think about how to answer that. When it was just her and Dad she'd been Maggie. Then once they'd somehow been absorbed into her mother's Night Church she'd been Sister Margaret. But neither of those names seemed to fit anymore. The first was too weighed down by loss and grief. The other was burdened by horror.

So—who was she?

Jolt squatted down, his muscular thighs bulging, his blond curls stirring as a hot breeze blew in off the sand. Even from thirty feet away, the girl could feel the impact of his stare. There was genuine interest there, and honest happiness.

The one thing she could not find, no matter how hard she searched in those bottomless blue eyes, was a single flicker of judgment.

"I . . . guess my name's Riot," she said.

"Booyah!" He rose and shouted through cupped hands. "Hey, Gummi Bear! Riot thinks you have mad bike skills."

The boy somehow lifted the back end of his bike and rolled forward on just the front tire, then popped the whole bike up, spun it in a 360-degree turn, and zoomed off.

Jolt laughed, then he turned to Riot. "You need to get back to somewhere?"

She said nothing.

"What about your people? Are you lost out here or—"

"I'm not lost and no one's waiting up for me," she said. "I don't belong nowhere."

As an after-echo she heard the deep bitterness in her voice. Vicious and hard.

Jolt's smile flickered as he studied her eyes. She had no idea what he saw there, or what he thought any of it meant, but for just a moment he looked very sad.

"Somebody hurt you?" he asked.

She did not answer the question.

"Okay," said Jolt, accepting her silence, or perhaps her right to silence. Then he beamed another of his bright smiles. "You can come with us, if you want. We got a camp up near the town, and we're going to play some games tomorrow. You in?"

"Games?" she asked suspiciously. "What kind of games?"

He frowned. "You serious?"

"Of course I'm serious," she barked. A dozen yards away a couple of the zees turned sharply toward her. Riot lowered her voice. "I just met y'all, boy, so how am I supposed to know what kind of games y'all are fixing to play?"

"Okay, okay, don't have a kitten. I thought you could figure it out from me and Gummi Bear. Him on his bike, me freerunning out here."

She said nothing.

"Z-Games?" he ventured.

She still said nothing.

He grunted. "Wow, you really aren't from around here, are you?"

"And y'all are taking the long way round the mountain just to answer a question."

The zees were moving toward them again, and more had joined in.

"Better to tell you at the camp—"

"Tell me now or I ain't going nowhere."

"Okay, fast version because, like—well, check it out." He nodded at the approaching dead. "I'm part of a scavenger crew that's been working the Ruin and—"

"The *what*?"

He frowned again and waved his hand to indicate everything. "This . . . the great Rot and Ruin. Used to be called America, now it's pretty much a breakfast buffet for the shambling wrinklers out there."

"Still called America, last I heard."

"Then you heard different than me," said Jolt. "You been as far west as California?"

"They nuked California, didn't they?"

"Just L.A. and, I think, San Francisco. Big state, though, and there's some towns scattered up and down the Sierra

Nevadas. Some small settlements farther out. Everything else—well, we just call it the great Rot and Ruin."

"It's not all ruined," said Riot, but her comment lacked conviction. She had seen her fair share of ruin. Some of it caused by the dead, some by other things. The Night Church was turning a lot of this part of the world into a silent grave-yard. So . . . *ruin* . . . that seemed to fit better than anything else she'd heard it called. "What are Z-Games?"

"Ah . . . well, that's the real fun," said Jolt. "Makes the whole scavenging thing worth it, you know? We go into towns to locate food, salvageable supplies, all sorts of stuff. We tag the buildings with spray-paint, and then the trade guards go in all armored up and collect the stuff."

"How is that a game?"

"It's all about *how* we go in. You have to go in clean. No weapons, no armor, nothing but the clothes you're standing up in and, depending on the category, your ride. Gummi Bear's a biker, or at least he's practicing to be one. Right now he's a pied piper. He uses the siren to call the zees. There are a bunch of bik-ers, though, real pros. And we have sticks—kids on skateboards—and cutters, the cats who cruise on inline roller skates."

"What are you?"

"I'm a bouncer. I do freerunning—it's a kind of acrobatic sport running. Used to be called parkour before things fell down. I used to be a stick, but I got pretty good at running and I won these kicks"—he waggled one of the sneakers he wore—"so I switched."

She goggled at him. "You do this for *fun*?"

"Sure, why else? Besides, it's a total rush. The whole thing's about wits and speed and cruising right there on the edge, where it's just what you know and what you can do matched against a bunch of biters with dead brains."

"One bite from those biters is enough."

"Sure, so the rule is don't get bit," he said simply. "Pretty easy rule to remember."

"*Do* people get bit?"

Jolt gave another shrug. "Yeah, but the incentive program is pretty strong. Mind you, the crew chiefs won't let a player in if they think he's off his game. They're not actually trying to feed to the biters. The teams that go in are primed, you know? They're ready to dance on a ray of light and hop over the sun."

Riot shook her head. "Y'all are crazier than an outhouse full of bats, y'know that, right?"

Jolt laughed out loud.

"What's so damn funny?"

"Wow, the *actual* apocalypse was twelve years ago. I mean, we are living in the epilogue to the end of the world, and you're telling me that we're crazy for finding ways to have some fun in the middle of it? That's fricking hilarious."

She grunted. "The Z-Games . . . is that how that young'un got his face all burned up?"

A shadow crossed Jolt's face. "Nah. We don't know how that happened. One of the trade guards, Solomon Jones, found Gummi out on the sand. He was burned and half dead. Maybe three years old. No one else around, and no way to find where he belonged. Solomon brought him to us 'cause that's what people do with orphans. Everyone in the Games is an orphan."

"You too?"

"Me too."

The dead had reached them now and were straining upward to reach them.

"Oops, time to boogie," said Jolt. "We're about a mile from the camp. It's Tuesday, right? That's chicken-and-bean burrito day. You hungry?"

"I—"

"Or did you fill up on Spam and pineapple?" he asked with a wicked grin. He laughed and ran on, leaping and jumping in the sunshine.

Riot—for that was now her name, and she knew that it was going to stay with her—nearly fell over.

"Well I'll be a . . . ," she began softly, but let the words blow away into the wind. In all the surprise and excitement of meeting these two boys she had somehow not connected them to the food placed in her traps. She thought that had been a kind act from a loner who wanted to help but didn't want to interact. Now she could see the prankishness of the act. The wildness of it.

"Hold on, I'm coming!" she cried, but her inner voice clucked at her. *Have a little self-control, girl.*

"Hush," she told that voice.

Riot ran to catch up.

14

During the last quarter mile the demands of running and jumping finally caught up with her. Twice she slipped and had to climb back up from the roadbed. To her satisfaction she saw that Jolt had slowed too. She hoped that he was getting tired—proof that he was human enough—and not that he was slowing down out of pity for her. The other boy, Gummi Bear, had sped on ahead.

Both times she fell, Riot's first reaction was to pull her knife and wheel to face the oncoming zee. Jolt was far ahead and wouldn't see her. She knew that she could make the kill quickly and be on her way without alerting him. But in each case she put the knife back, used a kick to knock the zee away from her, and hastily climbed up out of danger.

It made her feel strange and conflicted.

In the Night Church her mother and the elders occasionally had to silence the dead, though they always regretted it. There were complex spiritual reasons that were part of the church's mission to create what Mom called a "quiet world." At the same time the members of the church—called the Reapers in the Fields of the Lord or just reapers—wore colored streamers soaked in chemicals that somehow kept the gray people from attacking. And one of the elders, a strange and dangerous man known as Saint John, was trying to devise a way of controlling the countless hordes of living dead. The official church policy was to avoid killing the dead—though killing humans was allowed and even encouraged.

The farther Riot got from that group and the more she viewed it from a distance, the less sense it made.

After she'd fled, the girl realized that she had no choice but to deal harshly with any threat. She had no supply of the chemical that kept the reapers safe, and she had no sentries to watch over her as she slept, no teams of armed reapers to come to her aid if she was attacked by a dozen of the monsters. Since leaving the camp she had killed countless zees. It had become an automatic response.

Now she wondered if doing that had been wrong. How many of those kills had been unavoidable?

It was a dreadful question, and it throbbed like a canker in her mind. In light of Jolt's disapproval, it felt wrong. Now this kind of killing felt like *killing*. The word was the same, but the meaning had changed.

Now killing these monsters felt like murder.

There was something dangerous hiding in that thought, but now was not the time to sit and puzzle it out.

She ran and leaped and flew through the air. When she caught up, they grinned at each other and ran together.

Jolt ran ahead of her, looking over his shoulder to throw smiles behind him.

Then Brother Andrew stepped out from behind a big delivery van right in Jolt's path.

There was no time to warn Jolt as the wicked blade of the scythe flashed in the dry desert air.

15

Jolt fell backward, leaning, arching, his muscles contorting his big frame into an impossible backbend, lying almost flat as the blade cut through the air a tenth of an inch above him. The tip of the blade caught the loop of the silver chain and tore it from Jolt's neck. The skeleton key went spinning through the air to land at Riot's feet.

Brother Andrew was a bear of a man with biceps like

bowling balls and a back that was so crammed with muscle that he looked like a gargoyle. He had put every ounce of his strength into that swing, and had it connected, it would have cut Jolt in half. Easily.

Instead Jolt fell hard on his back on the hood of a red Chevy, and the scythe struck the curved windshield and caromed upward, gouging the glass, ripping loose a piece of silver molding, causing the reaper to spin in a full circle and then lose all balance. Brother Andrew crashed against the side of another car.

All of this . . . all of it . . . inside a fractured second.

Immediately Jolt twisted sideways and rolled off the front of the Chevy. He landed on the balls of his feet and leaped backward as two other reapers rose up from hiding and slashed at him with knives.

The blades glittered with reflected sunlight, and they cut absolutely nothing.

Jolt twisted out of reach, stepped on the bumper, and jumped over their heads. Before he landed, he shot one foot backward in a vicious kick that crashed one reaper into the other. The two of them slammed into Brother Andrew, and the three of them collapsed onto the blacktop. The scythe clattered to the ground nearby.

Jolt landed in a defensive crouch, hands open and ready, knees bent, face displaying equal parts confusion and rage.

"Hey! What the hell are you freaks doing?" he bellowed. "You could have fricking killed me. What, you think I'm a biter? Are you stupid or nuts or blind?"

Brother Andrew pushed himself out from under the two other reapers and climbed to his feet. As he rose, Jolt got his first clear look at the man and his eyes widened.

"Jolt—be careful!" warned Riot, climbing up onto a nearby car.

Brother Andrew bent to retrieve his weapon. He held it in one massive fist and pointed it at Jolt.

"You got one chance, pretty boy," he said in a voice that was low and gravelly. "Walk away. Leave the little witch with us. She belongs with us. She belongs *to* us. Walk off now while you can."

Jolt looked uncertain. "Who the hell are you?"

Brother Andrew cut a look at Riot. "Didn't she tell you?"

"Tell me what?"

The big reaper narrowed his eyes. "Who do you think she is?"

"Just a girl," said Jolt. "A friend. Why?"

Andrew laughed. The other reapers laughed too.

"Look, kid, you don't know what you stepped into. I don't know what kind of story Sister Margaret told you or how she convinced you to help her, but she is one of us." Andrew touched his tattooed scalp. "She bears the mark of the Night Church. She belongs to us."

Jolt turned his head slightly toward Riot. "What's he talking about?"

"Don't listen to him," she said quickly. "He's crazy. They all are. And they're dangerous."

"More dangerous than you know," said Brother Andrew. "Saint John and your mother charged me to bring you back. You think we're here to send you into the darkness, but you're wrong. That would be easy, and after what you've done you don't get 'easy.' You're going to come back with us, and then you're going to be on your knees before your mother. You're going to have to account for everything you've done. For all of your crimes. For all of your sins. For—"

"Shut up!" screamed Riot, clapping her hands to her ears. "Just shut up."

Brother Andrew stopped his tirade, but he laughed quietly, shaking his head with amusement.

"Listen, mister," said Jolt, "I think you'd better haul your fat butt out of here."

Brother Andrew took his scythe in both hands. "Boy, you don't know what kind of trouble you're asking for. I'm going to tell you one last time—walk away before something that isn't your business *becomes* your business. And believe me, you do not want that."

"What's going on?" asked a small voice, and they all turned as Gummi Bear appeared between two wrecked cars. He sat on his bike, leaning on one car for support. The crank siren hung around his neck, and his face was flushed with fear.

"Jolt—get him out of here," said Riot quickly. "They'll hurt him."

Brother Andrew clicked his tongue, and the two reapers with him began to move toward the boy.

"Whoa!" barked Jolt. "What are you cats doing?"

The closest one showed his knife to Jolt. "The greatest mercy of god is the release from pain. We will bless this boy. We will open red mouths in his flesh and give him the gift of darkness. Children should not have to suffer in this land of misery and woe."

"Gift of darkness? What are you talking about?"

"Jolt—they want to kill him," said Riot, and she moved

across the car tops toward Gummi Bear. "That's what they do—they kill. They think it's god's will, that it's a way to end suffering."

"It *is*," said Brother Andrew. He pointed at Gummi Bear. "Look at this child. Ugly and deformed. He's suffered terribly. Why perpetuate that suffering when we can bring him peace?"

"By *killing* him?" demanded Jolt. "I mean, that's what you're saying? Am I hearing this right? You want to help Gummi by cutting his throat."

"Um," said Gummi Bear as he walked his bike backward, "pass, thanks."

The two reapers moved to intercept him. Riot instantly moved across the car tops, ready to jump down between them and the boy. She drew her knife and pointed the tip at them.

"Y'all take another step toward that boy and I'll end you both, right here and now. Tell me if I'm lying."

"Go ahead," said Brother Andrew. "We are reapers—to die in the service of our god is but a pathway to paradise."

"Riot," said Jolt, "don't."

She looked at him. "What?"

"Don't kill them."

"Why the hell not?"

"Because," explained Jolt, "there's been enough death in the world. We don't kill. The players, the people in our camp— we don't kill."

She stared at him. "Jolt—don't you get it? These are *reapers*. That name wasn't picked 'cause it sounds cool. They want everyone and everything to *die*. It's who they are and what they are. . . ."

"But it's not who *we* are. We're scavengers—we find the

things that help people stay alive. Seven billion people have died already. . . . How many more will it take before the message gets through that killing isn't an answer to anything?"

Brother Andrew shook his head. "You're as much of a heretic as she is, and you're twice as much of a fool."

Jolt shrugged. "I don't really know exactly who you are, mister, but I'm beginning to get the idea. Reapers—yeah, I *grok* that. You think God wants you to kill everyone. Okay, fair enough, that's what you believe, and who am I to tell you you're wrong."

"Smart boy . . ."

"But," said Jolt, "here's the thing. That's *your* gig, man. That's what you believe. It sure as heck is a popular belief around here. We got this whole 'hey, we're alive and ain't it cool?' thing going on. I can respect you for your beliefs, man, but you're going to have to take them somewhere else. You can't come into my zone and force your ideas down my throat."

"This is the will of god."

"Dude, not really all that interested in a religious debate," said Jolt. "I'm telling you to leave us alone. You say 'walk away' to me? I'm giving you that same message. Beat it. Go."

"Or—?"

"Or I'll make you," said Jolt.

"I thought you said you were a pacifist."

Jolt suddenly jumped up and kicked Brother Andrew in the face with a lightning-fast snap kick. The big reaper went flying backward and crashed into the side of a car, then slid down to land on the ground, legs sprawled.

"I said that we don't believe in killing," said Jolt, smiling down at the fallen reaper. "And you ain't dead."

Before Andrew could shake off the shock and pain, Jolt whirled. "Gummi! Get out—go loud and long. Sound it!"

The boy picked his bike up, turned it around, and stood on the pedals to get into motion. The two reapers lunged for him, but then Riot leaped off the top of the car and was among them.

"No killing!" yelled Jolt.

Riot pretended not to hear him.

She crashed into one of the reapers and sent him sprawling, then she wheeled on the other. She and the reaper had knives of almost equal length. Riot knew this man—Brother Colin—and he was a superb knife fighter. He was in an entirely different league from Connie, Griff, and Jason. They began circling each other warily, feinting with their knives but not committing to any attacks yet, looking for an opening.

"Riot . . . please," implored Jolt.

Suddenly Brother Andrew surged off the ground, wrapped his arms around Jolt, drove him across ten feet of open space, and slammed into the side of a UPS truck. The impact drove the air from Jolt's lungs, and for a moment his eyes went blank, then he sagged to his knees.

"No!" cried Riot, and in that moment of distraction Brother Colin lunged, jabbing and slashing at her. Blood erupted from Riot's upper arm as the reaper's knife opened up a long gash.

Riot danced backward, hissing in pain, narrowly avoiding a second cut that would have torn open her throat.

In the distance she heard the rising scream of Gummi Bear's siren.

Was that what Jolt meant? To "sound it"? But why? Calling the living dead now would only take a terrible situation and collapse it into absolute defeat.

Nearby, Brother Andrew grabbed Jolt by the arms, hauled the boy upright, then flung him back against the truck.

The third reaper, Brother Max, climbed to his feet and shifted to Brother Colin's right. Riot knew that the moment was slipping away. They could come at her in a combined attack that would overwhelm her. She couldn't block two expert knife fighters at once. That's why Saint John had sent them out, and why Brother Andrew had picked them for this ambush. Their combined skill was more than a match for hers. The only chance she might have—and it would be a slim one—would be to slaughter them, to go in fast and use every bit of skill she had to cut them apart and kill them.

But Jolt's words kept ringing in her ears.

We don't kill.

There's been enough death in the world.

In a flash of a moment, Riot thought of all the lives she'd taken before she realized how horrible the Night Church was. She felt like she now stood ankle-deep in a river of blood. She could feel the bloodlust, the murderlust, burning in her heart and tingling in the fingers of the hand that held the knife. She realized with total horror that she wanted to kill these men; she *longed* to open red mouths in their flesh. To give them the gift of darkness.

It was everything her mother had ever taught her.

Everything Saint John had taught her.

It was the thing about her that allowed them to *own* her.

The blood hunger, the murder hunger, the need to kill in order to make the world right.

Riot thought she had escaped all of this when she'd run away from the Night Church.

But it was there in her hand. In her pounding ear.

In her *need*.

"Please," she said to the two reapers. "Please."

They rushed at her.

Something inside Riot's mind . . . twisted.

She moved.

So fast.

As she had been taught.

Their blades drove toward her flesh. She parried hard, knocking one hand aside so that the tip of the knife drove through the empty air an inch from her hip. With the other hand she snapped the tip of the blade down, finding flesh, finding bone.

There was a scream.

There was blood.

Brother Colin's knife dropped to clatter on the ground.

Riot moved, turning lithely. She may not have been able to dance a bicycle like Gummi Bear or run like the desert wind over every obstacle like Jolt, but in this, in the dance of blades and bodies, she was perfection in form and function. Elegant, in the way that perfect control can be elegant even in the commission of a violent act. Smooth, effortless, flawless.

Riot turned, and the blade whipped across Brother Max, cutting cloth and skin. Finding the redness beneath flesh. Drawing drops of it out in a spray of rubies. Drawing the scream out.

She turned in, completing a dancer's pirouette, coming to an abrupt stop as if painted on the canvas of the moment. Brother Max was on his knees, arms crossed over his chest, holding his blood inside. Brother Colin leaned against a car, one hand clamped over a ruined forearm. Both of them torn by her knife.

Both of the them *only* torn.

Both of them alive.

"Riot," said Jolt.

She stood there, panting, eyes wide and unfocused, staring through the world.

"Riot," he said again.

And she looked at him.

Jolt leaned against the truck; Brother Andrew held him in place with a flat palm on his chest and a fist the size of a bucket poised to deliver a killing blow.

Brother Andrew sneered at her, at her refusal to kill. "How far you've fallen, little witch."

He drove the punch at Jolt.

Jolt laughed.

He suddenly dropped into a low squat, letting his body simply go limp in a deadweight plunge. Andrew's hand slid with him, and the incoming punch missed Jolt's curly blond hair by ten inches.

It did not miss the side of the truck.

The impact was huge, a massive *ka-rang* that shook the whole vehicle.

The sound was so loud it masked the sound of all the bones in Andrew's fist breaking.

The echo of the sound bounced off all the cars. It drew

moans from the dead—the closest of which were now no more than a dozen paces away.

Brother Andrew did not scream.

He stared at his shattered fist, and for a moment the only sound he made, the only sound he was capable of making, was a high-pitched whistle that approached the ultra-sonic.

Jolt rose to his feet and shoved Brother Andrew away from him. The big reaper staggered back, his face flushing scarlet as he fought to articulate his agony.

"Finish it," cried Riot.

Jolt looked at her. "What?"

"Kill him!" begged Riot. "While you still have the chance."

The young man glanced at Andrew, who reeled away from him, cradling his hand against his chest and making small keening sounds.

"No," said Jolt. "It's over; he's done."

"He's *not*."

"Yes, he is." He looked past her at the two wounded reapers. "They all are."

"No . . . you don't understand. . . . There are more of them out there."

Jolt pointed past her and she turned. Beyond the line of cars, near the town and coming hard in their direction, was a mass of people. Fifty of them. A hundred. More. Riding in front of them, his siren still wailing, was Gummi Bear.

Riot lowered her knife.

The dead were getting closer now, climbing over the locked bumpers of crashed cars.

Jolt walked over to Brother Andrew's scythe, hooked his foot under the handle, kicked it into the air, caught it, and then spun his whole body and hurled the weapon as far away as he could. It arced over the cars and over the heads of the oncoming mass of zees. It fell out of sight, its clatter of impact lost beneath the moans of the dead.

Brother Andrew looked in the direction of his lost weapon and then turned slowly back to Jolt. His eyes were wet with unshed tears of pain, but his face was a mask of murderous fury.

"Jolt . . . ," pleaded Riot, "please . . . you have to. . . ."

But Jolt shook his head. "I told you already, Riot. There's been enough killing."

Brother Andrew managed a small, tight smile. "She's right, boy," he wheezed. "This is your only chance."

Jolt caught Andrew by the throat and stood him up, leaning in close to stare the man in the face. "Get your sick friends and get the hell out of here. You don't belong around decent folks."

He shoved the big reaper away from him and pointed to the only path through the cars that was not blocked by any of the living dead.

Andrew growled at the others to go, but he lingered at the mouth of the narrow path.

"You think you did something smart and noble here," he said. "But all you did was cry out for the wrath of god. The darkness will come for you. It will come for you and everyone you love . . . and I'll be there to see it happen."

Jolt just shook his head. "Go."

Brother Andrew looked past him at Riot.

"This is on you, girl. You know that we'll be back. You know what we'll do."

Riot pointed her knife at him. "If I ever see you again, Andrew, I'm going to kill you."

The reaper smiled. "Ah . . . now that's my girl."

He turned and lumbered away, trailed by his bleeding companions.

Riot hurried over to Jolt and got right up in his face. "He's not joking, Jolt; they *will* be back."

"I guess they will."

She studied him. "Y'all are barn-owl crazy."

Jolt grinned. "Been told that."

"Why are you doing this?" she demanded, her voice a fierce whisper. "Y'all are stepping into harm's way here, and you don't even *know* me."

"Does that matter? How long does a person have to know someone before they do what's right? You're a girl out here, starving and fighting for her life. Am I supposed to just ignore all that? What kind of person would that make me? What kind of world would that make? Look, Riot, I wasn't joking about what I said. How much killing is enough? How much pain is enough? When do we stop and say 'that's it, no more'?"

Riot opened her mouth to respond, but she didn't know how to answer those questions.

"The world that died couldn't answer those questions either," he said, and gave a small shrug. "The people Gummi and I travel with—we don't pretend to know *all* the answers, but we're working on them." His grin returned, brighter than ever. "And we're having some fun while we work it out."

"Y'all are definitely crazy," said Riot, and she too grinned.

The dead, smelling blood on the air, moaned in hunger. They crawled over the cars toward the living meat.

"Time to go," said Jolt, and he started to turn away. Then he paused and reached out a hand to her. "Want to come . . . ?"

She gave it a lot of thought. Maybe a full second.

Then she took his hand, and together they climbed onto the nearest car.

"Let's go!" bellowed Jolt. He let out a huge whoop of sheer joy, took two running steps across the hood, and then jumped high and wide, sailing over the heads and mouths and reaching arms of the biters.

Riot watched him—his strong back, his lithe body.

What in tarnation have you got yourself into, girl? she wondered.

Behind her the dead were massing, scrambling over the cars now like a swarm of wriggling worms. Off the road, hundreds of people were rushing toward her, coming to help her and Jolt. People she did not know. Orphans and refugees. Scavengers.

Friends?

Maybe. As strange as that concept was.

But what kind of friend could she be to them? Brother Andrew was right. He would be back. The reapers were out there, and there were so many of them. If they came in force, what could a couple of hundred people do?

"Please," she said to the hot air. But she did not know exactly what she was asking for. She watched Jolt run and leap and twist and land and run. "Please."

Riot cast one last look behind her, to where Brother Andrew had gone.

"Please," she begged.

The reapers would come for her.

No, that wasn't quite right. They would come for Sister Margaret. They would come for the girl who once belonged to them, to the Night Church.

Maybe they would not find her. Maybe by the time they came back the scavengers would have moved on to another town. And another. Maybe if it took too long to find her, the reapers would give up.

She hoped so.

She desperately wanted them to understand that the girl they were looking for did not exist anymore. Not a trace of her.

The girl she had been, Sister Margaret, was dead and gone.

She turned and ran and leaped and followed, hoping that she was free.

FROM NIX'S JOURNAL

ON REBELLION
(BEFORE *DUST & DECAY*)

Some of the people in town think that we're acting out. Because of training with Tom. Because we stood up to Charlie (and a lot of freaks in this town still think Charlie was a good guy!!!!). Because we go outside the gates and into the Ruin.

They say that Benny, Chong, Lilah, Morgie, and I are rebels.

Rebels.

Really?

Chong says that people are "stubbornly entrenched in convenient worldviews." Which is his way of saying that people don't want to think about anything but what they think about every day. Ever since they moved to Mountainside, people stopped thinking about the rest of the world. Tom says they can't afford that, because thinking about what's out there makes them have to remember what they've lost. I'm not sure that's it. I think they've given up, and they're okay with just waiting out the rest of their lives in what they think is comfort. They don't care about the future. They've given up on it.

So if they think about us, about why we're training, about that jet we saw, then they have to accept that there's something out there. That means they have to find the courage to become involved in the world again. They have to be alive again.

If having hope for the future and needing to go find what's out there makes us rebels, then . . . okay. I guess we're rebels.

Rags & Bones

(Thirteen years before the events of *Rot & Ruin*)

1

They called her Ragdoll.

Or sometimes just Rags.

She was small for her age. On the skinny side of thin. On the plain side of pretty. On the starving side of being alive. She was thirteen the last time her age mattered to anyone, even herself.

Once upon a time she'd had a name, but she never told anyone what it was. That name belonged to someone else. It belonged to a little brown teen who lived in a small town on the outskirts of San Jose. A girl who went to school. A girl who had friends. A girl who had her own room, the promise of a car when she was old enough, a great computer, a top-of-the-line tablet, nice clothes, great shoes, and a three-year-old brother.

It belonged to a girl who belonged. To friends, to places, to a family.

That girl had been happy. She'd been loved. She'd been protected.

That girl was dead as far as Rags was concerned.

Rags was alone and she was a loner.

Except for the dog. She hadn't named the dog yet. It

wasn't any dog she'd known before. Her own—the one she'd had since she was seven—was gone, and Rags didn't like to think about *how* she'd gone. PomPom had been small and cute and was scared of everyone, even the cat. It wasn't fair what had happened to her. And to the cat.

And to the world.

Rags tried never to think about any of that, because to think about PomPom meant thinking about what had happened.

What had happened when Mom came home.

Because Mom came home all wrong. All broken.

Red and strange and . . .

. . . and . . .

. . .

Rags sometimes had to scream to make her brain stop thinking about that.

Sometimes she ran down a road until she was pouring sweat and panting and the crazy lights started burning in the corners of her eyes.

Anything to keep her mind from replaying all of that.

It was like a streaming video that would show everything in high-def and then automatically begin again as soon as it was over.

If she exhausted herself, it helped.

When she was busy trying to find food, that helped too.

When she was running from the dead, that didn't help. That was part of the memory, even if these dead weren't the people she'd once been related to. Even if they didn't look like Mom or Dad, or Tyler or Gram or . . . or . . .

Taking care of the dog helped.

Trying to come up with a name for him was good. Especially when she kept trying different names on him to see if he'd respond to one.

The dog was big. Really big.

More than twice as big as her. The last time Rags had stood on her bathroom scale, she was eighty-six pounds. She'd lost weight since. Too much, really.

The dog had to be at least twice as heavy as she'd been on that day.

He was pretty. A little bit of this and a little bit of that. Rags loved dogs, and she could usually spot what breeds made up a mix. The Langstons next door had owned a cocka-poo and a Labradoodle.

PomPom had been a . . .

No.

No. Don't go there.

She told herself that fifty times a day. Most days she listened. Some days, no matter how much she did to her body or how much she crammed into her head, she couldn't help but go down that road.

It was on those days that she really learned how to scream.

It was on those days that she learned how to scream quietly. Into her backpack, into her hands. Sometimes into the crook of her arm when she huddled under a bush and smothered every single sound so the dead wouldn't find her.

It was a survival skill. One of the things she had to learn.

The dog, though.

The new dog. The dog she'd saved and who'd saved her. He was something else. Not a combination of a couple of miniature breeds. He was a brute. Rags thought that he was at least half white shepherd and half Irish wolfhound. Fur the color of dirty snow. Lots of teeth, lots of muscle.

The dog had been trapped in a wrecked car. There was no driver, no passengers. No one alive or dead. Just the dog.

Big. Wild-eyed. More than half-starved. Looking like a monster, like a werewolf from a horror movie.

When Rags first saw him, she almost broke and ran. She was instantly afraid of him, like she was taught to be afraid of things. Mom and Dad had been really good at teaching her to be afraid of stuff. People she didn't know. Animals. Bugs. The outdoors.

Stuff.

Since everything went crazy, Rags had become afraid of a lot more. The dead, of course. She always had to be afraid of them. They were never afraid of her.

Other things. Scavengers. Especially the male scavengers. Rags was young, but she wasn't naive.

Wild animals, too. When the end came, someone must have let the animals out of their cages at the zoos. Maybe in circuses, too. There were all kinds of things out there. She saw a tiger chasing a deer once. And a pair of zebras running along the side of a highway. There were monkeys in the trees, and last week she saw a pack of the dead hunkered down around a dead giraffe. Eating it.

The dead would eat anything.

Rags had met survivors who thought that the dead only went after people, but that was not true. They'd eat anything.

Being on the road, being out in the world, taught Rags the truth. The dead would eat anything as long as it was alive, or if it had just died. She didn't understand that. No one she knew did. Just like she didn't know why the dead would *stop* eating a person while they were mostly still whole, but they'd eat an animal all the way down to the bones.

It made no sense to her.

A lot of things made no sense.

Like why she'd let the big dog out of that car.

She shouldn't have.

The animal was starving, maybe crazy. Scared.

Letting it out was stupid. Suicidal. Way too risky a thing to even consider.

Rags had to think about it for a while, too. At first she stood on the bloodstained curb and studied the car. The dog was barking furiously.

There were no dead around. There was nothing but a couple of bodies that been shot in the head and left to rot. The stink was terrible, but Rags was used to it. Everything stank. She stank. She'd give a lot for a hot shower and clean underwear.

A lot.

The dog barked at her.

And then it stopped barking and stared at her.

It had strange eyes. One was such a dark brown that it looked almost black. The other was mint green. It wore a collar and had a tag, but Rags couldn't read it. Not through the cracked and dirty windows.

Rags came over and peered inside. The dog looked at her with its strange eyes. She expected it to growl. It didn't.

After a long time, Rags climbed up on the hood and sat

down, cross-legged, and laid her forehead against the windshield. The dog stared at her and did not move.

Rags had no idea how long she sat there. Shadows moved on the street around her. The air was still and there were no sounds in the distance. No moans or screams. No gunfire. Nothing.

Even the dog was silent. Watching her. Waiting.

There was so much going on in those eyes. Intelligence. And . . .

And what?

It was almost like looking into the eyes of a person rather than a dog. Even PomPom, much as she'd loved him, hadn't had this same quality. PomPom looked at her with a dog's eyes and a dog's mind and a dog's uncomplicated love.

This dog seemed different in ways she couldn't understand.

Rags straightened and then placed her palm flat over one of the cracks in the windshield. After a moment the dog bent forward and sniffed.

Then they sat and looked at each other for a while longer. Ten minutes maybe. Enough time for the shadows to slide around a bit more.

"Your family's gone," she said quietly.

The dog watched her.

"Mine, too."

The first of the evening crickets began chirping in the weeds that had grown thick in the cracks on the pavement.

"If I let you out," she said to the dog, "will you be nice?"

The dog watched her.

"I don't have much food, but I can give you some soup. I

have a couple of cans of beef soup. It has too much salt, but it's okay. Do you want some soup?"

The dog watched her.

"I'll give you half of what I have if you don't get all crazy on me."

Those eyes—dark brown and mint green—watched her.

"Okay . . . ?"

If there was anyone else to swear it to, Rags would have sworn on a stack of Bibles that the dog nodded.

It was a stupid thought, and a crazy one. But it was what she believed she saw.

Rags smiled. She felt it on her face, and it felt weird. She couldn't remember the last time she'd smiled.

No, that was wrong. She actually *could*.

It was that night, when she heard Mom's car pull into the driveway. Rags had gotten a new pair of tights she'd bought with money she made babysitting. She knew Mom would love them. Rags was smiling when Mom opened the door.

That was the last time she smiled.

But she smiled now, as she slid off the hood and walked around the car. The dog turned on the front seat to watch her. He was so big he filled the whole front of the car.

Rags reached out to try one of the door handles.

It was locked.

Of course it was locked.

She stood in the street and thought it through. There were shattered buildings, overturned cars. Bones. Debris. She nodded to herself and picked up a brick. Most of a brick. Enough of one for her purposes.

As she approached the car, the dog watched her. Rags showed him the brick.

"You have to get back," she said. "I have to smash the window. Get into the backseat, okay? You need to—"

The dog climbed over the seat backs and dropped down into the rear foot well.

That made Rags stop in her tracks.

That was very, very weird.

There was no doubt in her at all that the dog understood what she was saying. But . . . ?

It was just a dog.

The brick was heavy in Rags's hand. Doubt chewed at her. She hefted the brick and said, "Please."

To the dog, maybe. To the day. To whatever was left of the universe who might be listening.

She smashed the windshield. Even cracked, it took a lot to do it. The safety glass was tough. It resisted her, as if the car did not want to release its prisoner. Or maybe as if the car was trying to protect her from this strange dog.

The glass finally exploded. Not just broke—it exploded, showering her with little pellets of gummy glass, spraying everything inside the car with fragments.

The sound was louder than she expected. It echoed off the buildings around her.

And then the dog came surging over the seats and out through the windshield. He landed on the hood and stood there, even bigger than she'd thought, shaking glass from his thick coat, eyes blazing with bizarre light. Rags stumbled backward and fell on her butt right in the middle of the street.

The brick fell from her hand and rolled crookedly off.

The huge dog stared down at her, and then he bared his teeth.

Hair stood up along his neck and back. His ears went back and a low, dreadful growl rumbled from deep in his chest.

"N-no!" stammered Rags.

The dog snarled, and there was such deep, ferocious hatred in his eyes that Rags knew she had made a terrible mistake.

Then the dog crouched, muscles rippling, fangs gleaming, and with a bellow of pure animal rage, he sprang.

At her.

Over her.

Beyond her.

Rags fell backward and watched the monster dog sail through the air. Expecting him to land on her. Expecting to be crushed.

Except that it did not happen that way.

Instead he passed completely over her and struck something else.

On the ground, Rags turned and looked.

And saw.

Them.

Five of them.

Monsters.

Not the dead.

No, she would have smelled the dead.

Scavengers.

There were survivors, and everyone these days had to

scavenge. But the people that the survivors *called* scavengers were something else. They weren't out here looking for cans of food. They had darker, stranger, and more terrifying appetites.

And here were five of them.

Three men, two women.

All of them with knives. All of them with that *look* in their eyes that Rags had seen before. The look that promised awful things.

They must have heard her banging on the windshield, and on silent cat feet had come up behind her. With knives. With clubs. With ugly smiles and a hunger more frightening than what the dead had.

Rags knew that she couldn't outrun them. A couple of them, maybe. Not all of them. She couldn't outrun the two biggest men. And she certainly couldn't outfight them. Even so, she pulled her knife. It had a three-inch blade, and usually that was enough. Now it felt like a toothpick.

One of the scavengers spoke a single word. Maybe the most terrifying word Rags had ever heard.

"Meat . . ."

The five of them looked so hungry. Rags heard someone's stomach growl. One of the women licked her lips. If there was any sanity left inside the woman, it did not look out through those eyes. Those eyes—all of their eyes—were every bit as dead as the eyes of the walking corpses who filled the rest of the world.

"Please," said Rags.

"Please," echoed the scavengers. It meant something totally different.

Rags heard the dog growl. She turned. They all looked.

"Meat," said the man again. He bared his teeth in some kind of smile.

The dog bared his teeth too.

What happened next was unspeakable.

Rags screamed as she ran away. Her screams, though, were little things, small, kept locked inside her chest. The screams of a careful, frightened scavenger who needed to shriek aloud but absolutely could not.

2

Rags ran and ran.

There were so many places to hide. Empty cars, empty stores, empty homes. All kinds of empty buildings. She knew how to check for the dead, and she could almost always hide from the living. Today had been a mistake. The dog was a distraction, and it was stupid to let anything do that. As she ran, she hated herself for being so clumsy. And by mentally yelling at herself, it was easier to keep from screaming.

The things that dog did.

Even to scavengers. Even to people who did the kinds of things they did.

Rags wanted to scream. Probably needed to.

Instead she clamped down on the screams that boiled like hot water inside her chest. She screamed at herself inside her head.

And ran.

3

Rags was too smart to hide inside a house when she knew there were scavengers in the area. Houses had food, blankets, beds, toilet paper, medicines, weapons, clothes. Everyone raided places like that. No one hid there unless they wanted to be found.

The same went for stores that sold anything people could use for survival. She passed a big mall once, a few weeks after it all started. There had to be fifty thousand of the dead crowding the parking lot and hammering on the doors.

Schools were almost as bad. They had lunchrooms. They had gym equipment. Hockey sticks and football pads were worth more than gold. Rags had watched in horror as a fat man wearing only boxers fought two middle-aged women—all of them armed with lacrosse sticks and baseball bats. Rags wondered if all three of them had been teachers at the school. They were screaming and bleeding and Rags doubted they'd make it through the night. That was in the entrance to a middle school.

Other places to avoid included hardware stores, sporting goods shops, grocery and clothing stores, pharmacies, hospitals, police stations, military bases, and department stores.

The best places to hide were stores or warehouses filled with stuff no one needed. Computer centers, toy stores, gift shops. Like that. For Rags, though, her most reliable bolt-holes were museums. One in particular. The one that had been her home for weeks now.

Nobody went to museums anymore. Not unless they had

displays of military equipment, and those had already been looted.

Rags ran three blocks along the avenue, leaving the dog and the scavengers behind. Leaving the sounds of what was happening behind. Then she stopped behind a mailbox to study the Japanese American Museum on N Street at Taylor, right on the edge of Japantown.

The place was on the corner of a big intersection that was crammed with wrecked or abandoned cars. The burned shell of a big Marine Corps helicopter was smashed into the east wing of the museum, and the front doors were shut and locked. The building was made from blocks of tan stone, and there were no windows at all on the first floor; the ones on the second floor were covered with ornate brass grilles.

All of the first-floor doors were made from heavy steel. The words DEAD INSIDE had been spray-painted on the outside as a warning.

Rags had done that.

She put that mark on several of her favorite bolt-holes. She'd seen it on other buildings. Warnings left by travelers who cared. Or by the military back when they mattered.

There were no dead inside her place, though.

It had been shut up for the night when the world fell apart. No one had come to open those heavy doors in the morning. No one ever would. The helicopter that crashed on the east wing had burned, and as far as Rags could tell, none of the people onboard had survived. They hadn't walked out, they hadn't shambled out. They'd burned and stayed dead.

Rags envied them.

The street was clear of the dead.

She took a breath and moved away from the shelter of the mailbox, darting in a haphazard pattern from one car to another to another as she made her way around the fringes of the intersection. She stopped often, listened closely, watched everything. The only movement was what was pushed by the wind.

Crossing that intersection took five whole minutes, because Rags needed to know that no one saw her and nothing reacted to her. She got to the helicopter and paused again. The burned meat smell was long gone now.

With great care, Rags went around to the far side, climbed up onto the broken tail section, and crawled along it like a bug until she reached the place where the dying machine had punched through the outer wall. There was a small pile of pebbles there that Rags had left behind. She picked one up and then tossed it through the hole into the shadows of the museum. It clattered and bounced and then lay still. She bent forward and listened with all her might to whatever the shadows had to say.

They said nothing.

There were no moans, no soft and ungainly footfalls. There were no human cries of surprise.

Nothing.

She let out a breath and crawled inside.

Rags flicked on her solar-powered flashlight—an insanely valuable item she'd taken from the backpack of a dead hiker. Someone had shot the hiker in the head but left his gear intact. Half the good supplies Rags had in her own backpack had come from that person, and when she prayed at night, Rags always included a special thanks to Stanley Nogatowski.

She'd learned his name from stuff she'd found in his wallet. Mr. Nogatowski was thirty-four, was a house painter, had a library card, had a debit card and two credit cards, belonged to Sam's Club, and had a picture of him and another man holding hands as they cut a wedding cake.

The things she had found in his pack—PowerBars, a canteen, water purification tablets, a compass, a first aid kit, and a knife, not to mention the solar flashlight—had saved her life that day and a dozen times since. Maybe more. She sometimes prayed to Stanley as if he were her personal guardian angel. Maybe he was.

Holding Stanley's flashlight in one hand and his Buck lock-knife in the other, Rags descended a slope of rubble from the hole in the wall to the floor of the museum.

The east wing had a lot of displays about the architecture of ancient Japan. Rain and fire had ruined almost all of it.

The rest of the building was in good shape, though Rags hadn't yet fully explored it. She'd been to the art displays, the literature display, and one room on the second floor that was filled with all kinds of clothing. Kimonos in glass cases or hung on strings from the ceiling. They looked like giant butterflies. Rags had taken a dozen of them down and made a nest for herself in a niche behind two massive display cases filled with thousands of ivory combs and jeweled hairpins. No one would want to loot that stuff, so that was where she went. She was safe there.

She settled down and tried not to think about what had just happened outside. The room was dark and quiet and safe. There were a dozen ways out and she knew every one. She had weapons positioned around—sharp sticks, pipes, a few knives she'd taken from display cases of samurai stuff over in the west wing.

The last of the day's light fell in dusty, slanting lines through the high windows, and the grilles split the light into patterns of lotus flowers and cherry blossoms. She watched the way the patterns moved as the sun slowly set.

Rags thought about eating some of her soup, but her stomach rebelled. No. Not after what had happened.

So she pulled the ancient silk around her and tried to sleep.

The shakes began then, and they stayed with her. The shivers followed her all the way down into her dreams, and her dreams were no escape at all.

4

The dog found her.

In the deep of night, hours and hours after the thing with the scavengers, she woke from a troubled dream of broken teeth and grabbing hands. She woke to the certain knowledge that she was no longer alone.

Rags was too practiced a survivor to cry out even in terror. Instead she snatched up her knife and put her back to the wall, ready to run left or right, planning her route through the midnight darkness of the museum, certain she could navigate it better than any intruder.

Except she heard it coming.

It, not them. Not the living, not the dead. Not people on either side of that dividing line.

She heard it even though it moved very quietly. The dead are clumsy, and they don't understand stealth. Scavengers do, but Rags was alert. She was paying attention and analyzing the sounds she heard for reliable meaning.

She heard the dog coming. The faint click of nails on the marble floor. *Clickety-clickety-click.*

Panic flared in Rags.

That big dog was coming.

For her.

It had followed her here.

That monster of a dog.

Clickety-clickety-click.

The knife in her hand felt so small. She felt small.

That dog had killed five people. Five armed adults.

Clickety-clickety-click.

So close now. Right on the other side of the case behind which she crouched.

Then . . .

Silence.

Rags did not dare breathe.

A single ray of cold moonlight slanted down through one of the high windows. She rose slowly. So slowly, gripping the knife, holding the flashlight in her left hand, thumb on the button. Ready to flick on the light and stab in that moment of blinding surprise.

She tried to remember if dogs could see in the dark. If so, did that make them more vulnerable to sudden bursts of light?

Rags had no idea.

She moved very slowly down the edge of the case and peered around.

What she saw made her freeze into a pillar of ice.

The big dog sat there. Right in the middle of the patch

of light thrown down from the window. It was a huge male. Young and strong, but looking starved and a little wild. He sat upright and looked directly at her.

As if anticipating that she would come that way. Hearing, smelling, sensing. Whatever. *Knowing.*

And . . . *waiting* for her.

Watching her.

All that fur and muscle and size. Waiting. Like a statue. Patient.

But why? Why did he wait like that? Why not just come after her? If he could find her here, why didn't he simply pounce on her and do to her what he'done to the scavengers?

Why?

Rags licked her lips and swallowed a lump that felt as big as a rock.

The dog cocked his head at her.

And with a soft, heavy *thump-thump-thump*, he began wagging his tail. Beating it against the dusty marble floor.

That was how it started.

5

Trying to discover the dog's name went nowhere. She made her way through the entire alphabet, trying every dog name she could think of—Prince, King, even Fido. She was sure no one ever named their dog Fido unless they were trying to be ironic. She tried all the cool or semi-cool or corny names people she'd known used for their dogs. Sam, Max, Butch, Bo, a couple of dozen others.

The closest she got to a reaction was from Bo. The dog almost wagged his tail, but didn't. As if he was waiting for more of the name. She tried Bob, Bozo, Bono. Nothing.

The dog had a collar, and there was a bone-shaped tag on it, but instead of a name, there was a message that didn't tell her much.

PROPERTY OF THE

DEPARTMENT OF MILITARY SCIENCES

CAPT. J. LEDGER

There was a serial number, a phone number, and a website.

In the end, because the dog wore that tag and because it almost reacted to Bo, she decided to name him Bones.

The first time she called him that, the dog merely looked at her with those strange eyes.

The second time she called him, Bones came.

And Bones he was from then on.

6

Rags and Bones stayed in San Jose for nearly five months, and in their own way, they became scavengers.

Of a kind.

True scavengers, as she saw it. Not psychopaths.

They didn't hunt people. Not to rob, not to hurt, and certainly not to eat. Rags knew that with everything she'd been through she was probably more than half-crazy, but there was a lot of downhill road she'd need to travel before she let herself become *that* crazy.

The dog helped.

He was so smart. Weird smart, as Rags saw it. When she spoke to him, Bones listened. Not just heard her, but *listened*. As if he could understand her actual words.

It was strange, but even Rags had to admit that it was far from the strangest part of her world.

Rags had no idea what day of the week it was or what week of the month. She was pretty sure she was still thirteen, but that might not be true. If it was October, then she was fourteen. It still felt like September, though. Or the world wasn't getting as cool as it should. It was usually in the high seventies in September. By October it dropped down to the sixties during the day and into the fifties at night. This year it was hot even at night.

That was a weird thought. Rags figured that with all those dead people—none of them warmer than room temperature—the temperature should have dropped. But no.

Maybe it was the fires.

Maybe it was from all those bombs they'd released.

She didn't know. It was okay, though, because she was usually cold, and hotter days and warm nights weren't too bad. If it got really cold at some point, she figured she could cuddle up with Bones. He was always warm.

Since finding the dog, Rags had learned how to sleep again. Really sleep. Like all night, which was something she had not done once since she ran away from home.

It took a while for that to happen. A few weeks. But over time she began to trust Bones completely. And to trust that he would hear or smell something long before she did.

Being with Bones changed things for Rags.

She smiled. She laughed. She played.

That felt weird, because Rags thought that those things were extinct concepts.

At first their play was only an accidental version of fetch. They were picking through the ruins of a clothing store, trying to find a good sweater because fall was coming. Rags found a funny little hat that she thought would be warm, but it was too small. It was the tenth hat she'd tried on that didn't fit, and that annoyed her, so she threw it across the store.

Bones bounded after it and brought it back.

The world had changed so much that Rags didn't immediately understand why the dog did that. But Bones picked it up and dropped it again, a few inches closer to her sneakered toes. Bones wagged his big tail.

Rags stared at the brightly colored hat and then at the dog.

"Seriously?" she asked.

The tail whipped back and forth. He lowered his head and used his nose to put it closer.

She bent and picked it up.

"Fetch?"

More wags.

"You're weird," she told the dog.

Bones had his mouth open, tongue lolling. It made him look like he was grinning.

So Rags threw the hat.

Bones bounded after it, crashing through overturned display racks, leaping over fallen mannequins to retrieve the hat. He brought it back and dropped it on the top of her left shoe.

The tail kept wagging.

As Rags bent to pick up the hat, she told herself that this

wasn't smart, that they needed to stay focused and to keep hunting for supplies, clothes, and food.

Instead, she and Bones played fetch for nearly an hour. With hats. With fuzzy slippers. With balled-up socks.

The next day Rags and Bones went in search of a pet store.

The store had been looted. Hungry people will eat pet food if they can't get anything better. The shelves were bare of cans and bags. The cages had been torn open and most were splashed with blood. Either the hungry dead or the hungry living had been here.

The rest of the stuff was there, though.

Rags found a whole bunch of bright-green tennis balls, and she stuffed several of these into her backpack. Bones insisted that they play with one of them, and an hour blurred by. Rags laughed a lot because Bones acted like a big puppy when he was playing fetch. He was clumsy and pretended to hunt the ball.

None of the dog beds were big enough for him. People had taken all of those. But she found a set of saddlebags that buckled around the dog's barrel chest. She filled the pockets with toys, flea and tick medicine, and two bags of gluten-free dog treats that had been accidentally kicked under the front counter. She gave three of them to Bones, who nuzzled her afterward like he was in heaven.

Every day after that she took time to play with Bones. No matter where or how far she threw one of the fuzzy green balls, the big dog found it and brought it back.

He paid her back by helping her find food. He had an amazing nose, and he could scout up items she missed. In stores, in homes. Boxes of peanut butter crackers in a cabinet in an accountant's office. A box of instant rice in a cupboard of a house that had clearly been searched. Even canned food, which was something Rags couldn't understand. How could the dog smell food in sealed cans? She certainly couldn't.

Between the two of them, they survived. They both put on a little weight, and eating better helped them get stronger. Rags was still thin, but over time she became wiry rather than merely skinny.

Sometimes Bones went out hunting alone and came back with blood on his muzzle. Rags hoped that it was animal blood. There were rabbits and squirrels and raccoons every-where. If Bones was hunting like that, then it was okay. That was natural, even if it was a little disgusting.

But Rags remembered what Bones had done to those can-nibal scavengers. She made sure that she washed the dog's face of every last drop of blood before she'd let the animal cuddle up with her.

She washed his coat and applied the flea medicine. She found heartworm medicine and gave him regular doses.

She fell in love with the brute, and he clearly loved her.

Bones appointed himself her protector. He proved it many times.

Once, when they were creeping along the border between Northside and Japantown, Bones began growling very qui-etly. No barks. She hadn't heard him bark at all. Not once. But that growl stopped Rags in her tracks. The dog flattened out and crawled to the edge of a parked car and peered under it, so Rags dropped down and looked to see what it was.

A line of dead people were walking up the street. Why they were there or what they were following, Rags never found out.

Sometimes the dead just walked. Mostly they didn't; mostly they stopped moving if there was nothing for them to do, nothing to hunt or chase. A few, though, always seemed to be in motion.

Rags and Bones lay there and watched them. Nine of the dead. Adults and kids. Black and white, and a couple of Latinos. All of them pretty much gray now. Walking in a loose pack down Empire Street as if they had somewhere to go.

They didn't hear the growls. Bones did it very quietly and stopped as soon as it was clear Rags was seeing what he wanted her to see.

It was like that.

The dead passed, and then the two of them got up and went in a different direction.

Another time there was pack of men. Survivors for sure, and maybe scavengers. Or maybe something else. They didn't look as crazed as the cannibals, but they did not look friendly. Or safe. There were two really big men and a few others. One man had snow-white hair but he was young, probably no more than thirty. So many muscles, and a face that scared the crap out of Rags. Guns in holsters, knives strapped everywhere. And he looked around him with sharp, dangerous eyes. Red eyes. An albino, Rags thought, though she had never met one before.

The other big man was a few inches shorter but every bit as broad-shouldered and mean-looking. He had black hair and lots of scars, and instead of a gun or knife, he carried a two-foot-long length of black pipe wrapped in electrician's tape.

The other men were no prizes either, but compared to

the two big men, they seemed less important. Followers, thought Rags.

Bones had heard them coming and immediately took her wrist between his teeth and pulled her off the street. That was something he did, and even with all those fangs, he never once broke the skin or left a mark. She would only have gotten hurt if she'd tried to pull away. Rags didn't. She'd come to trust Bones. So she let him pull her into a burned-out beauty shop, and they crouched together in the shadows, watching as the men walked down the center of the street. They walked with the kind of bold confidence people had when they were afraid of absolutely nothing and absolutely no one. Not the living and not the dead.

The men talked in normal voices. No whispers. They made crude, disgusting jokes, and they laughed like donkeys. Rags hated them on sight. She feared them too. If they weren't cannibal scavengers, then they were clearly dangerous in some other way. If it hadn't been for Bones, she might have walked right into them.

Beside her, Bones bared his teeth in a silent snarl of animal hate. If he was afraid too, he showed it in a different way. The hairs on his spine stood up, though, and he did not blink once until the men had passed the store and moved on down the street.

A third time Bones saved her was when she began heading into the museum along her usual route, climbing the helicopter tail toward the smashed-in corner. Rags was reaching for her solar flashlight when Bones came running up the slanting tail, pushed past her, and stood at the edge of the hole, staring into the shadows. Once more the hairs stood up on his back and he bared his teeth, and once more he did not bark. He didn't growl this time either. He just stood there.

"What is it, boy?" she asked, kneeling beside him and pulling out her knife.

The dog stared and stared.

And then he began backing away.

"Hey," Rags said, "we have to go in. All our stuff's in there."

Bones stopped and glared at her. Not in a threatening way, but as if he was trying to tell her something.

"You can stay right here, scaredy-pants," Rags said, "but I need to get our stuff. We have a whole thing of food in there. My *backpack's* in there."

She straightened and took a step toward the hole.

Bones darted forward and blocked her way.

"If you're that freaked out, then come with me. We'll be quick," insisted Rags. "In and out."

The backpack was hidden beneath an empty display case, and it was crammed with twenty-six cans of food and all the rest of her supplies. All she had with her at the moment was the flashlight, the knife, and the first aid kit. She *had* to get it.

The dog stood there, blocking the entrance with his massive size.

"Hey, *your* food's in there too, Einstein," she said, trying to push past him.

Bones did something he had never done once before. Not to her.

He bared his teeth.

Nearly two hundred pounds of dog, with fangs that could

tear her apart. And all of that—muscle and teeth—right up in her face.

Rags was instantly and completely terrified. She stumbled backward.

Bones held his ground. He did not advance. Did not attack.

He stood there between her and the hole into darkness.

Slowly, slowly his lips settled back and he stopped snarling at her. Rags kept backing away. Not from the hole. From *him*.

Then Bones wagged his tail.

Two quick switches back and forth.

He cast one lingering look over his shoulder, and then he followed Rags down the tail of the helicopter and onto the cracked asphalt of N Street. When they were both down there, Bones stared up at her and made a soft whining sound. His tail flicked again.

Which was when Rags got it.

This wasn't about her. It was only about the museum. It was about the dog knowing something she didn't. Smelling, sensing, guessing. Whatever.

It was about the hard truth that the museum wasn't their home anymore.

It never would be again.

Whatever was in there, it wanted that place even more than Bones did. That was really scary.

Bones nudged her with his muzzle and kept nuzzling and whining until she broke down and touched him. Just a touch at first, then as he felt her hand on his fur, Bones pushed against her. Rags knelt down very slowly and wrapped her arms around the big dog. He licked her face as if in apology.

"Thanks," she said.

She wept for the food and supplies.

She wept for being alive.

Bones pressed himself against her and whined.

And they didn't die.

7

That night they slept in a shoe store that had been so thoroughly looted that even the little stocking things people wore when trying stuff on had been taken. There was nothing in the store but empty boxes, a smashed cash register, old animal bones, and dirt.

Out back, in a small courtyard shared by six different stores, they found three dead men and a lot of blood. Flies were heavy and the corpses stank. Rags looked at them through the screen door while Bones stood beside her. There were weapons on the ground and scuff marks. This had been a real fight. Rags was getting so that she could read signs of violent encounters. Fights with the dead left one kind of mark. Fights between living people left another.

This fight had definitely been between living people. What convinced her of that was that each of the corpses had their heads cut off.

The dead didn't return if their heads were cut off. Or if their brains were damaged. Someone had killed them and then made sure these three wouldn't rise.

Rags closed the door.

The presence of the rotting corpses, though completely disgusting, was useful. Rot did not attract the dead. Only living flesh did that. So, with nothing to steal and nothing to eat, the place was as safe as safe got these days.

Rags and Bones slept in the storeroom, curled together like pups in a litter.

All through the next week Rags looked for a new place. Some of the best prospects—places she'd taken note of to come back to—had been looted. A few had burned down, though whether it was arson or lightning was hard to say.

Almost every day they found more dead people. Not the walking dead. She found more people who had been killed.

And it was when she and Bones were examining the third fight scene that she noticed something. All the dead people had tattoos. Skulls, mostly. On their arms, on their necks. One had a big one on his chest. The tattoos were crude. Stuff that looked like it had been done recently and badly; not stuff from before.

Always skulls.

Every single dead person had a skull tattoo.

She began studying the bodies, trying to learn from them.

All the corpses were tough-looking. People with scars and with other, older tattoos. Although Rags had grown up in a nice neighborhood, she'd watched enough TV and rap videos to know what jailhouse tats looked like. Some of these people had those kinds of ink.

All of them were in bad shape. Like they'd been in a bad fight before they died. Almost all of them were men. She saw a couple of women, but these women looked every bit as rough and tough as the men.

At the seventh scene of slaughter, Rags began going through their pockets. She found stuff she didn't care about—cigarettes, money—and stuff she kept, like matches, folding knives, sealed packages of beef jerky and Slim Jims. Bottles of hand sanitizer, aspirin, vitamins. Even a little plastic container of breath mints.

She found a lot of rope, twine, metal handcuffs, and plastic pipe-ties. What her uncle Mark called Flex-Cuffs. Like cops used on TV. Every single corpse had that stuff.

She left that stuff there and took the useful items with her.

The days passed.

Twice she thought she heard the sound of yelling and then a few gunshots, but it was on the other side of town, and about the last thing she wanted to do was walk into someone else's trouble. Rags had gotten used to being alone. Just her and the dog.

Bones, though, sometimes he'd stand and listen, facing the direction of those kinds of sounds, head cocked, nose twitching. A few times he whined softly. But he never left her to investigate.

Bones never left her side.

8

They were walking under the deep shade of the trees in Backesto Park, down near the basketball courts on Empire Street. It was almost noon, and there were a million birds singing in the trees. Singing like the world was okay and things were normal.

Rags was hungry, and she knew Bones had to be too. The plan was to follow Empire all the way to the houses by Coyote Creek. Not all of them had been scavenged, and Rags was sure they'd find something to eat. Last month they'd gone into one of those places and found two canned hams. Entire hams, and the cans weren't swollen or anything. The can said they were fully cooked, and though Rags had never much liked ham, she ate a lot of it that day and loved every bite. Bones pretty much inhaled an entire ham by himself.

Maybe one of those houses would be a place to stay for a couple of nights while they worked the houses in the neighborhood. With any luck they'd find enough food that they could fill a shopping cart. Maybe some new clothes, too.

She was thinking about that as they left the trees and began walking along Empire. The street was empty, like most of San Jose. Rags had no idea why this town should be so deserted when there used to be so many people here. Either the town had somehow been evacuated during the crisis, or the dead had nearly all walked away since. Of the nearly one million people who used to live here, Rags guessed that there were no more than a few thousand of the dead. And a few dozen scavengers.

She had Bones, and they managed to steer clear of trouble. Most of the time.

Once they were on the street, Rags winced at the stink of a dead skunk that lay near a rusting FedEx truck and an Escalade sitting on four flat tires. Bones whined a little at the smell, and they both hurried past the dead creature, but as they did so the door of the Escalade suddenly swung open and two men stepped out.

Both of them wore leather jackets, hockey leg pads, football helmets, and thick gloves. One of them held a heavy wrench; the other had a long pole with a leather loop hanging from one end. Rags knew what that was; she'd seen it used on TV for catching wild animals. They drop the loop over the head, and the solid pole keeps the animal from getting close enough to bite.

Both men had tattoos of skulls on their forearms. Both men were smiling the kind of smile no girl ever wants to see.

Bones tensed, and there was that low growl again. Rags was scared, but not terrified. Two men against Bones. It would be ugly, but it would be short.

She pulled out her knife.

"That's cute," said the man with the wrench. "Little girl's got herself a knife."

His voice was crude, rough.

"Is that what that little thing is?" mused the man with the pole. "Thought it was a toothpick."

Rags clenched the knife and held it against her chest.

"Might have to show her how it works," said the first man. "Maybe carve some rules and regulations on her so she knows her place."

"I'm warning you," began Rags, but then Bones turned to look behind them. Rags turned too, and her heart froze in her chest.

Three more men were crossing the street. Two of them had poles with leather loops. The third had a fire ax.

All of them had skull tattoos.

A sound made her turn to the left, and there were two more men. Both of them big. Both with baseball bats. And with them walked a woman.

She was tall and thin, with dirty-blond hair pulled back into a ponytail. Skinny jeans and a tank top under an unzipped Oakland Raiders hoodie. She wore cheap sunglasses with white frames and dark lenses, and dark-orange lipstick. The woman walked with an exaggerated hip sway like she was all that, but Rags thought she was kind of hideous. Trashy and dangerous.

For a split second, seeing a woman made Rags wonder if this would be okay. Sometimes women looked out for each other.

Except when they were scavengers.

This crew, though . . . they looked better fed than the cannibals who roamed the dead cities. They were smiling, too, and Rags had never seen a scavenger smile. Maybe eating what they ate drove all the smiles from their faces. Maybe it made them crazy because they knew there was no coming back from where they'd gone.

Either way, these people looked different.

Every bit as dangerous, but not crazy. Or at least, not in the same way.

"Well, well, well," said the woman, drawing the three words out. She had a red skull tattoo on her upper chest and a silver skeleton on a chain around her neck. "What on earth do we have here?"

Bones growled at her and shifted to stand between Rags and the woman. It was clear to the dog, just as it was clear to Rags, that this woman was in charge.

The woman eyed the dog, and if her smile flickered, it did so for only a moment. She snapped her fingers, and the men with the poles began spacing themselves out in a loose circle. None of them were close enough to do anything yet, but there was also nowhere for Rags and Bones to run.

"What do you want?" demanded Rags, and she hated that her voice sounded so thin and defensive. It sounded like a kid's voice, and she wanted to sound strong.

"Pretty much what you think we want, little sister," said the woman. "You get to play with the boys. And Rover there gets to come play in the pits."

"Pits?"

"Oh heck yeah. We have a nice big pit up in Milpitas. Got us fifty dogs, 'bout a dozen good hogs, couple wild coyotes, and . . . oh, a few other surprises. Zoos are fun, let me just put it that way." She laughed, and all the men laughed with her. "Rover there has been on my to-do list for a while now. Been finding his leavings and all those footprints. Big ol' paws he has on 'im. What's he, a little wolfhound? Some husky or shepherd? Yeah, he's going to be a whole lot of fun. Maybe worth breeding if he turns out to be a good fighter. Love to have me a pack of dogs with that kind of muscle. If I had six, seven of them, I could wipe the floor with Danny-Boy and his pack of Rotties, oh hell yes."

Rags had no idea who Danny-Boy was, but if he had a pack of Rottweilers and was involved in some kind of dog-fights, then Rags hated him on principle. Just as she hated this woman and her crew of goons. Bones growled again, his anger in tune with hers.

The woman snapped her fingers. "C'mon now, let's make this easy. We don't need to leave hair on the walls here. That's for later. Be smart and this won't get any worse than it has to be. So, why don't you take one of those collars and put it on your pup? Do that for us, and maybe I'll give you something that'll make everything else all dreamy so you won't hardly be in your own head when stuff happens."

Stuff. The woman put the word out there like it was nothing. Like it was ordinary. Like it would destroy everything that Rags was, had been, or ever might be.

Stuff.

God.

Rags laid her hand on Bones's quivering back. The dog grew quiet, no longer growling, but he was incredibly tense. With the scavengers, maybe Bones knew he was going to win. Against these big men with the loops, there was no way. There were too many of them, and they had set a trap.

"Leave us alone," said Rags defiantly. "We haven't done anything to you. We don't have anything. Just let us go."

Everyone laughed at that. As if it was funny.

Rags felt tears in her eyes. "Please . . ."

"No, honey," said the woman. "You can say please all day and night and it won't matter much. School's out and the world went all to hell."

"Why are you doing this?" insisted Rags, gripping her knife. She was terrified, but she was also furious. To have survived so much, to have lasted this long when so many stronger, older people had died should mean something. It wasn't right that creeps like this could come along and decide that her life was over. That made less sense to Rags than what the dead did. It made less sense than what the cannibals did. The dead and the crazoid scavengers were out of their minds. These people—this woman and these men—

were not. They were in control of themselves, and yet this was what they chose to do.

Rags wanted to say all this, to lay it out, to build a case for the world not going in this direction. Gangs of postapocalyptic predators? That was so cliché. It was from old movies on the Syfy channel. It was video game stuff.

It shouldn't be allowed to be real.

"No," she barked, "you have to tell me why. What makes you think this is okay to do? What makes you think you can just *do* this?"

The woman grinned. "Because we can," she said, then shrugged. "And . . . because we want to. Because it's fun."

"I think," said a voice from behind Rags, "that the young miss here deserves a better answer than that."

Everyone whirled around. Everyone gaped. With the stink of the dead skunk polluting the air, not even Bones had smelled anyone else approach. Now the big dog suddenly let out a single, sharp bark, and his tail began whipping back and forth too fast to see. He barked again, and again. He didn't sound scared or shocked. No. He sounded happy.

Happy?

Rags frowned, because that concept didn't seem to fit into the day. Not in any way that made sense.

A man sat cross-legged on the top of the FedEx van, sitting as casually as if he was meditating, or sunning himself.

Rags hadn't seen him. None of the men had. And from the looks on their faces, they were as horrified to see him as Rags had been to see them.

The man was older than everyone there. Maybe forty or fifty, Rags guessed. He had blond hair streaked with gray, cold blue eyes, and a very white smile in a very tan face. There were laugh lines around his eyes and harsher, deeper lines around his mouth. He wore green fatigue pants, a well-worn pair of Timberlands, and a green muscle shirt with the words ECHO TEAM stenciled on the chest. Despite his age, the man was very muscular and looked as dangerous as a tiger. He had a wooden kitchen match between his teeth and made it wiggle up and down.

"Who the hell are you?" demanded the man with the wrench.

The blond man removed the matchstick and smiled. "On your best day, son, I'm bad news, and I'm afraid today is not going to be your best day."

One of the men leaned close to the woman and spoke quietly, though Rags was close enough to hear.

"That's him," he said. "That's the one I was telling you about."

The woman stiffened, and her smile went away to be replaced by a look that was colder and less human than anything Rags had ever seen on a human face. Even the dead looked more human than she did at that moment.

The woman said a name. She spat it out like a bad taste.

"Ledger."

Rags stiffened. That had been the name on Bones's tag. Captain J. Ledger.

"Yeah," said Ledger. He pointed to the woman with the matchstick. "I'm going to take a wild guess here and say that you're Mama Rat, am I right?"

The woman merely grunted.

"Mama Rat," repeated Ledger, nodding to himself. "And

these seven geniuses are what's left of the skull-riders. Geez. Skull-riders. I have to believe alcohol was involved in the process of coming up with that name." He shook his head. "So sad, really. You hear the rumors and you want to believe the hype. People in the refugee camps talk about the skull-riders like they're the biggest, baddest bunch of butt-kickers since the Visigoths. People tell *stories* about you ass-clowns, you know that?"

He sighed and shook his head.

Rags had no idea what was going on. There were seven armed men, all of them younger than this old guy. And yet he was making fun of them. Was he nuts? Was that it?

"You're that old ranger," said Mama Rat. "Joe Ledger."

"Guilty as charged," Ledger admitted as he rose slowly to his feet. He was very tall and had an empty holster on his right hip and a sheathed knife on his left. "And if you know my name, honey, then you know why I'm here. And you know that I don't take kindly to anyone messing with one of my dogs."

The woman cleared her throat. "Your . . . dogs . . . ?"

"Uh-huh. Dogs. Plural. Oops!" Ledger snapped his fingers, and with a clatter of nails and a deep-chested *whuff*, a second dog stepped out from between two cars.

It was massive, and its coat was the color of dirty snow.

It had one brown eye and one mint-colored eye.

It looked exactly like Bones.

Except that it was a lot bigger.

"Now ain't this a pickle?" said Ledger with a contented little chuckle.

9

Mama Rat and her seven brutish skull-riders gaped at this new dog. So did Rags. It was the biggest dog she had ever seen. Easily two hundred pounds, and probably closer to two-fifty. It wore a coat of leather studded with steel bolts whose shafts had been sharpened to deadly points. A metal cap was strapped to its head, and from its dome sprouted a dozen wickedly sharp blades. Another line of blades stood up along its spine like the plates of a stegosaurus.

"Let me make introductions," said Ledger. "Baskerville, meet the clown college. Clown college, meet my friend Baskerville. I'm sure you'll all get along swimmingly."

Baskerville bared his teeth. There were a lot of them, and his eyes blazed with such heat that Rags thought she could feel it. Beside her, Bones barked once, twice, again. Deep-chested and challenging. Baskerville responded with a booming bark that seemed to shake the street.

All seven men stepped back, fear blooming like weeds in their eyes.

Only Mama Rat held her ground, and despite everything, she smiled up at the big man with the big dog.

"Yeah," she said, "you're pretty darned impressive. You fit the stories people tell about you. The showmanship, the smart mouth."

Ledger gave her a small, comical bow.

"But there's still more of us than there are of you," said Mama Rat.

"You like those numbers? Seven idiots who couldn't find their own butts without a road map and a compass against me, Baskerville, and Boggart?"

Boggart? thought Rags. Beside her, Bones barked when he heard that name.

His real name.

In a strange way it made her sad to know that he wasn't really Bones. Not *her* Bones. The big dog belonged to this strange man. Bones—*Boggart*—was family to the other dog. Brother, maybe. Or son.

Either way, he didn't belong to her, and despite everything it made Rags want to cry.

Mam Rat said, "Eight to three is good enough odds most days. I'm sorry to spoil your bit of drama here, though." She reached into her hoodie pocket and produced a whistle, the kind coaches use. Mama Rat put it to her lips and blew a shrill, piercing note that rose high above the scene and floated away on the wind.

Both dogs barked at her, but Ledger snapped his fingers and they held their ground.

The moment stretched but nothing happened. Mama Rat looked at the surrounding buildings. Rags could see doubt flicker over her face.

"Go ahead," said Ledger quietly. "Try again."

Mama Rat blew the whistle again. And again. Her men looked nervously one to the other. They all turned to look down side streets and at the houses lining the street.

She blew once more, a long, protracted note that rose and rose, and then fell away as she lowered the whistle.

"Oops," said Ledger again. "Looks like your backup isn't coming."

"I—I don't—" began Mama Rat, and abruptly stopped as a figure stepped out of the shadows between two houses. He was average height, wearing jeans and a sweatshirt with the word CADET stenciled in fading black letters above the outline of a police department shield. The man was young, in his early twenties, and had a flat Japanese face with straight black hair. In his right hand he held the silk-wrapped handle of a sword. Rags recognized it from a thousand anime movies. A *katana*. The blade was covered in bright-red blood, and there were blood splashes all over the newcomer's clothes. Even a few drops on his face.

He walked into the street without haste. Then he paused, raised his sword, and with a sharp downward snap of his wrist whipped all the blood from the oiled steel. It left a pattern of red drops along the sidewalk.

Captain Ledger nodded to the man, and he nodded back.

"You okay, Tom?"

Tom, the swordsman, nodded again.

"How many?" asked Ledger.

"Six," said Tom. "I told them . . . not to . . ." He stopped and shook his head, and Rags realized that the man was very upset.

About what he had done.

Maybe about what he'd had to do.

Ledger sighed and turned to Mama Rat.

"Six men," he said, but Tom interrupted to correct him.

"Five men and a woman."

The captain sighed again. He did not look as upset as Tom was, but he clearly wasn't happy. He walked to the edge of the FedEx truck, bent to brace his hand on the edge, and jumped down, landing with a grunt and a flicker of pain.

"Knees are getting old," he said, more to himself than anyone else. He clicked his tongue and Baskerville vanished, but Rags heard a clatter from the rear of the truck, and a moment later the brute came trotting out to stand beside his master. Bones wagged his tail and whined softly, and Baskerville gave a single acknowledging *whuff.*

The seven skull-riders and their leader had drawn together now and stood in a defensive knot. Mama Rat stood closest to Rags, her face filled with doubt and anger.

And horror, too.

"You killed all six of them?" she asked in a small, hollow voice. Tears glittered in the corners of her eyes.

Tom met her eyes and Rags could see such a deep pain in him that it made her heart hurt. "I gave them a choice," he said. "They gave me none."

"All . . . six?" gasped Mama Rat. "How? *How?*"

Ledger answered that. "Tom has some real talent."

If it was meant as praise, it didn't come out that way. Ledger sounded sad, and Tom took a long, slow, deep breath and let it out.

"They gave me no choice at all," he repeated.

Two tears fell down Mama Rat's cheeks. "No . . . ," she whispered.

Joe Ledger walked up to Bones and held out his hand. The big dog licked him and danced around like a happy puppy. It twisted the knife in Rags's heart.

The big man seemed to sense that too. He smiled at her. "Looks like you've been taking good care of him for me," he said. "He's put some weight on. Nice."

The dog looked from him to Rags and back again.

"He's my friend," said Rags. "We've been helping each other."

Ledger nodded. "That's good. That's the only way we're ever going to get out of this mess."

He walked past her and stood in front of Mama Rat. Baskerville came trotting up behind him, gave Bones a quick sniff, allowed one in return, then went over to sit beside Ledger. His armor clanked.

The seven skull-riders clustered even more tightly behind Mama Rat. They each still held their weapons, but to Rags it seemed as if the men had forgotten what those items were used for.

Ledger stood and studied Mama Rat for a long time, his blue eyes filled with mysteries. Finally, when he spoke, he recited lines from an old story Rags had read in school.

"'The time has come, the Walrus said,'" murmured Ledger, "'to talk of many things. Of shoes—and ships—and sealing-wax— Of cabbages—and kings—And why the sea is boiling hot—And whether pigs have wings.'"

It was some nonsense poetry from *Through the Looking-Glass*, and its silly verses had no business on this troubled street in an abandoned city in a dying world.

Or, Rags wondered, did they?

In the stillness of the air there was magic hidden inside the ranger's recitation. The swordsman, Tom, came and stood ten feet to Ledger's left. The air around him seemed to crackle with a static charge of awful possibility. And Rags knew that whatever happened—and whatever *had* happened—it hurt the Japanese man every bit as much as those who felt his sword. Rags knew that with total certainty.

"What—what do you want?" asked Mama Rat, her voice soft and filled with cracks.

"That's up to you, sweetheart," said Ledger. "We're standing way, way out on the ledge here. You know what's down there if you take that step."

Another tear fell down the woman's cheek. "We're all dead anyway."

Ledger shook his head, but before he could say anything, Rags spoke. She hadn't meant to and didn't know she was going to.

"No," she said.

Everyone looked at her.

"That's not true," said Rags. "We're not all dead."

"Look around you, girl, the whole world's dead," snapped the woman. "The whole world's gone crazy, and anyone who says it's not is crazier than the rest."

"Maybe the world's crazy," said Rags, taking a hesitant step forward, "but that doesn't mean we are."

When she moved, Bones moved with her, standing right at her side, the way Baskerville stood beside the ranger. Captain Ledger seemed to take note of it, and he smiled to himself.

"What do you know about anything?" sneered Mama Rat. "You're a kid. You don't know anything."

Anger flared hot in Rags's chest. "I don't? Really? I know that this plague came and killed my mom. And after she died, my mom got up and killed my dad, and my little brother, and my gram. *She killed my dog.*" For some reason those last words were the hardest, and Rags's voice cracked on them. "My mom killed everyone in my house, and she tried to kill me. And I . . . and I . . ."

Tears fell like rain from her eyes as sobs broke over and over in her chest. They hurt so bad. Everything hurt so bad. And as she spoke, all the boards she'd hammered into place in the house of her memories began to come loose. Images thrust in through the windows like pale hands, doors burst open, and into her conscious mind came the shambling, lifeless things that had been her family. They filled her mind, coming for her, trying to crowd her into a corner so they could get at her and tear her apart.

"Do you know what I did?" yelled Rags, her voice rising to a shriek. "Do you know what I *did*?"

"Kid . . . ," began Ledger, reaching out for her, but Rags slapped his hand away.

"No! I want her to ask me what I did." She wheeled on Mama Rat and slapped her across the face so hard it sounded like a gunshot. "You're so tough. You're so scary. You ask me what I did! Go on—*ask me!*"

Mama Rat mouthed the words. She clearly could not speak them.

Her lips formed the four words.

What did you do?

Rags slapped her again. "I killed them!"

Another slap.

"I came back and killed them."

Slap.

"Mom."

Slap.

"Daddy."

Slap.

"Everyone."

Slap. Slap. Slap.

Mama Rat staggered backward into the arms of her men. Her face was so raw that tiny dots of blood sprang from her pores.

Tom stepped suddenly forward and wrapped an arm around Rags. She spun and pounded her fists on his chest, but he allowed it. Endured it. He used his free arm to gather her in, and while she screamed and wept, he held her to his chest.

Apart from the sound of her agony, the street was silent.

Then Joe Ledger said, "You people come here, hunting for little girls. Thinking they're nothing *but* little girls. You don't know anything, do you?"

Nobody said a word.

"Christ, do you know how much courage it took for her to do that? For a kid of her age to go into that house and do that?"

Silence.

"Do you know how much *love* it took?"

Rags stopped fighting Tom and wrapped her arms around him. Her knife fell to the ground, and she clung to him as if he was the only thing in the world that could keep her from drowning.

Ledger spat on the ground at Mama Rat's feet.

"You think your numbers and your knives make you

strong? Sister, you don't know what strength is." He pointed to Rags. "That? *That's* strength. That's power."

He took a step closer, and now he was so close to Mama Rat that they could kiss.

"That's hope," he said. "Do you understand me? Are you capable of understanding? This girl . . . and Tom here, and a few others . . . they are the future of this world. They have hope, they remember what love is, and they have the courage to do what's right."

He shook his head.

"When I met Tom, he was already hunting you people. Like me, he'd heard about a pack of human lice who were taking kids, taking lives."

In a movement that was too fast to see, Ledger drew his knife and pressed the edge against Mama Rat's throat. He spoke now in a deadly whisper.

"Tom Imura is a good man, and hunting scum like you is *killing* him. He's doing it because there are people trying to build something, trying to survive. He has a baby brother. He's helping to put together a town. He should be back in that town looking after his brother and planting crops. Instead people like you have turned him into a hunter and a killer. Now he's out here taking lives when we're so close to extinction that *every* life is precious."

He pressed the knife against her, lifting her onto her toes.

"I'm out here doing my part. Hunting, too, though unlike my friend Tom, I'm not as sentimental. I'm already a killer. I'm already a monster. Even before all this started I was out hunting monsters. Killing them. Monsters like you."

A bead of bright-red blood popped onto the edge of the

knife and slid down its silvery length. Ledger raised his voice.

"Tom . . . why don't you take our new friend out of here. Take her back to Mountainside, maybe."

"Joe," said Tom, "I can't just leave you here."

"Sure you can."

Rags pushed herself away from Tom and pawed the tears out of her eyes. "What are you going to do?"

Ledger smiled the most frightening smile she had ever seen. "I'm going to dance with Mama Rat here. Her and her boys."

Baskerville uttered a loud, sharp, single bark. Like a promise.

"Please . . . ," whispered Mama Rat. "Please don't."

"You called this play, darlin'," said Ledger. "You pushed us both right out onto this tightrope. What choice do either of us have?"

"Let her go," said one of the men, but his voice lacked all force and conviction. Bones and Baskerville growled him to silence.

"Go on, Tom," urged Ledger. "Get the girl out of here. She shouldn't have to see this."

"Let her go."

This time it was not any of the men who spoke. Nor was it Tom.

It was Rags.

Trembling, tear-streaked, flushed with psychological pain, she stood there and shook her head. "Please," she said, "just . . . let her go."

Ledger looked at her with a mixture of surprise, annoyance, and pity. "Seriously? You want me to cut them loose?"

Rags sniffed and wiped at her streaming eyes. "Y-yes."

"Why on earth would you want me to do that? I mean it," said Ledger. "Why?"

"Because we shouldn't kill each other."

A slow, sad smile formed on Ledger's mouth, but it didn't reach his eyes. "Do you have any idea what these freaks were going to do to you?"

Rags nodded.

Ledger kept the knife against Mama Rat's throat. "Do you think this witch or any of these scum-suckers would have carved off even a splinter of mercy for you?"

Rags shrugged.

"Think about the worst things that could happen to a person," growled Ledger, "then triple that because you're a girl. Now hold that in your mind and tell me again that you want me to let them go."

"It's you, isn't it?" Rags asked. "You and this other guy. I keep finding people with skull tattoos. Dead people. Not walking around dead, but left to rot. That's you two, isn't it?"

"It's us," said Tom Imura.

"Sure," agreed Ledger. "It's us. We're at war. The whole damn world is at war, or haven't you noticed, kid? Oh, wait, that's right, you're already a veteran of this war. You did what you had to do. That took courage. It also took smarts and compassion. Bottom line is, it *had* to be done. So does this."

"Why?"

"Why the hell do you think?" snapped Ledger.

Rags said nothing. She felt like she was standing on wobbly ground that was going to tilt under her. She turned to Tom, but his face was a mask, and he avoided her eyes.

Bones whuffed softly. He walked over to Rags and leaned against her. Rags knelt, wrapped her arms around his neck, and tried to lose herself in his fur.

"We have to stop killing each other," she said. "Or death is going to win."

The words seemed to hang in the air, and Rags heard them like an echo, as if it was someone else who spoke. Even to her own ears those words didn't sound like they came from her. Not from the little teenager who knelt in the dust surrounded by killers and madmen.

Rags closed her eyes. "I'm sorry," she said, and in that moment she wasn't sure if the words were meant for Ledger or for the people he wanted to kill.

Then she heard Joe Ledger sigh. And curse softly.

She looked up to see him lower his knife. Behind her, Rags heard Tom sigh too.

"Okay," said Ledger, and the frustration was there in his voice, woven into a fabric of anger and regret. "Okay. But there are conditions."

"Anything!" blurted Mama Rat, but Ledger growled at her.

"Shut up and listen. I don't want to hear any of you talk until I ask a question. You stand there and shut the hell up."

No one said a word.

"Like I said, there are conditions," repeated Ledger. He pointed to the ground. "First, drop the hardware. All of it. Poles, knives, anything you have. Do it now."

There were about three full seconds of hesitation as the men looked at one another and at Mama Rat and then into the eyes of Captain Ledger and Tom Imura. Baskerville stood and moved into a flanking position; and immediately Bones pulled away from Rags and did the same on the far side of the group. It was still eight to four, but the defeat was clear in the eyes of everyone there.

Mama Rat began pulling weapons from her pockets. Knives, a hatchet, a surgeon's scalpel. They clattered to the ground.

Then the others began doing the same. The catch-poles with their loops fell first, then knives and wrenches and other things. Rags saw a pair of nunchakus and a small pistol. She guessed it was out of ammunition or the man would have pulled it.

Baskerville padded over to the pile of weapons, hoisted a leg, and peed on it.

Everyone watched.

Joe Ledger was the only person who smiled.

"Tom—?" he said, and waited as the sad-faced swordsman moved among the men and patted them down, doing it exactly the way cops did on TV. Very quick, very thorough. "Be mighty sad if he finds something one of you idiots was trying to hide," observed Ledger.

One of the men cleared his throat, held up a hand, palm outward, and with two fingers of the other hand slipped a push-dagger from a concealed pocket. Tom got up in his face and took it from him. Their eyes locked and held until the skull-rider couldn't do it anymore and dropped his gaze.

For a moment Rags thought Tom was going to do something. His whole body trembled with potential, but instead he shook his head and finished patting down the men. When he was done he walked over to Mama Rat, who immediately laced her fingers together and placed them on the top of her head. She closed her eyes while Tom patted her down, but snapped them open again when the young man removed something from her jeans pocket.

"Hey!" she said, making a grab for it. "That's not a—"

Tom slapped her hand away and backed up. He showed the item to Ledger, but Rags could see it too. It was a silver locket with a broken chain. Tom opened it and stared at the picture, then held it out.

Rags saw the picture inside. It was a girl of about seven. Very pretty, with a pair of braided brown pigtails.

"That's mine," insisted Mama Rat. "Please—"

"Who's she?" asked Rags. "Is that your daughter?"

Mama Rat could not meet her eyes. She turned her head and looked at the nothingness down the empty street.

"Is it?"

"Yes."

"Did . . . did the dead people get her?"

Mama Rat shook her head.

"Where is she?" asked Tom.

It clearly cost Mama Rat to answer that. "Back . . . back at our camp."

Tom made a sick sound.

Ledger asked, "She's safe there, isn't she?"

Mama Rat nodded.

"Are there other kids there too?" Ledger demanded.

A nod.

"Kids who you people keep *safe*?" the big man growled.

Nod.

"And you bring kids like me back there?" asked Rags. "Not to keep us safe?"

No nod this time, but Rags could read the truth in the woman's eyes.

"Why?" asked Rags. "I mean . . . *how* can you be someone's mom and do that stuff to other kids? How can you be someone's mom and a monster at the same time?"

Mama Rat's knees buckled, and she sank slowly to the ground.

In that moment, Rags wanted to kill this woman herself. She could feel the need to destroy bursting like fireworks in her chest, behind her eyes. Her fists contracted into tight balls of bone and gristle and she wanted, needed, *ached* to kill. To slaughter. To destroy. Mama Rat and anyone like her. She could understand what made a person into a cold killer like Captain Ledger. She could understand what turned a gentle man like Tom Imura into the kind of person who could do the things he'd clearly done. She told herself that it wouldn't be murder. It would be no different from killing a scorpion that got into the house. Or a rattlesnake.

Bones and Baskerville seemed to feel her rage, and they both threw back their heads and let loose with howls as grim and loud as any wolf had ever thrown at a hunter's moon.

Rags held out her hand to Tom, and he gave her the locket. This tore a small cry from Mama Rat, and the woman made a half movement forward as if she wanted to grab it and take it back. But Rags stared her down, and the woman seemed to collapse back into herself.

The little girl in the picture was smiling.

No one else was.

"What's her name?" asked Rags.

"Caitlyn."

"It's a pretty name."

Mama Rat nodded.

"Did you have any other kids?"

"No."

"Where's Caitlyn's dad?"

"He left," said Mama Rat. "Long ago. Before."

"So it's you and her?"

A nod.

Rags showed her the picture, holding it up as if the little girl could see her mother through it. "Does she know what you do to people?"

No answer.

"Does she?"

"No."

"No," agreed Rags. "What do you think she'd say if she knew?"

No answer. Rags caught the glance Tom and Ledger shared between them. Ledger was about to say something, but Tom shook his head. They waited, letting Rags own this moment.

"I know what she'd say."

"You don't even know her."

Rags shrugged. "How's that matter?"

No answer.

"What would she say?" asked Tom.

Rags still held the locket out. "She'd hate you," she said to Mama Rat. "She'd hate you and she'd run away."

A breath of wind swept down the street, and it made the locket sway on its broken chain. It blew some of the stink of the dead skunk away. And it carried a distant sound, something that made everyone look. Both dogs growled softly. The sound was a moan.

Not one voice. Many.

Although she couldn't see them yet, Rags knew that the dead were coming.

The dead always came.

"We're drawing a crowd," said Ledger. "Put a button on this, kid, and let's get out of here."

Rags nodded. "I can't make you promise that you'll stop doing this stuff. I don't think I'd believe you even if you did promise. You're a monster. So are your friends. Monsters. Maybe you like being monsters. You seem to, and that's sick. It's sad and it's sick."

No one spoke.

The wind carried the hungry cries of the dead.

"I'm just a kid," said Rags, "so you probably don't care anything about me or what I have to say. Maybe I'm wasting my breath. Maybe I'm being stupid and naive. I don't know. I hope not, because I really don't want these two men and their dogs to kill you. They would, you know. If I hadn't asked them not to. If I wasn't here. They'd kill you." Rags shook her head. "Maybe even now, if I asked them to do it, they'd kill all of you. You can see that they would. That they could. They're killers."

Tom sighed again.

"But there's a difference," said Rags. "They're killers, but they're not monsters."

She went over and handed the locket back to Mama Rat.

"Maybe you can stop being monsters too."

Rags had to wait a long time before Mama Rat took

the locket back. The woman's hands were shaking as she wrapped them both around the locket, but Rags didn't immediately let go of the chain. The brief tug-of-war forced the woman to meet Rags's eyes.

"My family used to go to church," said Rags. "When my family was alive. When there was a world. Every Sunday we'd dress up nice and go. Since all this started, I think I stopped believing in God for a while. Not sure I believe even now. It's hard to believe in anything when everything is dying."

As if in agreement, the dead moaned louder.

They were in sight now. A dozen of them, shambling through the park, coming from different directions. Not dangerously close yet, but coming. Definitely coming.

"One of the stories I remember from church," continued Rags, "is the one about Cain and Abel. You know that one? Everyone does. They were brothers, and I forget why they had a fight, but Cain killed Abel. Bashed his head in. I guess that means Cain invented murder. When I first heard that story, I thought that it was going to end with God killing Cain. Like for punishment, you know? But he didn't. He let Cain live. Cain's pretty much the ancestor of everyone else. That's crazy when you think about it. Cain, the guy who committed the first murder, is the one ancestor we all share. You're white, I'm black, Tom's an Asian guy—but we all go back to Cain."

The moans of the dead floated on the breeze.

"Do you know what God did?" said Rags. "He told everyone that they weren't allowed to kill Cain. He made it a sin to do that. And he put a mark on Cain so that everyone would know who he was. They'd know, and they'd have to let him live. I never understood that story before." Rags let go of the chain. "Now I think maybe I do."

She reached out and touched the skull tattoo on Mama Rat's chest.

"Anyone who looks at you can see the same mark."

Mama Rat touched the tattoo as well, and for a brief moment their fingers touched. Something passed between them, like a static shock. Rags felt it, and she knew that Mama Rat did too.

"We're supposed to survive this, you know," said Rags, stepping back. "This plague, all this disease and stuff. We're supposed to survive it."

"How . . . how do you know that?"

Rags thought about it, then shrugged and shook her head.

"Because we're still alive. That has to mean something."

"What if it doesn't mean anything?" asked Mama Rat, clutching the locket to her breast. "What if none of this means anything?"

Rags shrugged again. "No. What if it does?"

With that she turned away. The dead were coming closer.

Captain Ledger and Tom stepped back and glanced at each other. Then they turned away too. The dogs were the last to leave.

The two men, the girl, and the two big dogs walked together along the street. Away from the dead, and away from the eight monsters who stood together near their pile of discarded weapons.

10

That night they camped on the top floor of an office building. Tom stayed with Rags while Ledger and the dogs cleared the building, checking for the dead. When it was clear, they went up to the fifth floor and found an office that had two couches and big windows. They made a cooking fire in a metal trash can, and Ledger produced cans of Spam from his pack. They ate in silence. In fact, none of them had spoken a word since they'd left Mama Rat.

When they were done eating, they sat on the couches and watched the sunset. Bones laid his big head on Rags's lap. Baskerville, free of his spiked and bladed armor, crawled under a big desk and began snoring.

It was Tom who broke the silence. "What you did back there?" he began, his voice soft. "What you said? That was very brave."

"Brave?" said Rags, surprised.

"Oh yeah," agreed Ledger. "You're something else, kid."

Rags shrugged.

"Want to tell us about your family?" asked Tom.

She shook her head.

They nodded.

The sun set and the stars came out. With no lights in the city, there were ten billion jewels in the nighttime sky. They sat and watched them and said nothing.

Finally Tom said, "Do you want to come with us? There's a small town out near Yosemite. It's an old reservoir, but we're building a fence and planting some crops. We have about a thousand people now. More coming in all the time. You'd be welcome. You'd be safe."

Instead of answering, Rags asked, "What do you think she'll do?"

"Mama Rat?" asked Ledger. Then he shrugged. "I know you'd like to believe that she and her crew are going to have a change of heart and devote the rest of their lives to good works. But . . ."

He let the rest hang.

"If she hurts another kid," said Rags, "is that on me? Will that be my fault?"

"Ooh," said Ledger, wincing, "that is one tough philosophical question."

"No," said Tom, "it's not. You're asking if mercy is wrong if the person who receives it goes out and does something wrong again."

"I guess I am," said Rags. "I've been sitting here thinking about it and wondering if I did something stupid or wrong."

The men gave it serious thought. They all did, and Ledger surprised her by being the first to answer. "No," he said. "If mercy's the wrong choice, then how screwed are we as a species?"

"But you'd have killed them," said Rags.

"Yes, I would have," he admitted. "And I still wish I had."

"But—"

"But that doesn't make me right. And showing mercy to a monster doesn't make you wrong."

She shook her head. "I don't really understand it."

Tom smiled for the first time. A sad and wistful smile. "Who ever does?" He leaned over and patted Rags on the knee. "But I have to tell you, the difference between what I would have done, and what Joe would have done, and what you did, is simple. And it's important. Maybe more important than anything. Maybe more important than mercy itself."

She studied his dark eyes, waiting.

"What you did was based on hope."

"Hope," she echoed.

"If we give up hope, then this world really will belong to the monsters and the dead." He smiled again. "And I thank you for that."

Ledger looked thoughtfully at Tom, then nodded to Rags. "Yeah. That says it. Hope." He grinned and shook his head. "In this day and age, who'd have thought there was any of that left?"

"Hope," Rags said again.

They watched the moon rise.

"You didn't answer my question," said Tom. "About coming back with us to Mountainside."

"I . . . don't know."

"What's your alternative?" asked Ledger.

She rose and walked to the window. "Does anyone know what's happening out there? In the rest of the world, I mean?"

"The plague is everywhere," said Ledger.

"That doesn't mean everyone's dead," said Rags. "We're not."

"No," agreed Tom. "We're not."

"I . . . ," she began, then faltered. She drew in a breath. "I think I want to go find out. I think I want to go and see what's out there. There has to be something. Who knows, maybe someone's trying to put it all back together. I need to find out. I want to find out."

"Alone?" said Tom, alarmed. "It's too dangerous."

Ledger leaned forward and rested his elbows on his knees. "She won't be alone."

"You're going with her?"

"Maybe I will," said the ranger. "Me, and a couple of flea-bitten mutts I happen to know."

Rags turned and stared at him. "Really?"

"Sure. Why not?"

"But . . . why?"

Ledger stood up and joined her at the window. "Because until today I'd given up hope too. I thought it was a sucker's game. Now . . . well, now I'm not so sure."

"Because of me?"

"Sure, kid. Why not?"

"I'm just a kid."

"So? Who ever said kids can't change things? Change people. Change minds." Ledger bent and kissed her on the forehead. "Who knows, you and me—? Maybe we'll go change the whole world." He laughed.

And Rags, despite everything, laughed too.

Bones jumped up and pushed between them, offering his head to whoever would pet it. They both did. After a moment, Baskerville joined them.

Only Tom sat apart, still on the couch, still wearing the same sad smile.

"Hope," he said, tasting the word.

"Hope," said Ledger, nodding.

"Hope," agreed Rags.

Above the city, the moon burned as bright as a promise.

And the night, like all nights, passed.

FROM NIX'S JOURNAL

ON DISCOVERING YOUR OWN PATH
(BEFORE *FLESH & BONE*)

Benny and I fight a lot.

I mean . . . a lot.

We love each other, but we don't always love everything about each other.

We want to be together, but we don't want the same things out of life. I know that, and he knows it . . . even if we don't always talk about it.

If this was a fairy tale, he'd be my Prince Charming and we'd live happily ever after.

If this was one of the epic fantasy stories Benny reads, then I'd be his princess and we'd live happily ever after.

Neither of us are those things. Not to ourselves and not to each other, so . . .

I don't know if happily ever after is a real thing.

Neither of us know if we're going to like the people each other becomes.

If so, we'll have to fall in love again and again as we change.

If not, I think we love each other enough as friends to stay friends.

But even that's not written in stone, is it?

PART THREE

ADRIFT IN THE ROT AND RUIN

Stay Calm and Be Warrior Smart!

In the Land of the Dead

The Fence

(Between the events of *Rot & Ruin* and *Dust & Decay*)

The teenager sat on a folding chair and stared through the fence at the zombie.

He was there most mornings. Sometimes in the afternoons, too.

At first the fence guards tried to chase him away.

"What the heck are you doing there, kid?" growled one, a new guard who didn't know who the boy was. The guard had come along the fence, a shotgun open at the breech crooked over one arm, a wad of pink chewing gum in his open mouth. When the kid did not move or even look at him, the guard came and stood right in front of him, blocking out the sun, blocking eye contact with the dead thing on the other side of the chain-link wall. "Hey? You deaf or dead?" the guard demanded.

Only then did the teenager raise his eyes to the big guard with the polished steel shotgun. He had dark-green eyes and brown hair, and the sunlight revealed streaks of red in his dark hair. A good-looking kid, fit and lean; the kind of kid the guard thought should be fishing for trout up at the stream or trying to lay some lumber on a breaking ball down at McGoran Field. He didn't look like the morbid kind of teen he sometimes met here at the fence; the kind who dressed in rags and painted their faces gray and pretended to be zoms.

The Gonnz, they called themselves. No, this kid looked like any other teenager from town.

"You okay?" the guard asked, his tone still sharp.

The teen did not say a word. He simply stared into the guard's eyes.

"You got to be careful around zoms, kid. They bite."

Something flicked through the kid's eyes; an emotion or reaction that the guard could not identify.

The guard was tough, big-chested and unshaven, a former trade route rider who had recently moved to Mountainside from Haven. The guard was used to staring down other people. He was that kind of man. He'd been out in the Ruin, he'd fought zoms, killed more than a few. No boy had ever stared him down, not even when the guard had *been* a boy. He met the boy's stare and stood his ground.

But it was the guard whose eyes broke contact first and slid away.

Before he did, the man's stern face changed, the harsh lines of his scowl softening into an uncertain frown. As he broke eye contact, he tried to hide it by pretending to turn and look at the zombie the kid had been staring at.

"What's so special about this one?" demanded the guard. "You know her?"

The zombie was dressed in the tattered rags of a party dress. Most people who worked the fence or ran the trade routes were pretty good at guessing how old a person had been before they'd zommed out, and this one looked to have been forty or fifty. A middle-aged woman dressed for some event. Maybe a graduation, maybe a wedding. The relentless California suns and fourteen brutal winters had bleached her rags to a paleness in which only the ghosts of wildflowers could still be seen. The dress must have been vibrant and pretty once. Expensive, too.

The guard turned back to the kid on the chair.

"Who was she?" he asked, and much of the gruffness was gone from his voice. He suddenly thought he knew, and he didn't want to know. "She your mom, kid?"

The teenager stood up and moved his chair a few feet to the left so that he had a clear view of the dead woman in the party dress.

"Hey," said the guard. "Did you hear me? I asked—"

"No," said the kid. "She's not my mother."

The guard's frown deepened. "Aunt?"

"No."

"Someone from your family—?"

"I don't know her," said the teen.

The guard looked from the boy to the zom and back again.

"Then what's she to you?"

The teen didn't answer. He sat down on his chair and rested his elbows on his thighs and looked through the fence. The zombie in the faded party dress shuffled clumsily through the tall grass, ignoring the guard and turning her dusty eyes on the boy. She stopped a foot from the fence; her arms hung limply at her sides, fingers twitching every once in a while. Her mouth opened and closed as if trying to speak. Or chewing on some imagined meal.

"Jeez, kid . . . haven't you ever seen a zom before?" asked the guard.

The teenager nodded. "One or two."

"So, what's the fascination?"

The boy almost smiled. "You wouldn't understand."

Minutes passed slowly. Flies crawled over the zombie's face. Sun-drowsy bees droned by, looking for flowers in the shade of the guard tower a hundred yards along the fence line. Five crows settled on the top bar of the fence and cawed to one another in their own ancient language.

The boy and the zombie stared at each other as if the guard, the fence, and the rest of the world did not exist.

"You shouldn't be out here," the guard said. "Ain't safe."

After a long, thoughtful moment, the teen said, "I know."

"There's been a lot of trouble lately, and not just with the zoms."

The teen nodded.

"Bunch of bounty hunters got themselves killed up in the hills last month."

Another nod.

"Charlie Pink-eye and the Motor City Hammer. Their whole crew. Got ambushed. Someone killed the whole bunch of them."

"Yes," said the boy. "I heard."

"If you heard, then you know it ain't safe out there. Weird stuff happening out in the Ruin, too. Zoms are all stirred up. People been seeing stuff. Wild animals and such, stuff nobody's seen for years, and I'm not talking about wolves and bears. There's talk about animals out of old zoos and circuses from before First Night. Tigers and lions and—"

The boy took a breath and exhaled it slowly and audibly.

He turned to look at the guard. "Is there a town law about sitting here?"

"Probably," the guard said bluntly. "Especially for underage—"

"I'm not underage," said the boy. "I'm fifteen."

"Fifteen? Then how come you're here all the time? Shouldn't you be working, earning your ration dollars?"

Another ghost of a smile flitted over the teen's mouth. "I *am* working."

"Gimme a break. You're just loafing out here."

The teen shrugged.

"Okay," said the guard in a challenging tone, "what kind of job are you *working* at, sitting out here looking at zoms all day?"

The boy's eyes burned with green fire. Cold and distant. "I'm a zombie hunter," he said.

That made the guard laugh. "Oh really?"

"Really. An apprentice, but, yeah . . . that's what I do."

"*You're* a bounty hunter? That's what you're trying to tell me? That's what I'm supposed to believe?"

The teen shrugged. "Believe what you want."

The guard gave a big braying laugh. "And who are you supposed to be apprenticing to?"

The cold green eyes were steady and unblinking. "My brother," he said.

"Yeah? And who's your brother?"

"Tom Imura," said the boy.

The mocking grin froze on the guard's face, and then slowly, slowly, it drained away. The guard's eyes flicked from the teen to the red zone that separated the fence line and the broad green fields that flanked them from the town.

"Tom Imura?" echoed the guard in a small voice. "You're Tom Imura's kid brother . . . ?"

"Yes," said Benny Imura. "My brother told me to come down here. He told me to do what I'm doing. Do you want me to go tell him that you said I couldn't?"

It wasn't said as a threat. Benny never raised his voice, never changed his expression. The guard stood near him, looking down at him, his mouth now working silently in an unconscious parody of the zombie.

"I'd like to be left alone," said Benny. "If that's not breaking any rules."

"Um . . . no. No, that's fine," said the guard. He unconsciously backed away from Benny, and his beefy shoulders bumped lightly against the chain-link wall.

Instantly the zombie lunged at him, thrusting her withered fingers through the links, clawing at the guard's shirt, biting at the chain-links with rotted gray teeth.

The guard cried out in alarm and tried to simultaneously pull himself away and close the shotgun breech; but before he could do either, Benny was out of his chair. Benny grabbed the guard's shirt with both hands and yanked him forward, away from the fence, away from the twisting pale fingers. As the guard staggered forward, his weight crashed toward Benny, but the teenager pivoted his hips and shoved the guard away from him so that the man staggered several yards toward the red zone. The shotgun fell to the grass with a muffled thud.

The moment seemed to freeze in place. The guard lay shocked and wide-eyed on the ground near the shotgun; the zom stood erect and motionless, her hunting frenzy stilled with no prey to attack. Benny Imura stood between them, legs planted wide, arms wide, palms pointing calmingly out toward guard and zom.

The guard looked up at the teenager as Benny slowly lowered his arms.

"You have to be careful around them," said the boy. "They bite."

Then Benny offered his hand to the guard and helped him up. He didn't touch the fallen shotgun, leaving it to the guard. Once he was up and dusted off, the guard checked the shotgun barrels and gave Benny a long, considering glare.

"I ought to chase you the heck out of here," he said.

"Because zoms are dangerous?" asked Benny, and now there was definitely wry humor in his eyes. Humor and something else that the guard at first could not identify. Some bigger emotion.

"Yeah, yeah, very funny."

They regarded each other for half a minute of silence, and then the guard chuckled and smiled. A small, rueful smile. Benny's smile was slower in coming, and smaller. But it was there.

And it was then that the guard identified the other emotion that hid behind the kid's green eyes. It was sadness. A vast and terrible sadness.

"You were out there," said the guard quietly. "Weren't you?"

Benny nodded.

"In the Ruin?"

Another nod.

"With Tom? When all that stuff happened to Charlie and the Hammer?"

One more nod, slower than the others.

The guard cleared his throat. He glanced at the chair, which had fallen over when Benny rushed in to save him from the zom. Without another word, the guard bent to pick up the chair. He righted it, glanced at the fence and the zom, then moved the chair back about six inches.

Benny watched him do it.

"You, um . . . you can never be too careful," mumbled the guard. "You know?"

"Yeah," said Benny. "I know."

The fence guard stepped back and took a breath. He gave Benny a brief nod, and then turned and trudged along the fence line the way he'd come, his head lowered in troubled thought, shotgun crooked over his arm.

After a while, Benny sat down on his chair again and stared through the fence at the zombie.

The Quick
and the Dead

(Set directly before the events of *Dust & Decay*)

1

The bounty hunter's name was Solomon Jones. He was medium height, built like a wrestler, and bald as an egg, with chocolate-brown skin and a small goatee shot through with streaks of white. The handles of a pair of machetes rose above his shoulders from where they hung in slings across his back.

He crouched on the gnarled limb of an ancient elm, completely hidden by the deep shadows of the forest's leafy canopy.

Solomon had once been a writer in the days before First Night. Now he was sure that there was no one alive who knew him as anything but a bounty hunter. He was a killer of the dead. There were no publishing houses any-more, no bookstores. And the only printing presses—old hand-crank jobs—were used to make bounty flyers, Zombie Cards, pamphlets of town rules, and religious tracts. No one printed novels anymore. It was too costly, and besides, there were millions of them lying unused in empty houses, deserted stores, and warehouses. Traders brought them by the wagonload, and they were as valuable to the people in the towns as food and water. The books were escape hatches, doorways out of the apocalypse.

He wished that he had the time and opportunity to write. Not anymore. Now he hunted in the Rot and Ruin, working bounty jobs on the zoms, guarding trade wagons, taking the occasional clean-out job. It was physical work. Horrible work.

Killing the dead.

The concept was absurd. It was so wild he wouldn't have put it in one of his novels. His readers would have thought he'd gone nuts.

Killing the already killed.

There was no phrasing in English—or any other language—that permitted a statement like that to make sense.

And yet . . .

He crouched on the tree limb, watching a spectacle unfold below him that was more real than anything he had ever put on the page, and yet even after all these years he felt that it was *not* real. That it, and he, were fantasies in the fevered dream of some madman.

But the firmness of the limb under his feet was real. The sweat that trickled down the sides of his face was real. The weight of the weapons strapped across his back and holstered at his hip. All real.

As was the madness below.

Zoms.

Not one or two of them. Not even the rare pack of half a dozen. Below him, shambling along the grass-choked country road, or staggering through the brush on the verge, were dozens of them. Many dozens.

He had rarely seen so many of them at once, and never moving with such purpose, such apparent focus. But . . . why? They were not following any prey. The woodland road wound through the forest, fed by a larger road that came west through farmlands. Beyond those farms was the vastness of the Yosemite National Park, and beyond that . . . the rest of America. The rest of the Rot and Ruin.

These zoms were coming from the east.

Coming in packs. Flocking like decaying birds.

Heading west.

Heading toward the line of small towns that huddled against the protection of the Sierra Nevada Mountains, here in Mariposa County and farther north. The small towns in which lived virtually everyone who was still alive. The last of humanity. Twenty-eight thousand people, give or take. All that was left of seven billion.

For fourteen years the zombies had followed a simple pattern. They hunted what they saw, and when there was no prey, they simply stood still. Like rotting tombstones to mark the place of their death.

Why were these zoms on the move?

What was drawing them toward the towns? Surely they could not smell the living flesh so many miles away. That was impossible, even in an age of impossible things. And with the dense forest and towering mountains, the zoms could not see the towns. What was drawing them?

Solomon did not move as the horde of the dead passed below him. He could handle himself against a small pack. He'd done it. More than once. But this was an army of the dead.

What was drawing them?

As he chewed on that, another thought occurred to him. Another question. An ugly, terrible question, and he rose slightly and looked out over the tops of the trees that covered the mountain slope down toward the farmlands.

Perhaps the question was not what was drawing them. Perhaps it was more frightening than that.

Maybe it was . . .

"What's chasing them?" he murmured aloud.

Was there something out there in the east that was driving all these zoms westward?

If so . . . dear God, what could it be?

Solomon Jones tried to swallow, but his throat had gone dry. Below him the last of the zoms lurched past.

He waited five more minutes, and then he dropped to the ground, landing in a tense crouch, eyes cutting left and right, looking for stragglers.

But the forest had become deathly quiet.

There was a bounty job waiting to be finished, but that was up north. However, Solomon turned to the southwest. He had to tell someone about this. People had to know. The *right* people.

He nodded to himself and set out at a run through the forest.

Looking for Tom Imura.

2

Girls

(Mountainside)

Lou Chong wondered if throwing himself off the guard tower would be better than going home. If he jumped over the rail, the worst that could happen would be a crushing impact on the ground, after which he'd be devoured by zoms.

"You are a total chicken," observed Benny Imura, who was sitting on a wooden crate in the far corner of the tower.

"Obviously," agreed Chong. "What's your point?"

Benny shook his head. "Dude, it's so easy. She *lives* at your house. You see her every day. All you have to do is *say* something to her."

"Really," replied Chong as he folded his arms and leaned against the rail. "That's all I have to do. I go up to a girl who is a year older than me; a girl who has lived alone for years doing nothing but killing zombies and rogue bounty hunters; a girl who knows more ways to kill me than I know how to die; a girl who fought in the zombie pits at Gameland when she was eleven; a girl—I might add—who is skilled with every kind of lethal weapon from handguns to swords . . . you want me to go up to that girl and just ask her to the summer dance? That's what you think is easy?"

"Sure."

"So, I was right all along. You *are* brain dead."

"Hey, I—"

"I mean, are you trying to get me killed?"

"You have to admit that she's hot."

Chong cocked his head to one side. "No, I don't think 'hot' is really adequate, do you?"

"And we both know that she doesn't have a boyfriend."

"She's never had a boyfriend," corrected Chong. "Because she is a feral zombie killer. She's killed everyone who ever tried to get near her."

"She didn't kill me."

"Hope springs eternal," murmured Chong.

"What's the worst that could happen?" demanded Benny.

Chong began ticking items off on his fingers. "Being beaten viciously about the head and shoulders. Comprehensive humiliation. Thrusting of sharp objects through my flesh . . ."

Benny made loud clucking sounds.

Chong stared at him through narrowed eyes. "I said I was afraid of Lilah," he said evenly. "I never said I was afraid of you. In fact, some recreational Benny-maiming might take the edge off the day."

"Ha! I'm a professional zombie hunter now. My body is a weapon, my arms are spears, my legs are swords."

He faked a kick at Chong, but the motion knocked Benny off his crate, and he crashed down onto the tower floor.

"Yes, a living weapon. I see," observed Chong drily.

Benny came off the floor and tackled him, and they wrestled from one end of the guard tower to the other, making loud fighting sounds like they had in old comic books. *POW!* and *KRUNCH!*

Chong was pretending to bash Benny's head against the wall when the shift supervisor bellowed up at them in a leather-throated voice. "What the bloody 'ell you two monkey-bangers doing up there? Do I have to come up and teach you how to act like adults?"

"We're not adults," Benny yelled, but before the words could get out, Chong clamped a hand over his mouth. All that escaped was a muffled nothing.

"Sorry!" Chong called down through the ladder hole. "There . . . um . . . was a wasp up here, and we were trying to swat it and—"

"Yeah, yeah," growled the supervisor. "Whatever you two delinquents are doing—*don't*."

He stalked away, and the boys peered over the edge of the tower to watch him go.

"Thanks for getting me in trouble," complained Chong.

"Happy to help."

They got to their feet, and Chong dug a couple of apples out of his backpack, which hung on a wooden peg. He and Benny ate them noisily as they watched the cloud shadows sweep with dark majesty across the field of tall grass and silent zoms.

After a long time, Chong asked, "How are things with you and Nix?"

Benny took his time with that. "She's going through some stuff. Her mom. Getting kidnapped. The fight. She's . . ."

He let his words drift away with the clouds.

Beside him, Chong nodded. He had not been with Benny and Tom when the brothers had gone out hunting for the men who had murdered Nix's mother and kidnapped Nix. Chong had stayed in Mountainside and spent a lot of time with Morgie Mitchell, who had been badly injured trying to protect Nix. Morgie had a skull fracture and concussion and was unconscious for four long, terrible days. All that time, Chong sat beside Morgie's hospital bed and read to him. Adventure stories from old books. The Mortal Instruments, Harry Potter, *The Maze Runner*. Books Chong knew that Morgie liked.

The stories filled the still air of the hospital room, but Morgie slept through most of it, and when he finally woke up, he said that he couldn't remember anything from the last few days. All of it was a blank, he insisted.

Chong looked in Morgie's eyes when he asked if his friend truly did not remember the bounty hunters taking Nix. Morgie swore that he did not, but there was a frightened, furtive look in his eyes that made Chong wonder.

That was a few days ago, and the world seemed to have changed since then.

"Benny?" Chong asked after a few moments.

"Yeah."

"About Nix. You falling in love?"

Benny didn't answer. Chong nodded to himself.

A few minutes later, Benny asked, "Chong?"

"Uh-huh?"

"What about you and Lilah? You falling in love with her?"

Chong sighed. "I don't know."

"You think she likes you?"

"Not a chance."

They thought about that. "She's been alone most of her life," said Benny. "She only knows about people 'cause she's read a million books."

"I know. We talk about books all the time."

"There's a lot of romantic stuff in books."

"Uh-huh."

Benny said, "Learning about that stuff in books isn't the same as *knowing* it, you know that, right?"

"Not being actually stupid, yes."

"Give her time."

"Yeah." Chong cut a look at him. "Nix, too."

"Oh yeah."

They stood side by side and watched the late afternoon shadows creep out from under the trees, hiding one by one the hundreds of living dead who stood like silent sentinels in the field beyond the fence.

3
Swords
(The Imura house, next day)

Benny Imura screamed like a ten-year-old girl.

He dodged, too, and the sword missed him by inches. Then he froze as the affect-echo of his shriek rolled back to him after bouncing off the line of trees. He looked around at the faces. Nix Riley, Morgie Mitchell, Lilah, Tom, Chong. All staring at him.

"Wow," said Chong, "that was manly."

Benny flushed a brilliant crimson and brought his wooden sword up in a defensive posture.

"I didn't hit you," said Nix Riley, who stood five feet away, the tip of her wooden sword pointing to the grass between them. Her pretty, freckled face glowed with effort and intensity. The wooden bokken and the insanely fast and accurate way she handled it were totally at odds with her short stature and curly ponytail. "No need to cry."

"I am not crying," growled Benny. "That was my *kiai*."

"Your *kiai*," echoed Chong. A smile trembled on his lips. "That's the spirit shout that's supposed to strike fear into the hearts of your enemies. You're going with a little-girl scream?"

"It wasn't a scream," insisted Benny. "It was a high-pitched yell."

"Uh-huh," said Chong.

"A hunting call."

"Right," said Nix.

"Like eagles use."

"Sure," said Tom.

"It was a battle cry—"

"Dude," said Morgie, who sat on the bench, his shaved head still bandaged. "You screamed like a little girl. I'm kind of embarrassed to know you."

"No," said Lilah before Benny could reply. The Lost Girl, with her snow-white hair and feral eyes, stood leaning on her spear. "Not like a little girl."

"Ha!" declared Benny. "You see? I told you it was a—"

"It was like a pig," said Lilah.

Benny whirled toward her. "No, it wasn't—"

"A little pig," she said. "They squeal like that when you try to catch them."

Benny turned away from her and saw this information register on the faces of each of the others. Even Tom was losing the battle to hide a smile.

"It's a war cry," Benny said between gritted teeth.

"The war cry of a ferocious piglet," suggested Nix.

Benny raised his sword and waited for Nix to do the same.

Tom called, *"Hajime!"* The Japanese command to begin.

Instantly both wooden swords flashed out, and there was a sharp *klack!* as blade met blade. Nix attacked with a flurry of overhand and lateral cuts, and Benny shifted in a circle, taking many small steps in order to keep his feet balanced and in constant contact with the ground. The blades slithered and crunched and *tokked* over and over again as they moved.

Benny ignored Morgie's constant oinking sounds and the fake eagle cries from Chong.

Nix was incredibly good with a sword, even though she had been training only as long as Benny—five short weeks. Benny was a reasonably good athlete, but better at baseball and wrestling than swordplay. Nix was a natural, and in the instant after Tom started each match, her face underwent a change from the smiling, freckly girl who Benny loved to something *else*. Infinitely more intense, incredibly focused. And ferocious. Even though she lacked Lilah's years of experience, Nix was every bit as aggressive.

It impressed Benny.

But it also scared him.

Her attack never faltered. She never backed off. Her sword flashed and moved in a blur, and it was all Benny could do to defend himself. Tom had taught him how to deal with aggression: evade and protect, then look for a lull and attack. But Nix never paused; there was no lull.

Gradually the catcalls and jokes from the others faded as the duel went on. And on.

Benny lost count of how many strikes he blocked; and the only attacks he managed were weak counterattacks intended to prevent a combination. He gave ground constantly.

Then Benny saw something that absolutely chilled him. Something that almost made him forget to block.

It was Nix's mouth. Her lips.

As she fought, with every strike of her sword, her lips formed a word.

A name.

Charlie.

The name of the man who had killed Nix's mother.

Charlie Pink-eye.

With sickening clarity, Benny realized that Nix was not sparring with him; she wasn't playing. She was *fighting*.

There was a wildness in her green eyes that scared Benny. It pierced his heart with all the force of an arrow.

"Nix," he said, but his voice was lost in the sound of wood battering against wood. When he looked into her eyes, he was sure—absolutely positive—that Nix was not seeing him. Not a chance. She was somewhere else entirely. Maybe in her house on that horrible night, when nothing she could do was enough to save her mother. Or out in the Ruin as a helpless prisoner of Charlie, the Hammer, and their men. Or in the bounty hunters' camp during the battle. Nix had wanted to strike Charlie down herself, but events had gone a different way. Nix had been robbed of that moment.

Of that *closure*.

Benny's arms began to tremble from the effort of blocking the attacks, but Nix's blows were every bit as sure and strong.

Does she know? he wondered. *Where is her head right now?*

"Nix," he said again, louder, and he could hear concern and maybe even a little panic in his own voice.

The sword kept coming, faster and harder. Benny didn't dare risk anything but defense. If he tried to simply step back, Nix's bokken would crush his skull.

"Nix!" This time he shouted it.

Her mouth formed the hated name. Over and over again.

"Nix!"

There was a blur of movement and a flash of silver, and

Nix's sword suddenly jerked to a stop in mid-strike, the edge slamming to a stop against a metal pole.

With another sharp cry, Benny staggered back and fell hard on his butt.

He stared at the tableau.

Lilah stood between him and Nix, her spear held high and in a wide grip. Nix's sword had met the shaft of that spear and stopped there. And then Tom was there, stepping in quickly and gently to take the bokken from Nix's hands. Nix barely noticed either of them. Instead she stared at Benny, who sat splay-legged on the grass.

Across the yard, Chong and Morgie stared with open mouths and unblinking eyes, all jokes forgotten.

Nix's eyes blazed with weird lights for a heartbeat longer.

Then she blinked, instantly confused by what she was seeing, what she was doing.

"W-what—?" she murmured, as if someone had asked her a question. A half smile wavered on her lips. "What?"

Tom cleared his throat. "Okay," he said softly, "let's call it a day? Pie and iced tea?"

Nix turned and looked at her hands. They were flushed red from holding the sword with such force. Then she looked at Benny, who still sat on the grass.

"I'm . . ." But that was all she got out; her face immediately crumpled into a wince of pain as the first heavy sobs broke from her chest. She whirled and ran out of the yard and up the path toward town.

Benny flung his sword away and scrambled to his feet to run after her, but Tom blocked him with a hand to his chest.

"Don't," he said.

"I have to," insisted Benny.

"What's going on?" demanded Morgie, getting heavily to his feet. Chong did too, and even though he said nothing, his intelligent eyes were cutting from Benny to Tom to Nix's diminishing figure.

Benny pushed Tom's hand away and headed for the gate, but Lilah moved faster. She thrust her spear into Benny's hand, vaulted the rail like a gazelle, and raced after Nix faster than Benny ever could.

"Hey!" Benny yelled.

Tom rested his hand on Benny's shoulder. "No, kiddo. Let them go."

Morgie and Chong came up to stand with them, and the four of them watched the figures dwindle in the distance.

"What's going on?" Morgie asked again, but there was less force in his question this time. When Benny glanced at him, he saw understanding blossoming in his friend's eyes. Chong was already there.

They watched the road for a long time, even though there was nothing to see.

Chong said, "On First Night, everybody saw someone they love die."

Tom nodded.

"That's why the whole town is like the way it is, isn't it?"

"Yes," said Tom. "They used to call it post-traumatic stress disorder. Now . . . it's just the way things are. Everyone has been damaged by grief, and most people think there's no escape."

"Is there?" asked Benny.

Tom sighed. "For my generation? I don't know. Maybe not. Most of the adults have given up hope."

"I meant . . . for Nix," said Benny. "Is she always going to be like this? I mean . . . it wasn't zoms who killed her mom. It was Charlie, and he's dead."

"I don't know," said Tom. "Everything in this town reminds Nix of her mom. Everything always will."

"That's why she wants to leave," said Morgie, and they all turned to look at him. "I know she says it's 'cause she wants to find that plane you guys saw, but that ain't it. She don't want to be *here* anymore. I don't think she can be here."

The comment was so unlike Morgie that they all stared at him. Morgie scratched at the edge of his bandage and kept looking down the road. After a while, Tom nodded.

"I know exactly how she feels," he said, and without further comment walked slowly back to the house.

The three boys stood at the wooden fence for long minutes.

"This is all going to change," murmured Morgie. "Ain't it?"

Benny and Chong didn't look at him.

"Nix. Tom. Us. All of it's over, ain't it?"

Chong opened the garden gate. "I'd better get home. I have work in the morning."

They watched him walk along the path under the summer trees.

After a moment, Morgie sighed and followed.

Benny Imura stood at the open fence, pulled in so many directions at once that all he could do was stand there.

Then he turned around, crossed the yard, and picked up his sword. The handle was cool from lying in the grass, and he adjusted his hold on it, feeling the balance.

He went over to the old car tire Tom had hung on a rope

from a tree. When he was little he'd swung on that tire, but he wasn't that little kid anymore.

With a whistle and thud he swung the sword and hit the tire. It was an awkward hit, poorly executed because his arms ached and his mind was splintered. He stepped back, took a breath, and swung again.

A more solid hit this time, but still not right.

He swung again. And again. Not letting up, not dropping the sword even when the ache in his arms turned to fire. He couldn't. To do that would allow him to be weak; it would keep his skills at too low a level. And he could not afford that. He could not risk that.

As much as he hated the thought, Benny Imura knew for sure that he would need to use that sword the right way. The *real* way. The way a fighter would. The way a zombie hunter would.

And . . . he would probably need it soon. The world seemed to be spinning him in that direction.

As he struck and struck and struck, he did not mouth the name of their enemy. He did not say "Charlie." Instead Benny mouthed a different word. One that tapped a different source of power than the well of hate from which Nix drank. He struck and struck and struck for what he thought and hoped was a better purpose. A cleaner one.

"Nix," he breathed, as he trained to fight the monsters he knew lived in his world. "Nix."

It put power into every single blow.

FROM NIX'S JOURNAL

ON BEING
WHO WE ARE
(BEFORE *FIRE & ASH*)

Benny isn't like he used to be.

I know I'm not.

Chong's changing too. Since we've come out to the Ruin, he's gotten tougher. But also more afraid. It's weird, because both things seem to be happening at the same time in him.

Even Lilah's changing. She used to be so sure about everything. I guess living alone for so long and having no one to answer to will do that. Now she's part of us, and she's part of a couple. Her and Chong. And she's part of a quest.

And we're all Tom's samurai. Even with

him gone. Or maybe more so because he's gone.

We're all changing into something else.

It's scary.

But I like it.

Hero Town

1

Then

New York City
(On First Night, fourteen years before Rot & Ruin)

Rachael Elle was a superhero.

Except when she was an elf queen.

Or when she was a sociopathic assassin clone.

Rachael was a lot of people.

Sixty-two people so far, with more planned.

Her friends included Star Wars stormtroopers, the many incarnations of Doctor Who and all his companions, tragic princesses from politically unstable fantasy lands, Jedi and Sith warriors, various members of the Avengers, the Justice League, the X-Men, the Guardians of the Galaxy, the crew of *Serenity*, the bridge crew of the *Enterprise*, hobbits, wizards, and at least one member each from Gryffindor, Slytherin, Hufflepuff, and Ravenclaw.

She had interesting friends.

Currently Rachael was dressed in skintight dark-blue trousers, a snug jacket, gun belt, and fingerless gloves. Her dark hair was pulled back into a severe ponytail, and there was a wicked cut on her cheek and another above her eye. Leftovers from when a mind-controlled Hawkeye invaded the SHIELD Helicarrier to free Loki.

Today Rachael was not Rachael. She was Maria Hill, a SHIELD agent and staunch supporter of freedom despite the constant and insidious threat of HYDRA.

Or she would be Maria Hill if she could get the grommet tool to work right so she could attach the holster to the leather gun belt. The holster, the belt, and the rest of the outfit had been made by her over many nights of painstaking research, design, materials shopping, measuring, cutting, and sewing. It was the eleventh of twelve outfits she had brought with her to New York for the big Comic Con at the Javits Center. The costumes hung on reinforced hangers that filled the closet in the small hotel room. Accessories were piled on both of the room's twin beds or arranged in careful groupings on the floor. Rachael stood in front of the mirror and studied her costume. The fit, the colors, the match between her version and the one worn by the actress in the Avengers movies and the SHIELD TV show. She rather thought hers was better. Cobie Smulders, though very pretty, was rail-thin. Rachael had a better figure and more muscle. She knew she rocked the costume. Brett, the nineteen-year-old who was going to be Thor for most of the weekend—styles from two different movie costumes, and four variations from the comics—would appreciate it, she was certain.

She certainly liked the way he fit his Asgardian clothes. He was tall, tan, and had a face a true Norse god would kill for, blue eyes that could stop the sun in the sky, and shoulder-length hair that wasn't a wig. He was Thor.

So, yes, Rachael wanted Brett to appreciate more than

her costume-making skills. She'd caught him looking, especially when she wore something tight or low-cut. When they went as Peeta and Katniss, he really paid attention to her. Working his role as her "boyfriend," at least in cosplay terms. Though frankly Rachael wasn't sure that it was just acting, that maybe Brett wasn't just role-playing his interest.

She certainly wasn't.

The age thing was the only real question. She would be seventeen in four weeks. Brett, like most of the guys in school, tended to focus on "older" women. Older as in college freshmen. As if two years made that much of a difference. Please.

Of course it didn't help at all when Gayla came to one of these conventions. Gayla was nineteen, and she always wore costumes that were more shock than style. Daenerys from *Game of Thrones*—one of her skimpier costumes. Or Power Girl, with the skintight white onesie with the huge cutout for cleavage. Or slave-girl Princess Leia. It was repulsive. Gayla was half-naked most of the time, and sure, she had a very nice figure, but everyone knew she wasn't born with those boobs. She went from a small B cup to whatever the heck you'd call those science-fiction plastic bowling balls she had now. That happened last summer, right after she graduated. She went away with a normal chest and came back looking like a Barbie doll. Brett and most of the other guys lost their damn minds.

They were plastic! They weren't real. What did it matter?

Rachael was real, head to toe. In this costume, Brett would absolutely be able to see that. And she was no stick figure herself. If Brett was able to grasp real from fake, then the choice would be obvious.

Rachael nodded to herself and unzipped her jacket a bit to show some cleavage.

Then she growled out loud and zipped it up most of the way, immediately disgusted with herself. She had never really been the kind to flaunt her curves to attract a boy, and hated that she was starting to head in that direction now.

"What are you doing?" she demanded of her reflection.

The image of Gayla seemed to wander through her imagination, barely dressed, with a love-struck Brett staggering along behind. Rachael's fingers lingered on the zipper pull. Maybe just a little . . .

"You are such a pig," she told herself. Or maybe she was talking to Brett.

Or Gayla.

She turned away, shaking her head, and went back to sit on the edge of the bed to continue working on the belt.

Across the room, on the big-screen TV, the reporter on CNN was telling some crazy story about a riot in Pittsburgh. People acting all weird, attacking one another. Biting one another.

"Everyone's insane," she told the screen.

The aerial video footage of a riot played out, but Rachael bent to her work and was soon lost in the detail-oriented task of working with grommets and leather and all the costumer's tools.

Like most people around the world, she did not pay much attention to these first reports.

Like most people, she should have.

2

Now

Doylestown, Pennsylvania
(This story takes place at the same time as Rot & Ruin*)*

Rags kept to the shadows as she moved along the road.

In the fifteen years since the dead rose, Mother Nature had been ferocious in her determination to reclaim the world. Most of the streets had been torn apart by the slow fingers of roots. Young trees rose above seas of pernicious weeds. Heavy, hairy vines clung to the sides of the trees like lampreys on the skin of sharks. Kudzu, once alien to America, now dominated the landscape, obscuring the facades of most stores and homes and covering many of the cars in green blankets. By day these streets ran with wild deer, foxes, horses, and packs of feral dogs. By night bears and wolves prowled the alleys and backyards, watched by owls and feared by everything.

Beside her, Ghoulie trotted along, sniffing everything, eyes alert, ears up. Like his father—Rags's old and much-missed friend, Bones—Ghoulie was a brute. He had the mixed shepherd–Irish wolfhound bulk and general shape of Bones; but he also had the heavier shoulders and broader snout of his mastiff mother. Rags estimated that Ghoulie was about two hundred pounds, slightly less than twice her weight. He wore a leather harness studded with rows of sixteen-penny nails that stood up like porcupine quills. Ghoulie had a bite-proof leather-and-plastic helmet that Rags had made from a jockey's helmet she'd taken from an abandoned racetrack in Kentucky.

The leather armor creaked a little as Ghoulie went sniffing along, but the sound was nearly lost beneath the continuous pulse of crickets and cicadas.

For her part, Rags wore jeans and a leather jacket, hiking boots and fingerless kickboxing gloves she'd taken from a sporting goods store in South Carolina and reinforced with small pieces of very hard plastic. Lightweight and strong. Her football helmet hung from her belt, ready to grab and put on if she encountered any of the dead. She made no sound at all as she walked. She'd learned that skill long ago. Captain Ledger was occasionally a jerk when it came to reinforcing his rules of safety, but Rags knew that she was alive because of him. She knew that she had survived a thousand instances when she would otherwise have died had it not been for the training he'd given her. Four years of it. Every single day that they'd traveled together. No days off.

"Will the dead take a day off?" he asked every time she complained.

"No," was her grudging, inevitable answer.

"Then you can't either. Not if you want to stay out here. Maybe if you went to Mountainside with that kid, Imura. Sure, behind fences you can take five. Or down in Asheville, in the new towns. But out here? Nope. You train, you prepare, you don't let up and don't lighten up and that way you . . . what?"

"You get to stay alive," she replied.

"Yeah you do."

It was a conversation they had so many times in a hundred different ways.

So, she was careful. Always. And in all ways.

She missed Ledger, though. Every night since he'd left to try to build a team of rangers, she wondered where he was, what he was doing, and if he was still alive.

Probably still alive, she generally concluded. Joe Ledger was a very hard man to kill.

Joe had taken Bones's older brother, Baskerville, with him, as well as Freya, the full-blood American mastiff mother of Ghoulie. Three hunters traveling in a pack, and one perhaps more of an animal than the other two.

The last time she saw them was nine years ago. Since then the world had grown quieter, older, less civilized, and far stranger.

Since then, Rags had crossed the country in a long, unplanned zigzag pattern, with no specific destination ever in mind. Going where the wind blew her was how she thought about it. Taking the road less traveled, in all the ways that phrase could be defined.

The years were long, and although sometimes she was completely content to share her life only with dogs—first Bones, then Ghoulie—she often wondered if she should turn and go back to the west. To find Ledger and maybe that other man, Tom Imura. To find people.

The dead were the poorest of company, and as the months crawled by, Rags became more disillusioned by talking to herself or imagining conversations in her head. She craved a simple conversation. She longed to belong somewhere. That hadn't been the case when she and Ledger parted company, but it was now. She was lonely, and the world had become so empty and so quiet. There weren't enough things to shelter her from her increasingly depressing thoughts.

One of which was the nagging question she so often asked herself.

Why?

Why keep going? Why keep fighting?

Why stay alive?

Why, why, why?

The more she asked herself those questions, the less often she could construct an answer. And over time, even the lies she told herself wore thin.

What terrified her most was the thought that staying alive had become nothing more than a habit. That was it. A reflex action without further or deeper purpose.

At night she dreamed about her family, lost to the plague all those years ago. She dreamed that they waited for her on the other side of a thin veil. All it would take to be with them again, to be happy again, to be needed and loved again, would be to cut through the veil. Ledger had taught her how to kill in a hundred different ways, and some of those ways could be applied to her own skin, her own veins, her own heart.

There were times when the presence of Ghoulie—of another beating heart a few feet away—was all that tethered her to the world on this side of the veil. With every day, with every endless night, that tether was fraying. She knew that someday it would snap.

Or she would cut it.

That day used to be far, far off.

Now, though . . .

Now she moved through the days and along the miles,

and she tried not to cry. She tried not to beg for someone or something to take her away.

Or to give her a reason to stay.

Her path led nowhere in particular. Today it brought her along a creek and down some overgrown roads and into a fence made of stout timbers that was set across the blacktop at the entrance to a town.

There was a sign.

DOYLESTOWN, PENNSYLVANIA

Once upon a time a population count had been painted in the lower left, but someone had scratched it out with real passion so that the board beneath was scored and splintered.

It was a small town north of Philadelphia and south of New York. Neither of those cities was ever on her list of possible destinations. Philadelphia was a radioactive hole in the ground. It had been one of the first cities nuked in the government's failed attempt to contain the spread of the zombies. Dumb.

New York, on the other hand, was a different case altogether. Rags had met a few travelers who had been there. Something had happened there. Or many weird things.

The stories were so strange and often contradictory, and she had never once met anyone who'd been there who was also sane enough to give a story Rags could believe. Worse things than zombies, the survivors all told. Worse things . . . but exactly what these horrors were, the survivors either could not or would not tell her.

Even though Rags told Ghoulie that they were never, ever going to go to such a place, their path seemed to be drifting in that direction.

Pure accident, of course. Nothing intended.

She told the dog that a lot.

Ghoulie did not appear to believe her, but being a dog, was unable to say so.

Her self-respect was comforted by the fact that at least they were not heading toward that city with anything approaching haste. Rags did not believe in haste. She had no use for it except in crisis moments, and she was smart enough to avoid most threats. So, without hurrying, she wandered through the years of her life.

There was a door in the fence, and it stood ajar.

Another place that had been fortified against the dead and whose defenses had either been abandoned or had failed.

Moving with great caution, Rags passed through the gate and walked along the empty road toward the town. Ghoulie trotted beside her, looking right and left to study the overgrown foliage that flanked the road.

They stopped at an intersection and spent some time on the porch of an old hotel. The front corner of the hotel had been a Starbucks once, but now it was home to rats that made their nests among piles of bones.

The streets were quiet and empty. The sun hung low in the west, casting deep shadows across the street, bathing nearly everything in purple darkness. The crickets had begun their concert early tonight, anticipating the quick twilight of late autumn. Somewhere off to her left a bull-frog croaked in a pond created by collapsed sewer pipes and seasonal flooding. Farther along the side street, a doe and two fawns foraged among wild bushes that flourished in the cracked asphalt.

That was good. Deer were as good a warning system as birds and crickets for signaling the presence of danger. The deer fled and the natural noisemakers fell silent in the presence of the dead. Deer also hightailed it away from dog packs, wolf packs, and hunting packs of the big cats.

So far, there were no obvious threats.

Ghoulie nuzzled her hand, letting her know that he thought it was safe for them to eat. Or rather, for her to feed him. He was less involved in how and when she fed herself.

"Okay, okay, don't nag," she told him as she unslung her pack and fished in it for the rest of a rabbit she'd trapped and cooked that morning. She tore off a leg for herself and then cocked an eyebrow at Ghoulie, who immediately sat down and looked well behaved and attentive.

"Here you go," said Rags, placing the rabbit onto the floor.

Ghoulie destroyed the rabbit, eating the meat and even crunching most of the bones. He kept his head down while he ate, reducing the noise.

They both had some water from a jug hung from Ghoulie's saddlebags, and they settled down to watch the fall of night. Everything was calm, even peaceful.

Until it wasn't.

Until a superhero walked out of the building across the street.

3

Then

New York City

"You decent?" yelled a voice. Male, deep, familiar.

Rachael felt her face go hot even though she was fully dressed and not—thanks to winning her inwardly directed battle of wills—flaunting anything. The zipper of her tunic was up to a level perhaps one inch above modesty. A bit of overcompensation. Even so, she felt suddenly naked as she opened the door to let Brett in.

If he noticed her burning face, he didn't comment.

"Oh, good, you're ready," he said as he crossed the room and went into the bathroom.

"Um . . . hello?" she said to the door as it closed.

"Got to pee," he called from inside.

So I hear, she thought sourly. He seemed to be making a career of it in there, so she killed a few moments checking her gear in the mirror. The gun belt had come out perfectly, and the pistol replica she carried looked like standard-issue SHIELD, but it was plastic and sealed with the orange peace bond required by the convention for all weapons. She had little pouches on the belt; they looked very official, but she'd filled them with lipstick, a compact, gum, cash, a debit card, her cell phone charger, a printed schedule that was folded neatly into a block, and a small stage makeup kit to keep her face freshly bruised. The version of Maria Hill she was playing today was specific to the Helicarrier attack scene from the first Avengers film and not the internal revolt by sleeper HYDRA agents from the second Captain

America movie. There were differences, and those differences mattered. It was all about attention to detail.

Rachael intended to leverage her costume making and pop culture purity of knowledge into a job in the film industry, or maybe at a Disney attraction. There were a lot of Hollywood people at the Comic Con. You never knew who might see her and ask. She wouldn't be the first cosplayer to get a nod from the gods of moviemaking.

There was another knock on the door, and Rachael gave her hair a final pat and went over to let her in. Gayla the Plastic Fantastic. Rachael took a breath and fixed an utterly false but hopefully believable friendly smile on her face, and then she opened the door.

Gayla stood there, dressed as Angela, the female version of Thor from the comics, with miles and miles of cleavage that had no origin in human biology.

Rachael stared at her.

And screamed.

Gayla's costume was perfect.

Her flesh was not.

There was a huge, gaping, bleeding wound on her upper arm, from which bright-red blood pumped.

Rachael screamed very loudly.

And . . . then she suddenly laughed.

"You *creep!*" she yelled. "You scared the crap out of me."

It was such an intensely realistic wound that Rachael was disgusted, impressed, and jealous all at the same time. She could do costumes, but makeup effects were a different skill set.

She gave Gayla a playful shove.

Gayla staggered backward and nearly fell.

"Oh, sorry," said Rachael quickly, snaking a hand out to catch her arm. "What's the theme? Is this a cross-theme thing? Like Thor after she gets mauled by dark elves, or . . ."

Gayla opened her mouth.

Not to answer.

Not to scream.

Instead of sound, she vomited a pint of blood that was so dark it was nearly black. It struck Rachael's chest.

And then Gayla was falling.

Falling.

And the world was falling too.

Completely and irrevocably off its hinges.

4

Now

Doylestown

Ghoulie shot to his feet, scattering bones and dried leaves.

Rags rose with him, her calm dissolving into immediate combat awareness. She did not carry a gun, favoring weapons that made little or no sound. So she whipped out the matched pair of fighting sticks Captain Ledger had taught her to use so many years ago. They were thirty-inch lengths of half-inch pipe fitted with lethal knobs with narrow tungsten-alloy blades on one side and slender spikes on the other.

The person across the street was dressed in a blue costume with red-and-white stripes around the torso and a white star on the chest. Red boots and gloves, a mask that covered the upper part of the head and had a white A on the forehead. The figure carried a round shield painted with concentric red-and-white circles around another white star.

Rags recognized the character. She'd spent endless hours over the long years reading what books she could find. Sometimes they were novels, sometimes they were old comics. Whatever survived and could be read. So, yes, she knew who Captain America was.

Except that in the comics Captain America was male, and this person was not.

This was a woman. Tall and slender, but definitely female.

And . . . this person was nobody's idea of a hero. Not anymore.

She was a zom.

The dead woman in the hero's costume staggered into the street, feet moving without grace, shuffling and tripping over the smallest thing and yet not falling. The shield was strapped to her arm and seemed to be fixed there so that it did not slip off. There was a huge rip in the blue material on her thigh, exposing a leg that was missing important muscle and flesh. The flesh around the wound was gray and veined with black lines. Blood was caked around her mouth and splashed in dark splotches on the tunic.

This made no sense at all to Rags.

She had been thirteen when the world fell, and she remembered Halloween. This dead woman was far too old to have been a trick-or-treater, and it was unlikely she had been at a costume party when it all went down. She hadn't been dead that long.

Not nearly that long.

Rags had seen every kind of walking corpse over the last fourteen years. The dead began to rot and then stopped. The oldest zombies looked like they were made from old leather—wrinkled and moistureless. Only the most recent of the dead had flesh that seemed to remember that it had once been soft and pliant and filled with blood.

This woman was somewhere in between.

Dead, but not withered enough to have been killed when the world ended.

So why was she in costume?

All these thoughts flashed through her head in a microsecond as she prepared herself for flight or combat. Beside her, Ghoulie stood as still and silent as a statue, waiting for her command.

This was a drama they had played out many times, just as she had done with Bones before that. One of the dead entered their world, and they got ready and waited to see what kind of reaction the moment would require.

Most of the time, Rags did nothing, allowing the dead the chance to follow whatever attracted it—some other prey, the wind, or something less understandable—and she would watch it go. Other times she might leave, outpacing the dead, or putting useful barriers between her and trouble. Sometimes, though, neither of those options were available to her. On those days, when the Fates were being playful in the ugly way they had, Rags would have to fight.

She was very good at it. She hated it, but experience had made her both cunning and strong. The slow and clumsy didn't survive out in the world. They became the shambling threats someone else would have to deal with; and in that transition from inept human to walking dead, they gained a greater measure of threat. A zombie child could bite. An old, crippled corpse crawling along the ground could bite. A bite was all it took.

The creature in the street took a few tentative steps toward the old hotel, then paused as a sound drew its focus. Rags turned too, but she did it slowly, without jerking her head around. Sudden movements drew the eye. Ledger had taught her that. One of ten thousand things he'd taught her.

Ghoulie made a small, soft sound. Not a growl, but enough of a noise to make sure she saw what he saw.

She did.

Across the intersection, moving along the side street, there were people.

Dead people.

Walking singly or in clusters.

Five of them.

Ten.

More.

Moving as fast as the dead ever moved, which was faster than many people knew. They were slow most of the time, but when there was an immediate promise of fresh meat, they could move almost as fast as the living. Some were even faster, moving with real speed. It was something Rags had encountered several times in her travels. Usually with zombies who came from the fringes of areas where nukes had fallen, or where reactors had melted down. The radiation was changing some of them. Not many. Some.

Enough.

Seeded among the zombies in this procession there were some of the faster ones. They loped along. Clumsy, but not as clumsy as the others. One of them scuttled forward on all fours because it had no feet.

They were heading directly toward the center of town, toward the intersection where the old hotel stood.

Directly toward Rags.

Yet with all this, there was something stranger, something that pulled a gasp from Rags's chest and made Ghoulie begin growling.

There was a person leading the procession, running in front of the pack, sometimes turning to run backward. Waving at them. Taunting them. Calling them.

It was a little girl.

5

Then
New York City

Rachael tore the cape from Gayla's costume, wadded it up, and pressed it to that terrible wound. She screamed at the top of her lungs.

"BRETT!"

"What?" came his muffled reply. "I'm still in here."

"Oh my God, Brett, it's Gayla!"

He whipped the door open and stared, half smiling, because he expected this to be a joke. That was their world. Little dramas, little bits of cosplay fun.

The smile and the color drained from his face.

"What happened? Is that blood?" he demanded. "Jesus—"

"Call 911," screeched Rachael. "She's really hurt. Oh my God, she's really bad."

He snatched up his cell and was hitting buttons as he dropped to his knees beside her. Rachael heard him shouting into the phone, giving name and room number, the hotel's location, and a shocked and almost incoherent description of what had happened. Gayla moaned softly and tried to raise her arms, but her movements were feeble and sloppy.

"What happened?" repeated Brett, trying to pull the cloth aside so he could examine the wound. "Did you two get into a fight or—?"

"No," snapped Rachael. "God, are you stupid? I didn't do this. Gayla just showed up like this. Someone must have attacked her."

"That looks like a bite," he said, recoiling from it, his brow knit in confusion.

Rachael snatched the cloth back and pressed it into place.

They both turned as they heard noises out in the hall.

"That was fast," said Brett as he shot to his feet and ran to guide the EMTs.

Rachael bent over Gayla, all their personal animosity swept away by what was happening. Jealousy and even mutual dislike did not matter when things were boiled down to the level of pain and suffering, of desperation and survival. "Hold on, sweetie. It'll be okay. They're coming. You're going to be fine. They'll take good care of you."

Gayla's eyelids fluttered, her hands twitched and spasmed.

Brett stepped into the hallway, raising his hand to wave for the paramedics.

He froze and stared at something Rachael could not see.

"What the hell . . . ?" he murmured. Then, a heartbeat later, he repeated the same words. Shouting them this time in a voice filled with confusion and fear. *"What the hell?"*

And then something hit Brett like a thunderbolt. A streak of red and blue slammed into him and knocked him into the wall on the other side of the doorway.

Rachael stared, unable to fully process what had happened. She'd only caught a glimpse.

Brett had been tackled with brutal ferocity.

By Superman.

6

Now

Doylestown

The little girl ran, and danced, and skipped, and whirled while a score of the hungry dead followed her. Rags gaped at her. At what was happening.

She was maybe ten years old.

Slender and pretty.

She was dressed in a costume. Black and sleek, with a stylized bat on the chest and a short cape that fluttered as she ran. Masses of curly red hair bobbed behind her.

Rags searched her oldest memories for the name of the character.

Batgirl.

Batgirl?

Rags felt as if the world had suddenly become insane. Or that maybe she had gone crazy. Had the years of isolation, of fear and violence, of constant danger finally pushed her over that delicate edge into genuine madness?

She could build a case for that. It made much more sense than what she was seeing.

A little girl dressed as a superhero, laughing as she led a pack of zombies down the streets of a dead town.

This was something from a fever dream. This was the sort of thing she imagined would happen every day in a mind that had become irreparably fractured. Rags had met several insane people, and it was clear from the looks in their eyes that they were seeing a different world than she was.

However, beside her, Ghoulie growled again.

He was seeing it too.

She hoped.

If he was seeing it, then it was real. As bizarre and unlikely as it was, these events were happening.

That was when Rags felt herself move.

It was nothing planned. One minute she stood gaping in shock, and the next she was in motion, leaping from the porch, racing across the intersection, hearing the clank of Ghoulie's armor as he ran with her.

"Hey, kid!" she yelled as she ran. "Over here. Over here!"

That made the girl whip around.

And stumble.

The zombies howled as they swarmed toward her.

7

Then

New York City

Rachael Elle screamed.

She had reason to.

Out in the hallway, Brett screamed too.

Other screams tore through the air and burst in through the open door.

So many voices torn by screams.

Rachael was caught in a moment of terrible indecision. Stay with Gayla, keep the pressure on the wound.

Or try to help Brett.

Which?

Which?

The decision was stolen from her in the next moment.

Gayla shuddered once, arched her back, went intensely rigid, eyes wide and staring.

And then she flopped back onto the floor. A long, ragged, empty breath hissed from between her teeth. Her eyes looked at Rachael, and through her, and into nothing at all.

Rachael said, "Gayla . . . ?"

But even in that fleeting moment, she knew that Gayla was no longer there.

Gayla was gone.

Gone.

And Brett was screaming.

She felt herself rise, felt herself move even though her mind seemed to be anchored to the girl who lay on the floor in a pool of blood. Her friend. Even in the blinding heat of the moment, Rachael realized and understood that Gayla was really her friend. A rival, sure. Even a hated rival. But on the ground floor of all things, she was a friend.

Brett was outside in the hallway. Screaming and fighting.

He was her friend too.

He was still alive.

Rachael was not a fighter. She played one at Comic Con and Dragon Con. At science fiction conventions all over the country. In photo shoots with her friends. Even the few karate classes she'd taken were more to get the form right when she cosplayed action heroes.

She was not a fighter.

No.

Not until that moment.

As she moved from the dead girl to whatever was happening in the hall, something changed. *She* changed.

She was dressed like a hero.

And this moment, against all possible variations on the reality of her actual life, required a hero.

Rachael raced into the hall and saw that it was not just she who had changed. The world had changed. It had gone wrong. Somehow . . . wrong.

People were fighting everywhere. Some of them dressed in costumes. Some of them in ordinary clothes. One man was naked except for bedroom slippers. Everyone was screaming and yelling. And bleeding.

And dying.

On the floor, Brett was wrestling with Superman.

With a tall, muscular man dressed as Superman.

They were locked together. Superman was clawing at Brett, tearing at his costume, scratching his face and throat. Superman's face was torn by horrible slashes, and part of his upper lip was gone. Just . . . gone. The injuries seemed to either be nothing to him, or the pain had driven him crazy. Either way, he kept darting his head forward, snapping at Brett with bloody teeth. Brett was on the bottom, and he had his big hands locked around the man's throat and was using sheer force to push the attacker upward away from him. The attacker, though savage and clearly undeterred by his injuries, was clumsy and awkward.

"Get off me!" screamed Brett. Blood ran from a dozen ragged cuts on his face. "Get off me."

Rachael front-kicked Superman.

Very, very hard.

She launched the kick while running, throwing herself into the air, snapping out with the heel of her boot, catching the attacker on the side of the face. Everything she had, everything she was, went into the force of that savage kick.

Superman's head snapped sideways and his body followed, his hands flailing but not trying to break his fall. He landed hard in the cleft between floor and wall, his head tilted over onto his shoulder, eyes bugging, mouth still trying to bite even though he was now more than four feet from Brett. Superman's legs thrashed and his heels hammered the floor as if in the grip of a wild seizure.

"Brett—are you okay?" Rachael yelled, but didn't even pause to listen. Superman was scrambling around to try to get up, and she kicked him again. This time it was with the flat of her foot, right in the face. The man pitched backward, hitting the wall again. His nose burst and his lip split, but instead of red the blood was dark and strange. Almost black.

Like Gayla's.

It terrified Rachael.

Superman rebounded from the wall and hissed at her, the pain and injury seeming to be of no consequence. He flung himself forward, grabbing at her leg.

Rachael kicked at him. Kicking the hands, the fingers, the arms.

Brett lay on the floor, too stunned to move, his mouth and eyes wide.

"Help me!" roared Rachael.

He didn't move.

Superman caught Rachael's ankle and jerked her foot toward his mouth, toward those bloody teeth. The sudden pull brought Rachael down hard and she landed on her side, facing the attacker. For one second they lay there and stared at each other. Her eyes met his, and she looked for some understanding.

There was nothing there.

Nothing.

No emotion, no expression, no connection.

It was like looking through an open window into the empty rooms of an abandoned house.

The mouth and the eyes seemed to belong to different faces. The madman's lips peeled back in an expression of avaricious hate, but there was no corresponding malevolence in those eyes. There was absolutely nothing there.

The creature—for in that moment Rachael's mind separated this *thing* from any connection to real humanity—darted forward and bit her. Its teeth sank into the soft leather of her boot, pinching her heel. The pain was massive. Huge.

Rachael screamed as she pulled back her other foot and lashed out, striking it in the face, the shoulders, the throat, the chest.

Over and over and over again while all around her the day was filled with blood and screams.

8

Now

Doylestown

Ghoulie raced ahead of Rags and slammed into the oncoming wall of zombies. The dog's two hundred pounds of lean muscle coupled with its spiked armor was like an artillery shell. Dried flesh and bits of bone exploded upward as bodies collapsed back. Ghoulie wheeled and rammed his shoulder into the next wave, ripping through withered tendons with the blades welded to his harness.

The little girl cowered back, her joy and laughter gone as her game had been transformed into a life-and-death struggle.

Then Rags was there.

She jumped over the girl, swinging her matched pipes in lethal arcs that smashed down through bone and brains. Two zombies fell back from her, and she pivoted to kick another in the knee so that it collapsed in front of the rest; then Rags turned again, using her hips to generate power for a series of brutal chopping hits. She crushed skulls and shattered jaws and reduced reaching arms to crooked uselessness. Ghoulie howled like some monstrous ghost dog and kept smashing into the legs of the dead, toppling them toward the whirling pipes.

The little girl stumbled backward. "They told me to get a few . . . but . . . but . . ."

Rags had no time for that conversation. More of the dead were coming; she could see their awkward shapes in the thickening gloom.

A burly zombie dressed in the ancient remnants of a firefighter's running gear closed in on Rags's left side while two middle-aged women with broken and jagged teeth came at her from the right. Rags front-kicked the fireman, driving him back, but as she swung around to deal with the women, something whipped through the air and the heads of both women simply leaped up. The headless corpses instantly collapsed.

Rags stared in shock.

As the bodies fell, she saw a bizarre sight.

A woman stood beyond the crumpling bodies. She was a few years older than Rags, with a pretty face and masses of dark, wavy hair that fell loose around her shoulders. She wore a short, red, tight-fitting dress that had a fur hem and a wide brown leather waistband, with brown leather pants under the dress and leather bite-proof bands around her forearms and thigh-high boots. She wore a molded leather breastplate and matching shoulder pads. A white leather belt slanted down to her left hip with an empty scabbard clipped to it. In her gloved hands she held a long, wickedly sharp Viking sword.

The woman smiled at her and said something that made no sense at all. "Welcome to Asgard."

Rags said, "What?"

"Nothing," said the woman. "Oh, crap—behind you."

Rags turned to see the fireman closing in on her. She moved into his attack, using one club to beat down his reaching hands and the other to crack his skull. It took five blows to drop him and shut down whatever strange force drove the zombie.

"There's more of them!" yelled a voice. A man's voice, and Rags turned to see a big blond man dressed as the superhero Thor. He had an eye patch, though, which did not look like it was part of a costume, because there was a ragged scar above and below the patch. He'd been badly hurt, but it was an old scar. Behind him were five other people in costumes. She recognized three of them, digging the names out of old memories from before the end of the world and from comics she'd read on lonely nights.

One of them wore a heavy leather jacket with yellow trim; his hair was in a weirdly pointed style with long sideburns. He wore metal braces around his forearms, from which sprouted three long sickle blades on each arm.

She mouthed the name. *Wolverine.*

He waded into the crowd of zoms, slashing at legs and throats. He grinned as if this was all big fun.

Next to him was a man wearing a costume that looked like it was made from layer upon layer of hockey pads that had been stitched together and spray-painted green. He was a brute of a man, easily six-foot-six and broad shouldered, and he swung a piece of pipe that had to weigh at least thirty pounds. His name was in her memories too.

The Incredible Hulk.

The last of the ones she recognized was easier to identify. Dark blue shorts speckled with white stars, a bloodred corset, stylized gold wings across the chest along with a gold belt, armbands, and a heavy lasso painted gold. She carried a Greek short sword. Lots of wild black hair.

Wonder Woman.

The other two were characters she did not know. A very muscular man in green spandex with a stylized dragon tattooed on his chest and yellow sashes tied around waist and head. He carried no weapon but used dynamic kicks and hand strikes to cripple the zoms so that his companion, a muscular black man with a steel headband, yellow shirt, blue pants, and a heavy length of steel-welded chain for a belt, could finish them using what looked like spiked gold-plated brass knuckles. The black man punched the heads of every fallen zombie, and the spikes dug deep, doing terrible damage.

The woman in red waved her sword. "Wolverine, Wonder Woman, take the left flank. Hulk, Iron Fist, Luke Cage, go right. Pincer formation. Go!"

The heroes split and ran to form lines in the path of the oncoming zombies.

Ghoulie ran back to stand by Rags, and the two of them watched in mingled shock and admiration as a group of people dressed as superheroes attacked the zombies with real zeal and a fair amount of style.

Except for the martial-arts guy in green—the hero the woman called Iron Fist—the others relied on speed and a few simple moves to do their grisly work. Rags could appreciate that. With zombies you did not have to know much about fighting—the dead never studied their enemies, never learned from the deaths of their companions, never adapted, never defended.

Even so, it was difficult work, and even the most seasoned of fighters soon became exhausted, especially when using great force over and over again.

Rags judged the fight with the eyes of experience and all the knowledge she had learned from Captain Ledger, who was the most dangerous man she had ever met. She saw some degree of care, some talent. And the woman in red kept yelling orders, reminding them to watch each other's backs, to hold their line, to fight rather than flail.

It was pretty good.

But Rags could tell it was not going to be enough.

Things started to fall apart—a little at first, and then faster, that way things will when a system breaks down. Some of the zombies in the crowd were also dressed in costumes. The tatters of costumes. She saw Batman and the Joker. Cyclops. A couple of others that she almost recognized but couldn't name.

None of those zombies looked to have died longer ago than a year. Most more recently.

The little girl began screaming, and Rags saw that more and more of the dead were circling the center of the fight, ignoring the combatants to pursue an easier target. They closed in, drawn by the shrill screams of the child.

"No," murmured Rags. Ghoulie gave a sharp warning bark. This whole fight was about to collapse into a feeding frenzy if it kept going like this.

Rags broke into a run and closed on where the girl cowered. In the heat of the battle, the heroes had lost track of her. Or they thought their two lines formed enough protection. The woman in red turned to look, but her eyes went wide as she realized too late that the mindless dead had outflanked her.

"Charlotte!" screamed the woman, but two zombies closed on her and blocked her way.

Rags skidded to a stop beside the girl, spun, and crouched with her back to the child, arms out, fighting sticks ready. Ghoulie took position on the other side, forming two sides of a box. Rags hoped it would be enough.

There were so many of the dead. The girl—Charlotte— started to bolt, to run toward the woman in red, but Rags growled at her.

"No! Stay behind me."

Charlotte dodged backward from the grasping hands of a man in a long black cape, like something a magician might have worn. Rags ended him with a one-two blow to the head.

As he fell, though, another staggered forward. And another.

Rags clanged her pipes together to give Ghoulie a combat command. This was what Ledger had taught her, and Rags had revised and developed the rhythm. First with Bones, and then with Ghoulie. Countless hours of training and practice, of refining their battle skills to suit her body type and his. To suit her fighting style and his. Now that shock and surprise were gone, they settled into the work that they had done in a hundred towns during their long journey.

Ghoulie bounded forward and smashed into the side of the pack of zombies. His sheer bulk knocked them back and down and sideways. As Ghoulie disrupted and destabilized them, Rags used her pipes to smash and destroy.

"Come on," she called, both to the dog and to Charlotte, as she began moving away from the center of the street.

Ghoulie backed up, forcing the girl to scuttle along behind Rags. All the time, though, the dead lunged in and were met by spiked armor and flailing metal rods. They fell.

And fell.

But still they came.

Rags could see the heroes, and she saw the exact moment when they realized their own danger, and the fact that they were in the presence of something tougher than them. Something more real and powerful.

"Get behind me!" yelled Rags to the heroes. "Spread out. Form a defensive circle. Everyone facing out. Protect the girl. Do it."

The heroes stared at her for one moment, not quite grasping what she meant, but then the woman in red nodded. She—the obvious leader of the group—began yelling to the others, pulling them away from the battle, shoving them into position until the bunch of them formed a protective ring around the little girl. Ghoulie ran up and down the lines, throwing his bulk at the dead to drive them staggering toward the heroes.

"Let them come to us," commanded Rags. "Don't chase—you'll just waste energy. They'll come to us."

They did.

Wave after wave of them.

"Work in teams," snapped Rags. "Short ones go for legs, big ones go for heads."

"Do it," ordered the woman with the sword. "Work in pairs. Iron Fist and Luke. Wolverine and Hulk. Tabby," she said to the black-haired fighter dressed as Wonder Woman, "you feed them to me."

And that was the rhythm. Four pairs, each knocking down, smashing skulls, or chopping necks.

Over and over and over again.

It was clear to Rags that the woman in red was the most effective of the heroes. Even more so than the one she called Iron Fist. Even so, Rags could tell that the woman had no formal training—some of her cuts were too big and required too much muscle rather than letting gravity do more of the work—but she had speed and instinct. And she was aggressive. That was good.

The zombies came at them in a relentless tidal surge of hunger.

Rags, Ghoulie, and the people dressed as heroes stood their ground.

One by one, the dead fell.

It took a long, long time.

Behind the town, beyond the trees, the last of the sun melted down into the west and darkness took possession of the world.

9

Now
Doylestown

They stood for a long time.

Bodies trembling with fatigue. Clothes streaked with black blood. Chests heaving, sweat running in lines down faces and arms and legs. Eyes bright with shock and the fires of destruction.

Around them, spread outward like some mad sculpture created in hell, lay the bodies of fifty-seven zombies. Not whole bodies. Limbs and heads, torsos and pieces were scattered in a pattern of artless slaughter. In the center of the debris field stood the survivors.

Rags and Ghoulie.

The child dressed as Batgirl.

The heroes.

The woman in red.

For a while all they could do was stare at what they had done. And then, slowly, they lowered their weapons and turned to look at one another. To confirm that others had survived, as they each had survived. To look at the living and remember that this was what they had fought for.

Rags watched them. She knew that she was often aloof, that she considered herself a warrior rather than merely a fighter, and with that came some elements of snobbery that she chose not to eliminate from her disposition. She waited to see if these people celebrated their victory, and if so, *how* they celebrated. If they mocked the dead, then they were of a kind she had seen too many times. People who had come to enjoy killing.

She wanted to see if they were mad. After all, they were dressed as comic-book characters.

She watched to see if they were the kind of people that Rags had spent so many years avoiding. And in that moment she remembered why it was that she'd never settled anywhere. Despite her loneliness, people had disappointed her too many times. So she waited. And watched.

She did not lower her weapons, and Ghoulie—alert to

her moods—stood wide-legged and ready to do whatever she asked of him.

The woman in red sheathed her sword, went over to the little girl and checked her for bites, found none, and pulled her into a fierce hug, kissing the girl's face, her hair, her cheeks. Then Thor came over and snatched the girl up and held her to his chest, burying his nose in her hair.

"Oh my God, Charlotte—why did you *do* that?" he demanded.

"But—but—you *said* to!" insisted the girl as she burst into tears.

"No, honey," said the woman in red gently. She came over and touched the child's hair. "Sweetie . . . don't you remember what Mommy told you? We went over and over it. All you were supposed to do was walk to the barrier and back. That was it. We just wanted them to see you so Donnie could let one of them inside. But you went outside, honey. You left the gate open."

Tears ran down the child's face. "No, Mommy, Donnie said he'd close the gate. I didn't go outside. I didn't leave the gate open. I—I'm sorry. . . ."

Rags cleared her throat. "The gate was open when I came through," she said. "Your man Donnie must have been sleeping on the job."

The woman in red studied Rags as she stroked her daughter's hair. "Brett," she said to the man dressed as Thor, "take her back. I want her to write out the rules fifty times and then she can have supper."

"But Mommy, I—"

"Shh, now, baby," said the woman in red. "It'll be okay. You do your lessons and we'll talk before bedtime. Go on now."

The big man—Brett—carried Charlotte away toward the other end of town.

Rags held her ground, waiting.

The woman in red turned toward her. "You saved my daughter's life."

Rags said nothing.

"You probably saved all our lives. Some of those things might have gotten us, or gotten past us."

"Both," said Rags bluntly. "You were going to lose this fight."

The woman studied her face for a long time, and then she nodded. "I guess so. It . . . um, wasn't what we had planned."

Rags said nothing.

"We teach the kids to draw them in, one at a time. The kids are fast."

"You risk your kids?" asked Rags, biting back harsher words.

"No, we train them. Charlotte's good at this. She's done it fifty times. Today . . . well, today she did it wrong. She left the gate open, and a whole bunch of them came in."

"I told you, there was no one at the gate," said Rags. "I know. I came in that way too."

"There was supposed to be someone there."

"There wasn't."

They both looked down the street. "Then," said the woman sadly, "either Donnie's dead or he ran off."

"He have a grudge against you? I mean . . . leaving the gate open and all."

The woman shrugged. "This was a training session. He's supposed to let one in every few minutes so some of our newbies can practice hunt, control, evasion. Like that. Donnie's supposed to keep it controlled. Not too many and such. But Donnie's lazy and he's not a very good team player. Maybe an even worse lookout."

She stopped, frowned, and then walked to the far side of the street to where three zombies lay in a heap. She bent, grabbed one of them by the shoulder, and hauled him off to reveal a fat woman and a thin man.

The woman had clearly been dead for years.

The man was different. His skin had gone pale from blood loss, but it wasn't weathered. Except for the color—and the deep impact crater on the top of his head from one of Rags's clubs—he could have been sleeping.

He was dressed as Robin from the old Batman comics.

"Ah . . . jeez," said the woman.

"Donnie?" asked Rags.

"Donnie."

Rags did not comment. The man had made a mistake—inattention or perhaps falling asleep—and had paid for it. The fact that his error could have resulted in a slaughter—not just of the little girl but of everyone—was obvious, so she left it all unsaid. The truth burned in the air all around them.

The woman straightened and began walking toward the gate at the far end of town. Rags fell into step beside her and sent Ghoulie ahead to scout for lurking dead.

"Look . . . who *are* you people?" asked Rags. "And what's going on here?"

Rachael smiled, and it was a bright and genuine smile, so at odds with the carnage spread around them.

"We're training."

"Training?"

"Sure. Teaching the kids, mostly. Helping some of the adults get better at fighting the Orcs."

"I'm sorry but . . . 'Orcs'?"

"Well, dead people. We call them Orcs," said Rachael. "Do . . . you know about Orcs?"

"I've read some Tolkien."

Rachael sighed. "I remember the movies. The movies were great."

"I was too young. My parents wouldn't let me see them. But . . . why Orcs? They weren't living dead."

"No, but they were horrible monsters. They ate people. There were a lot of them, and they made war on the world of men. And," she said, adjusting her tight-fitting dress as she walked, "the world of women, too."

"Ah," said Rags. "Orcs." It wasn't the strangest label she'd encountered for the zombies. There were monks out west who called them the Children of Lazarus. People called them rotters, stenches, walking dead, walkers, living dead, zombies, critters, ghost-people, harrowed, and a score of other things. Each isolated group came up with their own names, their own beliefs, their own rituals.

They reached the gate, which stood open as it had earlier. Rachael sighed and closed it, dropping the crossbar into place. Then she leaned back against it and blew out her cheeks. Sweat beaded her forehead, and she fished inside her broad leather waistband for a handkerchief.

Rags nodded to Rachael's costume. "What about this stuff? The superhero stuff? What's that all about?"

"The world needs heroes," said Rachael, and then, apparently realizing that more of an explanation was required, explained. "We're—or we *were*—cosplayers. Do you know what that is?"

Rags shook her head.

"Before the Fall, back when there was a world, they used to have these big conventions for pop culture stuff. Y'know, for people who were into comics and video games and movies and like that. The events were huge, and some people—like my friends and I—used to go to things like San Diego Comic Con, Dragon Con in Atlanta, Katsucon, Megacon . . . a slew of them. We'd make costumes and wear them. God, there were times I'd bring fourteen or sixteen different costumes. Really good stuff, too. I wanted to get into professional costuming, so I really put my heart into what I wore. I helped some of my friends, too."

"I'm confused. So . . . this is all fake?"

Rachael shook her head. And it was then that Rags took a closer, harder look at the woman. She had scars on her arms and face. Not bite marks, of course, but the kinds of scars a person gets from a hard life. From surviving, from fighting. Maybe from intense training while preparing for the realities of life out here. Rags had some similar scars. Despite the costume, she knew that this woman was a real fighter.

"No, it's not fake. Not anymore. It's how we live."

"Pretending to be superheroes?"

"Superheroes, video game characters, gods and demigods. Whatever."

"Why?" asked Rags.

Rachael looked at her. "Why not?"

"No, I—"

"I know what you mean. You think we're all crazy, right? That we're playacting while the world eats itself. But . . . we're not. That's not what's going on here. Or at least it's not what we're trying to do." Rachael smiled. "On that first night, when the plague broke out, Brett and I were in New York, at the big comic convention. One of our friends was bitten, and so were some people on the floor of the hotel we were all staying at. It was so wrong, so scary." She crossed her arms and shivered. "Even now, after all these years, it still gets me every time I think about it."

"You survived," said Rags.

"Sure. A bunch of us did," agreed Rachael, "and I think I know why."

Rags said nothing.

"We were *heroes*," explained Rachael. "That's what did it. Now . . . I know that sounds nuts."

Rags raised her hand and waggled it back and forth. "Just a bit. I've heard stranger stories."

Rachael told her what happened. How after the initial shock she and Brett rallied several other cosplayers on their floor of the hotel and they began working together—*fighting* together—as if that was something they'd always done. As if it was something they were used to doing for real. Together they cleared their floor, and as the night wore on and the outbreak spun out of all control, they invaded the other floors, saving who they could, killing the infected.

"It was like we were really superheroes. We weren't even all that afraid. Not really," said Rachael. "Being in costume while everything was falling apart, it kept us all together. And it made us want to stand with each other, you know? Like we were a real team. A few people split off, but a lot of people stayed with us. We blocked off the fire stairs and turned six floors of the hotel into our . . . um . . . headquarters. We even called it Avengers Tower." She paused, but when Rags made no comment and offered no criticism, the woman continued. "Later, when we realized that no one was going to come to rescue us, and when food started running low, we began taking over the lower floors. Our room was on the thirty-ninth floor. It took us two weeks to fight our way down to the street level."

"How many got out?"

Rachael looked away for a moment. The last fireflies of the season were drifting through the bushes. "When we left the thirty-third floor, we had forty-eight people. Seventeen cosplayers, and the other thirty-one were civilians."

Rags echoed the word. "Civilians."

"By the time we reached the street, there were only eight cosplayers left."

"How many civilians?"

Rachael smiled. "Thirty-one."

"You didn't lose any of them?"

She shook her head. "No. Not one. It was horrible—what happened, I mean—but it was also pretty amazing. Some of the cosplayers sacrificed themselves to save the rest. They stood up and fought the monsters so everyone else could run. Even though they *knew* they were going to die."

"Like heroes," said Rags softly.

"Like heroes."

They watched the fireflies.

"It took us three years to get back to Pennsylvania," said Rachael. "And when we did . . ."

She shook her head and didn't explain. It wasn't necessary. After three years, there would be nothing to come home to. Only heartbreak and horror.

"So it's just you guys now?" asked Rags. "You're still playing dress-up and pretending to be superheroes?"

"Pretty much," said Rachael, but there was an odd quality to her voice. "We recruit some more when we can. And I try to teach them how to fight."

"Do you have training?"

Rachael shook her head. "No, but I watched a lot of movies. Played a lot of video games."

"That's hardly the same thing."

Rachael shrugged. "I know. But it's what we have."

The fireflies danced and danced.

"How many of the civilians are still alive?" asked Rags. "Or . . . are any of them alive?"

Rachael turned to her and took a long time before answering. "We usually don't let people into town. If Donnie hadn't been . . . *taken* . . . he'd have rung the alarm and we'd have swarmed you."

Ghoulie growled softly. Rags said nothing.

"We'd have tried," said Rachael, hooking her long hair behind her ears. "We don't let people see what's going on here."

"If you want me to turn around and leave," said Rags, "just say the word. I'm not here to spy."

"I know. Or, at least I'm pretty sure you're not. But you're an amazing fighter. Better than anyone I've ever seen. Better than me, and better than Iron Fist. He knows some kung fu, but it's more fancy than anything."

"You're pretty good with that sword," said Rags, nodding to the weapon at Rachael's hip.

"Pretty good is nice. I'd like to be better."

Rags nodded.

"Do you know how to use a sword?" asked Rachael.

Rags shrugged. Nodded. Shrugged again.

"You can fight. You've been trained. Anyone can see that. And the way you stepped in tonight? That was so cool. You're a real hero."

"No, I'm not. I had a good teacher, though," said Rags. "Captain Ledger. He's an actual hero. He was Special Ops before the Fall. I trained with him for four years."

"Is he still alive?"

"I don't know. Maybe. Probably. Somewhere."

"Are you . . . looking for him?" asked Rachael.

"No."

"What are you looking for?"

Rags didn't answer. She shrugged again.

Rachael chewed her lip for a moment and made a soft, thoughtful noise as she watched the fireflies. Then she abruptly pushed off the fence and walked a few paces.

"Let me show you something, okay?" she asked.

"Show me what?"

"You'll see. It's . . . well, it's what we've been doing since we got here."

She led the way, and after a moment Rags followed. Ghoulie trotted along behind, huffing and clanking.

They passed through another gate—this one properly manned—and then turned and walked nearly half a mile down what had once been a broad street lined with big stores and automobile dealerships. They stopped at the top of a hill and stared at what lay beyond.

Rags gasped.

She took two clumsy steps and then sat down hard on the ground.

"How—how—how many—?"

Rachael knelt beside her, and they looked at the lights. Cooking fires and bonfires.

Hundreds of them, stretching along both sides of the road and then spreading back toward the distant gloom of nightfall. At the fringes of the fires were rows of tents, campers, RVs, trailer homes, and plywood shacks. Beyond those was farmland. Corn and wheat, pumpkins and apple groves. And more that Rags could not identify from that distance.

Her eyes, though, were drawn to the lights. To the fires.

There were hundreds of them.

Thousands.

And around each of them were people.

"At last count," said Rachael, "we had eleven thousand civilians. And I have two hundred and fifty-six heroes in training."

Tears burned in Rags's eyes and fell down her cheeks as a sob burst in her chest. Ghoulie whined and licked her face.

"So many people . . ."

"We're finding more all the time," said Rachael. "And once we train enough people, we'll send out more scouting parties. To find more. And to clear out the farmlands. Every year we take more of it back. Every year we get more of the world back."

"My God . . ."

Rachael leaned close to Rags. "We need to get tougher so we can save more of them," she said. "Tough like you. Like that man you mentioned, Captain Ledger. If we're going to save the world, then we need to become real heroes."

"You already are," said Rags thickly. "God . . . you're already heroes."

"Not yet," said Rachael. She touched the fighting sticks that were thrust through Rags's belt. "I'm not sure what you're out here looking for . . . but maybe it's this."

Rags put her face in her hands and wept.

Ghoulie howled.

Rachael placed her hand on Rags's shoulder.

Down the hill there was bright firelight and the sound of laughter. Of people.

Of life.

FROM NIX'S JOURNAL

ON NATURAL AND SUPERNATURAL

(BEFORE *FIRE & ASH*)

My mom believed in a lot of stuff. Ghosts and spirits. God, too. And angels.

I'm not sure what I believe in. I used to go along with her, with what she believed in. That's changed now. She's dead and I'm alive, and now I have to believe what I believe in.

But I don't know what that is.

Out here in the Ruin, especially late at night, when it's dark but the world isn't quiet because the night's never really quiet, sometimes I think I believe.

I keep thinking I see Mom's ghost. Standing just outside the light from our campfire. Not trying to scare us or anything. Just there.

There have been so many times when I know I should have been killed. In the pits at Gameland. Fighting zoms. Fighting Preacher Jack and his sons.

I didn't die, though.

Is Mom's ghost protecting me?

Or am I imagining it?

How will I ever know?

Tooth & Nail

(Between the events of *Flesh & Bone* and *Fire & Ash*)

1
Sanctuary
Area 51

Benny Imura stood at the edge of a concrete trench that was all that separated him from the reaching hands and hungry mouths of half a million zoms.

Half a million.

The dead stood there, pale and silent, most of them as unmoving as statues. They looked like tombstones to Benny, their moldering flesh marking the only grave the wandering dead would ever know.

None of the creatures could reach him; the trench was too wide. Those that tried fell down to the concrete floor and could never hope to climb up the sheer sides. Benny was safe.

Safe.

Such a weak and stupid word.

A year ago that word actually meant something to him. Safe was a concept he could grasp. Safe was his town of Mountainside. Safe was the chain-link fence, the tower guards, the armed men of the town watch. Safe was a sturdy oak door and good locks. Safe was shutters on the windows.

Safe was an illusion.

That illusion had been shattered when death came to town on a stormy night as a lightning-struck tree smashed part of the fence down. The concept of safety was battered by a zombie coming for him inside his own house.

The last fragments of the lie of safety had been ground to dust by the heavy boots of evil men—living men, not zoms—who'd brutalized Morgie Mitchell, one of Benny's best friends, when he tried to protect Nix Riley and her mother.

The men had killed Mrs. Riley and kidnapped Nix.

Benny and his brother, Tom, had gotten her back, but not easily. Not in any way that rebuilt the walls of safety, or that put a fresh coat of paint on the illusion that everything would be okay again.

It wouldn't be okay again.

It couldn't be.

Mrs. Riley was dead.

Morgie was gone too. In a way. He and Benny had traded hard words on the day Tom had left town. Benny and Nix had gone with him, along with Lou Chong and Lilah, the Lost Girl. All of Morgie's friends left town, and Morgie sent Benny on the road with a wish that they'd all die out here in the great Rot and Ruin.

Benny knew that Morgie was talking from a hurt place, not from his heart. But it was the last thing that had been said; it was the last memory.

Not even lifelong friendships were safe.

Not in the real world.

Not anymore.

Nothing was safe.

Tom was gone now too. Gone forever and for good.

His smile, his wisdom, his power.

Gone.

Benny looked beyond the closest ranks of zoms to a squat white blockhouse of a building that rose into the hot Nevada air. In there, behind those featureless walls, another of his friends was gone too.

Chong.

Infected, dying. Maybe already dead.

Maybe already returned from death as something inhuman. Something that, despite all their years of friendship, would try to kill Benny.

Try to eat his flesh.

No, he thought as tears burned in his eyes, *nothing is safe.*

He felt the weight of the sword he wore slung across his back. It was Tom's *kami katana*, a perfectly balanced weapon. It *had been* Tom's.

Had been.

Then, in a moment that was unavoidable and terrible and wild, Tom had used the last of his strength to try to draw that sword in order to stop a madman from slaughtering everyone. But Tom was already dying, and his strength failed him at last—but in that instant Benny reached for the handle, taking it from Tom, brushing his brother's fingers, drawing the weapon, completing the action. Doing what had to be done. Fighting the monster.

Saving Nix and Chong and Lilah.

Losing Tom.

And, in the act of killing to save lives—even with all the moral and cosmic justification that carried—Benny lost a little of himself. That blade cut more than the flesh of an evil man. It sliced away a piece of Benny's childhood and left it to die in the bloody grass around where Tom knelt.

Benny squatted down on the edge of the trench, took a handful of hot sand, and let it pour slowly out of his fist. The wind whipped it away from him.

Some of the zoms across the trench were dressed in black clothes with red tassels tied around their wrists and ankles, with white angel wings sewn onto the front of their shirts. Their shaved heads were elaborately tattooed with images of flowers, thorny vines, insects, and writhing snakes.

Reapers of the Night Church.

Because of them, no one was safe.

They were worse than the zombies. The dead meant no harm; they were driven by some impulse of their destroyed nature.

The reapers?

They actually believed that everyone—every man, woman, and child left alive—should die. They were converts to a new religion based on an ancient Greek god of death. Thanatos. And their leader, the cold and deadly madman Saint John, had trained them to be an army of superb and relentless killers.

Saint John believed that Thanatos had sent the zombie plague to eradicate the "infection" of humanity and thereby cleanse the world. Anyone who survived the plague and struggled to stay alive was going in direct defiance of Saint John's god. It made them heretics and blasphemers. They were like weeds in a bizarre version of the Garden of Eden, and Saint John used his reapers to mow them down.

Then, when the last of the heretics were gone, Saint John planned to lead his own people into an orgy of mass suicide.

The insanity of it was scary enough. The fact that so many

people joined the Night Church was insane. It was terrifying.

Benny and his friends had become embroiled in that unholy war.

Now they were injured, sick at heart, trapped, and dying.

And yet . . .

And yet.

Another emotion warred inside Benny's heart and mind, fighting back the terror, shoving back the despair over all that he'd lost.

Rage.

It burned inside him with a fire that was as cold as it was intense.

The thought that someone like Saint John would want to end life after all the years of struggle, of working together to overcome hardships, of finding a way to preserve the spark of life after plague and famine tried to blow it out . . . it made Benny burn.

He thought of everyone he knew who'd died, who'd sacrificed so much so that others—many others—could live.

Mrs. Riley, dying to try to protect her daughter.

Tom. Saving so many.

Maybe Chong, saving a little girl from reapers.

So many.

Too many.

If the reapers had their way, all of these deaths would be meaningless. To Benny, that was obscene.

Benny reached over his shoulder and touched the handle of his sword. He could feel his lips curl back in a feral snarl of hate. He imagined Saint John in front of him, within reaching, within cutting distance.

"No," Benny said.

It was all he said.

It was enough.

Because, with everything he had and everything he was, he absolutely meant it.

No.

2

South Fork Wildlife Area
Southern California

A voice rang out, sharp and full of threat.

"Who the hell do you think you are?"

The man who spoke was tall, broad-shouldered, bearded, and brutal-looking. He stepped out from behind an overturned tractor-trailer. He wore matched pistols in leather holsters at his hips and carried a working replica of a Scottish claymore sword in his knobby fist, the blade resting on one mountainous shoulder.

The man to whom he spoke was not nearly as bulky. Pale, short, slender, dressed in black clothes with angel wings embroidered in white thread on the front of his dark shirt. His garments were too big for him, and they bloused out around the red tassels tied to his wrists, elbows, ankles, and knees. He had a shaved head, and his scalp was covered in tattoos of bees crawling over a honey-rich hive.

"I'm just a humble traveler doing god's work," said the smaller man.

"Not on this road, pally," said the big man. "This road belongs to Boss Keffler."

As he spoke, there was an ominous sound. The smaller man turned to see other men step from concealment among the wrecked cars on the cracked highway. Four of them. All armed. One carried a shotgun in his hands.

"Ah," said the traveler. "Let me guess—there's a toll, am I right?"

That put a greasy smile on the big man's face. "Oh yeah, there's a toll."

"Does it matter at all that I'm a servant of god? No, don't look at me like that, I'm being serious here. I'm an actual servant of god. Doing god's work. That get me any play here?"

The beefy man looked momentarily confused. Then he grinned. "God's dead, ain't you heard? And he left this road to Boss Keffler in his will."

The big man guffawed, and the others joined him. The traveler smiled thinly, and as the laughter tapered off, he held up a hand.

"Yeah, yeah, okay, very hilarious," said the traveler, his tone calm and reasonable. "You look like you're the topkick of this crew. Am I right? What's your name, brother?"

"I ain't your brother."

"Figure of speech. What, sir, is your name?"

"Tony Grapes."

"Tony Grapes? Really? You're going with that? Yes? Okay, sure, Grapes. Whatever. Look, Mr. Grapes, my name's Marty Kirk. Brother Marty these days. We both know that you're a large, scary individual, and your colleagues there are tough as they come. That's obvious, that's a given, no need to go further with that discussion. We know that. Just like we know that I'm a hundred and sixty pounds of middle-aged nothing. I'm not armed, and even if I was, we both know you could take away anything I had and make me eat it, raw, with only a little soy sauce. We're there, am I right? We're on that page."

Tony stared at him with open mouth and narrowed eyes. Wary, but fascinated. "Yeah," he said. "That's about it."

"So, let's look at the last page of this script, 'cause I don't think we're reading from the same screenplay. In your version, I get my tuchus kicked and maybe my throat cut and you guys have a funny anecdote to tell the rest of the Neanderthals about how your combined weight of—I'm guessing here—three quarters of a ton of whale lard was able to stomp my skinny self into the dirt without so much as you bruising a hairy knuckle. I mean, let's face it, you got that script, you're reading those pages, am I right?"

"You've got a smart mouth."

"I've been told. My point is," continued Brother Marty, "my script has two different endings. One for the theaters, the other for the DVD extras, you follow? No? Forgot about all that already? Life's sad, so much is lost. Whatever. In one version, the version where we all end the day happy and still sucking air, you and your four chums here drop to your knees, renounce your false god like the carnival phony he is, embrace Thanatos—all praise to his darkness—and one-two-three, you guys are part of my team. This is a nice scenario, am I right? This is a Hallmark moment and a happy ending."

"This guy's totally monkey-bat crazy," said one of the gang.

"No kidding," said Tony. He swung the sword out and laid the flat of it on Brother Marty's shoulder. The weight of the blade made Marty's knees buckle for a moment.

"But," said Marty hastily, "let me get to the alternate ending. In that version we go for the edgy ending, the dark ending. The one that would play well at Cannes but score low in the word-of-mouth market. You dig where I'm going with this? No? Let me set the scene. In the alternate ending, you five goons don't forswear your false god, you don't accept the blessing of Thanatos—all praise to his darkness—and none of you are on call for the sequel to this summer blockbuster. Are you feeling me on this, Tony? You get where my GPS is taking us? That second ending sucks, neither of us like it. It's a tearjerker, am I right? And, come on, is that really the best ending for the whole family? I don't think so. I think we need to take a closer look at the first ending, the one the director wants to shoot, because, hey, it sells more popcorn and it's a crowd pleaser."

Tony Grapes said nothing. Neither did the others.

"No?" asked Marty. "Nothing? This is like talking to the screenwriter's union. Suddenly nobody has words."

One of the gang said, "Hey, Tony, it's bad luck to kill a crazy person, you know that, right?"

Tony sneered. "He ain't crazy. He's trying to tap-dance his way out of it, that's all." To Marty, Tony said, "What were you before First Night? Some kind of con man?"

"I was a producer, so . . . pretty much, yes. But here's my point, you fellas need to make a real career decision right here, right now. We could use some local talent, you dig? Someone who knows the ropes and knows the roads."

"How 'bout we just have some fun kicking your ass up and down the road?"

"Feel free to try, and I mean that sincerely, guys," said Marty. "But this is a one-time offer that expires . . . well, now, actually."

Tony abruptly looked up to see another man in black clothes and red tassels climb up on the hood of a wrecked car.

"Oh, please," he said with a gruff laugh. "It's gonna take a lot more than . . ."

His voice trailed off. There was sudden movement all around them. A second figure climbed onto a car, a third stepped out from between two SUVs. A third, a fourth. Ten more. Twenty.

Too many.

In front and behind and on both sides. They weren't there and then they were, the figures moving as silently as ghosts. They all carried weapons.

The closest ones were bigger, more muscular and more dangerous-looking than the others, and they had red hand-print tattoos over their faces. Their eyes burned with bloodlust.

The gang member with the shotgun raised it to point at the nearest figure.

"Whoa, whoa, whoa now," said Marty quickly. "Think it through. That there is a Remington model 870 pump shot-gun, am I right? You probably have a six-shot magazine and maybe one in the pipe. I'm using that word right? Pipe? So you got seven shots. Your friend there has a Glock 23 with a thirteen-shot capacity, and again one in the pipe. At best—at best I'm saying—if you guys are Deadeye Dicks, you can take out twenty, twenty-two of us. The rest of you have knives and swords, and I'm here to tell you that we like our odds in an edged-weapon tussle. Not bragging, just saying. So, you take out a coupla dozen of us, and the rest of us spend the whole afternoon and evening teaching you guys all sorts of songs. Hymns, if you catch where I'm going with this. It's a religious thing. Hymns to Thanatos—praise be to his darkness."

All around them dozens upon dozens of voices echoed the chant.

"So," said Marty, still being reasonable, "the math isn't good. I like you boys, you have some pluck, and central casting could've put you in anything by Tarantino or the Coen brothers. Seriously, you're great. But there's so many of us my head hurts to do the tallies."

Tony licked his lips but said nothing.

"Okay, I have your attention," said Marty. "Now, the whole reason I'm here and we're taking this meeting instead of just walking away from your bleeding corpses is that we need what's in your head more than we need what's in your veins. Okay, that's a bad line. I'm a producer, not a scriptwriter. Follow me, though. It was a threat, but it was couched so as to present an offer. You got that, right?"

"O-offer . . . ?" said Tony, so thrown off his game that he seemed to have forgotten the sword in his hands.

"Right. Like I said, we need someone who knows the area. Someone who can help us get around this part of California and up into the Sierra Nevadas. We need that more than we need to send all five of you into the darkness."

"I—I—"

"And, just to remove any confusion . . . we only need one

of you. Whoever knows the area best. The rest . . . well, sorry, kids, but that's how the Oreo crumbles."

"Just one?" echoed Tony.

"Just one."

"He's messing with your head, Tony," said the guy with the shotgun. "Don't let him—"

"Shut up, Ralphie," barked Tony. "I'm trying to think."

Marty nodded encouragingly. "Listen, Tony, you look like an enterprising fellow. You're a leader, you're a trusted man? These guys are here working for you, am I right?"

"Screw that," said another of the gang. "We work for Boss Keffler."

Marty glanced at him, said nothing, then addressed Tony. "Correct me if I'm totally wrong, but Boss Keffler isn't actually here. You are, Tony. And we are."

"Tony," said Ralphie, "don't listen to this clown. We can—"

Without a second's hesitation Tony spun and slashed him across the neck with the sword. Ralphie's head leaped two feet into the air, propelled by a fierce burst of blood. Before Ralphie's head even landed, Tony chopped down on the man with the Glock. The man screamed for half a second and then dropped to his knees, split from collarbone to groin. The other two gang members gaped for a moment; then they turned to run. Tony cut a look at Brother Marty, like a dog waiting for approval to do a trick.

"Earn it," suggested Marty.

Tony ran them down and his sword did quick, terrible work. It was over in seconds. Tony was splashed with blood, and as he turned back to Marty, the reapers closed in around him. Tony did not resist or protest when strong hands took his sword away. Nor did he fight when they pushed him down to his knees in front of Marty. The producer nodded and ran a palm over his tattooed scalp.

Marty smiled at Tony. Even kneeling, the gang leader was nearly as tall as the reaper. "Tony, I'm liking you more and more. You have pluck, you have common sense, and you have timing. All good qualities. Now . . . let's talk."

Tony Grapes licked his lips. His eyes were bright and wet and his chin trembled.

"Talk about what?"

"About where," corrected Marty. "My boss, a guy I'd knee-walk through broken glass for—and I don't joke when I say this—really wants to find a place called Mountainside." Marty leaned close so that his lips almost touched Tony's. "Let's all hope and pray that you can help us find it."

3

Sanctuary
Area 51

A big man with a bowie knife tried very hard to kill Benny Imura.

Benny yelled something loud and inarticulate as he flung himself out of the way of the slashing blade. He could feel the steel whistle past his ear. As he turned his panicked dive into a roll, he bumped and bounced to minimum safe distance, losing his sword in the process. The *katana*—Tom's sword—lay in the dirt between Benny and his attacker.

The man with the knife straightened and gave Benny a long, cold, harsh stare of contempt.

"I thought you said you could fight."

Benny spat dust out of his mouth and unloaded a string of comments that could have burned the paint off a steel drum.

"Nice," said the big man. "You kiss your mama with that mouth?"

"My mother's dead," Benny snarled. "Don't you—"

"Everybody's mother's dead, Sherlock. It's the apocalypse."

"Yeah, yeah, whatever." Benny climbed to his feet, eyeing the fallen sword. "Don't look so smug . . . you missed me."

"Sure, and missing you took some effort. It was all I could do to keep from carving a few pounds of stupid off you."

Benny laughed. "Oh, yeah, that's what happened. You missing had nothing to do with me dodging and evading and doing a combat roll. Yeah, you missed on purpose."

Suddenly everything seemed to blur. The big man threw the knife with incredible, insane speed. One moment it was in his hand, and the next instant the knife was buried three inches into the hard desert sand exactly between Benny's feet. But before it even stopped quivering the man hooked the toe of his boot under the sword, kicked it into the air, caught it one-handed, leaped forward, swung the sword, and then froze with the razor edge less than a hairbreadth from Benny's throat.

"Yeah," said the big man, "I did."

The world was frozen into a moment of impossibility. Benny tried to look down at the blade without daring to move his head.

He said, "Um . . . .urk . . ."

Behind him three pairs of hands began a slow, ironic round of applause.

The big man smiled—all white teeth and blue eyes in a seamed and scarred face—and stepped back half a pace. He reversed the sword in his grip and offered the handle to Benny.

Benny had to take a moment to remember how to breathe before he dared raise his hand to accept the weapon. His hand was shaking so badly he almost dropped it.

The audience was three girls—Nix Riley, Lilah the Lost Girl, and a former reaper named Riot. Nix and Riot were smiling, Lilah—typically—was not. The big man gestured for them to stop the applause and waved them over.

The four of them stood in a loose half circle around Captain Joe Ledger. The ranger's dog, Grimm, a massive American mastiff who usually wore armor fitted with blades and had been trained to hack zombies rather than bite them, sat nearby, watching Benny with undisguised dislike.

The ranger's own emotions were impossible to read. He had a sunbaked, scarred face that generally wore either a fake smile or a disapproving scowl. The man was still a bit unreal to Benny. He'd first read about him on a Zombie Card; Ledger was a hero of First Night, a former Special Operator. He had led a crew of world-class soldiers against terrorists who were armed with exotic bioweapons. In the weeks following First Night, Ledger was supposed to have saved thousands of people by organizing them, helping them find shelter, teaching them how to fight the limitless armies of the dead. He'd even fought alongside Solomon Jones, Fluffy McTeague, Hector Mexico, and Tom.

This man had known Tom.

The man had once been a great hero.

He was still fighting the zoms and leading the fight against the reapers. Without him, Benny and all his friends would have died in the Nevada desert.

He was a living legend.

And Benny wished he could bury the man up to his chin in an anthill and pour honey over him.

The feeling was clearly mutual.

"You know what your problem is?" asked Ledger.

"I'm standing too close to a jerk who thinks he's Captain Wonderful?"

"Cute. But no . . . the problem is that you have some skills. For the amount of training you say you've had, you're actually pretty good. And that's what's going to get you killed."

Grimm looked at Benny the way a hungry wolf might look at a limping gazelle. Drool hung from his rubbery jowls.

Benny waited for the other shoe to drop, and it hit with a thud.

Ledger said, "What you are is an arrogant little . . ."

There was more, a lot more, but Benny stopped listening. He turned and began walking away. He got a dozen steps before a strong hand grabbed him and whirled him around.

It wasn't Joe.

It was Nix.

She was beautiful even when she was furious, and right now she was absolutely furious. Her freckles glowed like hot embers and her green eyes were lethal. She pitched her voice into a low, fierce whisper that only he could hear.

"You listen to me, Benjamin Imura," she snapped. "Captain Ledger is trying to help us."

"I don't want his help."

"Don't be stupid. We need his help. We need to keep training."

"Tom trained us," he fired back, his voice rising. "Tom was the best, and he trained us and we've been warrior smart. We survived everything because of Tom."

Nix got right up in his face.

"Survived everything? Really? Why don't you go tell that to Chong."

It was worse than a slap across the face.

Chong.

God . . .

Benny tried to say something back, something witty and full of thorns, but the words caught in his throat; he couldn't spit them out. Instead he turned, slammed his sword into its sheath, and stalked away.

Nix Riley watched Benny go. She was angry and hurt and sorry for what she'd said. Tears began burning the corners of her eyes. When she turned away from him, Captain Ledger was right there. She hadn't heard him approach.

"He—he had to go and—" she began, but he stopped her with a smile and a shake of his head.

"Don't make excuses for him."

"He's been through a lot," she said quickly. "He's not usually like this. It's not his fault."

"Fault?" he echoed as they rejoined the others. "No. But it is his responsibility. We're at war, and we don't have the luxury of letting our emotions get in the way of preparing for the fight."

"No," agreed Lilah, and Riot nodded too.

"Besides," said Riot, "Benny don't hold the only license on pain and grief."

It was true enough. Each of them had suffered terrible losses.

And Lilah . . . she'd lost more than all of them. Lilah's pregnant mother had died in an old farmhouse and Lilah, two years old at the time, had watched first her natural death during childbirth and then a second and more brutal death as the survivors defended themselves after she resurrected as a zom. A man named George became Lilah's protector and guardian because he was the last survivor of that group of refugees in the farmhouse; but some years later he was murdered and his death made to look like a suicide. Around that time, Lilah and her little sister had been forced to fight in the zombie pits at Charlie Pink-eye's Gameland. During an abortive escape, little Annie was mortally wounded and left to die on a desolate rain-swept road. Lilah found her just as Annie reanimated. And the Lost Girl did what had to be done. After that, Lilah lived alone in the wilds of the Rot and Ruin, fending for herself and killing zombies and bounty hunters and in the process becoming remote and strange. And perhaps a little crazy. She'd begun to come out of that shell after she'd been rescued by Benny, Nix, and Tom, and more so when she and Chong had fallen in love.

Now Chong was lost. Dying or dead. Or maybe a monster.

The people in the blockhouse on the far side of the trench wouldn't tell them.

Benny had lost Tom. And that was hard enough. Tom was a bit larger than life, a man of great gentleness, wisdom, and power who ultimately saved the Nine Towns from the evil of Charlie Pink-eye and his family.

Nix cut a sideways glance at Captain Ledger, wondering what—and who—he'd lost; but the big ranger never spoke about himself. He didn't even comment on the things he was said to have done to earn himself a place on the Heroes of First Night subset of the Zombie Cards.

Ledger caught her looking at him. "He'll be back," he said, misreading her thought.

Nix shook her head. "I don't think so."

The ranger smiled. "He'll be back."

The day burned away and Benny did not come back.

4

Rattlesnake Valley
Southern California

They perched in the tree like a flock of birds. Five silent shapes, crouched on branches, their bodies and weapons dappled with sunlight and shadow. Only the fact that no actual birds shared the same tree hinted that they were there.

The tree was a stout and twisted cottonwood with many crooked arms reaching in improbable directions. Spring had come early this year and the branches were thick with leaves, but the early season had brought drought with it, and the leaves were already curling for want of water. It was the hottest spring any of them could remember. The sky above the valley was as hard and blue as bottle glass. Only a few small clouds moved above them, pushed along by a brisk wind that offered no relief from the heat.

A shadow cast by the largest cloud sailed down the far

side of the valley, moving like a dark stain across the fields of weed-choked grass. The five figures watched as several zombies staggered in pursuit of the cloud shadow.

The dead always followed movement. They were slow but relentless, walking on legs stiffened to sticks by withered tendons and nearly moistureless flesh. They would follow the shadow until it vanished or until the sun fell into the Pacific Ocean nearly four hundred miles away. They would chase it the way they chased anything else that moved, hoping for a meal they didn't need to satisfy a hunger that was as bottomless as forever. And if they caught up to the shadow and found that it was nothing but an illusion, with no substance, they would not cry out in despair, because that is an expression of emotion, and the dead were empty.

Nothing but empty shells.

As the watchers sat on their perches, they saw that the dead began angling toward one another while still pursuing the shadow. Soon a dozen of them were lumbering along in a loose and awkward cluster.

"See?" whispered Samantha, the oldest of the girls, pointing with the tip of her short spear. "I told you, they're moving in packs."

A second group of dead came in from another angle, staggering out from the ruins of a small factory where they had probably worked and where they'd almost certainly died. Seven of them, stepping into the sunlight through different open doorways, hearing the moans of the other zombies and catching sight of the shadow. Without pause the seven dead formed a new pack and moved off in pursuit of nothing.

"They're doing it too," said Laura, who was on a nearby

branch. She had spiked hair and her face was painted to match the dappled sunlight. A hunting bow was slung across her back. "They never used to do that."

"I know," agreed Samantha. "But they're doing it now. Amanda and I saw a bunch of groups like that while we were hunting last week."

Amanda nodded. She was generally the quietest of the group, deep and brooding, but fierce in combat. She wore a pair of matched hatchets tucked through her belt. "We saw one pack with nearly fifty of them in it."

Michelle, the second archer of the group, shook her head. "No, that's impossible."

"That's too many," agreed Laura.

"Amanda's right," countered Samantha. "At least fifty. We both counted."

The two packs out in the field followed the shadow for long minutes, but then it reached the top of the valley and vanished from sight. The packs slowed as confusion set in. They looked around, saw nothing else to chase, and one by one the dead slowed to a walk and then stopped.

And stood there.

The five girls knew that they would continue to stand there until something else drew their attention. Otherwise they had no reason to go anywhere.

Some of the dead, lacking an impetus to hunt, stood in fields with years of vines wrapped around them. Zombies like that were among the most dangerous. One of them could be lying on the ground covered by vines or fallen leaves or low-growing plants like pachysandra, and you'd never know until they smelled you. Or until you stepped on one.

The girls remembered that lesson very well, as they remembered all such lessons.

There used to be twenty-two of them. Girls, boys, and three adults.

Now there were six girls. Five in the tree and one . . . missing.

Tiffany had been on patrol in the woods surrounding the old motel where the girls lived, and sometime this morning she'd vanished. They found her weighted fighting sticks and a scuffle of footprints, but nothing else.

The other five girls had formed a party to hunt for her. A cold morning had caught fire to become an inferno afternoon. Each of them was sick with dread at losing Tiffany. They couldn't bear to lose another of their family.

Now they perched in a tree, letting the day tell them what was happening, what was there, what to expect.

They always paid attention to the lessons nature and experience provided. It was how they'd been raised. Samantha was the oldest of them by a few days. She'd been born one day before the world ended. The others had all been born in the days that followed. None of them ever knew their parents. Their mothers had been at a hospital near Sacramento. The nurses and doctors had tried to protect everyone from the dead, but they hadn't been able to. During one terrible battle the hospital caught fire. Nine adults gathered up the babies in the nursery and fled in a convoy of cramped ambulances. The leader of that group of adults was a tough-as-nails prenatal care nurse named Ida from Haiti, a place that probably didn't exist anymore. Because most places didn't exist anymore. Not with names, at least. Ida brought her small group of survivors out of the teeth of the zombie uprising and away, deep into the forests of California, where people were always sparse even before the nightmare. There they settled and learned to survive. To forage, to hunt, and to kill.

Or so the story went.

That tale was passed down from the survivors of the hospital to other refugees they met along the way and finally to the children as they grew old enough to understand.

The five girls were the last of that group.

Ida's main support and allies in the running of their group were Dolan, a man who used to be an actor, and Mirabel, who sold houses in Sacramento. Two springs ago Dolan had been attacked by a panther and dragged off. Ida said that the big cat probably escaped from a zoo during the End, or its parents did. There were all sorts of animals out here that used to be in zoos or circuses. Elephants and zebras and a huge white pregnant rhinoceros they saw heading north toward the Sierra Nevadas.

Mirabel and three boys had gone hunting one winter day, and none of them were ever seen again. The only trace of them that anyone ever found was Mirabel's locket—a beautiful thing with a cameo front. Samantha spotted it hanging from a tree branch. But its owner and the last of the boys were gone. That was nearly three years ago.

And Ida . . . she died of the flu early last year.

Ida came back almost at once, but it wasn't really Ida. It was a hungry thing that looked like her, but everything that had actually been her was gone.

The girls did what they had to do, what they'd been

trained all their lives to do. Afterward they buried Ida in the cemetery, which used to be someone's garden. Ida now slept in the cool, quiet ground along with the other kids and the adults who'd died at home.

Home.

They lived in what had once been known as the Rattlesnake Valley Motor Court. It was a V-shaped building with forty bedroom units, an empty pool, a tennis court, and a wall that had been meticulously built of tractor-trailers by previous tenants of the place who'd later died of plague. The tires of the big trucks had been slashed, and all the spaces under and around the vehicles had been packed with heavy stones and clay. There were a dozen ways out, but you had to know where they were and you had to have a working brain to use them. Even then, there were booby traps in case bands of human raiders tried to get in. A few tried every year. None had ever managed it. Not alive.

One thing Ida and the other adults had taught the girls was that they had to do whatever they needed to do in order to survive. The girls learned those lessons well, which is why these five were still alive. Along with the missing Tiffany, they were the top hunters, the best fighters. They were the fiercest of the little tribe that had lived—and died—at the Rattlesnake Valley Motor Court. They understood how to hunt, cook, do first aid, farm, observe, process, react, and fight.

They knew about their world, and they relied on what they'd been taught and what they'd learned from doing.

But now the rules were changing.

The dead were beginning to move in packs.

And Tiffany was missing.

Heather, the fifth and youngest girl in the hunting party, was the only one with a working pair of binoculars. While the others talked, she sat in silence and studied the dead through the high-powered lenses. When she finally spoke, her voice was filled with doubt and fear. "They look the same as always."

"What did you expect?" asked Laura sharply. "Little monkeys sitting on their backs, steering them?"

"No, stupid . . . but if they're the same, then why are they moving differently?"

None of the girls had an answer to that. When it came to the dead, their security, their hunting patterns, their lives depended on a total lack of change. So many other things in their world changed all the time—friends and adults dying, exotic and dangerous animals coming through, drought ravaging the crops, bad storms. Those things pushed them to their limits. If the dead somehow changed, then that could push them over the edge.

And they all knew it.

Michelle touched Heather's arm and in a small and fragile voice asked, "Do you see . . . ?"

She didn't finish the question. There was no point. They all knew what she was asking.

Did Heather see Tiffany out there?

Among the dead.

Heather was a long time answering. Not because she was afraid to answer the question, but because she was being sure, making certain. She moved the glasses from face to face, lingering long enough to study the features. Most of the dead were ravaged by old wounds—the injuries, bites, or bullets that had killed them—or pocked by the diseases that had swept through the fleeing human populations after the dead rose. The flesh of any zombie older than a week would be withered to a leathery mask of wrinkles. Once, when doing this kind of meticulous search among a cluster of zombies, Heather saw a torn and twisted figure whose body lacked arms and had much exposed bone showing through the remaining flesh. She could not be sure—and she didn't want to make sure—but in her heart she believed that it was Dolan. Or what had been left of him after the panther had done its awful work.

She let out a slow sigh.

"No," she said with real relief, "she's not down there."

As relief went, it was as thin and capricious as a brief waft of cool air. It did not mean that Tiffany was still alive. All it meant was that she was not part of this group of the dead.

Suddenly all the dead turned at the same time, twisting around to the east, raising their heads as if listening to a sound; however, none of the girls could hear or see anything. The dead seemed to tremble with indecision for a moment, their fingers twitching, mouths opening and closing, and then as one they began moving toward the tree line on the east part of the valley.

"What's going on?" gasped Michelle.

Samantha narrowed her eyes as she watched the dead move toward some very specific part of the forest. "I don't know. They must have heard something."

"Might be a deer," suggested Michelle, but Samantha shook her head.

"No, they heard something, and deer don't make enough noise to cause them all to react like that."

The other girls nodded.

Small, strong hands gripped the tree limbs and tightened around the handles of weapons.

Then a yell split the air.

A high, piercing scream of total terror.

A millisecond later Tiffany burst from between two shaggy shrubs and came running full tilt into the field the zombies had recently vacated. Her clothes were torn and streaked with blood; she held a broken spear in one hand, and her dark hair snapped in the wind as she ran.

Michelle opened her mouth to yell out, to let Tiffany know that her friends were close by, but Samantha silenced her with a sharp gesture. Laura leaned forward and pointed.

"Oh my God . . . look!"

The darkness under the trees roiled and twisted, and then the zombies staggered out into the sunlight. All the ones who had followed whatever lure had drawn them to the east . . . and many, many more.

At least a hundred of the tattered gray figures lurched after their fleeing prey, and as if in chorus they opened their mouths to utter a moan of unbearable hunger. It filled the sky and tore another scream from Tiffany.

"We have to do something," pleaded Michelle.

"If she makes it to the creek, she'll be okay," said Laura. A small ribbon of blue meandered through the valley floor. It was waist deep in places and the current, though not brisk, would nonetheless confuse the awkward feet of the mindless dead. They watched as Tiffany spotted the stream and cut right toward it, angling in the direction of the deepest section.

"Good," said Samantha under her breath. "Good . . ."

She took the field glasses from Heather and spent several long, agonizing moments studying the darkness under the tree line. Heather and Amanda must have seen some expression on her face, because they both asked, "What?" at the same time.

"Look!" snapped Samantha. "Behind the zombies."

They all looked, first by squinting and then as the binoculars were handed from one to the other. Soon they each wore identical expressions of mingled surprise, confusion, and fear.

"I don't understand," murmured Michelle.

"I don't either," said Laura.

None of them did, because what they saw made no sense in the world as they understood it.

As the dead continued to stagger out of the forest, a line of people walked slightly behind them. There were at least twenty of them, and they wore identical clothes: black pants and black shirts with some white design on them. Red cloth streamers were tied to their ankles, knees, waists, and wrists. Each of them held a weapon in one hand, a sword or ax or knife; and each of them held something to their mouths that flashed with silver light as they emerged from shadows into the sunny field.

None of them made a sound, though it looked like they were all blowing whistles.

Silent whistles.

"Are they . . . dog whistles?" wondered Michelle.

"I . . . think so," said Laura. "Dolan found one in that house we raided for food three years ago."

The people in black and red continued to walk forward without hurry, the silver whistles constantly held to their puffing mouths. Some came from different arms of the forest and stood waiting for the tide of dead to reach them.

The dead moved around them and past them, but not one of the cold zombies reached out a hand to touch what was clearly warm, living flesh.

It was a totally bizarre moment.

"What are they doing?" breathed Amanda.

Samantha shook her head.

But in fact it was clear what these strangers were doing. It simply seemed impossible.

Using their silent whistles, the strangers were driving the zombies into the field, calling them together, turning them into a pack.

And sending them after Tiffany.

There were now at least a hundred and fifty of the dead converging on Tiffany, and it was in no way certain that she'd reach the stream in time. The dead were coming from everywhere, some walking out of shadows to the north and south of the field, closing the teeth of this terrible trap. And now there were at least two dozen of the strangers. All of them were adults, and each of them carried a gleaming weapon.

Heather gripped Samantha's arm with desperate force. "We have to do something."

Samantha opened her mouth but she said nothing, gave no orders.

Because to go down there was certain death.

Absolutely certain.

Tiffany screamed again as she ran.

The dead moaned as they followed.

5

South Fork Wildlife Area
Southern California

Before Marty Kirk was a reaper, he'd been a top Hollywood producer. He put together movie deals that made hundreds of millions, he worked with the A-list of talent. His was a household name known even to people who didn't often go to the movies. Marty Kirk. He was a regular guest on Jon Stewart and Jay Leno and Conan O'Brien.

But that was before Jon and Jay and Conan and their audiences of millions were swept away by a tide of flesh-eating madness.

That was before the Fall.

Now he was known as Brother Marty.

Now he was a reaper of the Night Church.

He wore the black clothes, the red tassels, the white wings. He dabbed his tassels in a chemical mixture that kept the living dead—the gray people—from attacking. He spent hours each day reciting prayers and singing hymns and listening to sermons about a god that Brother Marty had never even heard of before the Fall.

A god that, even now, he didn't believe in.

Not at all. Not even a little.

And yet it was a god in whose name he had killed, and in whose name he had ordered other reapers to open red mouths in the flesh of the heretics and blasphemers.

Brother Marty never once spoke of his lack of personal faith. He never even hinted at it.

Brother Marty, above all else, wasn't stupid.

As the old saying goes, he knew on which side his bread was buttered.

Over the last nine years he had risen within the ranks of the Night Church, first from the least capable foot soldier in the service of Saint John, to a member of the logistics team, to the head of recruitment, all the way to his current position as a member of the Council of Sorrows and a personal aide to the saint.

Now he traveled everywhere with Saint John. He'd gone with him from Wyoming to Utah, to Idaho and Montana, and all through Nevada. Zigzagged throughout the west, raising armies of reapers, burning towns and settlements of blasphemers, carrying out the will of Thanatos.

Or, as Brother Marty privately viewed it, carrying out the master plan of an absolute total nutbag. Saint John was a monster by anyone's standards. A serial killer of legendary status before the Fall, a menace to society who had nonetheless been the inspiration for half a dozen movies and twice as many books, and who was now the charismatic leader of a vast army of killers. It was a crazy place to be, but in this world it was the only safe place left to stand. Marty always looked out for Marty. First and foremost. And to accomplish that, he did whatever he had to do, to whomever he had to do it.

He did not consider himself evil. Marty didn't believe in evil. Evil was something priests and rabbis droned on about, and Marty hadn't seen the inside of a synagogue since he was ten. He didn't believe that there was anything after death. All there was after this was bones in a box. No redemption, no paradise. Nothing, zip, nada.

So the only smart thing to do was stay alive as long as possible, and stay as well fed and protected as possible until the last gasp.

Nowhere was safer than with Saint John. The reapers were an unstoppable force.

And Saint John knew how to call on an even bigger and far more dangerous horde—the living dead. The saint and his reapers used their protective chemicals to be able to walk among the gray people, and employed dog whistles to call and direct the rotting walkers.

Who could ever stand in the way of that?

A few weeks ago Saint John had left Nevada, taking the main body of his reaper army with him in search of a string of nine previously unknown towns in central California. Nine towns packed with people whose flesh, according to the saint, ached to feel the kiss of the knife.

The problem was . . . California was a big darn state, and these towns hadn't existed back when maps were still being made. They were refugee camps that had grown into gated communities. Saint John wanted them destroyed. He wanted to burn them as a statement that no one may defy the will of Lord Thanatos.

All praise to his darkness, thought Brother Marty sourly. *All praise, yada yada yada.*

But as he approached the saint, he composed his face into one of reverence and humility.

He dropped to his knees. "Honored one," said Marty as he bent and kissed the dirt caked on Saint John's shoes. Then, like an obedient dog, he glanced up at the saint.

Saint John's dark eyes were so deeply set that they made

his pale face appear skeletal. His head was tattooed with a pattern of thorny vines. He wore black trousers and a billowy black shirt, his legs and arms wrapped with bloodred ribbons. On his chest was a beautifully rendered chalk drawing of angel wings. He was Saint John of the Knife, and the reapers were his flock, and he was the single most impressive and charismatic person Brother Marty had ever met. And he'd met everyone in Hollywood.

"Did you find a scout for me?" asked the saint.

Brother Marty hesitated for a moment. "I did . . . and I didn't. It's complicated."

"Stand up and talk to me," said Saint John. "Let me see your face."

Brother Marty got to his feet. He did not tremble, as many of the reapers did in the presence of Saint John. He had that much self-control; he was too practiced a performer, even as a producer, to show weakness during any meeting.

"We found a small gang of crooks. Lowlifes, you know the type," said Marty. "Their leader was a gun thug named—and I'm not joking—Tony Grapes. Real name. Anyway, I appealed to Tony's better nature, and he very willingly and enthusiastically, I might add, opened red mouths in all four of his own goons fast as you can say summer blockbuster. Wham, bam, and down they go."

Saint John nodded his approval. There was the slightest trace of a smile on his severe mouth, as there often was when he listened to Brother Marty.

"So, we do the whole conversion process, and our friend Tony here is an instant altar boy. He can't help us enough, he can't be more helpful. He's so helpful I want to tell him to shut up already, but since I just told him to talk, I can't very well turn that faucet off. Anyway, I ask him if he ever heard of a place called Mountainside, and he has. That's good, that's great, that's peaches and ice cream."

"But . . . ?" coaxed Saint John.

"But . . . he don't exactly know where it is."

Saint John said nothing. He was a patient man, and he allowed Brother Marty to get to his point in his own way.

"So, suddenly Brother Tony and I are having a new set of contract negotiations, and you know how that goes. Things get loud, things get wet. Long story short, he knows a guy who knows a guy who does know where Mountainside is."

"Was our new reaper able to tell us where to find this friend of a friend?"

"Ah, well, that's where it gets complicated," said Marty with a sad smile. "As it turns out, the guy he knows is a pal, but the guy his guy knows, the one who actually can tell us where Mountainside is—he's not exactly a friend of our Mr. Tony Grapes."

"Oh?"

"It seems Brother Tony used to run with a crowd who did considerable business with someone this other guy didn't like. There was some kind of wild craziness a while ago, and now this other guy would like to see Tony's head on a pole. Maybe metaphorically, maybe not, Tony wasn't clear on that point. This other guy scares the turkey stuffing out of Mr. Grapes."

"Who is this other man?" asked Saint John. "Who is this enemy of god and where can we find him?"

"That's what I asked Brother Tony, and he says that he

can take us right to him, but he wants protection because this fellow has made some vague threats about throat-cutting and spinal separation. Credible threats, apparently. The man's a trade guard who works all up and down the California border towns and outposts."

"His name?"

"Sweeney," said Brother Marty. "His name is Iron Mike Sweeney."

6

Sanctuary
Area 51

Benny Imura went as far as he could get from Captain Ledger, his stupid training methods, and everything related to that oversize old creep. He was so mad that he growled at several of the monks, who shied back away from him.

Every time Benny thought about how Ledger tried to lord it over him or prove that he was a better fighter than Tom, or knew more than Tom, or could teach better than Tom, it made Benny even madder. He bent and snatched up a big rock and threw it as hard as he could against the side of the nearest of the big gray airplane hangars. The impact made a loud *karooom* that Benny suddenly realized must have sounded like thunder inside.

He stopped and stared horrified at the spot where the rock had struck.

The hangar was filled with the sick and dying.

"Oh . . . jeez . . ."

The back door opened and a nun stepped out. Sister Hannahlily.

"Sorry!" yelled Benny, edging away.

The nun gave Benny a look that could have quieted a whole pack of zoms. He managed to endure it for two full seconds before he turned and fled. He could feel the heat of her disapproval stabbing him in the back like arrows.

Behind the hangars, foothills of red stone rose in broken walls to which tenacious vines clung. Spiky weeds sprouted up from the clefts. Benny caught movement out of the corner of his eye and glanced up to see a goat picking its way nimbly along a path so narrow that it wasn't even visible from ground level. The goat threaded its way along the face of the cliff, and Benny kept pace with it, trying to let a pointless and temporary fascination divert him from his own glum thoughts.

Benny marveled at the goat, wondering how it had gotten here. Sanctuary was so remote and supposedly impossible to find without a guide. And yet here was a goat that was walking with the kind of confidence that suggested it was familiar with these rocks.

He felt himself frowning and actually had to stop and take mental inventory.

Why was he reacting that way?

Was something wrong about this?

If so . . . what?

Benny looked around, but there was no one to ask. He didn't dare go ask one of the monks or nuns, not after the look Sister Hannahlily had given him. And there was no way in the world he was going to ask Captain Ledger. He'd rather kiss a zom than say another word to that jerk.

No, he decided, he'd find out for himself.

To satisfy his curiosity, he told himself.

To figure out why the presence of that goat bothered him so much.

He adjusted the *katana* that he wore strapped across his back. Tom's sword.

His sword now.

Benny took a breath, reached for the closest lip of rock, and began to climb.

7

Rattlesnake Valley
Southern California

The four girls kept shifting their desperate stares from the zombies converging on Tiffany, then to Samantha, and back again. For her part, Samantha was working it all out. Distance, speed, the presence of the two dozen strangers, the terrain, everything. She was the leader of their pack because she knew how to work things out. Ida had called it three-dimensional thinking.

Samantha had to weigh the safety of the remaining girls against the small chance of saving Tiffany, and factor in the personal risk for all six of them. A trap set for one could catch a rescue party as well. All too easily.

She also had to try to assess what total strangers would do if the girls made a rescue attempt. The people in black and red were clearly alive, and somehow—impossibly, or so it seemed—they'd discovered ways to both control the dead and keep themselves safe from them. Until a few minutes ago Samantha would have thought neither of those things could be done.

However . . . the evidence was clear and irrefutable; therefore it could be done. Her view of the world needed to change to accept that and work with it.

"Okay," she said quickly, an idea forming in her head. "Heather and Laura, I want you to go two hundred yards north. Stay low and stay hidden. Prep arrows and wait for my signal. Go!"

The two youngest girls, both of whom were superb archers, dropped from the tree, using the trunk to hide them. They melted into the high grass the way they'd been taught. Even Samantha, who was the best hunter in their group, lost sight of them at once.

"Good. Amanda, you and Michelle go south. Fifty yards will do it. Kindle a fire but use the driest brush you can find. No smoke. Wait for my call and then put wet stuff on the blaze. Soon as you do, leave it and go west. Find that old farm road and head for the barn. Wait as long as you can, but if we don't catch up in ten minutes, get out of there."

"What about you?" asked Michelle.

"I'll be right here. We have to move fast. Tiff is running out of time."

The girls nodded, dropped from the tree like squirrels, and vanished into the brush.

Tiffany had a lead of maybe thirty yards on the main body of the dead, but she had six hundred yards to go to reach the creek. Two lines of dead were converging, and Samantha judged they'd cut her off sixty or seventy yards shy of safety.

Samantha counted off the seconds she judged were required for the other girls to get into position. It was going to be tight. So tight.

She still had the binoculars and, while she waited, she took a longer look at the people in black and red. The field glasses were very powerful, and now she was able to see the design each of them had on their chests.

Wings.

White angel wings.

So strange a symbol for people who were driving the dead like a pack of dogs to try to murder a teenage girl.

What made it even worse was that the people with the wings and the knives were all smiling as they hunted Tiffany.

Smiling.

God.

Who were these people?

Over the years Samantha's ragtag family had met more than their share of wild loners, badlands human predators, bounty hunters, and worse. The fall of the world had driven so many people mad and corrupted so many others. That's what Ida always said, and she'd prayed for them to find their souls again.

Samantha studied these smiling hunters of innocent girls and wondered how long it had been since they'd lost their connection to either God or humanity. The fact that there were so many of them, and that they were acting in a coordinated way, suggested intelligence and control. And yet what they were doing was mad.

It made no sense to her.

There was a loud birdcall to her right, and she glanced

north. She could not see Heather and Laura, but she knew the call. They were in position. Samantha turned to the south and saw a few thin wisps of smoke. Amanda and Michelle were ready.

Samantha slung the binoculars over her shoulder, took a deep breath to steady her nerves, took her spear in both hands, and dropped out of the tree. She bent nearly in half and moved down to the closest point of concealment near the creek.

Tiffany was running as hard as she could, but by now she had to know that there was no chance she'd slip through the closing jaws of the trap.

Not unless . . .

Samantha set her spear down, cupped her hands around her mouth, and gave a sharp cry. The screech of a hunting hawk.

Instantly two threads of darkness stitched across the sky, and suddenly arrows struck quivering in the throats of the zombies closest to the right-hand part of the trap. One zombie fell at once, the brain stem clearly severed. The other staggered and crashed into another of the dead. They fell heavily, and the zombies behind them tripped and fell over them.

The zombies on that side of the field turned toward movement as first Heather and then Laura rose up, fired, dropped down, and rose up again a few yards away. Arrows flew across the creek, and each one hit a target. The girls were not trying for a kill, not at that distance, but they were good enough to hit heads and necks. Nerve and brain damage, even if not fatal, made the zombies far more erratic and confused. Within seconds that whole side of the trap was a jumble of falling bodies, thrashing limbs, frustrated snarls, and grasping hands.

Tiffany saw this and for an awful moment she slowed almost to a stop, wide-eyed and slack-jawed. Then there was another birdcall—an eagle's shriek—and within seconds thick white smoke billowed up from the south. Amanda and Michelle had thrown wet grass on the fire. The smoke was so dense that it did exactly what Samantha wanted it to do: It cast a writhing shadow on the waving marsh weeds. The zombies on that side of the trap staggered to a clumsy stop, and with Tiffany barely moving, their attention was now drawn by the column of smoke and its wavering shadow. The zombies turned and lumbered that way.

The path was now wide open, but Samantha knew it wouldn't be for long. The people in black and red had spotted the smoke and the arrow-struck dead. They began moving toward those points, weapons glinting in the sunlight.

Samantha rose up out of the grass and gave a third birdcall. The wild, mournful call of a marsh bird.

Tiffany jerked erect, looked the wrong way first, and then swung around toward the cottonwood. When she saw Samantha, she didn't waste a single moment gaping or waving. Instead she broke into a run again, pouring on the speed, racing with all her heart and fear and muscle toward the blue ribbon of water.

Samantha ran to meet her and as Tiffany splashed down into the deepest part, Samantha was there to catch her under the armpit and haul her to safety on the opposite bank.

"Who are those people?" demanded Samantha.

Tiffany was too breathless to say much, but she gasped out a single word.

"Reapers."

There was no time to learn more. The dead had heard the splashing and saw the movement of the two girls in the water. So had the people in black and red.

The reapers.

Holding on to Tiffany, lending strength to her exhausted friend, Samantha ran toward the high ground and the tall grass. The forest reached out with shadows and green arms to enfold them.

However, behind them they heard the moans of the dead, the splash of feet in the water, and the yells—the very human yells—of the reapers as they ran in pursuit of their prey.

8

South Fork Wildlife Area
Southern California

Saint John of the Knife stood in the shadows of a live oak and waited for the slaughter to begin. He stood on a grassy knoll, looking down on a country lane that wandered lazily through the countryside. Birds sang in all the trees, and the air was alive with the buzz of honeybees and bluebottle flies. Sunlight slanted through the boughs, dappling the road in yellow and purple.

The wagon clattered along the road, wheels crunching against the edges of ruts worn into the cracked blacktop. Four heavy-boned horses pulled the wagon, their bodies wrapped in carpet coats and draped with metal mesh. Two men sat on the wooden bench seat, one with the reins in his hands, the other with a shotgun across his knees. The wagon was an old-fashioned chuck wagon that had probably been looted from a cowboy museum. The sides had been reinforced with metal sheeting, and the words GUNDERSON TRADE GOODS had been painted in bright colors. Two men walked beside the wagon, one on each side, leading their horses. Fifty yards behind the wagon, another man rode slowly on a slate-gray Percheron that stood nineteen hands high and wore a helmet covered in spikes.

The man who sat astride the Percheron had flaming red hair gathered back into a ponytail, dusty jeans, cowboy boots, a Western shirt with flowers and hummingbirds stitched across the chest, and crisscrossed army gun belts around his lean hips, from which holstered Glocks hung. A compound bow protruded, slung from the saddle horn. It was a metal-and-fiberglass hunting bow fitted with cables and pulleys. A quiver heavy with arrows was slung across his back.

The man was big—tall, broad-shouldered, and muscular. His chest and arms were almost freakishly huge, nearly simian, but for all his mass there was something about him. A lurking potential to use that power with deadly speed. Saint John could see that right away; he was an excellent judge of combat potential.

This was the man they were looking for, he decided. He fit the description given by the Night Church's newest reaper, Brother Tony. This was the man who knew where Mountainside and the other eight towns could be found.

The trade wagon and its guards were walking through country that was virtually empty of the gray people, and it showed in the slack disinterest of each of those men. Only the big man seemed to be alert. In fact, Saint John saw the precise moment when the red-haired giant realized that the woods were not as empty as they appeared. His horse passed through a patch of shadow thrown across the road by a crooked willow. As the rider passed out of the shadow and into the sunlight, his head jerked up and he looked around. First to the right-hand side of the road, then to the left. His body language changed as he shifted forward in the saddle.

He raised his head, and Saint John had the strange impression that the redhead was sniffing the air the way an animal would. Could he somehow smell the chemicals on the tassels of the hidden reapers? With all the wildflowers that bloomed on either side of the road, it seemed unlikely, improbable. It was why Saint John had chosen this particular spot for the ambush.

"Bobby, Harv," called the big man. "Hold up."

The two men leading their horses turned to look back at him. "What's up, Mike?"

Iron Mike Sweeney used his thighs to guide his horse forward as he continued to look around.

"I don't know . . . something's . . ."

He let his voice trail off. And then it seemed to Saint John that the big man's whole body appeared to blur. His hands were empty and then they were not. He'd snatched up his bow so fast that the eye could not follow it. An arrow seemed to appear on the string as if by magic, there was a vibrating twang, and then a wet scream tore the air. A reaper staggered from between two thick bushes with that same arrow buried to the fletching in his chest. He took two wandering steps and then toppled forward onto his face with no attempt at all to catch his fall.

"Trap!" yelled Iron Mike.

Before Harv and Bobby could even react, Mike had begun filling the air with arrows. One after the other, so fast that Saint John felt an electric thrill race through him. It was like nothing he'd ever seen. Screams filled the air as each arrow plunged into dense shadows to find a chest or throat or eye socket. Reapers fell, writhing in agony or still in death.

The shotgun man on the wagon stood up and swung his barrel around, firing blindly into the trees. Then he shrieked and pitched backward, a hatchet chunked deep into his lower back.

There was a thunderous cry, and the reapers rose up from behind bushes and rocks. A wave of them crested the top of the grassy knoll and washed down toward the road.

Harv and Bobby drew their guns and fired.

And fired and fired.

The reapers were so closely packed that every bullet hit a target.

The guns clicked empty and the guards tried to reload.

Tried.

The reaper wave slammed into them, and they went down in a froth of red as silver knives ended them. Other reapers dragged the driver down and cut him into red inhumanity.

The arrows of the big trade guard never paused. He killed seven reapers, ten, fourteen. Twenty.

They surged toward him, and he hooked the string of the bow over his saddle horn and drew his Glocks. The reapers, the killers who served Saint John's god, ran into the storm of bullets. They screamed the name of Thanatos. They screamed the name of Saint John.

They screamed the names of their mothers as the bullets tore them down.

Iron Mike filled the road with the dead.

His mighty Percheron, twenty-six hundred pounds of warhorse, reared up and lashed out with steel-shod hooves. The elite killers of the Night Church were flung into the air with shattered skulls and arms and chests.

And then a blade whistled through the air, turning end over end, and its point bit deep into the Percheron's throat. The horse screamed and twisted sideways and fell.

Iron Mike leaped from the saddle and landed hard, tucking and rolling, coming up onto the balls of his feet, dropping empty magazines, swapping them out, turning, firing, killing. He dropped those magazines and slapped in his last two.

The reapers formed a wide circle around him, the diameter thirty feet across, the ranks of killers thirty deep. Hundreds of knives and swords and scythes glittered in the sunlight. The red-haired giant held the pistols out as he turned in a slow circle.

Everyone knew how this was going to end. He had fifteen rounds in each gun. He had no more magazines.

There were a thousand reapers around him.

Saint John walked slowly down from the top of the knoll. He paused to retrieve his knife from the horse's throat; then he gave an order and the reapers parted to create a corridor. The saint wiped his blade clean on his thigh and slid the throwing knife into its sheath as he strolled toward the last trade guard. He stopped ten feet away.

The big man said nothing, but he lowered his pistols.

"I am Saint John of the Knife," said the saint. "You understand that if I wanted you dead, you would be dead."

The big man shrugged. "Everybody dies."

His eyes were strange. The irises were red except for a rim of gold. Saint John had never seen eyes like that except in church paintings of vampires and demons.

"The question is, my friend," said Saint John, "do you want to live?"

9

Sanctuary
Area 51

It took twenty-five grueling, exhausting, sweaty minutes to climb all the way up to the goat path. For most of that time the goat stood there, quietly chewing on a tough piece of vegetable root, watching him with placid curiosity. Each time Benny slipped, he could swear there was a look of pitying amusement on the goat's face.

Only when Benny climbed onto a flat shelf near the goat did the animal move away. Even then it was at so leisurely a pace that it was as if the goat was daring Benny to give chase. The path it took was less than a hand's-width wide. Giving chase was very low on Benny's list of things to do in this lifetime.

Following, however, was another thing. He didn't want to catch the goat, but he definitely wanted to know how it had gotten into Sanctuary. On his climb he'd figured out what was bothering him.

If a goat could climb over the mountains and reach Sanctuary, so could a person.

Or a lot of people.

The dead would never be able to manage it, of course. They were too clumsy and mindless, and climbing required strength, coordination, observation, sharp wits, and good judgment.

The reapers had all those things.

Benny smiled grimly. If he was able to prove that Sanctuary was unsafe, that it was vulnerable to a sneak attack because of goat trails like this, then he would be able to throw that right in Captain Ledger's face.

This was being warrior smart.

That's what Benny's brother Tom called it. Warrior smart. Using training and good judgment, courage and determination to confront an obstacle and overcome it. The same rules of common sense and education applied. Faced with anything from finding food in the wasteland, avoiding the zoms, preparing a battle plan, to escaping a trap, or defeating an enemy.

Warrior smart was a better way of thinking than the gung-ho stuff Ledger wanted to teach.

Grinning, he began moving slowly and carefully along the goat path.

His courage and confidence stayed with him for almost three hundred yards, but after the first time the walkway cracked beneath his shoes, he began to doubt the wisdom of this plan.

Half an hour later he was only a third of the way to the crest of this broken hill, but the ground looked like it was a thousand miles down. Hot sweat ran down his face, but cold sweat tickled in lines beneath his clothes. His breath came in ragged gasps, and he tried to drill his fingers into the rock wall.

Once, when he closed his eyes, he thought he heard his brother Tom speaking to him.

Yo! Boy genius, said Tom. *Exactly what do you think you're doing?*

"Shut up," breathed Benny. "I'm trying not to die here."

How hard are you trying?

"Bite me."

Not even if I was alive.

They both laughed, but the laughs were ghostly and unreal. What Benny really wanted to do was sob. The ache he felt for his lost brother was almost unbearable at times. He kept seeing a hole in the world in the shape of Tom Imura, and he couldn't imagine anything filling it.

However, he believed that he was supposed to fill it. He was supposed to become the next Tom Imura.

Him.

Not some old guy who used to be a soldier back when something like that mattered. Before the dead rose and humanity fell. Now—and especially to Benny—meeting an actual soldier was like being handed proof that the old system was never good enough, that it wasn't strong enough. That it wasn't warrior smart enough. The world still ended.

Hot wind whistled past Benny, flapping the cuffs of his jeans and stinging his face.

"Tom . . . ?" murmured Benny.

Yeah, kiddo?

"I . . . I don't know if I can do it."

Tom laughed. A gentle laugh. *It's easy. Put one foot in front of the other and try not to fall.*

"That's not what I meant."

For a moment Benny could really see Tom, standing there in the shade under the big oak that anchored one corner of their gated yard back home. Tom standing with a cup of iced tea. The smell of hot apple pie wafting out through the kitchen window. Really good pie too. With walnuts and raisins, the way Tom made it. Sour apples so it wasn't too sweet.

"That's not what I meant," Benny said again.

I know what you meant, answered Tom.

"Tom, I—"

But Tom was gone.

The wind howled as it tore through the crags of the red rock wall.

Benny took as deep a breath as he could and sighed it out. Took another. And another. And then he continued climbing.

It took almost forty minutes to reach the top of the crest. By the time he did, his body was trembling with fatigue and jumpy from the residue of adrenaline in his blood. He staggered away from the edge onto a flat section that was covered with withered grass and strewn with huge boulders left over from the last glacier. Benny took two wobble-kneed steps and then sank down onto his knees.

His exhaustion was the only thing that kept him alive as something whipped over his head.

Benny flung himself sideways, thinking that it was the goat lashing out with hooves to defend its territory.

It wasn't a goat.

It wasn't an animal.

The thing that had nearly cut his head off was a broad-bladed field scythe.

And it was held in the fists of a reaper.

All around him, others reapers were emerging from hiding places among the glacial boulders.

10

Rattlesnake Valley
Southern California

Samantha and Tiffany plunged into the woods, and a veil of cool shadows dropped behind them. They ran hard and fast along a deer path for fifty yards and then cut sharply left toward a small stream that fed the larger creek. They stepped into the ankle-deep water and kept going, moving slower now, making sure they didn't splash water onto the dry mud along the banks or dampen any of the low-hanging leaves. There was no way to know if their pursuers understood anything about tracking, but the girls were long practiced at stealth and concealment.

Samantha bent close to Tiffany. "Who were those people? Who or what are reapers?"

The younger girl was gasping for breath after her exertions, but she managed to get out what she'd learned. "I . . . was hunting in the eastern woods . . . and I heard a scream. I went running, thinking the dead were attacking someone, but it wasn't that at all. Three men in black were chasing an old couple—they had to be seventy or eighty. The old lady saw me and begged for help." She looked at Samantha for approval. "What else could I do?"

"No, Tiff, you did the right thing, I'm sure," Samantha assured her. "Then what happened?"

Tiffany quickly told the tale. The old couple were the last of a small group of survivors who had been living in an old shopping mall. They barely had enough to eat, but they were safe from the dead. Then the people in black and red—the reapers—broke into the mall and just started killing everyone.

"Why?" asked Samantha sharply.

"That's just it . . . they didn't give any explanation. They kept yelling things about someone named Thanatos and about sending everyone into the darkness. Crazy stuff like that. The old couple and a few others escaped, but they were chased. They'd survived on the road, constantly heading west toward the mountains and forestlands, but the reapers picked them off one by one. Or they sent packs of the dead after them."

"How?"

"The old man said that the reapers made up some kind of chemical stuff that keeps the dead from attacking them. They dip pieces of cloth into it and tie the cloth around their ankles and like that."

Samantha nodded. "The red tassels," she said. "But how do they make the zombies do what they want?"

"The old man thinks they use dog whistles."

"But how does—?"

"The dead can hear it. Certain calls make the dead come to them, other calls make them go away. So, I guess they use the whistles to, I don't know, steer them? Crazy, isn't it?"

"It's smart," said Samantha. "Really smart."

There was a sound in the woods and they both stiffened, ready to run or fight, but it was only a couple of zebras. More zoo escapees. The striped animals turned to where the girls hid, sniffed the air, and then whinnied in irritation and trotted away.

"Why were these reapers chasing you?"

Tiffany flushed. "Well, what I left out was how I had the chance to talk to the two old folks."

"Tell me."

It was a simple thing to say, but Samantha knew that there was a lot behind it. There's always more to something than what it seems.

What Tiffany said was plain and honest and brutal. "They were trying to kill those two old people, so I killed them."

Samantha studied Tiffany's eyes. There were ghosts there, moving from one room of her mind to another. The reapers might have deserved the fate they got, but Tiffany would still carry the memory of what she'd done—what she'd been forced to do—for the rest of her life. Samantha saw similar ghosts when she looked in the mirror.

It made her wonder if the reapers were similarly haunted by the terrible things they were doing. Why, in fact, were they raiding camps and killing innocent folks? In a world where there was almost no one left, it was bad enough killing in defense of the innocent or oneself; but to kill for the joy of it, or for some other equally crazy reason, was a sin.

"What happened to the old people?" asked Samantha tentatively, afraid of the answer.

"I . . . was bringing them home. I thought we could help them. . . ."

"But . . . ?"

"But the reapers caught us. So many of them. They

attacked us, and before I knew it the old couple was down. It was awful, Sam. What they did to those people was bad."

Tiffany's voice was fragile with pain and anger. And with shock, and Samantha knew how dangerous that was.

"I took another of them down, but there were too many, and I ran. You know the rest."

"Reapers," echoed Samantha. "If they're coming this way, we may have to leave the motor court. We can't defend that place against an army, and if they can control the dead, then that's what they have."

Leaving the motor court would be a sad thing. They'd spent most of their lives there. Their friends were buried there. And there were too many supplies to carry if they had to simply pack and run. And they had no idea what was west of where they lived. Some travelers told rumors of a bunch of small towns somewhere in the mountains, but if they'd given any specific details, that knowledge had died with Dolan and Ida.

There were birds in all the trees, but suddenly there was a single sharp owl cry. Samantha and Tiffany stopped whispering and listened. Heard it again. Samantha responded with the sound a baby owl would use to call its mother. Immediately two figures stepped from the shadows beneath an old weeping willow, both of them with arrows nocked to the strings of yew-wood bows.

Heather and Laura lowered their bows and rushed forward to help.

"I have her," said Samantha, waving them off. "We need to get to the barn to meet the others. Buy us some time."

Tiffany, who was puffing and gasping, croaked, "I'm all right . . . I don't need help. . . ."

They ignored her.

However, Laura said, "I'm almost out of arrows. I'll take Tiff and find the others."

Samantha nodded and, despite Tiffany's breathless protests, let Laura take up the burden of supporting the exhausted Tiffany. Then Samantha took the short spear from the leather scabbard into which she'd thrust it. The weapon had a four-foot hickory shaft and a blade scavenged from a broken sword Dolan had recovered from an empty house. A Scottish claymore. Dolan said that the sword had been on the ground next to over a dozen corpses that had once been zoms. Someone had made a heroic last stand, but now that person was probably wandering the earth as one of the living dead. That was how it was in last-stand fights. The defender ultimately runs out of ammunition, or their weapons break, or they just fatigue out against an enemy that can never get tired.

However, twelve inches of that old sword now protruded from a sturdy knot of leather at the end of the spear. The metal was heavy enough to use as a cleaver, sturdy enough to block most blades, and sharp enough to cut through leather, flesh, and bone. Samantha called it her dragon's tooth, and with it she'd defended against a great number of enemies, living and dead.

She and Heather watched the other girls move off; then they addressed the ground. When Samantha and Tiffany came out of the water, they'd left a wet trail. That had to be erased. They set to work, using dry brush to remove all footprints, then scooping handfuls of dried leaves, sticks, and stones and laying them like a haphazard carpet over any wet piece of ground. Within seconds the trail looked old and disused.

Then they erased their own footprints as they crept into tall grass. They moved in silence, knowing that they were invisible to anyone except maybe a hunting tiger or wolf. Their route cut across the path most likely taken by the people in black.

The reapers.

Then they heard sounds.

Human voices.

"—this way, I'm sure of it—"

Samantha and Heather ducked down again and watched as three figures came hurrying along the deer path. Two men and a woman. All dressed identically, and at closer range Samantha could see that the white angel wings embroidered on their shirts were highly detailed. Good needlework, done with skill and care. They moved ineptly through the forest, either because they lacked woodcraft or because they simply did not care if they made noise.

She felt Heather trembling beside her. Her eyes were glassy with fear, but that was understandable. Samantha put a hand on the younger girl's arm and gave it a gentle squeeze. Heather flinched, but after a few moments her trembling eased a bit.

The reapers were getting closer, and the girls caught bits and pieces of their conversation.

"—be good to get some hot food once we catch up to the main army. I haven't had a cooked meal in—"

"—Saint John will open red mouths in the flesh of every—"

"—ought to skin that girl—"

Samantha touched Heather's bow and then pointed to the reaper out in front. He was the smaller of the two men and the one most likely to run out of bowshot faster than his companions.

Heather nodded and very quietly drew the fletched end of the arrow back to her ear.

"Now!" said Samantha in a sharp whisper, and the arrow vanished from the bow. There was a meaty *thuk*, and it appeared as if by magic between the reaper's shoulder blades.

Samantha was in full motion before the other two reapers could react. She struck the middle reaper—the woman—in the temple with the butt-end of her spear and with a grunt and a pivot drove the blade into the chest of the third killer. He opened his mouth to scream, but he died before the sound could escape. As he collapsed, Samantha wrenched her spear free and whirled toward the fallen woman, who was bleeding and dazed. The woman had lost her ax when she fell, but she scrabbled at her belt to draw a draw a long-bladed skinning knife. Samantha kicked it out of her hand and put the edge of her spear blade under the woman's throat.

"One word and you're dead," she hissed.

11

South Fork Wildlife Area
Southern California

"My name is Brother Martin," said the small man who stood next to Saint John. "But everyone calls me Brother Marty. I was never comfortable with Martin. I'm more of a Marty kind of guy."

Iron Mike Sweeney said nothing. The big red-haired trade

guard stood with his arms wide, wrists lashed to tree trunks, feet tied to roots, shirt stripped away, pale skin running with bright red blood. The woods around them were filled with silent reapers.

"What's your name?" asked Brother Marty.

Iron Mike didn't answer directly. Instead he made a suggestion that was rude, obscene, and physically impossible. Saint John's mouth compressed into a tight line. The closest reapers cut looks at him and then glared at the prisoner, ready to kill him for the insult.

Brother Marty merely sighed. "While that would make for an interesting little film back in the day when making interesting little films was how I earned a buck, I don't think your suggestion gets us very far. It doesn't open a dialogue."

Iron Mike said nothing.

One of the reapers, a big man marked with the tattoo of a red hand on his face, stepped close and whispered into Brother Marty's ear. The smaller man nodded and waved him away.

"Ah," said Brother Marty. "If I'm hearing this right, you're known as Iron Mike Sweeney. Also known as Big Mike Sweeney and Bloody Mike Sweeney."

Iron Mike said nothing.

"'Iron' Mike," said Brother Marty, putting the name out there to taste it. "Talk about truth in advertising." He glanced at Saint John. "He's as tough as iron, that's no joke."

The saint pursed his lips but did not comment.

To Iron Mike, Marty said, "On behalf of the Night Church and our Honored One, Saint John of the Knife, I got to say that you are one bad mamba-jamba, and we admire that. You got the stuff, man, you got that X factor that sets you apart from other men. You know how rare that is? Especially in these times? You could've been a star back in the day. The Rock, Bruce Willis, Clint Eastwood, Schwarzenegger—they had it, but I don't know how many of them could spend the kind of afternoon you're having without so much as a peep. I'm really impressed. You know how many reapers you killed? Between arrows, guns, and that horse? Thirty-four. Thirty-four. I couldn't sell a body count like that even in a summer blockbuster."

Iron Mike smiled at him. It was not a nice smile, and it erased the grin from Brother Marty's face.

Marty cleared his throat. "Okay, don't do that again, because it creeps me the heck out. And what's with the eyes? Red eyes? Really? And those aren't contact lenses?"

"I have my father's eyes," said Mike.

There was something in the way he said it that made Brother Marty want to run and hide. It did not make him want to ask who Mike's father had been. Or indeed *what* Mike's father had been. The world was too big and too scary already without exploring any new territory.

"Enough," said Saint John, and as he stepped forward Marty was more than happy to retreat. He faded to the edge of the clearing and watched the saint.

"You're boring me," said Iron Mike. There was no hint of pain or discomfort in his voice. That scared Marty too. "Say your piece. If you want to kill me, then go for it. If you have a deal, pitch it."

"Let's start with a deal, Mr. Sweeney," said Saint John. "And it's a simple deal."

"I'm listening."

"We want some information. The location of nine towns."

The prisoner snorted. "This is California, friend. Used to be the most populous state. There are a lot of towns here. Take your pick."

"We're looking for the town of Mountainside. It won't be on any map made before the Fall."

Iron Mike said nothing.

Saint John leaned closer to him. "As dear Brother Marty said, we are impressed with your strength. Of body and of will. But I am a saint abroad in a world of sin, and I am charged by god to cleanse the earth of the infection of life. This town of Mountainside is one of a group of towns that represent the largest population west of the Rockies. Its existence is an affront to god."

"Whose god?"

"The only god. Lord Thanatos."

"All praise to his darkness," chanted the reapers.

"Thanatos, huh? Minor Greek god of death," mused Mike. "Known as Mors to the Romans. Son of Nyx, the Night, and Erebos, the Darkness."

"You know your history," said Saint John, "but you don't understand the truth behind the historical propaganda."

"You don't know what I know," said Iron Mike. He craned his head forward to speak. Drops of blood fell from his chin and spattered on the saint's clothes. "I know you. I know who you are, Saint John of the Knife. I know who you were before the Reaper Plague began eating the world."

"Do you?"

The red eyes burned, and the mouth below them smiled. "I know. And even if I hadn't heard of the serial killer named Saint John in newspapers and books, all I have to do to know you is to look into your eyes. You know the saying—the eyes are the windows of the soul. Do you want to know what I see when I look into your eyes?"

Saint John did not answer.

"You want me to tell you?" asked Mike in a tone only Saint John and Brother Marty could hear. "In front of your 'flock'?"

The saint did not reply, but Marty raised his hand, snapped his fingers with a sound like a dry stick breaking, and waved the reapers back. He kept waving until they were well beyond earshot even of normal voices.

"You want me out of here, boss?" he asked.

Saint John nodded. "Question the last of the guards. Tear the truth from him if you must. Do it down the hill, but come when I call."

Before he left, Brother Marty looked up into Iron Mike's face. "You are one very spooky guy, you know that?"

"It's come up in conversation."

They smiled at each other for a moment.

"Be cool if you were on our side," said Brother Marty.

Iron Mike's smile grew cold. "I'm not on anybody's side."

Marty studied his eyes, then turned and moved quickly away.

When they were alone, Saint John said, "You try very hard to be impressive, Mr. Sweeney. Go ahead . . . impress me. Reveal your insights. What is it you think you know?"

"Seriously? You want to go there."

"Seriously," agreed the saint.

"Okay. Like I said, I know you. I look through the windows of your eyes and I know you. I can see what made you."

"I doubt that . . ."

"I can see the little boy you used to be. The tortured one. The abused one. The humiliated one."

"You'll have to do better than that. Before the Fall the newspapers ran all sorts of stories speculating about me. They trotted out FBI profilers who said that I was the product of an abusive home life. All very cliché."

"All very true."

"You're trying to buy your life back by teasing me with information anyone could have gotten."

Mike slowly shook his head. "I know the secret word. . . ."

Saint John froze.

"I know what it is and where it is," said Mike. "A word your father burned into your skin with cigarette butts. A word that he burned onto your mother's face right before she killed herself. Do you want me to tell you what that word is?"

The saint did not reply. His mouth went dry, and his heart beat with strange rhythms.

"I know what you did to your father," continued Iron Mike. "I know what you did to try to stop the pain. The horror. The ugliness."

"No."

"Yes."

"No . . . you can't know that. No one . . ." Saint John's voice died in his throat.

The prisoner shook his head slowly. "Look . . . you and I aren't as different as you might think. I did my own time in hell when I was a kid, and I have the scars to prove it. Inside and out. I know what it feels like to be turned from an innocent kid into a monster. Believe me . . . I know."

"You don't know my life," murmured the saint. "No one knows what happened. . . ."

"Look at me," said Iron Mike quietly, "and tell me if I'm like anyone you ever met."

Saint John shook his head.

"Look at me and tell me if you ever saw anyone like me except in the mirror."

"No."

Saint John tried to stare the man down, but the longer he looked into those burning red eyes, the more he felt the ground beneath him begin to melt, to turn to quicksand.

"What are you?" he demanded.

"I'm like you," said Mike Sweeney. "I'm a monster. We were both born in a furnace, raised by predators, and then vomited out into the world."

"Monster . . . ," echoed Saint John. His knees wanted to buckle.

"You call yourself a saint of god," mocked Mike Sweeney. "It's a front, it's a paint job you slap over bare stone walls. I know all about that. I wanted to remake myself too. I wanted to whitewash my soul. I couldn't do it before the world ended. Not really. But every day since, I've been trying to be a new person. Not the thing my father made me . . . no, I wanted to be the man I should have been if the old world had shown me even a splinter of grace." He laughed, short and bitter, full of nails and broken glass. "But maybe people like us can't really ever escape who we are. I was a monster before the Fall and I'm a monster now. A different kind of monster, sure, but then again it's a different world."

"I'm not a monster," said Saint John in a low, tight voice that was filled with menace. "I am a saint of god."

Iron Mike studied him for a long moment, then sighed and nodded. "Maybe you are. Maybe even heaven's broken and the old gods are fighting over the scraps. One of them might need a man like you to be his garbage collector down here. What do I know? But if you're a saint of your god, then maybe I'm a hound of mine."

Saint John's lips formed the words "hound of god."

Mike grinned with red-streaked teeth and eyes the color of blood.

The saint said, "You speak of mysteries. You speak as if you know about me."

"I do."

"You can't."

Iron Mike shrugged as best he could—a lift of muscular shoulders and a smile that seemed unable to acknowledge fear or the presence of death. Saint John searched the man's strange eyes, looking for a sliver of doubt, of fear, even of humanity. All he saw was something alien, something that did not fit into his world or his faith.

And that was an impossible thing.

That had never happened before.

Not once.

As if sensing his thoughts, Iron Mike gave a sad shake of his head. "You're looking in the wrong direction."

"What do you mean? We know the towns are in—"

"No," said the prisoner. "That's not what I mean. I'm talking about when you look at the world. All you can see is the world of machines and governments and science—all the things your kind hate; and when you look into the future, all you see is the end of all pain and the simplicity of your darkness. Tell me I'm wrong."

"What else is there?"

Iron Mike flexed his hands and gave a playful tug on his bonds. "You seem like a smart guy, educated. Ever read *Hamlet*? Remember the scene in the graveyard, that line everybody quotes? 'There are more things in heaven and earth, Horatio, than are dreamt of in your philosophy?'"

Saint John said nothing.

The prisoner nodded, however, as if the saint had acknowledged the quote and its meaning. "You treasure the darkness, and who knows, maybe you're really damaged enough to serve your version of the darkness with your whole heart, but—"

"My 'version'?" cut in Saint John. "There is only the darkness."

"Ah," said Iron Mike, "you'd better hope not. You'd better hope that there are many kinds of darkness. That's what I believe. Hell, I bet we even see different stars when we look up at the night sky. I believe there are worlds within worlds, shadows within shadows."

Saint John grunted with disgust. It was a dismissive sound. "What a pity," he said, "after all of this it turns out that you are merely mad. For a moment there, I will admit, I believed that you had insight, that you were some kind of damaged prophet. But . . . no. Merely another person driven mad by having to endure endless days in this world of flesh."

Something flickered in the prisoner's eyes, but Saint John could not accurately read it.

"It's okay if you believe that," said Iron Mike. "Sometimes even I think I'm nuts. If you've seen the things I've seen, done the things I've done, saw the world through my eyes . . ." The prisoner laughed quietly and shook his head. "Being insane would be nice. It would be a kindness, and I can't remember the last time this universe threw me a bone. Everything I've ever loved has died or been torn away from me. Am I crazy? I wish to god—any god who will listen, even your god—that I was."

"I pity you," said Saint John, and he mostly meant it. This man disturbed him on so many levels. His words, as mad as they were, threatened to open doors in his head that had long since been nailed shut and bricked up. "Tell me where the Nine Towns are and I will end your pain and your suffering. I will send you on into the darkness."

"Killing me would be a blessing," said Iron Mike, "but not in the way you think."

"What is that supposed to mean?"

"Nothing, nothing . . . but . . ."

"But what?"

Iron Mike looked up at the trees, above which the sun was a bright ball of fire. He closed his eyes and took in a long, deep breath.

"It's going to be a full moon tonight," he said, eyes still closed. "Did you know that?"

"So what?"

Iron Mike opened his eyes, and they seemed to burn with palpable heat.

"You really don't understand this world," he said in a voice that was not at all human. It was low and wild and wrong. "There's darkness and then there's darkness. Real darkness.

You think you understand what's on the other side? You want to go into the darkness? You crave it. Keep thinking that, keep bringing pain to people who aren't as strong or as crazy as you. But when it's your time, when you step through the door into the big black . . . I'll be waiting there for you. And I'll show you what darkness really means."

In a flash, before he knew he was going to do it, Saint John drew a knife and buried the blade in Mike Sweeney's chest.

The big man made a single sound. It was not a grunt of pain. Not even of surprise.

It sounded more like a snort of mocking laughter.

Saint John tore his knife free and stared numbly at the bloody blade, watching in detached fascination as the red dripped down onto his hand. With a cry he flung the knife into the woods.

Then he spun away and fled.

When he reached his bodyguards, he waved them away and hurried toward the road where the army waited. Brother Marty followed at a run.

"Honored one," panted Marty, "what happened down there? What did he say to you?"

Saint John suddenly wheeled, and one bloody hand darted out and caught Marty by the front of his shirt. He lifted the smaller man to his toes, pulled him so close that spit flecked Marty's face as the saint spoke in a fierce whisper.

"We will never speak of this again. Never. I will personally flay the skin from anyone who mentions that man's name. I will cut his tongue out and nail it to his—"

"Honored one," croaked Marty, "please, please . . . it's okay, it's all cool. We don't need that freak."

Saint John's eyes blazed at him, and it took a visible effort of will to stop the flow of his words and respond with a modicum of calm. "What do you mean?"

"Look at this." Marty reached into his pocket and removed a folded paper and, with a flick of his wrist, shook it out. He held it up to show the saint. It was an old AAA road map of California. Dozens of notations had been handwritten onto the map. "The wagon driver had this under the seat. Look there . . . see? Haven, Mountainside, New Town . . . and six others. All nine towns are marked clear as day."

Slowly, slowly . . . Saint John eased the force of his grip on Brother Marty's shirt, letting the smaller man settle back onto his feet. Marty held the map out like it was an offering, or a shield. Saint John snatched it from him and stared at it.

Saint John closed his eyes and took a steadying breath. When he opened them, the look of wild panic in the saint's eyes scared Marty more than anything had since the dead rose. This was not a man who was ever frightened. Not of the living or the dead.

The map seemed to work some magic on Saint John. Calming him, driving the wildness from his eyes. The saint took another breath and let it out slowly.

"There is great evil all around us, my friend," he said in a ragged voice. "The sooner this world is destroyed, the safer all our souls will be."

He turned and walked away.

Brother Marty stood there, quivering, bathed in cold sweat.

Marty cast a nervous look down the slope to where the red-haired man hung between two trees. Even now, even slumped in death, there was something about the prisoner.

Something deeply, deeply wrong.

Marty backed away, spun, and ran to catch up with Saint John.

12

Sanctuary
Area 51

Benny whirled and saw more reapers emerge from points of concealment. Six of them.

No . . . seven.

His mouth went instantly dry, and his heart sank all the way to his feet.

"Oh God . . . ," he whispered.

One reaper, a tall man with a hook nose and tattooed beetles and scorpions covering every inch of his shaved head, pointed at Benny with a two-handed field scythe, but spoke to the other reapers. "You see, my brothers and sisters? He calls on a false god when confronted by the servants of the only true god. All hail Thanatos."

"Praise be to his darkness," intoned the others in unison.

Benny licked his lips, which were so dry it felt like they were covered with sand. "I don't want any trouble."

It sounded as lame as it was, and the reapers smiled.

"Unless you accept the darkness, you are lost in a world of trouble."

Benny looked quickly around. There were five men and two women, all of them lean and hard-looking, all of them armed with knives and swords. Their white angel wings seemed to glow with inner light on their chests, as if the intensity of their strange beliefs burned with real fire.

"Kneel, brother," said the man with the scythe. "Humble yourself and pray for release, and in the name of our god we will send you into the sweet and perfect darkness."

Benny stood and considered the man and his offer. Then he reached over his shoulder and slowly drew the *kami katana*.

"Or not," he said.

The reapers looked at the sword and then at the teenage boy who held it.

They burst out laughing.

It was, Benny mused, not exactly the ideal reaction.

His mind was racing furiously, trying to remember every lesson Tom had ever taught him. The path he'd used to come up here was behind him and he could reach it, but it was impossible to negotiate it fast enough to stay alive. Even though none of these reapers carried bows and arrows—and none of them ever carried guns—they could simply stand at the edge of the cliff wall and throw stones at him. They'd batter him off the wall and send him plunging down into the jagged rocks below.

All other potential routes out of here were blocked by reapers. Benny could see some paths beyond them. One wending through dry grass looked well trodden. Benny realized with a jolt that the reapers must have been using this spot to observe Sanctuary. Why weren't there soldiers up here? There were soldiers across the trench below; Benny had seen a few. Why wouldn't they have people up here?

Or . . . had some of these reapers once been soldiers who'd been forced to kneel and kiss the knife, to accept membership into a church built on total human extinction?

Too many questions. Not enough time to discover answers.

All that was left for Benny to do was fight.

The reaper with the scythe had been watching him very closely and must have seen the acceptance of the inevitable in Benny's eyes. He raised his scythe.

"Kill him," he said.

And the reapers, with their smiling faces and gleaming knives, attacked.

13

Rattlesnake Valley Motor Court
Southern California

"Heather," snarled Samantha as she crouched over the female reaper. "Watch her."

Heather had another arrow fitted and she drew it back, aiming at the woman's chest. Samantha quickly searched the woman and removed four other knives. Two were very good and she pocketed those; the rest she flung into the brush, where they vanished completely. She did the same with the ax and the weapons of the men. Then, while Heather kept watch, Samantha ran quickly down the path to survey the forest. There were no other reapers that she could see, which meant that they had split up to search the woods. That was good for the moment, but she and Heather would have to get out of here soon and warn the others. As she started to turn away, she caught sight of several figures farther down the slope. Slow, clumsy figures, but they were coming this way.

Zombies.

She turned and ran back to the site of the ambush.

The reaper woman was still semi-dazed from the vicious blow of Samantha's spear, and her eyes were glassy.

Samantha knelt in front of her and once more put the knife edge against her throat.

"Who are you and why are you killing people?"

The woman sneered. "A killer asks a question like that?"

"Self-defense, sister. You started this when you tried to kill my friend. So what's with that? World's full of zombies and you want to start killing some of the people who are trying to survive?"

The woman actually managed to smile. "You're a heathen and a blasphemer and you wouldn't understand."

Samantha had heard those words "heathen" and "blasphemer" only in old Bible stories. She couldn't imagine how they applied to something like this.

"Try me," she said, and emphasized the request by pressing harder with her knife.

"We are reapers of the Night Church, faithful servants of the Lord Thanatos, all praise his darkness. We are the soldiers of our god. We are sent into the wasteland to find all those who defy our god's will by clinging to the lie that is life."

"What? That doesn't make any sense."

"Not to the unenlightened." The woman continued to smile. "When the old world ended, many people believed that it was the judgment of their god. And in a way it was, but the god of the old world, the god of the Christians and Jews and Muslims, and the heathen gods of the Hindus and all those other false idols were proven to be lies told by blasphemers. The truth is that Lord Thanatos—all praise to his darkness—is the one true god, and he has judged mankind and found it wanting. He raised the dead, his holy gray people, to open red mouths in the flesh of all who live in this world of sin. Through the sacred doorway of death the impure are made pure, and in the vast and formless darkness they know true peace and joy."

Samantha almost smiled. "Wait, let me get this straight . . . you people believe that we have to die to be saved?"

"Of course."

"And that's why you're killing everyone you meet?"

"We bring the blessings of Saint John of the Knife, the holy minister of our god. With the sacred blades we open the doorways to—"

"Paradise, right, I got it. But you guys have a weird double standard. You believe in death, but you're still breathing and running around causing problems."

"No," said the woman, "we remain clothed in flesh only until the full will of god is completed. And then, with joy and songs on our lips, we will open the red mouths in each other's—"

"Something's coming," said Heather, swinging around to aim her arrow into the woods.

"Zombies," said Samantha. "I saw them a minute ago."

"We have to go."

"I know."

The reaper said, "Why not stay and let the gray people send you into the blessed darkness?"

Samantha shook her head. "Thanks, but I think we'll pass."

She closed her hand around the silver dog whistle that hung around the woman's neck. "You use this to control the zombies?"

"Yes. It is a gift from Lord Thanatos, all praise his—"

"Darkness, right." With a grunt she yanked the whistle hard enough to snap the chain, looked at it for a moment, then stuffed it into a pocket. "Heather, get the other whistles."

The younger girl hesitated, casting a nervous eye at the woods, then nodded and ran to comply.

"Get those red streamers, too."

"They stink!"

"They smell like death," said Samantha. "Kind of useful, don't you think?"

Heather thought about it for a moment, then gave a small smile of understanding. She drew a knife and began sawing at the tassels on the two dead men. They could hear the zombies thrashing through the brush as they came.

Time was just about up.

Samantha looked at the woman.

"What you're doing is wrong."

"It is the will of god."

"Not a chance. No god would want his people to do this much harm. If someone told you that, they were either lying to you or they're crazy. Either way, what you're doing is wrong."

She removed the edge of the spear blade and stepped back.

"It is the will of god," growled the reaper, her smile gone now.

Samantha shook her head.

"Go ahead, then," said the reaper. "Kill me. Use your weapon and open the red doors in my flesh. You'll see the joy on my face as I cross into the darkness."

The zombies were less than a hundred feet way now, and they were closing in from all sides. Heather whimpered softly and restrung her arrow.

Samantha holstered her spear and drew one of the knives she'd taken from the reaper. The woman smiled again as if in welcome of what she thought was coming. But behind that smile, Samantha thought she detected a flicker of something else.

Doubt, maybe.

Or fear.

With a flash of silver, Samantha crouched and slashed away the red tassels the woman wore, then quickly gathered them up and stuffed them into her pocket. Then she backed away from the reaper. The zombies were entering the small clearing. A circle of them, their gray faces slack, their eyes empty, their mouths working as if biting the air.

Samantha began backing away, pushing Heather as she did so.

"You have those tassels?" she asked.

"Y-yes," stammered Heather.

"Then let's go. No! Don't run . . . follow me and we walk out of here."

The reaper woman looked at them in horror.

"Wait—you can't leave me here."

"Why not?" asked Samantha.

"Give me my tassels back."

"Not a chance."

The zombies were a dozen feet away now, reaching with pale hands.

"My whistle . . ."

"No."

"But . . . but . . ."

Samantha could feel the coldness of her own expression. "You said that the dead were here to complete your god's will. Who am I to interfere?"

"Please!" begged the woman.

Samantha pushed Heather backward, and then the girls turned as two zombies closed in on them. Heather still had her arrow ready, and Samantha once more held her spear.

The zombies sniffed the air and their fingers grasped in their direction, but then they moved around the girls, indifferent to them, and shambled toward the woman who knelt on the ground.

"Please . . . god, please . . ."

"Don't look," said Samantha. "Just go and don't look."

Together they fled the scene, first walking, and then running, pursued only by the echo of the woman's dreadful screams.

The last cry of "Please!" sounded like it had been torn from her throat.

Serves you right, thought Samantha coldly.

The echo of that last cry seemed to hang in the air, refusing to faded into nothingness.

Samantha tried to feel good about what she'd just done. She wanted to feel smug about how she'd spun the situation on the reaper. She tried, but by the time they reached the barn and the other girls, she was sobbing so hard she could barely run.

"I'm sorry," she kept saying. "I'm sorry."

Heather told the other girls what happened, and they in turn tried to tell Samantha that she had done the right thing. That it was justice. That it was okay.

But they all knew they were lying.

Please . . .

Without another word, they headed off to the Rattlesnake Valley Motor Court to pack what few things they needed. The woods were full of reapers and zombies. The day was closing like a fist around them.

14

South Fork Wildlife Area
Southern California

As the reapers marched away into the hills, Brother Marty found himself unable to stop thinking about the big man Saint John had killed. The one who must have said something that had ignited fear in the saint's eyes—a thing Marty did not think was possible.

Who was Iron Mike Sweeney?

There was something about the man.

Something very wrong.

Something weirdly wrong.

Although Marty had accepted the path of the darkness and the way of the knife, part of him was still an ordinary man. A pre–First Night man. He'd been raised in a Jewish household, but not a strict one, and over the years agnosticism had drawn him away from his faith and his traditions.

He was, however, always a very superstitious man, though he ascribed that to working in Hollywood. The movie business seemed to swing between the poles of very good or very bad luck. The superstitions that became part of him were in no way tied to his previous faith—or any faith. Luck was luck, and the world was always a little weird to him. The angels he sometimes prayed to never appeared in anyone's holy books. Then or now.

As the reaper army marched on, he sat on his quad and rumbled down the center of the road behind Saint John, who was flanked by his personal guard, the Red Brotherhood.

Marty tried to shake his weird feeling and simply could not.

Finally he peeled off from the procession and signaled for four of the Red Brothers, and with them in tow he made a U-turn and headed back down the road to the place where the trade wagon had been ambushed. They reached the spot in less than thirty minutes. Marty pulled to a stop in the woods where he had a good view of the scene of slaughter. Most of the dead had risen and wandered off. A few—those with traumatic head wounds—lay where they'd fallen. The wagon stood there. Saint John had ordered the quartermasters of his army to take the uninjured horses and to slaughter the rest. The massive Percheron lay sprawled and dead beneath a crowd of vultures. Up the slope loomed the place where Iron Mike Sweeney had been executed by Saint John.

The two trees that had held him stood as silent as mourners. Ragged ends of rope hung from each, flapping weakly in the breeze.

But the man was gone.

Brother Marty sat immobile for a long moment. Then he signaled to one of the Red Brothers.

"Come on, guys. I want to know who cut him down and what happened to his body."

The four Red Brothers dismounted and followed Marty up the slope. They stayed off the path to prevent any useful footprints from being obscured by their own shoes. When they reached the two trees, one of them—Brother Zeke—crept forward, knees bent, body bowed low to read the tale of the ground. Brother Marty followed close behind.

Zeke suddenly stopped, and from his posture it was clear there was something puzzling about the scene. He squatted down and poked at the ground, then picked up the pieces of rope that had been used to tie Mike Sweeney to the tree. Frowning, he turned to Marty.

"What is it?"

"Something's weird about this, boss," said Zeke.

"Don't talk to me about weird," said Marty. "We don't want weird. We don't like weird. This Iron Mike fellow is dead, and either he's *dead* dead and some maniac body-snatched him, or he's walking around dead-ish looking for a hot meal. That's ordinary, that's what I want to hear. So, tell me what I want to hear."

The reaper's expression was difficult to read beneath the flaring red of the hand tattooed across his face, but even so the lift of his eyebrow and the tilt of his head conveyed plenty of meaning. He held out the ropes. They were torn apart, shredded. It was clear even to Marty that it hadn't been done with a knife, either.

The rope ends looked gnawed.

Zeke squatted down and touched the dirt at the base of the trees, where deep marks were cut into the ground. Footprints.

But they were not made by human feet.

Each print was huge, bare of shoes, with wide-splayed toes. The tip of each toe print was gouged deep into the dirt as if by a savage claw. The reaper placed one palm over the clearest of the prints. It was bigger than his whole hand.

"That ain't no dog," muttered Zeke. He looked genuinely frightened. Sweat beaded on the red ink tattooed across his face. "And it's too big to be a wolf. Or . . . at least not any kind of wolf I ever want to see. Except . . ."

"What?" asked Brother Marty.

"I don't know. Something my granddad told me once. Some old legends from the deep woods in Canada where I grew up." He half smiled, then shook his head. "No, that's stupid stuff. That's fairy-tale crap. Forget I said anything."

"No, I want you to tell me," insisted Brother Marty. "What exactly are you saying here?"

Zeke looked at him for a long five count, then down at the prints, then off into the woods. Finally he shook his head.

"I'm not saying anything, brother," he said in a wooden voice.

"Where's the body? Who took it? What'd they do with it?"

"It's gone."

"I can see that it's gone, genius. I'm asking you to tell me what you're suggesting?"

"I'm not suggesting anything, brother," said Zeke. He paused, and in a more confidential tone said, "Look, Marty, all kidding aside here, you know me. I can track pretty much anything. My dad and granddad took me hunting soon as I could walk. They taught me how to track like a pro. I can read signs. I can do that like you read a book. But I got to tell you, man, I don't want no part of this. No sir. Tell on me to the Honored One if you got to, but I've said all I'm going to say." He got to his feet and pointed into the woods. "And I will not go looking for whatever made those tracks. Not for anything."

Brother Marty glared at him, but Zeke shook his head. He dropped the pieces of chewed rope and backed away from the paw prints. Then he turned and stalked back to his quad, muttering, "This is too weird for me, man. This is way too weird for me."

Then he stopped and came back to Marty. "I'm just a grunt, brother," he said quietly, "and you're on the Council of Sorrows, so my opinion doesn't mean either jack or squat. But we've been friends ever since we got scooped up by the Night Church. I thought we could, you know, talk to each other."

"Say what you want to say, Zeke," said Marty irritably.

Zeke pointed to the place of execution. "I think we should bug the heck out of here and not tell anyone about this. Not Saint John, not the Council . . . not anyone."

"Why?"

"Because this spooks me, man." The big reaper actually shivered. "Whatever this is . . . it's wrong. Wrong in ways I can't put into words. It's creeping me out. I say we bug out and write this off."

Marty studied him. Before he knelt to kiss the knife, Brother Zeke had been an enforcer for a group of road pirates working the Dakota badlands. Before that he'd run with a biker gang. He was not an imaginative or fanciful person. He was also not stupid. If he was scared—and that was evident from the man's tight face, nervous glances, and twitchy eyes— then Marty did not want to stick around to try to prove that this was all nonsense.

Not for one second longer.

"Okay. We're out of here right now," Marty told the reaper. They exchanged a look that was equal parts under- standing and agreement and moved quickly down the slope to their quads.

They fired up the quads and roared away at full speed.

It was a very large, very strange world, and not all of that strangeness belonged to the plague. Marty wondered if they had just cruised the edge of something older and less defined even than the dead rising to eat the living.

They never once looked back.

Marty was afraid that something would be watching them go.

15

Sanctuary
Area 51

Tom Imura had taught Benny and his friends to be warrior smart.

It was all about a way of thinking. A way of acting and reacting to the world. A way of working with the world in the way that it actually was rather than in the way one assumed it was.

Tom was a practical man. That he had died was no fault of his own.

Benny was seldom practical, but he was working it. Flexing that muscle. If he lived long enough, he figured he'd get there.

The current odds on that, however, were pretty crappy.

He dodged under the whooshing swing of the wicked scythe and tried to cut the leader of the reapers down, but he missed. The force of his swing sent him sprawling on his face, and for a moment all the reapers had a perfect chance to slaughter him.

If any one or two of them had tried, Benny would have died right there.

As it was, all of them attacked at once, each of them so eager and desperate to make the kill that they gave absolutely no thought to themselves or one another.

They crowded in, and stabbing knives met reaper flesh, shoulders collided with shoulders, heads cracked together. Like a clown act from a May Day festival, the reapers reeled back from one another. Not one blade had touched him.

With a whimper of mingled joy and shame, he quickly rolled sideways and scrambled to his feet. His mind burned with the thought that the only reason he was still alive was because he'd been so incredibly clumsy that he'd somehow infected the reapers with stupidity.

He knew, however, that it was going to be a momentary thing.

"Come on, Tom," he said under his breath, "some Zen wisdom would be good right about now."

Tom did not say a word, and Benny could imagine his

brother doing a face-palm and walking away in embarrassed disgust.

"Thanks," muttered Benny.

Three of the reapers were hurt, two badly. They reeled away from their fellows, one clutching an arm that had been laid open from biceps to wrist, the other clamping hands over a chest wound that pumped bright blood.

That left five, one of whom had a deep cut on his forearm, but that didn't seem to keep him from gripping his ax with fierce intent.

Benny's mind raced through the countless hours of warrior-smart training, the endless scenarios Tom had drilled into Benny, Nix, Lilah, Chong, and Morgie. Solo attacks, group attacks, all sorts of variations.

One of Tom's most important rules started shouting at him inside his head.

Stay in motion.

Suddenly Benny felt himself move, felt his arms lift, felt the sword come alive in his hands. It was an illusion, of course; it was the training kicking in, those hours of repetition. It was muscle memory and reflex and his deepest need to survive.

Fight a single enemy, never a group.

He rushed at the closest reaper and battered aside the fall of a butcher knife that was aimed for his heart. As he parried it, Benny stepped to the side so that for a moment the reaper was between him and the others.

Isolate an enemy and engage.

Benny cut the man across the upper shoulder, aiming to wound rather than kill. The reaper shrieked in pain and staggered back. Right into the arms of two others who'd been trying to circle him to get at Benny.

If retreat is impossible, attack without hesitation.

Benny lunged to one side, going behind the tangle of reapers, chopping and slashing at their arms and thighs. Two of the three reapers buckled, falling into the third and bearing him to the ground. Benny leaped over the closest reaper and then leaped backward as another of the killers hacked at him with a meat cleaver. As the big blade sliced downward an inch from his nose, Benny pivoted and kicked him sharply in the knee. As the man crumpled, Benny kicked him again, this time in the chest, knocking him backward against a woman reaper who had a pair of hatchets. One of the blades flew straight up into the air, and Benny struck the other with his sword, taking it and part of the woman's hand in one slice.

Out of the corner of his eye, Benny saw the leader come charging at him with the scythe.

Benny began to smile. He was winning this.

He was going to win.

He rushed forward into the attack, bringing his sword up in a graceful, powerful sweep, his body set and balanced for the parry and the counter-cut that would destroy this reaper.

Sword met scythe blade.

Benny felt the shock of the impact shiver through his hands and vibrate along his arms. The force was ten times what he'd expected, and he found himself falling backward, the sword dropping from nerveless fingers. It clanged onto the hard ground, and Benny thumped down onto his back.

The reaper with the scythe stood over him, panting with fury.

Benny twisted and kicked out, aiming for the man's knee with a ground-fighting kick Tom had taught him.

With a snarl of contempt the reaper moved his leg, and as Benny's foot shot past, the man snapped out with a kick of his own. It caught Benny in the back of the calf. The man pivoted on the ball of his foot and side-kicked Benny in the chest, knocking him flat and breathless.

Benny tried to roll over to hands and knees. But couldn't.

He tried to reach for his fallen sword. But couldn't.

Tried to come up with one of Tom's rules for a situation like this. For anything that would save him.

But couldn't.

The scythe rose into the air. The other reapers—those who could still stand—clustered around to watch him die. The blade reached the apex of its lift, and golden sunlight ignited along the wickedly sharp edge.

"No!" cried Benny.

And the reaper said, "Unnh . . ."

It was a soft, surprised grunt.

The scythe trembled in the air and then fell backward as the reaper's fingers uncurled from it. It landed hard.

The reaper's knees began to bend. Slowly, slowly . . . until he dropped down into a kneeling position directly in front of Benny.

He said, "Unhh . . ." again.

Then the reaper fell flat on his face and did not move.

The other reapers stared in shocked horror.

Not at the fallen body. Nor at the leather-wrapped handle of the knife that stood up from between the reaper's shoulder blades.

They stared past their leader's corpse.

As did Benny.

A man stood there.

Tall. Grizzled. A scarred and tanned face and the coldest blue eyes Benny had ever seen. Beside the man stood a monster of a dog. Two hundred and fifty pounds of mastiff, but with armored plates all over him and a spiked helmet.

Joe Ledger said, "Sic 'em."

Benny could swear the dog laughed as it leaped forward to attack the reapers.

And they, armed and in greater numbers, stood no chance at all.

16

South Fork Wildlife Area
Southern California

Hard miles broke slowly under their feet as they ran.

The woods all around them were filled with the dead, though, and every way they turned they encountered teams of reapers leading packs of zombies. Some packs had only a dozen of the dead, but the farther west they went, the larger the packs grew. Once they had to stop for ten minutes as a swarm of at least a thousand of the dead shambled by.

Samantha and Heather shared out the tassels among the girls, and there were enough for each of them to tie half a dozen to their clothes. For a while they worried whether that would be enough, but as the afternoon burned toward sunset, it became clear that the dead were not drawn to them. Either they could not smell living flesh through the chemical stench, or the stench deceived them into thinking the girls were other zombies.

All the time that they were running and hiding Samantha was trying to understand what she'd done back in the clearing. She could have given the reaper a chance to run, could have left her with at least a tassel. She could even have cut her throat and given her the quick death the woman apparently wanted.

Instead she'd left her to be consumed by monsters.

Please . . .

Even though the reaper's screams had faded into nothingness hours ago, Samantha knew that they would echo inside the caverns of her soul forever.

Like all the girls, Samantha had grown up hard and along the way had been forced to spill blood many times. Human in defense, animals when hunting. Zombies constantly.

But never once had she been cruel.

Never once had she treated life without regard.

Never once had she been as much of a monster as the things that haunted and hunted her.

Until today.

Please.

With the hard miles her tears had dried, but she never ceased wanting to stop where she was and simply collapse in tears. Maybe in the path of the reapers.

As they ran, she occasionally caught quick looks from the other girls. Each of them assessing her, judging her, measuring themselves and their own potential for darkness against what she'd done. None of them met her eye. Maybe it was contempt, pity, or perhaps to prevent Samantha from seeing a familiar darkness in the eyes of a friend.

The sun seemed to expand into a supernova as it fell down behind the western haze.

The six of them moved downland through rougher country than the reapers chose to use, cutting into ravines and through dense brush. It was slow, but it gave them safety, and the terrain would slow down any attackers, human or otherwise. The dying sun spilled its paint box across the sky, splashing the horizon with gaudy shades of blood and fire.

Michelle ran point and she suddenly stopped, her fist raised in the way Dolan had taught them. They all saw the closed fist and froze, hands on weapons, eyes and ears alert.

Michelle waved them on and they clustered around her, looking where she pointed. "There's something down there."

A hundred feet downslope was a road, and through the leaves they could see the humped back of an old-fashioned wagon like the ones in storybooks of the Old West.

"Something's dead down there," said Laura.

They all nodded. Although the tassels blocked their sense of smell, they could hear the drone of blowflies. Samantha looked up to see that the sky was filled with crows and vultures turning in slow circles.

"Really dead," she said. The others nodded at that, too. In the perversion of death that was the zombie plague, carrion birds did not feed on the living dead. Only corpses whose life force had been totally extinguished by injury to the brain or brain stem rotted in a way that attracted scavengers.

Samantha took point now and led them down through the brush. The closer they got to the road, the more the trees and shrubs thinned out and the more a horror was revealed.

The wagon was an old-fashioned chuck wagon that had probably been looted from a cowboy museum. The sides had been reinforced with metal sheeting, and on the sides the words GUNDERSON TRADE GOODS had been painted in bright colors. There were bodies everywhere. Humans and horses. They had been killed in ugly ways, and they'd been left to rot. The ground was splashed with blood and littered with shell casings from pistols and shotguns.

Nothing moved except the flies.

If any of the victims of this massacre had reanimated, their living corpses had wandered off.

The girls fanned out across the road, looking at the dead, checking the wagon, scanning the surrounding woods.

"Reapers?" asked Laura.

Tiffany nodded. "Has to be. Who else would do something like this?"

"Why'd they kill the horses?" asked Heather. Ida had found an old wild horse years ago, and they'd had it for seven years before it died. Heather was destroyed when the horse was found dead in its stall. She stood looking down at the body of a massive Percheron. "Why would anyone kill a horse?"

Samantha shook her head but didn't say anything about the slaughter. She knelt for a moment and looked at tracks that were cut into the bloody soil.

"What's that?" asked Laura.

"I don't know."

"A wolf?" asked Michelle.

"Too big."

"A dog?" suggested Amanda. "Like a mastiff?"

Years ago, when the adults were still alive, a traveler had come through the area. A big man accompanied by a monstrous American mastiff. He'd stopped only for a cup of coffee before moving on, and afterward Samantha and the girls had looked at the prints left behind in the road. They were similar to these.

"It's not a mastiff," Samantha decided. "These are too big."

They looked around at the darkening woods. There were so many strange animals out there. Wild creatures that had escaped from zoos or come in packs from other countries like Mexico and farther south. There was no way to identify these prints now, and no time to waste in trying.

Samantha said, "It's getting dark. We need to find a place for tonight."

One by one the girls turned away, sickened and saddened by the senseless death. Samantha watched them head up the road, moving off the road and preparing to cut across country. There were plenty of empty houses and old buildings everywhere, and they hadn't seen a reaper now for almost two hours.

Samantha lingered for a moment longer, thinking about the killings. She wanted to find some justification for what she'd done. These dead bodies were proof that the reapers were evil.

Right? she asked herself. *What I did to that woman wasn't wrong. It was justice. Right?*

The questions echoed inside her head like thunder.

She wiped at her eyes, turned away, and hurried after the others.

But then she jerked to a halt as she saw something in the

thickening gloom. It was a figure sitting slumped over against a tree. Big, bulky, bleeding.

It was in near-total darkness, except for one slack, out-stretched arm that was covered with blood.

The blood looked fresh.

Had it moved? Did the fingers of that slack arm twitch?

Was it a victim of the attack reanimating as a zom?

That fit the circumstances but not the timing. This massacre was hours old, maybe as much as half a day. Any dead would have risen.

Unless . . .

There were two real possibilities. A person who'd been injured and had recently passed, and was now reanimating. Or a person who was injured and perhaps dying. Alive, but badly wounded.

Samantha wanted to turn and run. This wasn't her matter; it had nothing to do with her. If it was a zombie, then dispatching it was a dangerous waste of time. If it was a wounded person, then it would be a drag on resources and a burden when efficient flight might be the only thing that would help Samantha and her little tribe survive.

She started to turn. She actually took three small steps away from the slumped fingers, but then she stopped again.

The hand twitched again.

Samantha backed away. She wanted no part of this; she wasn't sure she could be a participant to another death. She'd had her fill.

She turned her back on the figure and began to jog along the path taken by the other girls.

"Please . . ."

It was a single word, and she could have imagined it.

Perhaps it was not even a word.

She stopped and squeezed her eyes shut.

The word echoed in her head.

Please.

Up ahead the other girls were making good time, but Heather, the last in the line, glanced back.

"Come on!" called the girl.

Samantha nodded.

But not to Heather.

She abruptly turned and walked back to the slumped figure.

That one arm lay in the last of the day's fading light. Pale skin with red hair that was coarse as wire. A thick wrist, corded muscles. Blood. Beneath the gore the arm was crisscrossed with scars, old and new. Samantha had seen every kind of injury in her young life, and she could recognize the marks of violence. Knife cuts and other trauma. Whoever this person was, he'd been hurt over and over again. Some of the scars were so faint that it was evident they were very old, perhaps wounds suffered in childhood.

The figure spoke again. Hoarse, a damaged croak of a voice.

"Please . . ."

Samantha licked her lips. "Are . . . are you one of them?"

"Please . . ."

"Are you one of them? Are you a killer?"

The shadow-shrouded body moved, and with a hiss of pain and a grunt of effort, the man leaned his head and shoulders out of the shadows. He had pale eyes that seemed to reflect the fiery light of sunset. His face was lined with pain and white with blood loss.

"I'm a killer," he said in a voice that was filled with darkness and cold winds. A voice filled with a great and terrible sadness. "But . . . not like them."

Samantha said nothing. Her spear felt like it weighed a million pounds.

The man spoke very softly. "I'm . . . like you."

"Like me?"

He nodded and gave her the faintest of smiles. "Like you."

Samantha bristled. "You don't even know me."

He didn't reply to that, but instead reached out his bloody hand. "Please," he said, "help me."

She took a small step backward. "Why should I?"

The man didn't answer, and his hand remained out for her to take.

"Come out where I can see you," ordered Samantha. "If I see a gun or knife, I'll put you down like a dog."

The man made a sound. It could have been a laugh.

But then he moved, his bulk shifting inside the bank of shadows. He got clumsily and slowly to his knees; then, with small grunts and hisses of pain, he managed to get to his feet. He took two trembling steps forward and then stood swaying in the fiery light.

"God . . . ," breathed Samantha.

The man was huge, with massive muscles that seemed molded onto him like lumps of clay. His clothes were torn and slashed, and there were barely enough left to cover him. The ruined shirt and trousers revealed limbs and a torso that were covered with scars and old burns and what looked like healed-over bullet wounds. Even with all the refugees and survivors of the Fall she'd seen, Samantha had never once beheld a person who had suffered a tenth as many injuries as this man.

There was a fresh wound on his chest, almost directly over his heart, but it could not have been as deep as it looked. Blood was painted across his body and down each limb.

He looked down at her with the strangest and least human eyes she had ever seen. The irises seemed to be as red as the sunset, and they were rimmed with burning gold.

"What—what—happened to you?" stammered Samantha.

Those eyes were filled with sadness.

"Too much," he said.

He carried no weapon, and despite his muscles he seemed on the verge of collapse. His face was pale, almost gray, and his lips were dry and cracked.

For reasons Samantha wasn't able to explain, she stepped close to the man, reached out a hand, and lightly touched the edge of the wound over his heart.

"Are you going to die?" she asked.

"No."

"Are you sure?"

"Yes," he said, but if anything the sadness in his eyes intensified as he said it.

"Can you walk?"

He shook his head. "Not yet," he said. "Not alone."

"Are you safe?" Samantha raised her hand from his chest to his cheek. "Will you hurt me?"

"No," he said. "I'm not safe."

She almost pulled her hand away.

"But I won't hurt you, Samantha."

She stiffened. "But—but—how do you know my name?"

He did not answer the question. "My name's Mike."

In the gathering dusk, caught in the web of so strange an encounter, Samantha remembered two things. The first was something Ida had said to them once about twilight when all the girls were little.

"Twilight is a strange time, my girls," Ida had said. "In daylight you can see things the way they are. At night everything's a guess, 'cause so many things are hidden by shadows. But twilight is a little of both. It's real and unreal. You see things, but you can't be sure of what you see. People used to believe that twilight was when the world of what's real and what's unreal creaks open. If you're not careful, you can step right through into who knows where. Or maybe something from over there can step through."

Heather had asked, "Something from where?"

And Ida had answered, "From anywhere that isn't here."

"That doesn't make sense," declared Samantha, who, even when young, was not given to fancy.

Ida gave them all a wink and a knowing smile. "During twilight nothing has to make sense."

Now it was twilight, and things seemed to have stopped making clear sense. It was like the sharp edges that defined the world during the day had been sanded down to a point where they were indistinct and untrustworthy.

"Listen to me," said Mike, wincing as pain flashed through him. "I'll make you a deal."

"What kind of deal?" asked Samantha suspiciously.

He shivered with the onset of shock and fever. "If you

help me now, tonight . . . then I'll make sure nothing ever happens to you and your friends."

"You can't make a promise like that."

He smiled. It was the most human thing about him. Despite the blood and his wounds, despite the strangeness of his eyes and the impossibility of his knowing her name, despite everything that made this encounter seem like something out of a dream, that smile held no trace of threat. None.

"Yes," he said, "I can make that promise."

She started to back away.

"Please," he said.

Please.

In the woods far behind them, they could hear the dead moan as they followed the silent calls of the reapers.

Without realizing that she was going to do it, Samantha turned sideways to him.

"Come on," she said, "lean on me."

He hesitated. "Are you sure? You can still walk away."

She looked down at the ground. His feet were bare, and there was dirt caked under his toenails as if he'd dug them into the ground. His clothes did not look like they'd been cut. They looked like they'd burst apart.

Samantha knew that she should have been terrified. She knew that she should shove this man away from her, that she should run to find her friends and then run farther until this place was far behind her.

She knew that.

And yet.

There was something about this man.

Here was a person who had suffered so much, survived so much, had so much will to live that he risked making promises despite being on the edge of death. And in the woods here were the living dead and those whose purpose was to exterminate all life.

It came down to that choice.

Between the takers of life and a man who clearly fought harder than anyone she had ever met to belong to life.

If it was a strange choice for her to make, then she blamed it on twilight.

Somehow she knew Ida would approve.

She took the big man's arm and laid it across her shoulders.

"Come on," she said. "I'll help you."

Together Samantha and Iron Mike Sweeney made their slow and careful way past evidence of carnage, away from death, toward life.

17

Sanctuary
Area 51

It took a long time to walk down the mountain.

They didn't take the goat path. Instead they went a back way that was easier but longer. Fifty feet down that road they came to a spot where two soldiers lay. Both were dressed in the uniforms of the American Nation, the new government that had formed after the destruction of the old world. It was clear that these men had been on guard but had been surprised, overwhelmed, and murdered by the reapers. It was equally clear that Captain Ledger had quieted them. Both of them had distinctive knife wounds in the backs of their heads, right at the weak point where the spine enters the skull. What Tom had once called the "sweet spot."

"I didn't know there were guards up here," said Benny.

"Of course there are guards up here," said Ledger. "There are also a crapload of land mines and you're lucky you didn't step on one."

"The reapers didn't step on any mines."

"Not this time," said the ranger, "but over the years? Yeah, a whole bunch of them have gone into the darkness at high velocity."

"It's not funny," said Benny.

"No," admitted the ranger, "it's not."

Benny considered the two soldiers. "What were their names?"

"Private Andy Beale and Private Huck Somerton."

"Do they have family?"

"Back home. They're from Asheville, North Carolina."

"I'm sorry," Benny said.

"Yeah," said Ledger. "But at least we know that the reapers have found a way through our back door. I'll make sure it's nailed shut again."

"Is that worth two people's lives?"

The ranger shook his head. "No. But we take what we can to save more lives down the road."

"The reapers . . . they'll keep trying, won't they?"

"Yes."

"Won't they ever give up?"

"Not as long as Saint John is driving them."

"They're afraid of him," said Benny.

"It's worse than that," said Ledger. "They love him. They really do think he has the answer. They think he's going to solve all their problems."

The kept walking. Grimm trotted along behind, his armor clanking. Joe carried the dog's spiked helmet.

After a while Benny asked, "How'd you know I was up here?"

"I didn't. But I was looking for you and didn't find you anywhere else. You didn't take a quad, and you weren't in one of the hangars. There's not too many other places you could be."

They walked and the sun slid red and swollen into the west.

"I'm not going to say I'm sorry," said Benny.

"I didn't think you would."

They looked at each other. Harshly at first, then with small smiles of acknowledgment. Like chess players.

"Thanks, though," said Benny.

"Jeez, kid, that sounded like it actually hurt to say."

"It did. My gums are bleeding."

Ledger laughed, and the sound of it bounced off the stone walls. They walked for another ten minutes without speaking.

"There's a war coming," said Benny at last, "and I'm not ready for it."

The ranger gave a slow nod of approval.

"It takes a . . . ," Joe began, but stopped.

"What?" demanded Benny, some sharp edges still evident in his tone. "What were you going to say? That it takes a 'man' to make a decision like that? Don't bother, we both know I'm not a man. I'm a kid, and I'm doing the best I can."

Captain Ledger gave him a small smile. "No, kid, that's not what I was going to say. What I was trying to say was that it takes a real warrior to make a decision like that. To accept the world for what it is. To ask for help. That's what your brother would call being 'warrior smart' . . . and that has nothing to do with how old you are."

He held out a big, tough, calloused hand.

After looking at it for a long moment, Benny took it.

18
South Fork Wildlife Area
Southern California

Saint John sat near the glow of a massive campfire. He'd ordered it built big tonight, and there were three times as many guards posted. Most of the reapers were already asleep. Even Brother Marty was dozing.

Saint John sat apart from everyone and stared deep into the chaotic heart of the fire, watching the snakes of flame twist and tangle and writhe.

He listened to the crackle and pop of the wood as the purifying fire consumed it.

And he listened to the sounds of the night.

Listening for . . .

For what?

The sad laughter of a stranger?

The howl of a wolf?

"I will cleanse this world of all flesh, all life," he told the flames, speaking in a voice so soft he could barely hear his own words. "I am a saint of the Night Church. We own the night, we hold it in the palm of our hand. There is no force in this world or any other that can stand against us."

Although his voice was quiet, he spoke with the force and cadence of a litany. Repeating each phrase, each promise, each vow.

Repeating and repeating it until he believed it once again.

That, however, took all night.

Tomorrow, with the dawn, he would take his army of the living and the dead and set out with a will toward Haven. Toward the first of the Nine Towns. There were hard weeks of forced marches ahead of him. His army would have to forage and provision, and that would lose them hours, days. It didn't matter.

Even if there were things out in the night that he didn't understand, he had his army and he served the will of Thanatos, all praise to his darkness.

He finally slept, and for the first time since his troops attacked the caravan, he had a smile burned onto his hard mouth.

FROM NIX'S JOURNAL

ON HOPE
(BEFORE *FLESH & BONE*)

The jet's out here somewhere.

Somewhere.

Somewhere.

Out here.

We all saw it. Lilah, Benny, and me.
Tom saw it too.

It's out here.

Sometimes knowing that is the only thing
that keeps me from screaming.

BONUS MATERIAL

ROT & RUIN
Issue #1
Warrior Smart

The Complete
Comic Book Script

PAGE 1:

1.

Full page panel. BENNY IMURA, fifteen, sits on a grassy slope as the sun rises. He leans on a sheathed *katana*.

CAPTION: I'M BENNY IMURA.

CAPTION: MY PARENTS ARE DEAD.

CAPTION: MOST OF THE WORLD'S DEAD.

CAPTION: MY BROTHER TOM'S DEAD TOO.

CAPTION: HE WAS TRAINING ME TO BE LIKE HIM. TO BE A ZOMBIE HUNTER AND A SAMURAI.

CAPTION: HE DIED SAVING A LOT OF PEOPLE. SAVING ME AND MY FRIENDS.

CAPTION: WE COULDN'T GO HOME. BACK TO MOUNTAINSIDE.

CAPTION: WE SAW SOMETHING THAT COULDN'T BE.

CAPTION: A PLANE. WAY HIGH IN THE AIR. A JUMBO JET.

CAPTION: NOW THE FOUR OF US ARE LOOKING FOR IT. ME. MY GIRLFRIEND, NIX. MY BEST FRIEND, CHONG.

AND LILAH, A GIRL WE FOUND LIVING WILD IN THE FOREST. FOUR KIDS. FOUR SAMURAI.

CAPTION: KIND OF.

CAPTION: IT'S A BIG WORLD. THAT PLANE COULD BE ANYWHERE. BUT WE HAVE TO FIND IT.

CAPTION: AFTER ALL . . . WHAT ELSE IS THERE?

PAGE 2:

NOTE: On pages 2–5 there is a slim vertical panel that shows the exact same view of a sword blade held downward so that the tip is nearly touching the ground. In each panel the sword will be increasingly bloody; and in each it will reflect a different image.

Each of the other panels are wide and horizontal, running from the edge of the vertical sword panel across the rest of the page.

1.
Flashback begins. Sword panel. This panel hugs the left side of the page and runs the whole length. The sword blade is clean. In the bright, polished steel we see a reflection of a baby crying.

2.
Flashback continues. We see four members of a family. TOM, twenty, a handsome Japanese-American in a police academy uniform; BENNY, eighteen months, a half-Japanese toddler; MOM, Irish-American and very pretty, wearing a white long-sleeved casual dress; DAD, Japanese, dressed in a police patrol sergeant's uniform, tie askew. Dad sits on a dining-room chair as Mom bends to examine a bloody bite.

CAPTION: NOBODY KNOWS HOW IT STARTED.

CAPTION: DAD GOT BIT AT WORK. SOME CRAZY HE ARRESTED.

3.
Flashback continues. Dad, semiconscious on the couch, sweating and gray as Mom frets over him.

4.
Flashback continues. In the foreground, Dad's dead face, slack and gray. Tom holding Mom (who is holding a wailing Benny) as she screams in horror at her husband's death.

CAPTION: HE GOT REALLY SICK REALLY FAST. HE DIED BEFORE WE COULD EVEN GET AN AMBULANCE.

CAPTION: JUST LIKE THAT.

5.
Flashback continues. Same angle, but Dad's eyes are open now. They are gray-green zombie eyes. Tom and Mom stare in horror. Even the baby seems to be shocked.

CAPTION: BUT *DEATH* KIND OF DIED TOO.

PAGE 3:

1.

Flashback continues. Vertical sword panel. The orientation of the panel now shifts to one-quarter of the way across the page. The blade has a single line of blood running down the gleaming steel. In the bright, polished steel we see a reflection of a male zombie, Japanese, reaching for whoever is holding the sword. This is Tom and Benny's dad.

2.

Flashback continues. Mom shoves Benny into Tom's arms as she begins to rush toward her husband, who is now standing. Tom yells out a warning.

CAPTION: AT FIRST NO ONE KNEW WHAT A ZOMBIE WAS.

3.

Flashback continues. Dad bites Mom's arm.

CAPTION: GUESS WE LEARNED THE HARD WAY.

CAPTION: THE WRONG WAY.

4.

Flashback continues. Switch to a bedroom. The door is closed. Mom pushes Tom to the window, forcing Benny into his arms. Sleeves are now drenched with blood.

CAPTION: MOM MADE TOM TAKE ME AND RUN.

CAPTION: SHE WAS ALREADY STARTING TO CHANGE.

5.
Flashback continues. The bedroom door bursts open and Dad is there, rushing at Mom.

CAPTION: WHAT ELSE COULD TOM DO?

PAGE 4:

1.

Flashback continues. Vertical sword panel. The orientation of the panel now shifts to halfway across the page. The blade has several lines of blood on it, and some of the blood is very dark, almost black. In the steel and gore we see the reflection of a little girl zombie.

2.

Flashback continues. Tom huddles with Benny on the lawn, crying and wretched. Benny screams.

CAPTION: IT KILLED HIM TO LEAVE HER.

3.

Flashback continues. Tom stands by the open trunk of his car. We can see his police gear bag and his martial arts bag, from which the handle of his sword can be seen. Shadows fall across Tom's back, and a few hands reach into frame.

CAPTION: BUT IT WOULD HAVE KILLED US BOTH IF HE DIDN'T DO WHAT HE *HAD* TO DO.

4.

Flashback continues. Tom whirls to see that the neighbors are there. All are zombies.

CAPTION: WHATEVER HE HAD TO DO.

5.

Flashback continues. A view from inside the trunk as Tom, having clearly placed Benny inside, closes it. He has his *katana* in his right hand.

CAPTION: NO MATTER WHAT IT COST HIM.

PAGE 5:

1.

Flashback continues. Vertical sword panel. The orientation of the panel now shifts three-quarters of the way across the page. The blade is mostly covered in blood. We see the reflection of a burning city and a mushroom cloud.

2.

Flashback continues. Also seen from inside. Tom opens the trunk. He is covered with blood and he looks crazed.

CAPTION: NO MATTER HOW MUCH OF HIMSELF HE LOST DOING IT.

3.

Flashback continues. Tom and Benny in the front seat. Tom, still streaked with gore, drives; Benny is in the car seat, screaming. Tom looks absolutely shell-shocked and crazed.

CAPTION: BACK THEN—ON *FIRST NIGHT*—IT WAS FIGHT, RUN, OR DIE.

4.

Flashback continues. A long traffic jam into a city.

CAPTION: EVERYTHING FELL APART REALLY FAST. EVERY CHOICE WAS A HARD CHOICE.

5.

Flashback continues. The city is in the rearview mirror, very small. A mushroom cloud rises above it.

CAPTION: MOST OF THE CHOICES PEOPLE MADE WERE THE WRONG ONES.

CAPTION: UNTIL IT ALL FELL APART.

PAGE 6:

1.

Flashback continues. Vertical sword panel. The orientation of the panel now shifts all the way across the page so that it hugs the right-hand side of the page. The blade is completely bloody, and the glistening blood reflects the image of a horde of zombies. Rotting fingers with broken nails begin to intrude into the panel.

2.

Flashback continues. Tom and Benny abandon the dead car.

CAPTION: WHEN THEY NUKED THE CITIES, THEY DIDN'T STOP THE ZOMS. BUT THE EMPS KILLED ALL THE POWER.

CAPTION: THE WORLD WENT DEAD TOO.

3.

Flashback continues. They pass a crashed Black Hawk helicopter.

CAPTION: THE DEAD ROSE.

CAPTION: WE FELL.

4.

Flashback continues. Benny sits on the ground, still crying, as Tom fights two living men—one with a club, the other with a sledgehammer.

CAPTION: PEOPLE WENT CRAZY, OR THEY TURNED BAD 'CAUSE THEY THOUGHT IT WAS THE ONLY WAY TO LIVE.

CAPTION: EXCEPT TOM. HE ALWAYS HELD ON TO WHO AND WHAT HE WAS.

5.

Flashback continues. Tom, in his thirties now, and a teenage Benny train together. Tom has the steel sword that Benny will carry throughout the series; Benny has a plain wooden bokken.

CAPTION: TOM FOUND US A HOME. HE HELPED BUILD A TOWN. HE KEPT PEOPLE SAFE. HE HELPED THEM WANT TO BE ALIVE.

CAPTION: WHEN I WAS OLD ENOUGH, HE STARTED TEACHING ME HOW TO BE TOUGH, AND FAIR, AND HONORABLE.

CAPTION: LIKE HIM.

PAGE 7:

1.

Flashback ends. Benny stands up to put on his carpet coat. (This is designed like an Old West duster, but made of thick carpet. It hangs down past Benny's knees.)

CAPTION: NOW HE'S GONE. I HAD A CHOICE. BE WEAK AND DIE BEHIND A FENCE. OR GET TOUGH. TO BECOME *WARRIOR SMART* LIKE TOM.

CAPTION: AT FIRST I DIDN'T WANT TO.

CAPTION: NOW I KNOW I HAVE TO.

2.

We look past him down the hill. There's a small cottage there with an overgrown front yard. There are two zombies in the yard. An old man and a young woman. He wears farmer's overalls. She wears the remnants of a waitress's uniform.

CAPTION: THERE ARE MAYBE THIRTY THOUSAND PEOPLE LEFT ALIVE. THAT WE KNOW OF.

CAPTION: AND SEVEN BILLION ZOMS.

3.

Reverse view, looking past the zombies—who don't yet

see Benny coming down the hill. His sword is slung over his shoulder.

CAPTION: THEY'RE NOT EVIL. THEY'RE NOT ANYTHING.

CAPTION: WE DON'T UNDERSTAND WHY THEY DON'T DIE. OR WHY THEY WANT TO EAT PEOPLE.

4.

View of the legs of the zombies, with the waitress in the foreground. Creeper vines have grown up and tangled around their ankles and calves. Clearly they haven't moved in a long time.

CAPTION: UNLESS THEY HAVE PREY TO FOLLOW, ZOMS WON'T GO ANYWHERE. SOME OF THEM JUST STAND IN PLACE FOR YEARS. I USED TO THINK THAT WAS FREAKY. NOW I THINK IT'S JUST SAD.

PAGE 8:

1.

Benny stands on the other side of the garden fence as he sprinkles some liquid from a small jar onto his sleeve.

CAPTION: WE USE CADAVERINE. IT SMELLS LIKE ROTTING MEAT.

2.

The zombies look at him as he cautiously approaches.

CAPTION: ZOMS DON'T EAT THEIR OWN KIND.

3.

Benny sidles carefully past them toward the front door. The zombies are alert, but they still haven't moved.

CAPTION: THE TRICK IS TO MOVE VERY SLOWLY. ZOMS REACT TO QUICK MOVEMENT, SOUND. THE SMELL OF LIVING FLESH.

4.

Inside the kitchen, Benny begins stuffing items into a satchel. Knives, a metal saucepan, a bar of soap.

CAPTION: SCAVENGING KEEPS US GOING. ALL THE FOOD'S TOO OLD, BUT THERE'S ALWAYS OTHER STUFF.

5.

In the bedroom, Benny takes underwear from a drawer. Men's boxers now hang from his satchel, but he's taking a bra and functional-looking panties, too.

CAPTION: CLEAN UNDERWEAR? WORTH A LOT MORE THAN GOLD.

PAGE 9:

1.

Benny walks away from the house. The zombies stare at him. Benny's satchel is full.

2.

He walks down a weed-choked road. There are bones in the weeds and the burned-out shell of a Charlie Chu-Chu Chicken stand.

CAPTION: WE'RE CAMPED IN YOSEMITE. I CAME OUT TO DO SOME SEARCHING. PICK UP SOME STUFF.

3.

Benny crouches in the tall grass, eating a chicken drumstick. A pair of giraffes walk by.

CAPTION: THE WILDLIFE IS CRAZY. ALL THE ANIMALS THAT ESCAPED FROM ZOOS AND CIRCUSES ON FIRST NIGHT ARE BREEDING OUT HERE.

CAPTION: WE EVEN SAW A RHINO ONCE. WEIRD.

4.

Big panel. He stands on a rise above a small camp. We can see tiny figures in the distance.

CAPTION: LAST YEAR I LIVED IN A TOWN. LAST YEAR

I DIDN'T KNOW HOW TO FIGHT. LAST YEAR I HADN'T EVER KILLED A ZOM. OR A PERSON.

CAPTION: LAST YEAR WE HADN'T SEEN THE PLANE.

CAPTION: LAST YEAR TOM WAS ALIVE.

CAPTION: I NEVER KNEW SO MUCH COULD CHANGE IN A YEAR.

PAGE 10:

1.

Big panel. Benny walks toward camp. We see his three companions. All are about fifteen. NIX is short, curvy, freckled and has lots of wild wavy red hair. She has a scar across her forehead. She is very pretty. LILAH is taller, lean, athletic, sexy in a feral kind of way; with long blond hair so pale it looks white. She has honey-colored eyes, a good tan, and looks a bit aloof and strange. CHONG is Chinese-American. He's a skinny, bony nerd with glasses. Highly intelligent face.

CAPTION: TOM TRAINED ALL OF US.

CAPTION: NIX RILEY. MY GIRLFRIEND. QUEEN OF FRECKLES. VERY COMPLICATED.

CAPTION: LOU CHONG. BEST FRIEND. SMARTEST PERSON I KNOW. TOTAL KLUTZ IN THE WOODS.

CAPTION: LILAH. CRAZY AND WAY DANGEROUS. SPENT FIVE YEARS LIVING IN A CAVE, KILLING ZOMS AND BOUNTY HUNTERS.

CAPTION: SHE AND CHONG ARE A THING. A VERY STRANGE, DYSFUNCTIONAL THING.

2.

On Nix, who holds Benny's satchel and is removing a bra from it.

BENNY: I FOUND SOME GOOD STUFF.

NIX (reading a tag): WONDERBRA?

3.

On Lilah as she leans on her spear (a length of black pipe with a Marine Corps Ka-Bar attached to one end).

LILAH: YOU DIDN'T FIND ANYTHING USEFUL? AMMUNITION? WE'RE DOWN TO FOURTEEN BULLETS.

BENNY: NAH. THE PLACE HAD BEEN LOOTED ALREADY.

4.

On Chong as he holds up a folded map of Yosemite National Park.

CHONG: THERE'S A SMALL TOWN JUST OUTSIDE THE PARK. A HOSPITAL. POLICE STATION. LIKE THAT.

CHONG: WE MIGHT FIND SOME STUFF THERE.

PAGE 11:

1.

Benny and Nix are alone on a rock that's half-submerged in a pretty forest stream. They sit together with their feet in the water. They lean their heads together. It's a romantic and very personal moment.

NIX: YOU WERE GONE SO LONG I WAS STARTING TO WORRY.

NIX: THINKING ABOUT TOM?

BENNY: YEAH. STILL CAN'T BELIEVE HE'S GONE.

2.

On Nix, who smiles at him.

NIX: YOU'RE A LOT LIKE HIM.

BENNY: I WISH.

NIX: I'M SERIOUS. YOU ARE. YOU'RE STRONGER THAN YOU USED TO BE.

BENNY: YEAH, WELL—I NEED TO GET A WHOLE LOT STRONGER IF WE'RE GOING TO SURVIVE OUT HERE.

3.

Small panel. On Nix's face, showing some concern as Benny speaks.

BENNY: WE CAN'T BE KIDS ANYMORE.

4.

Small panel. They sit in silence.

5.

They see Lilah and Chong in the distance. She has a couple of dead rabbits she's caught.

BENNY: HOW ARE THE LOVEBIRDS?

NIX: SHE HASN'T THREATENED HIS LIFE YET TODAY.

BENNY: LET'S CALL THAT A WIN.

6.

Lilah squats next to Chong and is watching him skin a rabbit. Her expression is cold indifference. He is turning green and getting sick.

LILAH: YOU MAKE A CUT AT THE GROIN AND OPEN IT UP ALL THE WAY TO THE THROAT. HEY! ARE YOU PAYING ATTENTION?

CHONG: URK.

PAGE 12:

1.

Cut to next morning. The four of them are packing up their camp.

BENNY: OKAY. IT'S TWELVE MILES TO THE HOSPITAL. WE CAN MAKE IT BY THIS AFTERNOON AND THEN CAMP IN THE WOODS OVERNIGHT.

BENNY: THEN WE HAVE A WHOLE DAY TO SEARCH THE PLACE.

LILAH: GOOD PLAN. FOR A CHANGE.

BENNY (small): THANKS.

2.

The four of them are walking down a deserted road.

CHONG: SO—JUST SO I'M CLEAR ON THE GREAT MASTER PLAN, WE'RE JUST GOING MORE OR LESS EAST IN THE HOPES OF SEEING THAT PLANE AGAIN. OR SOMEONE WHO SAW IT? OR . . . SOMETHING?

BENNY: PRETTY MUCH.

NIX: YOU HAVE A BETTER PLAN?

3.

Small panel. Chong waves his hands dismissively.

CHONG: NO. ALL MY PLANS WOULD ACTUALLY MAKE *SENSE*.

LILAH: STOP COMPLAINING.

4.

Big panel. Chong plods along with the others. Little word balloons seem to follow him, getting smaller and smaller.

CHONG: WHO'S COMPLAINING? I'M NOT COMPLAINING.

CHONG: WHAT'S TO COMPLAIN ABOUT?

CHONG: EXCEPT FOR FLEAS.

CHONG: NO TOILET PAPER.

CHONG: NO HOT SHOWERS.

CHONG: ZOMBIES.

CHONG: WILD ANIMALS.

CHONG: MORE ZOMBIES.

CHONG: AND NO TOILET PAPER.

CHONG: DID I MENTION THE COMPLETE LACK OF TOILET PAPER?

PAGE 13:

1.

Lilah freezes and blocks them all with one outstretched arm as she grips her spear with her other hand.

CHONG: *WHAT THE—?*

LILAH: STOP.

2.

Another angle, looking past them, as a bear comes out of the woods.

3.

We then see that it is wounded and dying.

4.

Then we see why. A pack of zoms comes out of the woods. There are a lot of them. Many show marks from having been mauled or slashed by the bear. All of the zombies are in hospital gowns except for a few dressed as nurses or doctors.

BENNY: OH . . . CRAP.

PAGE 14:

1.

The zombies pile onto the bear.

2.

They begin tearing it to pieces as it howls its last. It's all very messy. Blood, meat, and fur fly everywhere.

3.

On the faces of the four kids. Benny looks sad; Nix winces; Chong turns away; Lilah's face is cold.

4.

One of the zombies looks up from the chunk of meat it's eating. We see its face.

ZOM: UH—?

5.

Reverse view and we see that it has noticed the four kids.

ALL FOUR KIDS: OH.

ALL FOUR KIDS: CRAP.

PAGE 15:

1.

The zombies all notice the kids now. They begin rising from the fallen bear.

CHONG: UM . . . ANYONE HAVE A PLAN THAT DOESN'T INVOLVE US DYING?

LILAH: YES. WE FIGHT LIKE WARRIORS, TOWN BOY.

CHONG: ANYONE HAVE A PLAN THAT INVOLVES RUNNING AWAY?

2.

The kids pull their weapons. Nix and Chong have wooden bokken. Lilah has her spear. Benny has the *kami katana* sword.

BENNY: I'M OKAY WITH THE RUNNING-AWAY PLAN.

NIX: WORKS FOR ME.

3.

They try to back away.

LILAH: THEN SHUT UP AND DO IT.

4.

Chong hears a sound, and turns.

CHONG: UM . . . GUYS . . . ?

5.

There are many more zombies behind them.

PAGES 16–17:

1.

Big two-page spread as the four kids fight a major battle. Lilah and Nix face one direction, and both girls are fierce. Lilah leaps upward, decapitating a zom with her spear; Nix does a lateral cut; Benny does a rising cut to take off the arm and head of a zom. Chong falls backward as a zom tackles him.

PAGE 18:

1.

A zom lunges close to bite Chong. He shoves his carpet-covered forearm in its mouth, though it's clear he still feels the pain of the bite.

CHONG: AIIIEEE!

2.

Lilah spears the zom from behind so that the tip of her blade comes out of the zom's mouth, inches from Chong's face. He gets gore on his face but not in his mouth.

LILAH: STUPID TOWN BOY.

LILAH: ARE YOU *TRYING* TO GET YOURSELF KILLED?

CHONG (small): Wasn't—gak—on my—gak—to-do list.

3.

Benny and Nix fight desperately back-to-back. Parts fly everywhere but it still doesn't look like they're winning.

NIX: THERE'S TOO MANY OF THEM!

BENNY: I KNOW. I KNOW.

BENNY: *RUN!*

4.

Benny shoves Nix though a gap in the zoms. Zoms pluck at their clothes, shredding them. One grabs Nix's hair . . .

BENNY: GO—GO—GO!

5.

. . . and Benny slices through Nix's hair with a sword.

6.

The four of them flee into the forest.

PAGE 19:

1.
They run down a tree-lined road. The zoms are pursuing. And more come out of the woods on either side of the road.

CHONG: THE MAP—*PUFF*—SAYS THAT THE—*PUFF*—HOSPITAL IS—RIGHT AHEAD.

NIX: IT COULD BE FULL OF ZOMS. WE'LL BE TRAPPED IN THERE.

LILAH: WE'LL DIE OUT HERE.

2.
Ahead they see the ruins of a hospital. Zoms all around it.

3.
They climb in through a window as decaying hands reach for them. Lilah stabs backward with her spear.

BENNY: HURRY!

4.
Exterior shot of a pile of zombies against the wall and the topmost climbing in through the windows.

LILAH: MAYBE THEY WON'T SEE OR SMELL US IN HERE.

BENNY: YEAH, I THINK WE'RE SAFE.

5.

Inside the hospital. Lilah and Nix fight the zoms as Chong points to a corridor.

CHONG: IT LOOKS CLEAR. THIS WAY!

6.

They push through a door. The grimy and hard-to-read sign says SPECIAL CARE NURSERY, but most of the last word is covered with old, dried blood and is hard to read.

CHONG: C'MON. WE CAN BARRICADE THE DOOR. WE'LL BE—

PAGE 20:

1.

They stand together in horrified silence. The room is the hospital nursery. There are dozens of small beds. On each is an infant zombie.

CHONG: —SAFE?

NIX (small): OH GOD.

TITLE CREDITS:
ROT & RUIN #1: WARRIOR SMART
Story by Jonathan Maberry
Pencils by Tony Vargas
Edited by David Hedgecock
Published by IDW 2014

CHASE CARD

N⁰ 4

RAGS AND BONES

There are plenty of tall tales about a little girl named Rags and her fierce canine protector, Bones. They've been spotted all over the Rot & Ruin, from the wastelands of Canada to the edges of the southern forests. How a girl and a dog have survived all these years in the wild is anyone's guess.

THE RANGERS

№ R.303

TOP AND BUNNY

The Rot & Ruin is a dangerous place, and only the toughest and bravest venture into it. Two of the most daring deep-Ruin explorers are a reckless pair known only as Top and Bunny—who are rumored to be part of Captain Joe Ledger's team of rangers.

WILDERNESS HEROES

№ 991

RACHAEL ELLE

Travelers have brought many wild rumors back from the Ruin, but few stranger than the one about a town where the residents dress up as superheroes in order to fight zombies. Reports of this so-called "Hero Town" are all second- and thirdhand, but many believe it may actually exist deep inside the zombie lands.

MYSTERIES OF THE RUIN № 8

BONUS CARD

THE WOLF

The Rot & Ruin is a place of mystery, but nothing is more mysterious than the legend of the Wolf. Some claim that it is a giant wolf that hunts both humans and zoms. Others whisper that it's a werewolf! Whatever it is, when the Wolf hunts, nothing can stop it.

VILLAINS OF FIRST NIGHT

№ 801

MAMA RAT AND THE SKULL-RIDERS

Lawless groups of raiders, scavengers, and cannibals make the Rot & Ruin every bit as dangerous as the hordes of zoms do. In the early years after First Night, few groups were as savage or dangerous as Mama Rat and her skull-riders.